Michael L. Clark

Raven's Destiny

Library of Congress Control Number: 2024924788

Historic Traces Publishing

Hardback: 978-1-965756-08-9

Paperback: 978-1-965756-07-2

Ebook: 978-1-965756-06-5

RAVEN'S DESTINY

CHAPTER 1

October 20, 1707

Somewhere in the Atlantic

Morning broke to the sounds of insects chirping in the distance, tropical birds singing in the treetops, and the waves crashing against the hull of *Raven's Destiny*. *Destiny* had once been a merchant ship transporting slaves and other goods from the continent of Africa to the Carolinas in Colonial America. She was now used as a pirate ship attacking other merchant ships and freeing them of their trade goods, especially slaves.

Her captain was eighteen-year-old Raven Ashworth, originally from Bristol, England. Raven began sailing the seas at age twelve, disguised as a boy. Her father, John, took her along with him after her mother had died. Raven, then known as Richard, served as Ship's Boy aboard the former ship known as *Destiny,* which Horatio Billings captained. Billings never suspected that Richard was a girl. He took particular interest in training the lad to be a good sailor. Billings found Richard to be a quick learner of the sea and smart as a whip to the business aspects of running a ship. Richard convinced the captain that if he fed the men and the slaves aboard his vessel proper nutrition, they would survive the long, arduous journey through the open seas.

Most captains were losing nearly eighty percent of their slave cargo to disease, starvation, and malnutrition. Richard helped educate Billings that even if it took longer for them to reach their destination, they would make more money in the long run by stopping along the way and replenishing their food stores, especially fresh fruits and vegetables.

Richard seized the opportunity to free some of the slaves along the way by using his hard-earned money to buy their freedom. First, there was only one, Batimkoo, whom Richard had renamed Pharaoh. On his second voyage, Richard freed two more: Caesar and Attila. Then, on the third trip, he freed two more slaves: Nero and Alexander.

Richard renamed all his companions after famous kings and leaders he had read about in books he had borrowed from Mr. Greer, the ship's doctor. After *Destiny* sank during a hurricane, Richard revealed his secret to his men: He was not Richard, but Raven. They and the rest of her crew have faithfully served her in their quests ever since.

Raven awoke groggily from the sound of a screech from the monkey who lay at her head on her pillow. Captain Billings, named after Raven's former captain, was her constant companion. Raven found the monkey lying next to his dead mother on an island in the Atlantic, which Raven and her crew had reached after the shipwreck of the *Destiny*.

As Raven stirred from sleep, she slid out of bed and dressed. She pulled on her white stockings, then pulled on her leather breeches. She slipped on a white linen shirt with billowy sleeves, then added a leather waistcoat. She then buckled on her belt with her sword hanging from it and slid two braces criss-crossed over her shoulders. The braces held two pistols and two knives. She then tossed her long, curly, red locks of hair from underneath her blouse and let them spill down her back. Raven was a beautiful young woman, but men mistakenly thought she was weak or frail. She could outfight most men with ease. She was an avid swordsman and a crack shot with either pistol or long rifle.

Raven stepped out of her quarters, walked across the ship's deck to the officer's quarters, and opened the door to Jeffrey's cabin. Jeffrey Hamilton was a former captive of Raven, who now served as her quartermaster. He was two years older than Raven and had served aboard the *Matilda* as the ship's second mate. *Matilda* was the second ship that Raven and her crew captured after leaving the island that had served as their home for a few months after the original *Destiny* sank. The first ship Raven captured was the *Scarlett Marie*, which Raven and her crew had captured off the coast of their little island by using hand–built dugout canoes to row out and overtake the ship. Once it was captured, Raven renamed the ship *Raven's Destiny* in honor of her former ship.

Raven spoke to her quartermaster, saying, "Jeffrey. Jeffery!"

She then pulled the pillow from underneath his head, struck him with it, and called, "Jeffrey! Get up!"

Startled by the striking of the pillow and shouting of his name, Jeffrey woke up. He wiped the sleep from his eyes as he looked up and saw Raven standing over him as she faced him.

"Good morning." he said.

"Get up! We've lots to do!"

Jeffrey dressed, not wanting to leave the bed just yet.
"What's your hurry?"

Raven replied, "We've been hiding here long enough. I want to get back to the seas and find some ships to raid."

It had been only a month since her crew had rescued her from the gallows of the French government after having been captured at Port St. Felix on the southwest coast of Madagascar. Raven's crew left the docks of La Rochelle, and the ships moored there, supposedly in disrepair, as they rescued their captain from losing her head. They had spent the past week at their hide-out, the Robin's Nest, re-supplying for their next voyage.

Raven was down to two ships, *Matilda* and *Raven's Destiny*. *Tryton* had been sunk by the French navy when they captured Raven. Raven's long-time friends and crew members, Caesar and Nero, were among those who were lost when the French frigate sank *Tryton*.

Their first order of business was to make sure the ships were supplied with ammunition. She wanted to return to Port St. Felix to see her old friend Señor Oscar Alejandro Rivera. The last time she had tried to meet with him, she was captured by French soldiers who had set a trap for Raven using Rivera as the bait.

Raven had three things she wanted to accomplish shortly – to establish her trade with Rivera once again, to establish trading with the people who occupied the mountain she and her men had discovered north of Mbini, and to further explore Lomé in Togo. She once spoke to a man claiming to have more than six hundred slaves at his disposal. Raven wanted to see for herself whether or not his claims were valid.

Raven's ships still carried some of the gold they had traded for on what she referred to as the Grey Coast. She had determined the people there had access to more gold than she had ever seen, and they were willing to trade with her exclusively. She needed to return to Port St. Felix to buy rum and textiles, which her new friends coveted.

Raven was not ready to raid another ship or announce her position in the sea, so she ordered the white sails to be unfurled as *Destiny* and *Matilda* sailed west out of the Gulf of Guinea.

Pharaoh and his crew sailed within a quarter-mile of *Destiny* to hear the call from *Destiny* should it be made. From the beginning, Raven and her men had developed a series of signals using conch shells to communicate.

The winds coming from the northwest were cold on this October morning. *Destiny's* sails billowed out, catching the wind quickly and propelling her at twelve . They were making excellent time.

Seven days out, Raven witnessed the coast at Port Gentil, where Andre Arsenault once ran a trading post and forge where weapons and ammunition were manufactured. Arsenault's body still hung from a tree near the beach where Raven had left it as a warning to other slave traders who didn't heed her words. Raven had warned Arsenault to refrain from slave trading, allowing him to continue the manufacturing of his guns, cannons, and ammunition. However, Arsenault thought Raven's warning to be wanting in credibility. Unfortunately, he and his men learned the hard way not to cross the Red Raven.

Raven remembered watching Arsenault's body sway in the wind as she left him there, choking to his death, with his men hanging in the trees surrounding him. She didn't delight in seeing men die, but she felt it was no more cruel than what they had done to the natives on the African continent.

Raven stood next to her papa as he steered *Destiny* past Port Gentil. John Ashworth caught a glimpse of Raven as she stared at the hanging lifeless bodies. All that was left after several months were the bones and torn clothing hanging from them. Scavenger birds and insects had removed all the flesh from each body, producing a grizzly sight to warn slave traders who might happen upon Port Gentil. Word spread quickly among merchant vessels who were involved in slave trading. The Red Raven was no one to be trifled with, and she and her crew should be avoided at all costs.

John Ashworth was ordered by Alexander, Raven's first mate, to turn the ship southward, sailing toward the Cape of Good Hope. John turned the wheel of the helm twenty degrees southward to steer *Destiny* toward the southern tip of Africa. *Matilda* took its cue from *Destiny* and turned south. The ships continued to sail together throughout the night. The skies were clear, not a cloud in them. The stars shown brightly amid the glow of the full moon.

Fourteen hours into their voyage, Isaac took over the helm. John was now below decks in his hammock. Alexander occasionally climbed to the quarterdeck throughout the night to check their progress. Daktari was in the crow's nest at the top of the main mast. The night winds whistled past him as he stared into the distance. He lifted the spyglass to his face occasionally and searched the distant horizons for other vessels in the area.

Destiny continued to sail five miles off the coast of West Africa. On their twenty-ninth hour, Alexander measured their distance and found they had traveled nearly three hundred miles. A young man, Mtoto Jasiri (Brave Child), who took over the crow's nest for Daktari, called out to Alexander, "Ship ahoy off the starboard bow!"

Alexander climbed to the bowcastle and looked through his spyglass. He slowly moved his spyglass across the horizon, searching for the ship. Finally, he saw it—thirty degrees off the starboard bow and about a mile away. Alexander could see three masts but couldn't determine what flag she was flying.

Alexander called out to thirteen-year-old Jeremy, standing on the main deck.

"Jeremy, run and find Raven!"

"Aye, Alexander!"

The boy ran to Raven's cabin and knocked on the door.

"Enter!"

Jeremy quickly opened the door and found Raven and Jeffrey standing at her table, looking over a chart of the Atlantic.

"What is it, Jeremy?"

"Raven, Alexander needs you on the bow castle! A ship has been spotted!"

Raven quickly glanced at Jeffrey and said, "Come on!"

All three escaped her cabin and trotted to the bowcastle to meet Alexander. Alexander handed Raven his spyglass and pointed in the direction she should look. Raven slowly moved the spyglass from left to right, searching for the ship. She thought she must have missed it, so she swung the glass back to the left, this time more slowly. There it was!

Raven asked Alexander, "How far do you think it is?"

"I measure it to be about a mile."

Raven replied, "I agree. I still can't make out what type of ship she is. Let's see if we can get closer. If she is a merchant ship and riding low in the water, she might be worth taking."

Jeremy asked, "Why would the ship be riding low in the water, Raven?"

Raven turned to Jeremy and replied, "It means she is probably full of cargo. Could be slaves, could be rum, or maybe even gold."

Jeremy's eyes lit up with intrigue. "Will we capture it?"

"That's the plan! Are you ready?"

"Aye, Raven!"

Raven ordered Alexander, "Ninety degrees starboard. Let's see if we can cut her off or at least get a closer look."

"Aye, Raven!"

Alexander turned back to the quarterdeck and called out to Isaac, who was still at the helm. "Isaac, ninety degrees starboard!"

"Aye, Alexander! Ninety degrees starboard!"

Then Alexander called to the crew on deck, "All hands ready at the sails!"

All the crew scrambled to their positions to receive further orders.

John Ashworth came up from his hammock below the deck and looked around to see what was happening with the crew. He saw Raven and Alexander standing on the bow castle, looking at something in the distance. John moved to the quarterdeck and stood beside Isaac at the helm.

"What's happening?"

Isaac replied, "We've spotted a ship off the starboard bow. Raven wants a closer look."

Excitement rose within John as he heard the news. He enjoyed a good sea chase.

Isaac turned the wheel to the right, and the ship smoothly changed direction as it bounced through the waves of the Atlantic. Raven watched as the horizon changed before her. The sun eventually moved directly in front of her. She watched seven pelicans fly across the bow in a perfect V-formation. She wondered to herself how it must feel to fly. She had always felt a sense of freedom on the seas, no matter which ship she had been aboard. But she couldn't imagine there being a more free way to live than to be a bird and be able to fly among the clouds.

Half an hour later, the distant ship became more visible. Raven checked her spyglass and saw that the boat was *indeed* a merchant's vessel riding low in the water. Raven told Alexander, "Lower the blood sails."

Alexander called out to the crew, "Lower the blood sails!"

The crew set into action, switching out the white billowing sails for the blood-red sails displaying the black raven. *Destiny* slowed slightly as the crew changed out the sails, but their speed increased once the sails were in place.

Pharaoh noticed that the blood sails were lowered and knew that the hunt for prey was afoot. He ordered his crew to prepare their guns and be ready to board the ship that occupied the waters before them.

Raven's crew onboard *Destiny* began preparing their guns as well. Ammunition was running low for the cannons, but they would be sufficient for an unarmed merchant ship. Alexander ordered his gun crew to load the bow cannon. They would fire a four-pound shot across the bow of the merchant ship to warn them of impending doom should they try to run. Few merchant ships ever armed themselves with anything more than blades and small firearms. That's why they were so susceptible to pirate attacks – the pirates needed only to fire a warning shot to overtake the merchant vessel. Crews aboard the merchant ships valued their lives more than the pockets of their employers. Earning sometimes less than £30 per year while serving on board a vessel that many were forced upon in the first place, most men would drop their arms and surrender at the first sign of danger. Some men would even join the pirates to find a more financially stable life among them.

Raven watched the vessel as it approached. Eventually, she was able to read the name of the ship upon its bow: "*Nightingale.*"

Raven was familiar with the *Nightingale.* She was captained by Nicholas Hornsby, a crusty old man notorious for treating his crew as severely as his cargo. He was in the business of hauling slaves to the Americas, but most of his cargo would never make it to its destination. The slaves he carried and his crew often suffered from starvation and malnutrition. If it hadn't been for his loyal officers, Hornsby would have succumbed to mutiny many times throughout the years. However, if any of the *Nightingale's* officers even suspected someone of initiating a mutiny, the man was strung up from the yardarm. Raven would take great delight in relieving Hornsby of his ship.

Hornsby saw two ships sailing toward him. When he took out his spyglass, he saw one of the ships sailing under red sails. He cursed out loud when he realized one of the ships making way for his ship was none other than *Raven's Destiny*. He had never encountered her before but knew of her reputation. He knew Raven was friendly to those he often profited from, namely slaves, and dangerous to those who would profit from slavery.

Thirty minutes later, *Destiny was* just a quarter mile from the *Nightingale*. Raven looked over at Alexander and nodded. Alexander called out to the gun crew on the bow, "Ready one across the bow!"

"Ready, Alexander!"

"Fire!"

The four-pound iron ball whistled through the air as it left the cannon and whizzed past the bow of the *Nightingale*. The shot, meant only as a warning, landed harmlessly in the water ten yards from the *Nightingale*.

A voice from the *Nightingale* called out to its crew, "Raise the sails and come about."

The ship's crew scrambled to work, raising and wrapping the sails against the yardarms of the three masts that towered above the deck. The first mate ordered, "Prepare to be boarded!"

Destiny and *Matilda* pulled alongside the merchant vessel, one on the port, the other on the starboard. Sandbags were draped over the rails to cushion the ships from each other as they were tied together. Raven and Pharaoh's men tossed grappling lines over to the *Nightingale* to pull their ships together. Raven's men scrambled to the trapped ship, brandishing their blades and pistols as they surrounded Hornsby's crew.

Raven swung from a mast line over the side onto the *Nightingale* and landed on their quarterdeck. She landed face to face with Hornsby, who smugly greeted her, saying, "Well, might I presume you are the Red Raven of whom I have heard so much about?"

CHAPTER 2

R aven stood before the old man, her sword drawn as she asked, "Are you Hornsby?"

"Captain Hornsby!" he replied.

"Well, Captain Hornsby, consider yourself and your ship captured. Have all of your crew assembled on the main deck at once."

Hornsby stared into Raven's eyes with disgust for several seconds before relenting. He looked at his first mate and nodded. The first mate called out with a loud, clear voice, "All hands! All hands on the main deck!"

Men climbed down from the tops of the masts – others from below decks until all thirty of the *Nightingale's* crew stood on the main deck.

Raven then sent twenty of her crew down below to check out the cargo with Alexander in the lead. Pharaoh's crew stood by, keeping watch over Hornsby and his crew. Men could be heard below the decks rummaging through and tossing things around as they searched for anything of value. Alexander took a lantern with him to check the lowest deck, where most cargo would be stored. When he opened the hatch, a familiar smell of human waste and rotting flesh emitted from below. Alexander slowly climbed down the steps leading to the lower deck while holding the lantern in front of him. As he reached the deck floor, he looked around and found pairs of frightened eyes peering at him in the darkness. He heard coughs and sniffles. A voice began speaking to him in a language that was familiar to him.

A man sitting on the deck shackled to a beam just before Alexander cried out, "Have mercy on us!"

Alexander responded to the man, "Don't worry, my friend. We are here to free you from your bonds. You will be free again."

Gasps of relief could be heard throughout the lower deck as Alexander instructed his men to free the people from their shackles. As their chains were unlocked, each one was escorted to the top deck and moved to one of Raven's ships. Jeffrey tallied the number of slaves as they were removed from the hull of the *Nightingale*. It took more than an hour to free the three hundred and forty people who had been shackled below.

Once they were all placed on their new ships, Alexander's men began carrying out the lifeless bodies of the individuals who had already expired below decks. Twenty-three bodies were laid out on the main deck before Hornsby and his crew. Usually, when someone would die on a slave ship, the body was immediately tossed overboard. Hornsby didn't bother to send anyone below decks more than once or twice a week for feeding. So, bodies were left to rot rather than disposed of into the sea.

Raven watched as the dead were brought out and placed on the deck. Her contempt for Hornsby grew with every corpse that was pulled from below. Raven finally ordered, "Bring the officers to the quarterdeck.

Five men were escorted to the quarterdeck and stood next to Hornsby. Twenty-five men who had served under Hornsby were left standing on the main deck. Raven began to address these men.

"You men of the *Nightingale* who stand before me have a choice to make. I suspect that many of you were forced into serving onboard this ship. I also suspect that many of you have been mistreated by Hornsby or his officers. Consider yourselves freed from their oppression."

Someone from the crowd called out, "Who are you, Miss?"

Raven walked to the rail at the edge of the quarterdeck and looked at every man standing before her on the lower deck as if she were searching for the voice who had asked the question. She then replied, "I am the Red Raven."

Gasps and murmurs could be heard throughout the ship until Raven raised her hands to quiet them all.

"I take it that you have heard of me? Well, be sure that much of what you have heard is probably fable. I am not here to kill you men. I am here to make an offer. As you have probably noticed, most of my crew is made up of Africans, men and women who were forcefully removed from their homes and taken captive. I will allow you to join my crew and serve alongside these men and women. You will receive the same share as any of them according to rank. If you want to come and sail with me, you will be expected to work alongside these fine sailors of mine. If that does not agree with you, you will not be harmed. You will, however, be expected to work for your passage to the next available port where you can find work on another vessel."

Another voice called out, "What about our officers?"

Raven replied, "These men are guilty of atrocities against God and man. They will be punished accordingly."

The crowd spoke among themselves for a few minutes before Raven finally silenced them again.

"Well? What will it be? If you are willing to sail with me, step forward."

One by one, men began to step forward. However, only five were willing to sail with Raven. The other twenty chose to seek refuge at another port.

Raven asked again, "Will that be all?"

No one else stepped forward.

"Very well. Three of you will come to *Raven's Destiny*. The other two will climb aboard *Matilda*. Captain Pharaoh will attend to your needs. If you men have belongings you'd like to bring with you, gather them now."

The five men scrambled below decks to retrieve their gear and returned to receive instructions. Several remaining men sneered at them when they returned on deck, calling them traitors.

Raven then said, "You three men, climb onto *Destiny*. You two, over to *Matilda*."

They did as they were instructed. The men of the *Nightingale* continued to murmur.

Raven raised her voice again and spoke to the crowd, "Now I want to speak about these poor souls who lie before you who have fallen under the care of your dear captain, or lack there of if you will. I ask you, what did they do to deserve this sort of death – this lack of concern? You, dear Captain, and your officers will die for the restitution of murdering these twenty-three souls and the kidnapping of three hundred and forty others."

The murmuring grew louder among *Nightingale's* men. Raven's men pressed against those who murmured, causing them to quiet themselves. Hornsby raised his chin in defiance against the young woman who made such threats against him and his officers. As Raven walked past him along the quarterdeck, Hornsby slipped a small knife from underneath his shirt sleeve and drove it into the small of Raven's back. Raven gasped and fell to her knees. Daktari, who was guarding the officers on the quarterdeck, went to Raven's aid. Haskins, another of Raven's crew who had been guarding the officers, quickly smashed Hornsby in the back of the head with the butt of his rifle, driving Hornsby to the deck. Haskins then recovered the knife when Hornsby dropped it from his grip. The other men guarding the officers forced them to their knees and held them in place with sword blades pressed against their throats.

With Daktari's help, Raven stood again, wincing from the pain of her wound. She felt foolish, momentarily dropping her guard, allowing the captain to attack her. Within her mind, she vowed it would never happen again.

Raven stepped up to Hornsby as he knelt on the deck before her, blood seeping from his head wound. She drew her knife, not so small, grabbed him by his thinning hair, and sliced his throat from his left ear to his right. Hornsby's eyes widened as the knife slid across his throat. He tried to cry out but was unable to speak. He could only gurgle and choke on his blood. Raven released him, and he dropped face-first onto the deck.

Hornsby's men and his officers were all dumbfounded to see what this young woman had done to their fearless captain. Raven stepped up to each of the officers one at a time and drove her knife into each man's throat under their chins. She raked her blade through, severing the jugular of each one. When she was done, six lifeless bodies lay on the quarterdeck, and Raven was covered in their blood.

Raven turned to the crowd below and ordered, "Take the rest of them below and shackle them!"

Twenty men were escorted below decks and shackled in the same manner that the slaves had been. Raven's men left the lower deck and slammed the hatch down, rejecting them all in darkness.

Mr. Greer climbed over to the *Nightingale* from *Destiny* to check on Raven's wound. Raven refused Greer's care, saying under her breath, "Not here. I'll meet you in my cabin soon."

Greer nodded his understanding. He realized she didn't want anyone to see her in a weak moment. Her crew needed to know she was still in charge and capable of leading her crew.

Raven stood by while her men tossed the lifeless bodies of Hornsby and his officers over the rail of the *Nightingale*. Her men watched as each body splashed in the dark waters below. Blood mixed with salt water spread away from the ships as they slowly dispersed into the sea. It didn't take long for the bodies to be discovered by sharks swimming nearby. Suddenly, more sharks than could be counted had found their meal for the day, and a feeding frenzy commenced. Tails and fins flipped through the water's surface, splashing and stirring the blood and water mixture.

Raven beckoned Alexander over to her. "Congratulations, Captain Alexander! The *Nightingale* is now your ship to sail under my flag."

Alexander smiled in response, "Thank you, Raven."

"I'm leaving you with Daktari to serve as your first mate, I believe him to be capable. I'll send you ten men from *Destiny* and Pharaoh will send another five, so you can man this vessel properly. Some of the people we have just rescued will likely fill in some of the gaps along the way. For now, you and Daktari should go over and grab your gear. We'll ready your ship for you in the meantime."

"Thank you, Raven. I will not let you down."

Alexander called Daktari over to him, and they climbed back onto *Destiny* to retrieve their gear.

Raven slowly walked over to *Matilda* and softly spoke to Pharaoh, "I am assigning Alexander as captain of the *Nightingale*. Would you please send over five of your men to serve on his crew?"

"Aye, Raven! Alexander will make a good captain I think."

Raven said, "I need you to talk to the rescued people. Find out where they are from so we can get them closer to their homes. I'm going back to *Destiny* now. Would you please help prepare the

Nightingale to sail while Alexander and Daktari bring over their gear. When you find out where we need to go from here, call me over?"

"Aye! That I will do. Raven? Are you alright?"

Raven looked at Pharaoh and only gave a slight nod. Then, she turned and walked across the deck of the *Nightingale* and climbed back onto *Destiny*. Her strength faded quickly, but she didn't want her men to see her this way. She walked to her cabin as soon as she could. John, seeing his daughter struggle as he stood on the quarterdeck, stepped down to her but did not try to help her. He followed her into her cabin, where Mr. Greer was waiting.

Greer helped Raven remove her waistcoat and blouse, then had her lie face–down on her bed. He cleaned her wound with warm water and bathed her arms and face as well to clear the blood that had spilled on her as she executed the *Nightingale's* officers. Upon closer examination of the knife wound, Greer discovered that none of her vital organs had been damaged. He flushed the wound with alcohol and then began stitching the wound together to help stop the bleeding.

"Raven, you need to take it easy for a few days. Give that wound a chance to heal before you go ripping out my stitches."

"Don't worry, Mr. Greer. I know the routine. You forget that you taught me how to tend to wounds."

"I haven't forgotten, I just know you. You're not likely to sit still for more than a minute or two before you're off starting a fight with someone. Now, I mean it! Let your officers take care of things for now."

Raven said, "Speaking of which, would you please send Papa and Jeffrey in please?"

Greer packed up his sewing kit and headed for the door. He turned once more as if to say something else, but Raven said it first.

"Don't worry! I'm not going anywhere soon."

Raven sat up slowly, then finally stood. She moved over to her wardrobe, where she found another blouse. Raven carefully slipped her arms through the sleeves and began buttoning the blouse as someone knocked on her door.

"Just a minute!" she called out.

Once she had finished dressing, she walked to the door and opened it. There stood Jeffrey and John waiting to enter.

"Come in."

Jeffrey and John both noticed that Raven's face was pale. They could see her pain in the expressions she made.

John said, "Sit down, daughter. You need to rest."

Raven shuffled over to her bed and sat down on the edge. Then, she began to speak.

"I'm going to make some changes around here. Alexander has been made captain of the *Nightingale*. Daktari will be his first mate. Papa, I want you to be my first mate. I know you are as good a sailor as anyone aboard these ships, including myself. The men trust you and will follow you and I know you won't make them feel as if you are usurping your authority."

John was surprised by her comments, "Thank you, Raven! I'll do my best."

"I'm going to make Hadari my second mate. Jeffrey, I need you to help him get the hang of things. He's a good sailor, but I'm not sure how much of a leader he will be. He is very quiet around me. We'll need a new helmsman too. I think maybe Kifaru would make a good helmsman."

Jeffrey remained quiet. Raven could tell by the look on his face that he was disappointed.

"What? Were you expecting to be made first mate?"

Jeffrey shrugged and replied, "Well, I have served as second mate before, as you know, and I thought naturally . . ."

"You thought it would be a natural progression for you."

Jeffrey was silent.

"Jeffrey, I need you to remain as quartermaster. You're not quartermaster as a punishment. You are the only one qualified and whom I trust to carry out the position. You're not quartermaster just for *Destiny*, but for all my ships. It is a very important position and I trust no one else with the job."

Jeffrey's countenance changed. He nodded to Raven in agreement, giving her a slight nod.

Raven said, "Now, we should head back to the coast of Africa. Pharaoh is questioning the people we rescued to determine where they were taken from. We'll try to get them back to their homes if possible. As soon as you hear from Pharaoh, let me know."

"Aye, Raven."

"Jeffrey, please be so kind as to introduce the crew to their new officers. Tell everyone I'm fine but I need rest. Oh, and would you please send Jeremy in to me?"

"Aye, Raven."

The two men left Raven's cabin and closed the door behind them. Jeffrey turned to John and presented his hand to congratulate him. John took his hand and asked, "You're not upset?"

"Rather the opposite. It's strange, but Raven makes me feel all the more important to her even after having passed me over for a promotion."

John replied, "She is a rare individual."

They both walked out onto the deck and climbed to the quarterdeck, where Jeffrey called all hands to assemble. When everyone gathered on the main deck, Jeffrey called, "Hadari and Kifaru, please join us on the quarterdeck."

Both men climbed the steps leading to the quarterdeck and stood beside John.

Jeffrey began, "The following changes have been made by your captain. Alexander is now captain of the *Nightingale*. Daktari will be his first mate. John Ashworth will now be first mate of *Destiny* and Hardari will be second mate. Kifaru will take Mr. Ashworth's place at the helm. Raven expects all of you to congratulate these men and serve them as well as you have served her. She has been injured, but Mr. Greer has tended to her and she should recover quickly enough. She asks that you respect her privacy as she heals. That will be all. Dismissed!"

The crew began rummaging around, returning to their duties. Many of them walked by the quarterdeck and congratulated the new officers and the new helmsman. As they all got back to work, Jeffrey caught sight of Jeremy.

"Jeremy! Jeremy!"

Jeremy looked around to see who was calling for him. He saw Jeffrey beckoning him over, so Jeremy approached the quarterdeck.

"Jeremy, Raven has asked that I send you to her. She is resting, so don't bother knocking. Go on in quietly and see what she needs."

"Aye, Mr. Hamilton!"

CHAPTER 3

Jeremy quietly entered Raven's cabin. Captain Billings squeaked at him as he entered. Jeremy and Captain Billings became close friends after Jeremy and his father, Isaac, joined the crew. He cared for the monkey whenever Raven left the little creature onboard. Jeremy cared for Captain Billings when Raven was arrested and held in prison.

Jeremy quietly stepped to Raven's bed. The monkey jumped on his shoulder, waking Raven as he did.

"Oh, Jeremy! There you are."

"Do you need me to do anything for you?"

"Yes, I'm thirsty. Could you please go to Mr. Hardy and fetch me a pint of ale?"

"Aye, Raven. Would you like anything to eat?"

Raven replied, "No, I'm not hungry. Just the ale and some rest."

Jeremy left Raven's cabin and walked across the ship to the ship's kitchen. Louis Hardy was busy preparing the next meal for the crew.

"Jeremy lad! Have you come to help me?"

"No, Mr. Hardy. Raven sent me to fetch her a pint of ale."

"How is she?"

"She seems weak to me. She needs to rest, but she said she was thirsty and wanted a pint of ale."

Hardy took a tankard from the cabinet, filled it with ale, and handed it to Jeremy.

"Now make sure none of that finds it's way past your lips on the way to Raven." Hardy chuckled.

Jeremy carefully took the tankard from Hardy and returned across the ship to Raven's cabin. He returned to the room and found Raven sitting on her bed.

"Just set it on the table, Jeremy."

Jeremy did as she asked.

"Would you mind watching Captain Billings for me today? It's hard for me to rest with him crawling all over me."

"Aye, Raven! I would be happy to do so."

As Jeremy began to leave with Captain Billings, John Ashworth met him at the door.

"Oh hello, Jeremy! How's Raven doing?"

"She's fine, Mr. Ashworth. She just needs her rest."

"Don't worry, I won't be long."

Jeremy allowed John to come into Raven's cabin as he exited with Captain Billings on his shoulder. Raven saw John enter the cabin and asked, "What is it, Papa?"

"I just spoke to Pharaoh. He said that the slaves were bought in Lomé port. The people we loaded onto *Destiny* are telling the same story. Isn't that where you found the wanted poster?"

"Yes. There was a man who claimed to have six hundred slaves for sale there. I thought it was just a trap, but maybe he was telling the truth. Have they said anything else?"

"Those aboard *Destiny* have said they don't want to go back to Lomé. They said that their tribal leaders gave them to the white men as slaves in order that the slavers don't attack their villages."

"Extortion! Another case of the strong feeding on the weak. Inform the other captains that we will go to Port Gentil."

"Port Gentil?"

"Yes, we'll set up an encampment for the people there until we can resupply the ships. They should be safe there until we return."

"Aye, Raven! I'll let them know right away."

John left Raven and went up to the quarterdeck, where he gave instructions to head back to Port Gentil. He then blew the conch shell to signal the other ships to follow.

"Hadari, have the men strike the blood sails and drop the main sails. We're heading for Port Gentil."

"Aye, Mr. Ashworth!"

Hadari told the crew, "Raise the blood sails and unfurl the main sails. Mr. Finch, come about twenty degrees east."

"Aye, Hadari! Twenty degrees east."

Hadari felt a little odd giving his first order to the crew. He felt nervous and proud. Hadari was never thought of as a leader among his people. However, he was a quick learner, and Raven saw this in him. What he lacked in confidence, he made up for in intelligence.

The evening sun was setting at their backs as the ships pulled through the waves toward the Gulf of Guinea. A drizzle of rain misted the ships as they sailed to their next destination.

Skies were clear, and the sun was warm as the three ships approached the coast of Port Gentil. Many of the freed Africans stood at the rail of their respective ship as they sailed into port. They stared at the skeletons hanging from the trees along the coast and wondered where they were and why they had been brought here.

The refugees stared, wondering what type of evil spirits resided here, what unholy beings haunted the beaches along this coast.

The ships were secured at the docks, and each captain prepared for the passengers to disembark. Most of the people were frightened by the dead bodies hanging near the beach. They didn't like the idea of being left here; they wanted to stay on the ships.

Pharaoh, Alexander, and Raven met the people on the beach to inform them of their plight. Three hundred and forty African refugees stood on the beach as Raven began to speak. Pharaoh translated for her.

"I know this is not your homeland. From what my captains have discovered, many of you were subjected to slavery by your tribal chiefs in order to keep your villages from being raided by the slavers. This is a place that my crew and I cleared several months ago. The people who lived at this place were involved in slave trade. I warned them to stop, but they continued, so my men and I executed them. They now hang from these trees as a warning to anyone who would force people into slavery. I have been informed that many of you can't go home. That's why we brought you here. This will make a suitable home for you. There is large building about a mile from the coast. It can be the beginning of a village for those of you who want to stay here. There are plenty of fish here for you to catch and fruit trees are plentiful. I will also take as many as thirty able bodied men or women who want to sail on one of my ships. Those of you who want to sail with me, remain here on the beach. Some of you may qualify, some will not. Those of you who wish to stay here and build a new community may follow Pharaoh to the new campsite. He will show you the way."

Pharaoh and five of his men began leading most of the people through the deserted village and away from the beach to discover their new home. The people were furnished with several machetes and other tools to help them build huts. It took only thirty minutes for them to reach the clearing where the old slave barn was. Pharaoh and his men helped divide the people into groups to get them started on building the huts and gathering food and firewood to begin their new lives of freedom.

One hundred men and women remained on the beach, hoping to earn a place on Raven's crew. Alexander, Raven, Daktari, and Hadari questioned the people to determine their skill levels and physical capabilities. Young girls and old men were turned away immediately. Six strong women were selected to become part of the crew, and thirty of the most fit men were also selected.

Raven divided the thirty–six recruits among the three ships, where they would be trained as sailors, gunmen, and cooks. Raven's crew and officers now totaled a strong one hundred souls.

Raven called John over before going back to her ship.

"Papa, I will be in my cabin should you need me."

"What should we do with the prisoners onboard the *Nightingale?*"

"I don't want to leave them here. It wouldn't be safe for them or the people making their homes here. When we leave the Gulf there is a kidney shaped island due west by southwest of here. Let's drop them off there."

"I'll see to it."

Raven retreated to her cabin, depending on her officers to replenish food stores from the island for the voyage to Port St. Felix. John, Alexander, and Pharaoh saw to the supply of the ships while their junior officers remained aboard to prepare them for sailing.

By the time the sun had set, all the ships had been supplied, and all crews were back on their ships. They weighed anchor and set sail for Kidney Island under the guidance of John Ashworth, who had charted the course. Twenty hours later, they sailed into the southern beach of Kidney Island. There weren't any docks, so they had to use the dories to shuttle the prisoners to the island. The twenty former crew of *Nightingale* were dropped off by Raven, Alexander, and ten other men. The prisoners were ordered to leave the dories when they reached the beach. They were each given a knife, and the group was given two machetes.

One of the men asked, "Is this all you leave with us? How can we survive?"

Raven replied, "Would you rather I have fed your corpses to the sharks like your officers?"

Another man said, "At least we wouldn't have starved to death. We'd be better off if you killed us quickly."

Raven replied, "I'm not in the habit of killing innocent men. If you want to die quickly, ask one of your friends to help you. I have other matters to attend to, so I bid you farewell."

Raven and her crew rowed away from the island to screams and curses being hurled at them. Raven ignored their comments and rowed away with a clear conscience. She looked back once and saw two men fighting over a machete on the beach. One man struck the other with the machete and wounded him. The wounded man then stabbed the first with his knife and killed him. Raven thought to herself, "Men are such cowards."

When they reached the ships, the dories were lifted back onto them, and the fleet sailed away. Raven resumed her original voyage to Madagascar to resupply the ships. Although Raven was still healing from her injury, she spent as much time as possible on the quarterdeck to observe the new men as they trained in their duties.

Raven recalled going through some of the same training when she was only thirteen, working as a ship's boy on the original *Destiny*. Raven took to the sea immediately, under the training of Captain Horatio Billings. It all seemed like a lifetime ago.

Raven's Destiny had traveled 2,800 miles when they finally changed course near the Cape of Good Hope's entrance. Raven was suspicious of sailing into Madagascar without precautions. Port St. Felix happened to be where the French navy had captured her only three months earlier.

Raven called for Pharaoh and Alexander to come alongside *Destiny*. *Matilda* and *Nightingale* sailed up to *Destiny* to converse with Raven. Pharaoh and Alexander climbed onto *Destiny* to meet with Raven in her cabin. They all sat around the table with John to discuss Raven's plan.

Raven said, "I don't want us all going into port all at once. Let's stagger the ships two hours apart. *Destiny* will go in alone, then *Matilda*, then *Nightingale*. Since *Nightingale* is not yet armed, it would be wise that you come in last should a fight break out. If you see us engaged in a battle from ship to shore, then don't approach. Anchor at bay and standby in case we need you to help us escape."

Alexander nodded his understanding.

"Pharaoh, after you see *Destiny* sail away, standby for two hours before you set sail. If someone is waiting for me at Port St. Felix, that will be long enough for them to show themselves and their intentions. Alexander, you will begin two hours after Pharaoh has sailed."

Pharaoh replied, "Aye, Raven."

"If we all become separated, we will meet back at the Robin's Nest in two months. If anyone has not made it back by three months time, we will assume they have either perished or have been captured. We will begin at first light."

Both captains replied, "Aye."

Pharaoh and Alexander returned to their ships and waited for dawn.

As the sun climbed above the eastern horizon, *Raven's Destiny* pulled away from the other two ships and began the last 1,600 miles to Port St. Felix. Seven days later, *Destiny* reached the bay at the mouth of St. Felix.

Raven scanned the horizon through her spyglass. Everything seemed normal at the port. No ships were docked, and she saw none mooring or sailing nearby. Raven told John, "Prepare to dock."

John nodded and announced to the crew, "All hands, prepare to dock. Mr. Finch, bring us in at port side please."

"Aye, Mr. Ashworth!"

Raven continued to search the docks and the village for anything out of the ordinary. Something suddenly caught her eye as she scanned the streets past the docks. A familiar figure was quickly walking toward the piers. She checked her spyglass and was relieved to see Señor Rivera walking toward her with his trusty assistant, Juan, alongside.

Rivera and Juan waited on the pier as *Destiny* slowly came alongside them and docked.

Oscar Alejandro Rivera smiled when he saw his old friend Raven onboard *Destiny*. The last he had heard was when the French navy had captured her at his little port village.

Rivera called out to her, "Señorita Raven, it is so good to see you! I was afraid we would never meet again."

Raven smiled, waved to Rivera, and waited for her crew to finish docking and extending the gangplank before responding.

"Señor Rivera, it is good to see you again. Are you well?"

"Si, Señorita! I am well, but I have been so worried about you. How is it you are here? I thought you would either be in a French prison or worse."

"I was in a French prison, and I was to be executed, but my crew found and rescued me before it could happen."

"Ah, well I am happy you escaped and are free again! Shall we go back to my hacienda for some refreshments?"

"Under her breath, Raven quietly asked Rivera, "Is it safe?"

"Si, Raven. It is safe. No one has been here since you were captured, other than merchant ships."

Raven replied, "Refreshments sound good, then."

She returned to the ship and called Jeffrey, "Mr. Hamilton, would you please join me? Mr. Ashworth, please set up a guard around our perimeter and keep an eye on the seas."

"Aye, Raven!"

John still felt odd that his daughter referred to him as Mr. Ashworth instead of Papa.

Raven and Rivera walked along the street to his hacienda, with Jeffrey and Juan following behind.

Rivera said as they walked, "I am so sorry that you lost the *Tryton* and her crew."

Raven asked, "Were you able to salvage anything?"

"I am afraid not. All the cannons, ammunition, and everyone aboard were lost. I don't have the equipment to make a deep sea salvage either."

"How deep do you think the water is there?"

"I would guess at least one hundred feet deep."

Raven replied, "Maybe if we had some pearl divers they could reach it and see what could be salvaged, but it might not be worth the trouble or the danger."

"Si, I think you are correct."

Raven then changed the subject, "By the way, I think it would be prudent for us to set up a safety signal to let me and my crew know when it is safe to sail into port."

"Si, I have been thinking the same thing. If you will notice, I have had a flag pole installed near the port. She is flying the Spanish flag right now and underneath my country's flag is a white banner. The white banner will give you a signal that all is safe. There is another banner that has a red 'x' in the center which is visible only by using a spyglass. If you see that flag, you should not come into port."

"Excellent! Only, how many of your people know of this? I wouldn't want it to be known by just anyone who might betray us for a reward."

"Only Juan and I know of this. Juan is my most trusted amigo. You have nothing to worry about."

Raven glanced back at Juan and asked, "Is this true, Juan?"

"Si, Señorita! I am very reliable for you!"

CHAPTER 4

Raven, Jeffrey, Juan, and Rivera all sat together in Rivera's study, sharing wine and cheese. Raven had never been to the hacienda before; she had always done business with Rivera at the edge of town near the docks.

"Señorita Raven, what brings you to St. Felix this time? Do you have goods to trade?"

"I do! I also have a new ship that will need outfitting with cannons and ammunition if you have any left."

"Oh, where is this ship? I only saw the one come into port."

"My other two ships will be here shortly. *Matilda* should be here in less than two hours. The *Nightingale* will arrive two hours later."

"You have gold to trade for the cannons?"

"I have gold, yes. But I will also need other supplies. Do you have rum?"

"Si, I have many barrels of rum. How many do you need?"

"How many do you have?"

"Hmm, I'm not sure. Juan?"

"Señor Rivera, we have more than two hundred barrels."

Rivera asked, "Why do you need so much rum? Are you going to throw a fiesta?"

"No, I have a new client. They also want tools and textiles."

"Okay, I have textiles. Do you want silk?"

"No, silk would be too fine. This client needs sturdy cloth. Cotton would be better."

"Si, I have much cotton fabric. You say you have gold to trade?"

Raven replied, "I have gold, only it isn't gold coins; it's golden trinkets – cups, statues, jewelry, and such."

"Ah! So we will weigh it out to determine the value, eh?"

"That is agreeable. Shall we begin?"

"Yes. We can start unloading it and weigh it out to determine its value if you like."

Rivera smiled and said, "I am ready to see your gold. Por favor, lead the way."

John and his crew brought up cargo from below decks in preparation for Raven's return. A young man named Mtu Mdago was standing in the crow's nest with his spyglass, searching the bay west of *Destiny*. He suddenly saw a ship sailing from the north heading for Port St. Felix. The ship was sailing along the eastern coast of the African continent. Mdago cried out, "Ship ahoy! Starboard stern!"

John looked around to find the vessel in question. Without his spyglass, he could only make out a ship that appeared to be out about two miles.

"Mdago, can you see what flag it flies?"

"The flag has three colors. They run like this."

He held his hand with three fingers pointing down. He stroked each finger with his forefinger from his other hand to indicate the flag's colors.

"Blue, white, and then red!"

John cursed under his breath.

"All hands on deck! He shouted.

Everyone scrambled to the main deck and awaited John's orders.

"Listen, the ship sailing toward us is French. They no doubt will be looking for Raven. If anyone should ask you about her, you haven't seen her since she was captured months ago. You new men, you don't even know who Raven is. You have never met her. Understand?"

"Aye, Mr. Ashworth!" they all said.

"We are here to trade for rum and supplies, that is all."

"Aye!"

"Hadari, make ready the guns on the starboard rail. Have your gunmen ready, but not obvious."

"Aye, Mr. Ashworth."

"Now, go!"

Everyone quickly continued their work except the gun crew, who loaded the cannons.

John called Jeremy over and said in a low tone, "Jeremy, I need you to go find Raven. Tell her that a French ship is coming into port. Tell her to hide!"

"Aye, Mr. Ashworth!"

Jeremy started to run from the ship when John stopped him, "Jeremy, leave that blasted monkey here!"

Jeremy suddenly stopped, turned around, and carried Captain Billings into Raven's cabin, where he left the monkey on the bed. He turned around and ran away from the ship as fast as possible.

Jeremy ran down a street on the left side of the village where he had seen Raven and Rivera walking earlier. He searched high and low for anyone who could point him in the direction to find

Señor Rivera. He saw a young woman hanging out laundry up the street. He called to her as he approached her, "Señor Rivera?"

The woman pointed up the street and said something in Spanish Jeremy did not understand. He continued forward, taking deep breaths as he ran. His heart was pounding in his chest. The fourteen-year-old was youthful but not used to running that hard for so long. Still, he wouldn't stop until he found Raven.

The street sloped upward the farther he went into the village. His breathing became labored. He stopped momentarily to catch his breath, then he continued.

Jeremy saw four individuals walking toward him a quarter of a mile away, up the hill. He waved his hand as he ran, trying to catch their attention.

"Raven!" he cried out. "Raven!"

The four individuals noticed Jeremy and walked more quickly toward him. When they realized who he was, they began to trot. Moments later, they all met. Jeremy was so breathless he could barely speak.

"Raven, a French ship is coming toward us. Mr. Ashworth says you must hide. He has told everyone to say no one has seen you since you were arrested."

Raven's eyes widened, realizing she was in danger of being arrested again. She looked at Rivera for answers.

He told his servant, "Juan, take her! You know where to hide her."

"Si, Señor Rivera. I hide her good!"

The two of them trotted off back the way they had come. Rivera then turned to Jeffrey and said, "You and I are in a negotiation of trade. We have nothing to hide, understand?"

"I understand."

The two and Jeremy walked casually toward the docks as if they were old friends discussing nothing. As they got closer,

Rivera said to Jeffrey, "Congratulations, Señor Hamilton! You are now captain of *Raven's Destiny*."

Jeffrey looked at Rivera as if he were mad and asked, "What?"

"Ah, just for today."

Jeffrey then replied. "Oh, I understand."

Jeffrey began to walk alongside Rivera with more confidence. He walked proudly like a peacock. Jeremy watched and snickered under his breath. As they reached the docks, the French vessel pulled up to *Destiny* and anchored at her starboard rail to keep *Destiny* from fleeing if her crew chose to do so.

Rivera, Jeffrey, and Jeremy met John at the gangplank.

"Señor Ashworth, have you met your Captain Hamilton?"

John looked at Rivera questioningly, then realized his game.

"Welcome back Captain Hamilton. The men are ready to unload the cargo whenever you are ready."

A French voice came from behind them, saying, "You there! Stand still! Prepare to be boarded by His Majesty's Navy."

Jeffrey and John walked to the other side of the ship and greeted the man who had made his announcement.

"I am Captain Jeffrey Hamilton. Who might you be?"

"Captain Michaud Jacques de Francois, captain of His Majesty's Guard."

Jeffrey asked, "How may I be of service, Captain?"

"We are looking for the Red Raven."

Jeffrey acted dumbfounded as he replied, "Red Raven? We haven't seen or heard from her since your soldiers carried her away several months ago from this very port. Do you mean she has escaped?"

"Oui, and you already know it!"

"Well, I know no such thing, Captain. My men and I have been at sea these past several months. The last thing we heard was that Raven was taken back to France and executed. Are you saying she's not dead?"

"Captain Hamilton, I believe you know where she is and that you are hiding her. You and your men will exit the ship at once while my men search the ship."

"Captain, I will have my men leave the ship while you search, but my officers and I will remain to watch your men search my ship. We have valuable merchandise onboard and I wouldn't want any of it to find its way into the pockets of your soldiers."

"My men are honorable! They do not need you to watch over them. You must leave!"

The two captains continued to volley their concerns and reassurances to one another when suddenly, two cannonballs whistled through the air, striking the French frigate in its starboard hull at the waterline.

Matilda sailed into view of St Felix right on time. Daktari was checking the port with his spyglass as they moved closer to the port. He called Pharaoh over when he witnessed a second ship at the docks along with *Destiny*.

"Pharaoh, there is a French ship blocking *Destiny* at the port!"

Pharaoh looked through the spyglass and confirmed what Daktari had said.

"Daktari, prepare to come about when we are within gun range. Fire our two starboard guns into their hull near the waterline. We need to sink that ship!"

"Aye, Pharaoh!"

Daktari ordered his gun crew to prepare the starboard cannons at five degrees elevation. The men scrambled to prepare their cannons, loading them with powder and cannon shot. Then, they stood by with the match, a slow-burning fuse on the end of a stick. When Daktari was convinced they were within 1,500 yards from their target, he ordered the helmsman to come about so that the starboard guns could be presented. Once the guns were properly lined up with their target, Daktari ordered, "Fire!"

Both guns erupted, billowing smoke from their pipes and expelling the six-pound iron ball toward the frigate. Both shots reached their target, blowing two holes in the starboard hull of the enemy ship – one just above the waterline and the other just below. The blasts were enough to cause the frigate to begin taking on water.

Pharaoh commanded, "Prepare to fire again!"

The gun crew quickly swabbed out the cylinders and, reloaded the cannons with gunpowder and shot. The gunmen raised their hands to signal that their cannons were again ready to fire.

"Daktari ordered again, "Fire!"

Again, the cannons fired their blasts into the air, and the iron balls whistled toward the French frigate, whose men were already scrambling in a panic as they were unexpectedly attacked.

Captain Francois ordered his men to load their cannons and return fire. He would have the upper hand even though he was caught off guard. His frigate carried many more cannons aboard than the *Matilda*; Francois needed to get two or three shots off to make it a fight. However, he hadn't realized that his ship was already sinking from the two holes in his starboard hull. The frigate's guns were located below decks, and the water leaking into its hull had already soaked the gunpowder they needed to fire his weapons. The French gunmen didn't realize it until they tried to fire the cannons, and the powder wouldn't ignite.

Francois stood on the main deck continuously, calling for the guns to be fired. Everyone seemed to be ignoring him, which exacerbated him. Meanwhile, Jeffery's crew had already begun attacking the vessel, too.

Both of their starboard guns were fired at the frigate, both at point-blank range. One shot hit the quarterdeck, while the other blasted the base of the main mast. French bodies began to fly everywhere as the shots landed, exploding the ship into pieces. Splinters and shards of the wooden vessel struck the French sailors and soldiers like bullets being fired from hundreds of muskets all at once.

Matilda's second shot hit the frigate in the starboard hull, opening up two more holes. She quickly began to sink, and many of her crew could be seen diving over the rail to avoid sinking with the ship.

Pharaoh ordered the ship to come around again. "Turn back around and head right for her. Don't let anyone escape!"

Pharaoh's men picked up muskets and lined up at the ship's bow to begin firing at the men bobbing up and down in the sea. Many of them tried to swim for the docks but were shot before they could climb up out of the water.

Jeffrey ordered the crew of *Destiny* to fire their muskets at any Frenchmen still on the ship's deck. It was like shooting rats in a barrel – there was nowhere for them to escape.

Twenty minutes later, the French vessel and all her crew were either at the bottom of the bay or floating lifelessly on top of the water. No one from either *Destiny's* or *Matilda's* crews was injured. Raven's men raised their guns in the air and cheered one another in victory over their enemies.

Pharaoh docked *Matilda* a few slips down from *Destiny* and left the ship to meet with Jeffrey and John. They all met along the boardwalk with Rivera to discuss what had happened.

Pharaoh asked, "Where is Raven?"

Rivera replied, "Señorita Raven is fine. I had my man Juan take her to a safe hiding place. We will go and get her momentarily."

Jeffrey suggested, "Why don't we get started unloading our cargo and get this deal done. The *Nightingale* should be here in about an hour. We'll need to get her outfitted with cannons as soon as possible. While you two get everything unloaded, I'll go with Señor Rivera to find Raven and bring her back."

John said, "No Jeffery, I'll go."

Jeffrey looked at the concerned father's face and knew he should relent. "Of course, John. I understand. I'll see to *Destiny* while you're gone."

"Thanks!" John replied.

John and Rivera quickly walked up the street on the north side of the village.

John asked, "How far is it?"

"It is not far. She is at my hacienda."

"Your hacienda? That would be the first place they would have looked for her had they made it off that ship!"

"Señor John, it isn't where you hide someone or how far away that you hide them, it is how you conceal them."

Ten minutes later, John and Rivera walked into Rivera's study. There, they found Juan sitting at a desk tending to the accounts for Rivera.

John looked around, then asked, "Well, where is she?"

Rivera looked at Juan and said, "Juan, if you please?"

Juan stood up and moved to the end of his desk while Rivera stood at the other end. They lifted the desk a few inches off the floor and shuffled it over to a new location. Juan pulled away the carpet under his desk, revealing a hidden hatch. With much effort, Juan pulled at the latch on the trap door to lower it open.

Then Juan called out to the darkness, "Señorita Raven? You can come out now."

Raven's face appeared from the darkness as she climbed a ladder leading up to Rivera's office.

Raven asked, "Papa? What happened? Is *Destiny* alright?"

"Everyone is alright, daughter. Pharaoh came into port at just the right time and fired against the French ship and sank her. None of our men were harmed."

"How about the French?"

"They have all perished and their ship is at the bottom of the bay."

Raven embraced her father with tears in her eyes and said, "I'm so thankful that everyone is alright."

CHAPTER 5

When Raven returned to the docks, *Nightingale* appeared on the western horizon. Thirty minutes later, the ship docked next to *Matilda*. Raven greeted Alexander and told him what had happened after *Destiny* arrived. She also informed Alexander and Pharaoh of the new signal that Rivera had set up to inform them of safe docking.

Rivera's men inspected all the golden items that Raven had brought him. They weighed it all and discovered she had brought nearly seven hundred pounds of gold.

Raven asked Rivera, "What kind of deal can we work out?"

Rivera asked in return, "What are you needing?"

"I need new cannons for the new ship, ammunition for all my ships, food supplies, cotton fabric, rum, tools to trade, and coinage to pay my crew."

Rivera thought, then said, "Let's see, the gold trinkets will have to be processed to make them easier to trade with. I'll have my men melt them down into gold bars. I think we can call it £500 gold after it is melted down."

"Let's call it £600." Raven replied.

Rivera suddenly remembered how savvy Raven could be in her trading.

"Alright, £600. So, £200 for the cannons and ammunition, £100 for one hundred barrels of rum, £50 for one hundred bolts of fabric, £25 for fifty various tools of your choice, and £100 for a month's worth of supplies for your three ships. That leaves you . . . £125 to pay your crew. How does that sound?"

"It sounds like you're the pirate. £200 for the cannons and ammunition, £100 for one hundred and fifty barrels of rum, £50 for two hundred bolts of fabric, £25 for the tools and £100 for three month's worth of supplies."

Rivera countered, "One hundred and twenty-five barrels of rum, one hundred and fifty bolts of fabric, and two month's worth of supplies."

Raven replied, "Deal!"

"Very fine! Let us go back to my hacienda and we can get you the balance of your gold."

Raven said, "Give me a moment to get my people started on loading the ships. Will Juan be overseeing our transaction?"

"Si!"

Raven asked, "Then, Juan, would you mind coming along with me while I instruct my officers?"

"Si, Señorita! I come with you."

Raven told Rivera, "Why don't I meet you at your hacienda in half an hour, Señor Rivera?"

"Bueno! I will see you, then."

Raven and Juan walked over to each ship so Raven could gather her officers. Pharaoh, Attila, Daktari, Alexander, John, Hadari, and Jeffrey were gathered together with Raven and Juan as they were given instructions.

"Alexander and Daktari, you will be responsible for supplying all the ships with ammunition and installing the new cannons onto the *Nightingale*."

Alexander replied, "Aye, Raven."

"Pharaoh, you will have some of your men load one hundred and twenty-five barrels of rum onto the ships. Split the load up between all three ships."

"Aye, Raven."

"Attila, I need you to have men load one hundred and fifty bolts of cotton fabric and split the load between the three ships."

"Aye, Raven."

"Hadari, you will select fifty tools to trade with the mountain people. Just put them all on *Destiny*."

"What kind of tools, Raven?"

"Hammers, picks, and spades mostly. Anything that will make it easier for them. You've seen their village. Think about what you would need if you were in their situation."

"Aye, Raven."

"And, Papa, would you please gather enough food and water supplies for two months for all three ships?"

"Aye, Raven."

"Jeffrey, I need you to accompany me please. The rest of you, Juan will be here to answer any questions you have regarding where to collect your supplies. I will be at Rivera's hacienda finalizing our deal."

Raven and Jeffrey walked silently together for a while before Jeffrey finally asked, "I guess the French are still searching for you, then?"

"It seems to be the case."

Jeffrey suggested, "Maybe we should lay low for a while until things settle down."

"That doesn't work for me. I have too many people counting on me and there are too many people who are being captured and placed into slavery."

"Yes, but we are only a small fleet of three ships and very little fire power. What will we do when a whole fleet of frigates come for us?"

Raven replied, "We have to be smarter than they are, and we will need to increase our fleet whenever the opportunity presents itself."

Jeffrey said, "These square rigged ships are not built for fighting. We need to capture a faster vessel, maybe a schooner, that we can use as a gun ship to help block attacking ships from firing upon our other ships."

"That's a good idea. Too bad we had to sink that frigate. It would have made an excellent gun ship for us. Maybe Rivera has some ideas about that."

They continued to walk together until they finally reached the hacienda. Raven knocked on the door and waited until a young, dark-skinned woman opened it. The girl wore a bright-colored dress, and her feet were bare.

"Si? Puedo ayudarlo?"

Raven replied, "Donde es Señor Rivera?"

"Ven conmigo, por favor."

Raven and Jeffrey followed as the young woman led them through the hacienda into Rivera's study.

When Rivera saw Raven being led into his study, he told the young woman, "Ah, gracias, Teresa."

Rivera smiled as he sat at his desk-like table. "Raven, I have your money all ready for you."

He presented Raven with a small chest, about eight inches wide, twelve inches long, and six inches tall, with leather handles. When Raven tried to take the chest from Rivera, it was heavier than expected.

"Humph!" she grunted.

"Here, Jeffrey. You take it, you're the quartermaster."

Jeffrey strained as he took the chest from Raven and looked for a place to check its contents.

Rivera said, "Señor Hamilton, you may use that other table to count the money if you like."

Jeffrey nodded, placed the chest on the table, and opened it to see it was nearly full of gold coins engraved with Spanish symbols and writing. The coins were valued at various amounts – some were worth about one-fourth of a British pound, while others were one-half. As Jeffrey began counting the coins, Rivera and Raven entered into a conversation concerning their future together.

Raven began, "Señor Rivera?"

"Please, Raven. Don't you think it is time to begin calling me Oscar? We are, after all, amigos, are we not?"

"Of course, Oscar. Do you know of any small ships that might be suitable for use as a gunship for my small fleet?"

"Are you talking about a purchase?

"No. . . not necessarily. If we happened to find a ship like that frigate that is already outfitted for battle, that would be ideal."

Rivera replied, "Si, however capturing a ship of this sort would be most unlikely with your large merchant ships, would it not?"

"Yes, unless we could manage to set a trap for one."

"Si, this would take careful planning. The frigate carries one hundred and fifty fighting men. How many men do you have on your three ships?"

"Not that many, maybe one hundred at best."

Rivera suggested, "Maybe you should increase the number of soldiers under your command before you try to take on the French navy again. I realize you just sank a frigate in my bay, but much of that was due to luck and timing, was it not?"

"You are right. Thank you for your counsel. I will think on this a little more."

Jeffrey walked over to where Raven was standing and announced, "It's all there."

Raven nodded her response as Rivera said, "Bueno! Bueno! Is there anything else I can do for you today?"

Raven replied, "No thank you. As always you have been very accommodating. We will finish loading our ships and prepare to launch tomorrow morning."

Rivera replied, "Raven, it is always good to see you and to do business with you. Until next time, my dear."

Raven shook Oscar's hand and said, "Hasta que nos encontremos de nuevos!"

Raven and Jeffrey then left the hacienda, carrying the chest by one of the leather handles.

Raven commented, "Next time, remind me to bring more men to carry the money."

Jeffrey said, "Don't worry, we only have about a mile or so to reach the ship."

They struggled as they made their way down the village street, stopping occasionally to catch their breath and relax their muscles. Half an hour after leaving Rivera's hacienda, they arrived at the docks.

Alexander's men were still installing the cannons on the *Nightingale*, but all the other supplies had already been loaded onto the ships. Pharaoh and all the other officers pitched in to install the new cannons and supply the three ships with a whole load of gunpowder and cannon shot.

When the installation was completed, Jeffrey set up a small table on the dock to begin paying the crew. John sat next to Jeffrey and counted out the proper amount of money for each man or woman who was paid according to their rank by the Articles of Code Raven had established when she and her crew began.

Before they made the first payment, Jeffrey called Raven over to ask, "What about the men who have just joined us? Do they get their full share?"

Raven replied, "Why shouldn't they?"

"Well, they haven't been here as long as the others. Do they deserve a full share?"

Raven asked, "Tell me this, if a new man had died in battle on the way here, would he be only half-dead?"

"Well, no . . . it's just that, what will the others think?"

"Why don't you ask them?"

John sat at the table listening to their conversation, his head bowed, and his mouth curved into a smile. He knew Jeffrey was not going to win an argument with his daughter. Raven could see far in advance above most other people. She knew human nature could create jealousy among the crew. However, she also understood that the risk was equal among them all. Any one of them could die at any moment. It didn't matter if you had been with her from the beginning or had come aboard last week. You were one of her crew members and got paid like any other crew member. She also knew that paying the new men and women the total share would encourage their loyalty to her.

Jeffrey finally sat beside John, and the two began paying the crew. The crew lined up in front of the table by ships. *Matilda* was the first crew to get paid. Pharaoh and Attila stood next to the table as their crew received their pay. Jeffrey had a ledger in which each crew member's name was listed. He entered the amount each man or woman was paid as John counted the proper number of coins. The *Nightingale* crew was paid next as Alexander and Daktari stood by at the table. Then, finally, *Destiny's crew* stepped forward to receive their wages while Hadari stood by. The officers were paid last receiving their proper shares.

Raven then addressed the crews of all three ships, "Did everyone get paid?"

All her people cheered happily, "Yes!"

"Good! Now go and have some fun. Spend your money however you like, but be back on your ships before dawn tomorrow. We will be leaving at first light. I expect all of you to be sober and ready for duty. There is work to be done, ships to be captured, and men and women to be freed from the bonds of slavery."

Again, all her crew cheered, and they slowly dispersed into the village to discover how to spend their money.

As Raven started up *Destiny's* gangplank, Jeffrey stepped next to her and said, "I didn't mean to question your authority back there."

Raven replied, "You didn't. You were simply asking a question, and I simply gave you an answer. Was there malice in your question?"

"Well no, but I didn't want you to think there was either."

"I thought no such thing. Do you think me so fragile that you have to worry about my feelings?"

"But I do worry about your feelings. I don't ever want to offend you."

"Jeffrey, if you offend me, I will certainly let you know. Did I hurt your tender little feelings?" she asked with a wry smile.

Jeffrey smiled back and replied, "Maybe. Just a little."

"Ah, you pitiful little thing." she said as she turned and walked away.

John then approached Jeffrey and said, "Careful, lad. I have a feeling that girl is going to break your heart someday."

CHAPTER 6

Morning broke under a dark clouded sky. Raven stood on the quarterdeck of her ship, looking toward the village. Many of her people were walking quickly toward their respective ships.

Raven exclaimed to Hadari, "Sound the signal! Get those people onboard!"

Hadari blew the conch shell to announce *Destiny's* readiness to depart. Raven waited for a response from the other captains.

Raven asked John, "Is everyone aboard *Destiny*?"

"We're missing three – Mwanamke Mtamu, Mvuvi, and Seremala."

Once the conch was blown, the men and women began to sprint toward the ships. Some were carrying parcels, others were wearing new clothes, and others were staggering as if they had been drinking all night.

Hadari said to Raven, "There is Mvuvi!"

Mvuvi was running toward the ship with a bundle under his arm. He galloped up the gangplank and avoided eye contact with anyone on the quarterdeck.

Raven yelled at Mvuvi, "Mvuvi, why are you keeping my ship from leaving on time?"

Mvuvi replied as he continued to the lower deck, "Sorry, Raven!"

Seremala was the next to arrive. He was only half-dressed as he scrambled up the gangplank. "I'm sorry Seremala, did we wake you too early!"

"No, Raven!"

Finally, but not the last of the stragglers, was Mwanamke Mtamu.

"Mwanamke Mtamu, how nice of you to join us this morning! Is it alright if we leave now?"

"Sorry, Raven!"

Destiny's crew was complete. Raven continued to wait until she received the response call from *Matilda* and *Nightingale* that all hands were aboard. She watched as several more scrambled up the gangplanks of the other two ships. When she thought she had seen the final crew member board his ship, Raven noticed one more just now stepping out of the village into the docks area. He was one of the white sailors who had joined Raven's crew and seemed to be in no hurry.

Raven asked Hadari, "Who is that man?"

Hadari looked through his spyglass and responded, "He is one of the new men that previously served onboard the *Nightingale*, Raven."

Raven ordered, "Signal Pharaoh to set sail right away!"

"Aye, Raven!"

Hadari blew the signal for *Matilda* to leave immediately. A few seconds later, *Matilda* called back, acknowledging the order. *Matilda* loosed her lines from the docks, keeping them tied to the pier, and began floating away. A call came from the *Nightingale* that she was ready to sail.

Raven said, "Give *Nightingale* the signal to set sail."

Then she told John, "Mr. Ashworth, set sail, please."

John smiled as he realized Raven was teaching the new man who had failed to be on time and her whole crew that tardiness would not be tolerated.

"Aye, Captain!"

When the unnamed man noticed the ships pulling away, he panicked and ran to the docks. By the time he reached the end of the pier, *Matilda* was already ten feet away. He called out, trying to get their attention.

"Hey! Wait! I'm right here!"

He heard his fellow shipmates laughing at him as the ship slowly floated away. The man saw Pharaoh standing on the quarterdeck, looking straight at him with his arms folded. Pharaoh never said a word to the man. He asked Attilla, "What is his name?"

"Henry Bleaker."

Bleaker cried out, "Wait, don't leave me!"

All three ships floated away from St. Felix, heading west to the Cape.

A month later, Raven had her ships pull into Port Gentil to check on the people she had left there. She noticed four men on the beach working on constructing a boat she assumed would be used for fishing. The men stood when they saw the ships pull into port, watching to see who was coming. They were relieved when they saw Raven standing on the quarterdeck, her red hair waving in the breeze. They waved to her.

Raven and John met Pharaoh and Alexander on the docks to meet the four men. The men all smiled when Raven approached them, happy to see the one who had rescued them from tragedy.

"Salamu!" Raven greeted the men.

"Salamu, Shujaa Mkubwa!" which translates, "Greetings, great warrior!"

Raven asked, "How are your people? Is everyone still safe?"

One of the men replied, "The ones who are still here are well. Many of the people left to find their homes."

"How many of you are left?"

"Only about fifty, and most of them are women."

Raven asked, "Why did so many leave? I thought they were afraid to go back to their villages because their leaders traded them into slavery."

"They are all afraid. They think that more white men will find them here at this beach and take them away again."

"Why did you men stay?"

"We have nowhere else to go. We have no families to go back to and we are unwanted."

"Unwanted?"

Alexander spoke up, "Banished!"

Raven asked the man, "Why were you banished?"

"We were a part of the royal guard for our chief. The chief's younger brother sought to take over as chief. We fought to protect the chief, but when he was killed by his brother, the brother humiliated us in front of the people, making them think that we were responsible for the chief's death. The people threw stones and sticks at us and tried to kill us. We ran from the village and we were captured by white men who put us on the ship."

"Raven asked, "Did you men come to the beach when we were here before? Did you ask to sail with us?"

The man replied, "No, we do not like the sea. We feel better on the land."

Raven asked, "So, you plan to stay here?"

"Yes, we will hunt and fish. Maybe we can set up a trading post. Many of the women are excellent weavers. There are many women here for just four men. Maybe we will all have many wives. We will all be kings." The man laughed.

Raven smiled at his joke. "Is there anything you need?"

"Do you have any more machetes? All of the machetes were taken by the ones who left."

"Yes!"

She turned to Alexander and asked, "Will you see to it?"

"Aye, Raven!"

Moments later, Alexander arrived with a machete for each man and handed it to them. Each man received his machete and bowed as he acknowledged his gratitude.

Raven said, "I want to see your progress in setting up your new village."

One of the men, Shujaa wa Mfalme, led Raven and her officers to the village while the other three men remained working on their boat. The party followed Mfalme through the jungle trail that led to the clearing where the women were working to make their new dwellings inhabitable. Some women gathered firewood, some picked fruit, and others made reed baskets.

Mfalme said to Raven as they entered the clearing, "We found a large house to the north. It seems to be abandoned. We were afraid to go in for fear that the owner would find us and kill us."

Raven said, "The man who owned that house is now hanging from a tree on the beach. His name was Arsenault. You don't have to fear him. Take the house and use it as you like. You might find something useful in there – something worth trading for other things you need."

"Who would we trade with?"

"I will trade with you. Is there anything you need?"

"Goats! We need goats!"

Raven replied, "Ah, we can do that. How many do you want?"

"Two bucks and seven does will be a good start. We can grow the herd from that."

Raven then noticed the baskets the women were constructing. They were various sizes and shapes—some large with handles, while others were small, bowl-shaped. They were all exquisite.

"Have your women make as many baskets as they can, all shapes and sizes. I will trade you the goats for as many baskets as you can make until I return."

Mfalme smiled as he said, "We can do this."

Then Raven said, "Go to the house and pull out anything you think is of value. I'll trade for those too."

"Thank you, Red Raven!"

As they walked farther into the clearing, Mfalme announced to the women, "Look who has come to visit! It is the Red Raven!"

The women looked up from their chores and began to sing out their greetings to Raven as she approached. Everyone gathered around Raven and her men, laying their hands upon them as if blessing them. Then, the women began singing a song to Raven as they bounced around her like kangaroos.

"Kunguru Mwekundu anasafiri juu ya maji
(The Red Raven sails on the water)
Yeye ni shujaa hodari
(She is a mighty warrior)

Ametuweka huru kutoka kwa wafungwa wetu
(She has freed us from our captives)
Tunakuheshimu Kunguru Mwekundu
(We honor you, the Red Raven)
Kunguru Mwekundu ametuokoa
(The Red Raven has saved us)
Kunguru ametuokoa.
(The Raven has saved us.)"

The singing went on and on as Raven was led into the village. When they reached the structure that had once served as a prison for slaves, Raven noticed an image of a red raven had been painted on the door. Suddenly, she was overwhelmed with the honor these people had placed on her. Tears welled up in her eyes and began to run down her face. She was speechless.

Mfalme asked Raven, "Will you and your men join us in celebration of your return?"

Raven asked, "All of my men?"

"Yes, all of your men. We have gathered much food from the jungle around us. There will be plenty."

"We would be honored."

Raven sent John, Alexander, and Pharaoh back to the ships to invite the men to the village for the celebration. Twelve men would be left behind to stand watch.

As the evening sun began to lower itself behind the horizon, the celebration had started. The nearly one hundred of Raven's men dispersed throughout the clearing, mingling with the villagers. People were laughing, singing, and eating. Drums were brought out and set up around the fire at the center of the clearing. A rhythmic beat began, then chants entered in, and finally, singing as everyone celebrated.

Several village women danced around the fire to the beat of the drums and the singing. Raven had never witnessed such a display of pure joy. One of the women reached out and took Raven by the hand. She led Raven into the dance procession and encouraged her to dance with the other women. Raven felt self-conscious at first, then allowed her inhibitions to leave. She danced with the women around the fire until she could dance no more. Raven plopped down next to Jeffrey, who had been watching her dance around the fire.

Jeffrey commented, "I never knew you could dance like that."

"Neither did I!"

The party lasted until nearly midnight. People slowly began leaving the clearing, searching for a place to sleep for the night. Raven and her officers returned to the ships, climbed aboard, and found their beds.

Raven lay in bed thinking about the night. She couldn't remember ever having so much fun in her life. So much of her life was involved with work, problems, and danger. There was little time for fun. She thought she would need to change that about her life. Then, she closed her eyes and quickly fell asleep.

Raven awoke to the sound of rain pelting the roof of her cabin. A chill filled the air as the winds blew against the ship's hull. Raven heard her men above and below as they prepared to launch the ships back into the sea—their destination – the mountain people.

It had been nearly a year since Raven and her crew had met the people who mined for gold on a mountain that had been undiscovered by anyone except the primitive people who lived at its base.

Raven stayed in her cabin most of the day due to the rain. She didn't mind the rain so much but felt a little melancholy this morning. Raven sat on her bed, looking out the port hole into the distance and at nothing. She thought about her losses. She had lost her mother at such an early age. Typhus had been rampant in Bristol at that time. She remembered her father dressing her up like a boy, cutting her hair, and changing her name to Richard so she could go on the merchant vessels with him.

Captain Billings crawled into her lap, which made her think of Captain Horatio Billings, her first captain. She had feared him initially but learned quickly that he could be a gentle soul that she grew very fond of. He taught her everything she now knew about sailing, fighting, and business. He had leaned on her as a consultant when he realized how sharp her mind was. She had a flare for seeing things plainly before others could even catch a glimpse of them.

Raven then began to think of Caesar, Nero, Birdie, and Whisper – people she had saved from slavery and had added to her crew. Caesar and Nero were among the first five – she bought their freedom with money she earned onboard the original *Destiny.* Birdie and Whisper were two young women among the many that Raven had rescued from *Destiny* when she went down in a hurricane.

Pharaoh, Attila, and Alexander were the remaining of her original five. They had paired themselves with Rose, April, and Melody from the *Destiny* shipwreck.

A knock came to her door. "Enter!" Raven called out.

Jeremy opened the door and entered with Raven's breakfast.

"Set it down, Jeremy, then come sit with me."

Jeremy carefully set the tray on Raven's table, then walked over to her bed. He paused before he sat next to her and the monkey.

"Are you alright, Raven?"

"Yes, I'm fine. I've just been thinking of all that has happened to me since I was your age."

Jeremy asked, "How old were you when you first sailed?"

"I was twelve years old."

"I didn't know they allowed young girls aboard ships at such a young age."

Raven replied, "They didn't. My papa dressed me like a boy. He cut my hair really short and he named me Richard. Has no one told you this?"

"Aye, I heard some stories. But, I never know what to believe. The crew make up all sorts of stories."

Raven asked, "Have they told you about Davy Jones?"

Jeremy paused with a lump in his throat, then replied, "I've heard of him."

"Well? What have you heard?"

"Well, some say he's none other than Jonah himself, from the Bible. Living under the sea in a great cavern. He calls out to you during heavy storms and those that hear his call find themselves dragged under never to return to dry land. I also heard some say, he doesn't live under water, but runs a tavern in London. He's the devil himself he is. He wallops men on their noggins and throws them into his locker until he can sell them to ships sailing out of port. The men are never heard from again. Who do you think he is, Raven?"

Raven decided to ease Jeremy's mind with her version of the story. "Jeremy, have you ever heard of a metaphor?"

"A metal what?"

"Not metal! A metaphor. It's like an example people make up to describe something that is unknown or complicated. I think that's what Davy Jones is. He's a metaphor of death that comes to men on the open seas. Have you ever heard of someone on a ship being called a Jonah by his ship mates?"

"Yes, but I never knew why."

"It's because he seems to be an unlucky sort. Everything goes wrong for him. In the Bible, Jonah was one of the most unlucky of all sailors. Think about it. All the men on that boat out in the sea with him, he gets tossed overboard and swallowed up by a whale. Now, how unlucky can you get? So, that's why unlucky sailors are referred to as Jonahs. Now, I think that Davy Jones' locker is just a reference to where men go to be buried when they die at sea. It's a sailor's graveyard. It's nothing to fear unless you're afraid of death."

Jeremy asked, "Are you afraid of death?"

"No."

"Not even your own death?"

"Jeremy, the way I see it is, death is just sleep. You fall asleep and you sleep forever. It's nothing to fear."

"But aren't you afraid of it hurting if you are killed?"

"Lot's of things hurt. Did you ever stump your toe? That hurts alright! But, not for long."

Jeremy then asked, "Aren't you afraid when you get into a fight that you might get killed?"

"Jeremy, when you're in a fight with someone, you have to think of yourself as already dead. Fear is a powerful thing. It can make a man freeze in his tracks so he can't move. If you have fear when in a fight, you might as well lay down and die. When I fight I have no fear for myself. I imagine myself as already dead, that removes my fear and allows me to fight at my best."

Jeremy asked, "So, you want to die?"

"No, I don't want to die. That's why I live so freely though. I live everyday of my life as if it's my last day in this world."

Chapter 7

Nine hours after they left Port Gentil, Raven's ships sailed past the inlet they called their home base, the Robin's Nest. They were fully supplied, so there was no need to stop there. They continued sailing eastward toward Mbini, a port in Equatorial Guinea. They followed the coastal line, turning slightly north, and continued until they reached the point Raven had marked on her chart. Raven had dubbed the location Mlima wa Dhahabu the Gold Mountain.

The mountain was about seven miles off the coast. The ships entered a bay from the gulf – the bay was shaped like a star with seven points. Raven's destination was the middle of the seven points. All three ships moored off the coast because there weren't any docks along the beach to park their ships. Raven's men would have to use the dories to reach the dry land and begin their trek to the mountain. Their journey to the village of the mountain people would require nearly all of Raven's crew.

Each of the three ships carried two dories. Each dory would shuttle over ten men plus supplies. Each dory made four trips from a ship to the beach before the trade goods and the men were offloaded from the ships. Five men were left aboard each ship. An officer was left in charge of each ship among the five men. Pharaoh remained with *Matilda*, Alexander with the *Nightingale*, and John with *Destiny*.

It was nearly noon before the ships were unloaded, and Raven was ready to begin the trek through the jungle to meet with the mountain people. Raven felt excited to see the people once again. It had been nearly a year since she had seen them last. Abobtu, the king's son, was friendly enough at their previous meeting. However, he looked intimidating, with the bone sticking through his nose. He looked like a wild man who wouldn't mind having her for dinner and not as a guest.

Abobtu's father was Al Bagani, a man Raven thought to be about forty years old. He had been accommodating at their last visit once he had learned that Raven could supply him with rum.

Raven had only eighty-five men at her disposal to transport one hundred and twenty-five barrels of rum, one hundred and fifty bolts of fabric, and fifty digging instruments to the village seven miles away. Raven and Attila left Daktari behind to organize the transportation of the goods through the jungle. They left ahead of everyone else to find Abobtu. The trail wasn't obvious, but Raven had traveled it before, so she knew at least where they wanted to end their trek. She and Attila took two hours to make the seven-mile trip through the jungle. Long before they reached their destination, Raven heard familiar bird calls following her as she walked the hidden trail. Raven knew the jungle's inhabitants had seen them and were being watched all the way. She kept hoping that Abobtu would come and find her so that her anxiety would leave.

Suddenly, a figure appeared before her, blocking the trail. A large man, about six feet tall, stood in her path. His face was painted with white stripes, and a bone pierced his nose. It was Abobtu. He held a long spear in his right hand and a leather shield in his left. Raven greeted him.

"Salamu, Abobtu!"

Abobtu stood still, not saying a word.

"Abobtu, do you not remember me? I am Raven. I am here to trade with Al Bagani. We have brought rum and cloth as well as tools for digging."

Abobtu asked, "Where are these things you speak of?"

"My men are bringing them as we speak. They should be here within the hour. There is too much for them to bring all at once though. They will need to make two more trips through the jungle to get it all here."

"I will send men to help carry the load. Come, let's go into the village and I will get my men to help you. Al Bagani will want to speak with you."

Abobtu led Raven and Attila down an unseen path to their village at the mountain's base. They witnessed the familiar mud huts scattered about the clearing as they entered the village. As they walked into the clearing, Al Bagani exited his hut to meet them.

Raven greeted Al Bagani, saying, "Salamu, Al Bagani!"

Al Bagani raised his hand in greeting, saying, "Salamu."

Raven said, "We have returned to trade with you, great Al Bagani. My men are bringing rum, cloth, and tools to your village as we speak."

"I remember you, Red Raven. You brought us the drink that made us laugh. You wanted gold in exchange for more of the laughing drink. We need something else now. We need the weapons used by the white men."

Raven looked at the chief, puzzled, and asked, "What has happened since we last saw you, Al Bagani?"

White men came to our beach. We thought they were you returning to trade with us, but they were not. They captured many of my warriors and many women and took them away. They put them on big boats and sailed somewhere to the north."

Raven realized now why Abobtu had not been so cordial when he met her in the jungle. He must have been expecting them to be more slavers coming to take more of his people.

"How many of your people did they take?" Raven asked.

"Fifty men and twenty women. My youngest daughter, Mshijana Mwimbaji, was among them. She is only sixteen."

"How long ago did they leave?"

"The moon has finished its change two times since she has been gone. Do you know where they have taken her?"

"No, I don't. But, there are places we can look.

That night, Raven sat with Al Bagani, Abobtu, and Atilla to discuss plans for getting the captives back from the slavers. Raven had been thinking about a plan all afternoon after hearing that Al Bagani's people had been stolen. As they sat by the fire near the center of the village, Raven laid out her plan.

"Abobtu, would you be willing to go with me as I search for your people? I need someone who will recognize them should we find them."

Abobtu looked at his father for permission to follow Raven. Al Bagani nodded to his son, signifying he would allow him to leave.

"I will go with you."

"Al Bagani, I will leave one of my ships here to protect your people while Abobtu is gone. There is a place on the north side of the Gulf of Guinea that claims to have many slaves to sell. We will check there first."

Al Bagani asked, "When will you leave?"

"We will start at first light tomorrow. Al Bagani, I will need gold to take with me to trade for your people should we find them. If they are where I think they are, it is a fortified city. I can't go in there and steal them away. I will have to buy their freedom. After we have rescued your people, we will go back and make sure they never take your people again."

Al Bagani replied, "Take whatever you need, only bring back Mshijana Mwimbaji and the rest of my people."

Raven then said, "I will leave now. Abobtu, I will leave Attila and my men here until your supplies have been delivered. Then, my men will bring back the gold we will need to make the trade. Come with them and be ready to sail with me."

"I will be ready."

Raven got up from her seat and said, "Attila, will you please walk me back to the ship?"

"Aye, Raven!"

The two of them walked back to *Destiny*, and Attila listened as Raven began to lay out her plan. They met many of their men still carrying kegs of rum into the village from along the path. As Raven and Attila neared the beach, Raven instructed, "I'm going to leave the *Nightingale* here to protect this place from slavers. I need Alexander and Daktari to look after these people. You and Pharaoh will be on a mission back to Port St. Felix."

"Why will we go to Port St. Felix?"

"We're going to set a trap. I'll explain it all later."

Once Raven and Attila reached the beach, they met six of the crew who had finished delivering the goods to the village and were now waiting for the return of the others. Raven had them take her and Attila back to the ships in one of the dories so she could meet with her captains. They rowed first to *Matilda*, where they picked up Pharaoh, and then to the *Nightingale*, where they picked up Alexander. Then, they rowed over to *Destiny* and climbed aboard the ship together.

Everyone followed Raven into her cabin, along with John and Jeffrey. They all stood around the table in Raven's cabin, discussing her plan of attack.

Pharaoh had objections to her plan.

"Raven, we should not split up. We are too weak when we are divided."

"I know Pharaoh, but our strength will come from the element of surprise. If we all arrive together it will look suspicious. Besides, I have already told King Al Bagani we would protect his village. I can't change my mind on that. The *Nightingale* will remain here to protect the mountain people. *Matilda* will sail to Port St. Felix. *Destiny* will sail to Lomé. We will meet back here as soon as each phase of the mission is completed. It will take us three days to reach Lomé and another two days to see if they have Al Bagani's people and if so make the deal. It should take you six weeks for you to complete the journey to Port St. Felix and return. We will meet back here to supply Al Bagani with weapons, then sail back to the Robin's Nest to complete the second phase of our plan. Pharaoh, remember the signal that Señor Rivera has set up for us. Don't get trapped."

"I won't, Raven."

"Alexander, you and the *Nightingale* will remain here to protect the village from any more slavers."

"Aye, Raven!"

"One more thing – I want to make some changes to each of the ships' crews. *Destiny* needs to look like a slave ship, so I need all the white men on *Destiny*. I'll send my African sailors to divide among the other two ships."

Pharaoh, Alexander, and John switched up their crews, so all the white sailors were aboard *Raven's Destiny*. It was nearly midnight when Abobtu arrived with the rest of Raven's men and the gold. The gold was loaded onto the dories to be shuttled over to *Destiny*. Abobtu nervously climbed into one of the dories and clinched the side of the boat as it rocked up and down in the waves.

Attila said, "Don't worry, my friend. You will get used to it soon. We won't let you come to any harm."

When the dories arrived at *Destiny*, Abobtu was the first to climb onboard. Raven met him at the rail and helped him onto the ship.

"Welcome aboard."

Abobtu replied, "I have never seen such a large boat! It is like a village on the water!"

Raven smiled and said, "Well, I hope we can make you feel comfortable while you are with us. Don't be surprised if you feel sick the first day or so. It will pass as you get used to the motion of the ship in the waves. Be sure to drink plenty of water."

When the gold was finally loaded onto *Destiny*, Raven sent her officers back to their respective ships. Each captain made sure their ships were prepared for duty at first light. Raven had Hadari show Abobtu where he could sleep in the officers' quarters.

Raven was exhausted as she entered her cabin. She was greeted by Captain Billings, who squealed his welcome and then jumped onto her shoulder as she moved toward her bed. She sat and stroked the monkey's furry head as she thought of recent events and what she needed to do over the next several weeks. She finally decided to undress and lie under the covers of her bed, Captain Billings by her head. She closed her eyes and quickly fell asleep.

Raven awoke startled to the sound of someone blowing a conch shell. Another conch shell answered, and Raven heard men above her shuffling around, manning their post. She quickly dressed and went to the quarterdeck to observe as *Destiny* pulled away, heading northwesterly. Raven glanced across the port rail and witnessed *Matilda* weighing anchor and dropping her sail to travel west out of the Gulf of Guinea. She then looked at the *Nightingale* and raised a hand toward Alexander, standing on his quarterdeck. She hated leaving Alexander behind but knew it was the only way to keep the mountain people safe for now.

Abobtu came out of his cabin to see what was happening. He slowly walked across the deck, using his hands to grasp anything he could find to steady himself. He saw Raven on the quarterdeck and began to climb the steps to meet her. A wave tossed the ship, causing Abobtu to lose his grip and fall back to the main deck. Again, he tried climbing the steps to reach the upper deck, eventually reaching Raven wide-eyed and breathing heavily.

Raven asked, "Are you alright?"

Abobtu could only shake his head no as he grasped the rail to hold himself steady. Raven smiled at him and said, "You'll get used to it."

The sun rose over the mountains in the eastern sky as *Destiny* sailed forward, passing a small group of islands off her port bow. Once they cleared the islands, they would have a clear path to Lomé. With luck, they would reach Lomé in two and a half days.

On the second morning, Abobtu stayed in his bunk. His head was swimming, and his stomach was churning. He couldn't keep any food down – he was constantly vomiting into a bucket at his bedside. Mr. Greer came to his aid by providing some ginger root for Abobtu to chew on. Eventually, the ginger began to work its magic, and Abobtu's urge to purge subsided.

By late that afternoon, Abobtu joined Raven and the others on the quarterdeck as they sailed into the evening. On their left, the sun began its decline into the western sky, beautifully painted with azure, orange, and yellow hues. A strong breeze smashed their faces as they turned directly north toward Lomé.

Raven realized that Abobtu was still dressed in his native garb and was shivering from the wind.

"Hadari, take Abobtu below and find him some warm clothing to wear. He needs to look more like the rest of us when we go into port."

"Aye, Raven!"

Hadari escorted Abobtu down to the second deck to find suitable clothing. Abobtu was larger than most men – he was muscular and over six feet tall. The only pants Hadari found that would fit him in the waist were too short. He wore them anyway. They were still warmer than the loin cloth he had been wearing. Hadari found a shirt and a coat for the big man. No shoes were large enough for his feet, so he would have to go barefoot.

When Hadari and Abobtu returned to the quarterdeck, Raven looked him over.

"There's just one more thing. Abobtu, would you mind removing the bone from your nose? I'm afraid it will make you look out of place. We need you to look like you belong with us, not like the mighty warrior you are."

Abobtu reached up, removed the bone protruding through his nose, and looked for a place to put it. Hadari showed him that the coat he wore had pockets. Abobtu placed the bone in one of the pockets and looked to Raven to see if she was satisfied.

"Much better!" Raven commented. "How do your new clothes feel?"

"They are warm, but I can't move very well in them. It will be hard to fight in them."

"Don't worry, you'll get used to them. Besides, I hope we won't have to fight. If my plan works, we can free your people without anyone getting hurt."

Abobtu raised his voice as he said, "But, I want to hurt the men who took my people!"

"Don't worry. They will be dealt with in due time, but now is not the time. We need to make sure everyone is safe back home first."

Abobtu wasn't sure he agreed with Raven. He wanted to see the men who took his people suffer. He wanted them to die.

Raven reassured Abobtu, "Patience my friend. They will get their due when it is the right time. Patience."

CHAPTER 8

Raven's ship pulled into port at Lomé near noon on the third day. Two other merchant ships were docked at the pier when they arrived, the *Pierre Léon* from France and the *Chica Cantando* from Spain.

Raven knew she had to be careful here in Lomé. It was here she had discovered the wanted poster displaying a likeness of her face. Raven would need a disguise, so she donned her only dress and looked for a local dress shop. The dress she wore was old, tattered, and ill-fitting. She had Jeffrey accompany her, playing the part of her husband. Instead of his officer's uniform, Jeffrey wore a gentleman's garb. They left the ship together, leaving the crew behind temporarily.

They found a suitable dress shop about a quarter of a mile from the docks. Raven entered the shop with Jeffery following. A bell rang as the door opened and then closed behind them. A middle-aged woman came from the store's back room when she heard the bell ring. The woman's smile quickly faded when she saw the young woman wearing the tattered dress.

"Bon jour."

Raven replied, "Bon jour, Madame. Parlez vous anglais?"

"Yes, I speak English."

Raven said in her best snobbish demeanor, "I apologize for my appearance, Madame. I have had an unfortunate accident in which all my trunks were lost at sea. I had to borrow this awful thing from a young lady of poor circumstances. Could you help me with an outfit to sustain me until I return to England?"

Relieved, the woman replied, "But of course, Madame is it?"

"Yes, Mrs Ashworth. And this is my husband, Daniel."

The woman bowed to Jeffrey, and then Jeffrey returned her gesture.

"I have some dresses already made that I think might fit you, Madame. Come this way, please."

Raven followed the woman to the back of the store, and the two of them rummaged through racks of dresses of all sorts and colors.

"Do you see anything you like?"

Raven fingered through the racks of dresses that hung one behind the other. Suddenly, one caught her eye. She pulled out a green silk dress with white lace. The color was a beautiful jade that she thought would go well with her bright red hair. Raven held the dress in front of her and looked in a full-length mirror hanging on the wall.

Raven said, "I'd like to try this on, please."

"Oui, Madame! This way!"

Raven was led into the back room and behind a screen where she could dress privately. She quickly switched the tattered mess for the beautiful silk jade—the dress fit ideally even without a corset. Raven stepped out from behind the screen and met the woman, who responded, "Aah! Madame, you are beautiful! This dress is perfect for you!"

"Thank you, Madame! I'll need some shoes, a hat, and maybe a parasol too."

"Oui, but of course."

Raven tried on several pairs of shoes but settled on ankle-high taupe boots. Her hat was made of straw with a jade-colored ribbon and white feathers. Her parasol was white with green lace ribbons sewn around it.

Raven exited the back room to show Jeffrey what she had selected. Jeffrey was speechless when he saw Raven exit the back room.

Raven said as she walked toward him, "Your mouth is opened, Mr. Ashworth. Be careful, your teeth might try to escape."

Jeffrey closed his mouth and tried to gather his composure. "My dear, you look marvelous!"

"Thank you, darling. Now, pay the lady won't you."

Jeffrey asked the storekeeper, "How much do we owe you, Madame?"

The lady proudly announced, "This fine outfit only cost £10!"

Jeffrey tried to hide his shock when he heard the extravagant price. He managed to smile as he said, "And worth every shilling."

Jeffrey reached into his purse, pulled out several gold coins, then counted out £10 and handed it to the storekeeper.

"Merci, Monsieur!"

Jeffrey bowed to the lady and said, "Au revoir, Madame!"

Raven and Jeffrey walked out of the store and moved arm-in-arm down the streets of Lomé. They took their time walking back to the ship, ensuring everyone they met saw the beautiful red-headed woman who had come to their fair city. When they arrived back onboard *Destiny*, John greeted his daughter with a smile of delight.

"Daughter, I have always dreamed of seeing you dressed in this manner. You are beautiful my girl!"

"Thank you, Papa. Now, we must get busy. Oh, look! Someone has already taken our bait."

A man approached the ship and called out in English, using a French accent, "Ahoy there! Is the master of the ship about?"

Raven spoke quietly to Jeffrey, "Alright Master, it's time to go to work."

Jeffrey stepped to the rail and replied, "How may I help you, my good man?"

"I am Jean Louis d' Etienne. I wondered if you are in the market for anything in particular."

Jeffrey replied, "I understand this is a port where a business man might find cargo of a human nature."

"Oui, Monsieur! I can help you with that. We have many slaves to sell."

"Fine, when can we see them?"

"I can take you to them now if you like."

"Yes, give me just a moment and my party and I will be right with you."

Raven and Jeffrey prepared to leave the ship, taking Mr. Greer and Abobtu. They followed Etienne to a large carriage he had waiting one street over. His driver was standing by when they all arrived. Raven instructed Abobtu to climb up next to the driver while Etienne, Mr. Greer, Jeffery, and Raven climbed into the back.

The driver whipped the horses forward, and they trotted down the city's cobblestone streets. They drove for a mile or so, angling upward toward a large stone building on a hill. As they reached the front gate of the building, Raven noticed a sign engraved in the stone header reading Fortresse d' Pierre.

As they entered the fort, the horses' hooves on the road echoed throughout the stone walls that encased them. The walls were built in a perfect square with a courtyard in the center. The walls stood twenty feet high and were divided into three tiers of cells stacked upon each other. Each corner of the fort contained a guard tower, and there were armed guards every thirty feet throughout the structure and on all floors of the prison.

Etienne led them all to a covered porch near the center of the courtyard, where they could inspect the merchandise out of the hot sun.

Etienne asked, "How many slaves are you looking for?"

Jeffrey replied, "I don't have a certain number in mind, but each one has to have a special quality to them."

"Male or female?"

Jeffrey replied, "Both!"

"Very well then, let us begin."

Cells were emptied one at a time as slaves were marched in front of the porch for their inspection. Abobtu stood next to Jeffery with his hand gripping Jeffrey's elbow. Whenever one of Abobtu's people happen to come past, Jeffrey received a squeeze to let him know. Jeffrey then instructed Mr. Greer to look closer at the slave in question. As Mr. Greer confronted the slaves, he made a pretense of examining them for head lice, checking their teeth, and feeling their arm muscles. As he did so, he whispered to the individual he was examining, "Usiogope, Abobtu yuk haha kukuokoa. (Fear not, Abobtu is here to save you)."

Those selected were placed in a pen near the porch to wait for transportation back to the ship.

The process took hours. At first, they didn't find any of Abobtu's people. After searching through at least ten cells without finding anyone, they finally discovered a woman belonging to Abobtu's village. After five hours of searching, they found only forty-three men and fifteen women belonging to the mountain people. Thankfully, Mshijana Mwimbaji, Abobtu's sister, was among them. The rest had already been sold.

When Mshijana Mwimbaji saw her brother standing under the porch, she started to cry out as she looked him in the eyes. However, she noticed that he slightly shook his head at her, and she realized she should remain silent.

Etienne and Jeffrey haggled over the price of the slaves to be purchased, finally agreeing on a price.

Jeffrey asked Etienne, "Can you deliver them immediately? I would like to leave as soon as possible. We are already late for an engagement in the Caribbean."

"But of course! Would you like to pay now or upon delivery?"

"Why don't you take us back to the ship, and we will get your gold? Once the delivery is made, we will release the gold to you."

Etienne replied, "That will be fine."

They all climbed back into the carriage and rode back to the docks. Etienne followed them onto *Destiny* and waited on the main deck while Jeffery retrieved enough gold to make the agreed payment of £500 gold.

Etienne waited on the ship along with the others for the slaves to arrive. Fifty-eight men and women were led through the streets of Lomé chained together. They were then walked onto the ship, where they were sent down into the depths of the hull where Abobtu was waiting for them. The people were all asking him questions in their native tongue until he spoke to them to quiet them. Once the last person was sent down into the lower decks, the hatch was closed, and Abobtu began freeing his people from their chains. He told his people, "Remain quiet until the hatch is opened. These people are going to take us home."

One man questioned Abobtu's sanity when he asked, "Do you believe these people are actually going to take us home? They are going to take us far away from here. We will never see our families again."

"You are wrong, Kaka! It is the Red Raven! She has come to free you. She can be trusted."

After an hour of sitting in the dark with his people, Abobtu was beginning to doubt freedom for his people. Suddenly, the hatch opened, and Raven stuck her head down through the hatch and called, "Abobtu? Abobtu, you can come out now."

Abobtu climbed up the ladder and out of the hull into the sunlight. He squinted his eyes and said, "I was beginning to wonder if you had lied to me. My people said I was a fool for trusting you."

"No, Abobtu! I will never lie to you. We had to wait until we were out of sight of Lomé before we brought you up. We are heading toward your village now. You should all be home in three days."

"Thank you, Raven!"

Raven's Destiny had just pulled away from the *Nightingale* when Alexander told his men to lower one of the dories into the sea. Alexander placed a rolled-up parchment inside his buttoned jacket before climbing into the dory. Six of his men joined him as they rowed back to the beach. Once they reached the shore, they secured the dory and walked toward the village.

Raven and her crew had made several trips down the trail, which was pretty well-worn. Alexander and his men made the trek in only an hour and a half. When they arrived, they saw Al Bagani sitting outside his hut petting a goat kid.

Alexander approached him and asked, "How many goats do you have?"

"I have hundreds of goats."

"Why have we not ever seen them?"

"Most of the time they are on the other side of that small mountain. My herders brought this little one to me because his mother was killed by a leopard last night."

"Does Raven know you have goats?"

"I don't think so. Why?"

"We freed some people a few months ago who were going to be sold into slavery. We recently went back to check on them to see if they needed anything. They told us they want some goats."

"How many goats do they need?"

"Two bucks and seven does."

Al Bagani thought momentarily, then replied, "If Raven brings back Mshijana Mwimbaji, I will gladly give her two bucks, and seven does."

Alexander smiled and said, "That is wonderful! There is something else Raven would like you to do if you don't mind."

"What is it?"

"The gold things you make to trade with her are wonderful, but they are more difficult for us to trade than if you were to make gold coins for her like this."

Alexander pulled out the parchment to show Al Bagani a drawing of a gold coin with two offset R's to represent the Red Raven. Al Bagani stared at the drawing momentarily, then asked, "Do you have a coin of the size you want them to be?"

Alexander reached into his coat pocket and pulled out a gold coin.

"This would be the correct size and shape. Can you do it?"

"We can do it. It will take a while for us to make enough molds to cast the metal, but we can do it."

"Very good, my friend. This will make Raven happy."

"Raven will make me very happy when she brings back Mshijana Mwimbaji. We will begin making the molds for the coins right away."

Alexander asked, "Would you mind if my men and I gather food from the jungle between here and the beach? I don't know how long we will be here until Raven returns, and our food stores are dwindling."

"Don't bother yourselves with gathering food, my friend. Our women have gathered enough food to supply your needs for a week. If you need more, come back next week and there will be more."

"Thank you, Al Bagani!"

Al Bagani instructed some women to bring out several large fruits, vegetables, and dried meat baskets. He then had his men help Alexander and his crew carry the baskets back to the beach. When they reached the shore, Alexander called out to the *Nightingale* for Daktari to send out the other dory to help bring back all the food they had been given.

When the second dory arrived, they dumped the baskets into both dories and rowed back to the ship. Once they reached the ship, the crew lowered the lift lines for each of the dories and lifted the two boats, their passengers, and all the food onto the ship's deck. They had more than enough food for a week.

CHAPTER 9

The *Matilda* left the inlet as *Destiny* did, turning southwest to sail out of the Gulf of Guinea. Pharaoh still wasn't comfortable leaving Raven behind for such a long time. He knew she could take care of herself, but he felt they were all vulnerable when separated.

The wind was in their favor as they sailed toward the Atlantic. Thirty-three hours later, they were sailing out of the gulf and turning southward along the west coast of Africa. They reached the Cape of Good Hope on the twelfth day and turned east. All weather was in their favor. The winds were steady, and the skies were clear, making for quick travel through the seas. Pharaoh hoped they might make it back to Raven earlier than expected.

It took less than three days to make it around the Cape, and four more days found them pulling into Port St. Felix. As they sailed closer to the port, Pharaoh took out his spyglass to check the flag flying above the little village. He carefully watched the white banner as it drooped down the pole from which it hung. The wind wasn't blowing enough for it to stand up to reveal its signal. Finally, a gust of wind moved the flag enough that it stood out momentarily. The signal was all clear.

Pharaoh gave the order to pull into port and prepare to dock. His men scrambled, raising the sails except for two smaller ones that would give them enough wind to pull into the docks. When they were close enough to drift into the docks, the last two sails were raised and tied up. Attila had his helmsman steer *Matilda* in and dock her at the pier with the starboard side facing St. Felix.

One of the crew leaped from the starboard rail with a bow line in hand to tie the ship at the pier. Another man did the same on the stern. Once *Matilda* was tied up, they lowered the gangplank onto the dock.

As usual, Señor Rivera met them before they finished securing the ship to the dock.

"Hola, mi amigos! So good to see you. Where is Señorita Raven?"

Pharaoh replied, "She did not come this time. She had other business to attend to, so she sent us instead."

"Well, Señor Pharaoh what may I do for you today?"

"We have a client in need of guns and ammunition."

"Ah yes, and how many do you need?"

"At least one hundred of the long guns. Do you have that many?"

"Oh si! I still have most of the guns I bought from Raven the last time. We can take care of your needs, no problem."

"Good! How much for the guns and ammunition?"

"Well let's see, one hundred rifles with ammunition at my rate will be £5 each. So, £500 will cover it."

"Yes, that's what Raven said you would ask. She says she won't pay a shilling over £3."

Rivera's smile faded as he realized the Red Raven had already given Pharaoh a price. He also knew she would pay more than £3 for a rifle.

"Okay, señor. I know where this will end. Raven has told you she will pay £4 each, so you may have them for £400."

"You know her well."

"That I do, and right now I'm wondering why I put up with her."

"It's because you know you can trust her. She will never try to cheat you, she only wants the best deal possible."

"You are right, my friend. She is the best! I will have Juan show your men where they can find the guns and ammunition you need. Is there anything else I can help you with?"

"We just need to gather enough supplies to make the trip back home."

"Oh, and where is home?"

Pharaoh smirked, "Señor Rivera, Raven may trust you but I do not."

"Of course, Señor. I was only curious. I would never tell anyone of her whereabouts."

"Maybe not intentionally, but what if you were tortured? Men will give away secrets about their mother when tortured."

Rivera asked, "Well, would you like to join me for some refreshments?"

"No thank you. I have other matters to attend to while my men load the ship."

"Then I must say, adios to you my friend."

"Until next time."

As *Matilda's* crew loaded the rifles and ammunition onto the ship, Pharaoh walked along the docks and on the outskirts of the village as he watched the men work. As the last load was being taken to the ship, a man approached Pharaoh as he walked by a tavern. Attila watched the two men in conversation while he stood on the quarterdeck.

"Captain Pharaoh!"

Pharaoh turned to see who had called his name.

"Mr. Bleaker is it?"

"Aye, Captain. I was wondering if I might join your crew once more. I apologize for being late the last time you were here. It won't happen again."

"Mr. Bleaker, I am sorry but I can not let you sail with us at this time. Maybe the next time we come through here."

As they continued their conversation, Attila watched with great intent. Pharaoh and Henry Bleaker talked for several minutes before Pharaoh finally excused himself and walked back to the ship. As Pharaoh crossed the gangplank, he looked up to Attila and asked, "Attila, are we ready to sail?"

"Aye, Pharaoh!"

"Then let go the lines and shove off, please."

Attila gave the orders to sail and watched Pharaoh as he walked into his quarters. Attila wondered about the conversation Pharaoh had with Henry Bleaker. He wasn't shocked that Bleaker was not allowed back on the ship. But why would it take him so long to refuse Bleaker?

Henry Bleaker watched as *Matilda* sailed away from the port. He then opened up his right hand to examine five gold coins he held. He shook his hand a couple of times to hear the coins jingle together, then placed them in his pocket and walked back into the tavern.

Eight days after leaving the *Nightingale* behind, *Raven's Destiny* found her way back to her sister ship. Alexander had Daktari blow the conch shell to welcome *Destiny* back. Nearly one hundred people stood on the deck of *Destiny* as she rolled through the waves toward the shore. They all cheered and waved at the sailors on the other ship's deck.

Once Raven had moored her ship next to Alexander's, she called out to him, "Send your dories over so we can get these people back to their homes."

Alexander replied, "Aye, Raven!"

He ordered four men to be lowered into the two dories so they could row over to the other ship. Alexander joined them so he could go along and speak with Raven. Fifty-nine mountain people climbed into the four dories, along with Raven and Jeffrey.

As they rowed to shore, Alexander told Raven about his conversation with Al Bagani while she was gone.

"Raven, Al Bagani has goats. He said if you bring back his daughter, Mshijana Mwimbaji, he will give us the goats we need."

"Really? That's wonderful!"

"You did find her, then?"

"Yes we did. Unfortunately we weren't able to find all of his people. Twelve of them had already been sold."

Then Raven asked, "How about the other item? Is Al Bagani willing to turn the gold into coins?"

"Yes, he had his men working on the molds as soon as we discussed it."

"Perfect! Now if the rest of our plan comes together we should be set."

"What will we do next?"

"Rope! We will need a lot of rope. Once we get these people back home, let's bring a work crew over to have them begin making rope and some other items we will need to set our trap."

"A trap for who, Raven?"

"I want a gunship. Preferably a schooner or a sloop. I want to be able to battle against the frigates if we come up against them again. We got lucky last time, but we need to be able to hold our own against the warships."

"Aye, Raven!"

When the dories reached the shore, everyone stepped out of the boats and began walking to the village at the mountain's base. Abobtu's people were happy, laughing and singing as they strolled along the trail.

Alexander asked Raven, "What kind of trap will we set?"

"The bait has already been set. The trap will need to be built right here in this bay. We will need five or six thousand feet of rope and some spools to wind the rope up onto. In the meantime I need you to deliver the goats Al Bagani has given us to the people of Port Gentil."

When they reached the village, everyone cheered as they saw their relatives had been freed and brought home. A celebration broke out as singing and dancing began spontaneously.

Raven went to find Al Bagani, who was hugging his daughter, Mshijana Mwimbaji. Al Bagani smiled at Raven and held out his hand to her. Raven took his hand and received his blessing.

"Red Raven, you have done what you said you would do. You have brought back my people and my family. I am eternally grateful to you."

"You're welcome, Great King Al Bagani! I am forever at your service."

The celebration continued for the rest of the day and into the night. Raven and her crew left before dark to return to the ships. Tomorrow would be a new day of hard work and preparation.

The next morning, Raven awoke to goats bleating in the distance. She quickly rose from bed and dressed before leaving her cabin to see what was happening. A group of mountain people stood on the beach with a large herd of goats. When they saw Raven standing at the rail, they began calling to her and waving.

Raven called Hadari to lower the dories into the water so she could meet the goat herders on the beach. She took four men with her. When they reached the shore, Raven asked one of the men about the goats.

"What do we have here?"

The man replied, "Al Bagani has sent these goats to you for what you have done for our people."

"But, I only requested two bucks and seven does. How many are there?"

"Four bucks and thirty does. Don't worry, he has plenty more if you need them."

Raven smiled and replied, "Oh no! This is more than enough. How will we get them to the ships without them jumping out of my boats?"

"We have brought rope to tie their feet. They will not be able to jump or even walk."

The herdsman showed Raven's men how to tie the goats' feet and then helped place the goats into the dories. Once the goats were loaded and secured, Raven's crew began rowing back to the ships. She took the goats to the *Nightingale* so Alexander could deliver them to Port Gentil.

Alexander met Raven at the starboard rail as her dories reached the ship. Alexander suggested, "Maybe we should keep a few for ourselves since the king has provided more than we needed."

"I think you're right. It certainly wouldn't hurt to have fresh milk onboard."

Raven decided to keep two does for each ship and one buck to share among them. The two does that would belong to *Matilda* were placed on the *Nightingale* until Pharaoh returned. Raven kept two does in her dory and delivered them to her ship so Louis Hardy would have fresh milk whenever he needed it for the meals.

When the goats were secured onboard the *Nightingale*, Alexander ordered them to set sail. They weighed anchor and unfurled the sails, moving southwesterly out of the star-shaped cove. Thirty miles and three hours later, Alexander had his helmsman turn south into the Gulf of Guinea. Less than thirty hours later, they pulled into the docks at Port Gentil.

The *Nightingale* was tied up at the docks three hours past noon, and Alexander's men were unloading the goats. The loud bleating of twenty-five goats was nearly ear-splitting. Alexander wasn't completely unfamiliar with goat herding – his family back home had raised a few. He had one of his men tie a lead rope around the head of one of the bucks and led the way as the rest of the goats followed along. They walked the path leading to the small village, bleating. When they reached the clearing about a mile from the beach, the people were delighted to see the herd of goats walking into their camp. Shujaa wa Mfalme came forward to meet Alexander and said, "Salamu, Shujaa Mkubwa!"

"Salamu, Shujaa wa Mfalme! Here are the goats you request-ed."

"This is so much more than we had hoped for, Alexander. How can we repay you?"

"Do you have any baskets ready yet?"

"Yes, we have many baskets for you. Oh, and there is something else."

Mfalme ran to his hut and then returned with a small sea chest.

"I went into the big house to look around when Raven said it was okay. I found this chest and I want Raven to have it. It isn't nearly enough for all she has done for us but I know she will like it."

Alexander set the chest on the ground and lifted the lid. Inside, the chest was full of gold and silver coins as well as diamonds, rubies, and other gemstones. Alexander couldn't believe his eyes. "Where did you find this, Mfalme?"

"It was hidden behind a wall I found as I was pulling wood down to use in my hut."

"Did you tear the whole house apart?"

"Not yet. It will be gone by the time we get all of our huts built."

"If you find any more chests like this one, Raven will trade for it. They are very valuable so she will make sure you are well paid."

"I know the Red Raven is a fair woman. I trust her very much."

It was a rainy morning when a schooner operating under a French flag sailed into the docks at Port St. Felix. Captain Michaud d'Arnaud of the French Navy stood on the deck as his ship came to port. He ordered his crew to tie up the vessel and prepare to go ashore.

Once the ship was secured, d'Arnaud gathered his boarding crew on the pier to give further instructions. Oscar Rivera saw the ship from the top floor of his hacienda.

"Juan! Juan!"

"Si, Señor Rivera?"

"Go and change the signal flag! The French have arrived!"

Juan scrambled from the hacienda and trotted through the streets of St. Felix, trying to reach the flag mast as quickly as possible. He untied the rope holding the flags atop the pole and lowered them to the ground. He looked around before changing the white flag that usually flew beneath the Spanish flag with another white flag with a tiny red X on it. Juan then raised both flags back into place.

Captain d'Arnaud's men dispersed throughout the city, searching for anything they deemed illegal. The captain and his lieutenant walked up the street leading to Rivera's hacienda. They knocked on the door and waited to be greeted. A young woman answered the door and greeted the men, "Buenos Dias!"

The captain returned the greeting, speaking Spanish. "Buenos Dias, Señorita."

Then he asked. "Where is Señor Rivera?"

"Please, come in."

The two men were shown into Rivera's study, waiting for his arrival. As Oscar entered the study with his best smile, he said, "Ah, Capitán d'Arnaud, how good to see you again."

The captain replied, "Forget it, Rivera. I know how you detest these visits. I detest making them, but I will not stop until that infuriating woman is captured."

"Well, Capitán, I assure you she is not here at the moment. I have not seen her in many months."

"What was she doing here?"

"Well, trading of course. That is the business I do here you realize?"

"Among others no doubt. Exactly what did she bring to trade?"

Knowing the answer, Rivera made a pretense of looking up her transaction in his ledger. "I see here that she bought food, supplies, some bolts of cloth, and a few digging tools. Oh, and some rum."

"And how did she pay for these supplies?"

"The usual way, gold."

"Did she say where she was heading?"

"No, she never trusts me with such information. Although I did ask. Even so, she is a sly one. She would never tell me her true destination."

"Rivera, I am going to leave a detail here to camp at your pier. You will supply anything they need while they are stationed here. Do you understand?"

"Si, El Capitán! But who will be paying for these supplies that your men might require?"

"Keep an account. I will pay you when I return."

"But of course."

The captain and his lieutenant left the hacienda and returned to the docks.

When they reached the pier, one of his men came running to him.

"Capitaine! Capitaine! I have found someone who has seen the Red Raven!"

"Where is this person?"

"He is in the tavern just around the corner from here!"

"Take me to him!"

They quickly walked to the tavern and entered. The room quieted as the crowd saw the captain and the other officer enter.

The sailor led Captain d'Arnaud over to a table near the back of the room.

"This is the man, Capitaine!"

Captain d'Arnaud asked, "Who are you?"

"My name is Henry Bleaker, Captain."

"You say that you have seen the Red Raven?"

"Depends. Is there still a reward on her?"

"There is."

"How much is the reward now?"

"£1,000!"

"My, my! How do I collect my reward?"

"You won't until she is captured, and only if your information is correct and leads to her arrest."

"So, I'm just supposed to wait here for it?"

"Yes, we will get back to you eventually."

"Tell you what, Captain, how about I go along with you. Then, when you capture her you can pay me on the spot."

"That's highly irregular. You should wait here."

"No offense, Captain, but I don't trust you to come back. I know where she's going, so I'll go with you and show you the way."

"How is it you know where she is going?"

"I was on a ship called the *Nightingale*. She captured it and took some of us prisoner. When we arrived here about, oh, five or six months ago, I escaped. But I know where she's going. I've seen her charts."

The captain instructed his lieutenant, "Bring him along."

Chapter 10

Once Henry was loaded onto the schooner, the captain ordered his men to return to the ship and cast off. Henry was led to the captain's cabin and kept under guard until d'Arnaud could return. Once the schooner had drifted away from the docks, Captain d'Arnaud walked to his cabin to begin questioning Henry.

"Monsieur Bleaker, where should we begin looking for the Red Raven?"

"Do you have a chart of the Gulf of Guinea? I can show you where."

The captain rummaged through several charts on a shelf, searching for the correct one. When he finally found it, he spread it out on the table. Henry searched the map, looking for the right place.

"There it is! This cove that looks like a seven point star. The middle point of the star is where she will be."

"How do you know she will be there?"

"I overheard one of her captains talking about it to another of the officers."

"Are you sure this is the place?"

"Yes! If she isn't there right now, she will be."

Captain d'Arnaud was satisfied for now, so he instructed one of his crew members, "Take this man below decks and lock him up until we can verify his story."

Henry protested, "Wait, Captain! Why are you going to lock me up? I have done nothing wrong."

"On the contrary, Monsieur. You have consorted with pirates. That makes you a pirate. You will be hanged with the rest of your compatriots."

Henry struggled against the grip the sailors had on him as they dragged him to the hatch and lowered him below decks. They then took him down to the lowest deck, placing him in a cage made of iron bars. The sailors threw Henry into the cage, slammed the door behind him, and locked it. It was dark, dank, and smelled of human waste.

Henry called out as the sailors climbed to the main deck, "Wait! Help me! I am not your enemy!"

Raven's men spent most of their time on dry land, gathering materials to build their traps. Palm fronds and snake plants were used to make the rope. The rope needed to be extremely strong and long, so the men worked tediously at winding the fibers together to make the rope. Raven wanted the rope to be three inches in diameter and two strands at least four thousand feet long.

Raven had others working on constructing a wheel and pulley system that the rope could be wound onto. Two wheels, about six feet in diameter, were made into a spool by building them onto a barrel about two feet in diameter and three feet long. The spool was then mounted onto legs that raised it off the ground so it would rotate. A long pole was run through the spool, and cogs were built on both ends of the pole. The cogs were placed within the cogs of another wheel system with a handle long enough for six men to turn. Two of these gadgets were built and placed at different points off the coast. Each end of the rope would be fed into one of the spools, then dragged through the water about two thousand feet off the beach. Once everything was built and the rope was taken out as far as it would reach, Raven's men wove a two hundred by six-foot net onto the rope to snag any ship that came too far into the bay. After the net was attached, Raven's men weighted it with heavy stones to drag it beneath the water's surface so it couldn't be seen and ships could pass through without becoming snagged.

It took a month for Raven's men to complete the trap construction. Once finished, the waiting game began.

Al Bagani's men continued working on molds for the gold coins Raven wanted. Making gold coins was more time-consuming than making the trinkets they usually made. Once they were finished, they also made wooden chests with leather hinges and clasps to store the gold coins.

Six weeks had passed since *Matilda* had left to complete their mission. Two hundred and seven days after leaving Port St. Felix, Pharaoh, and his crew sailed back into the star-shaped cove of the mountain people.

Raven instructed all three ships to be moored at the easternmost part of the bay to lure any attacking ships into her trap. She wasn't sure anyone would be searching for her here; she could only hope that a French vessel would come calling.

Pharaoh's men unloaded the guns and ammunition from his ship and carried them to the beach, where they would be distributed to Al Bagani's men. Raven and her men worked with the mountain people, showing them how to load, aim, and fire the weapons. At first, the loud report of the rifles frightened the mountain people. However, they quickly became proficient at hitting their targets once they got used to the noise.

Every day, while they waited for someone to wander into their cove, Raven ordered a practice run so that everyone knew exactly what they should do when the time came. She had a team of twenty men on *Destiny* responsible for manning and cutting loose the net weights. Another dory was placed at the bay's south end, where another team of twenty men was camping. Men armed with rifles were stationed near the beach. They stayed in a campsite near the area where the two spools were set up. Others in the camp were assigned to operate the spools once their prey reached the inside of the snare. Whenever the alarm was blown, everyone scrambled to their positions. Those on the beach baring rifles would climb a tree to a position where they could fire against the trapped ship. The dories rowed out to the outermost part of the snare, and men dove into the water at positions indicated by floats attached to the unseen net below the surface. Each man was responsible for cutting away a weight from the net, allowing it to float to the water's surface. The weights were spread about twenty yards apart from each other. During these trial runs, they never actually cut the ropes; they only dove below the surface to practice diving and holding their breath for long periods.

After two weeks of waiting, Raven decided it would be prudent for her to send out a ship to the mouth of the Star Cove to spot any approaching vessels. The *Nightingale*, captained by Alexander, was chosen for the task. The ship was fully stocked with food and water so that they could stay out as long as necessary. Alexander had only ten men with him as they cruised the gulf at the mouth of the star cove. The rest of his crew were manning the net spools at two different points on the beach.

Day after day, Alexander and his crew patrolled the waters southwest of the cove, never venturing too far away. The days became monotonous as they waited for any approaching ships. Eight men rotated shifts in the crow's nest, searching for ships in the area.

Ten days after they began their patrol, Mwindaji spotted a ship to the west. He called down to Alexander to alert him of the approaching ship.

"Ship off the starboard rail!"

Alexander asked, "What kind of ship is it?"

"It's too far away to tell!"

They nervously waited for the ship to come close enough for Mwindaji to identify it. Half an hour passed before the ship finally came close enough to see that it supported three masts.

"She is a British merchant ship!"

Everyone onboard the *Nightingale* felt the adrenaline drain from their bodies. Alexander asked, "Which way are they sailing?"

Mwindaji replied after a long pause, "They seem to be sailing northeast toward Port Harcourt!"

Alexander ordered his helmsman, "Let's move back into the cove enough to avoid the ship as it passes."

Mkimbiaji turned the ship's wheel, moving the *Nightingale* back into the cove far enough that the oncoming ship would not see them. They waited two hours, which allowed enough time for the merchant vessel to pass by before they moved back into the open waters of the gulf.

Mchungaji took over duties in the crow's nest once they reached the gulf waters. Half an hour after reaching the gulf, Mchungaji spotted another approaching vessel.

"Ship off the port bow!"

Alexander waited for more information. Thirty minutes passed before Mchungaji announced, "She is sailing fast! Looks like a schooner! She's flying a French flag!"

Everyone on board the ship felt adrenaline rush through their bodies once again. Would this be what they had been waiting for? Alexander ordered Mkimbiaji to turn the ship back toward the cove if they needed to retreat. They waited to see if the ship would continue its present course. The French vessel was just west of Kidney Island when Alexander found himself holding his breath. He made himself breathe as he watched the schooner move quickly through the water.

Alexander ordered *Nightingale* to sail back into the cove. She sailed deep into the cove but not so far that they couldn't see the mouth of the gulf. They all waited with bated breath, hoping that the time had finally come. Mchungaji finally announced, "The ship has turned! It is coming toward us!"

Alexander ordered, "Full sails! Make for home!"

The small crew scrambled to drop all sails to achieve full speed. They sailed directly to the center point of the star cove with the French ship gaining on them. Alexander ordered his men, "Prepare the stern gun!"

Three men ran to the quarterdeck and loaded the cannon at the ship's stern. Mwindaji yelled, "Ready at the stern!"

Alexander ordered, "Fire!"

Boom!

A shot rang out as the cannonball flew directly at the schooner. The shot was too short to hit the vessel. However, it wasn't Alexander's intent to damage the ship. The cannon shot was both an enticement for the schooner to pursue them and a warning for Raven and those waiting.

Raven heard the cannon fire's retort and at once ordered, "Get ready! They're coming!"

Hadari blew the conch shell to let those on land know that a ship was approaching. Men everywhere scrambled to their assignments. The mountain men climbed into the trees to take aim and fire their weapons should the enemy come close enough. Raven's men on land manned the net spools. Twenty men from *Destiny* climbed into their dory, ready to row out to the net. Another group on shore made their dory, ready to launch from the beach.

Everyone watched as the *Nightingale* sailed into the cove at full sail. Alexander turned her toward the other two ships on the east side of the cove. When they reached the other ships, Alexander ordered the sails to be raised. The *Nightingale* slowed and came to rest next to the other two ships.

Moments later, everyone watched as the French schooner sailed into their midst. Captain d'Arnaud pointed his spyglass at the ships moored in the waters near the shore. He moved the glass from ship to ship before finally discovering what he had hoped to see. He muttered to himself, *"It's the Raven."*

The captain announced to his men, "Man the guns! We've found her!"

The schooner continued sailing closer to the shore until Raven saw it sail past the point of no return. She ordered Hadari to blow the conch shell.

"Wooo!"

The dories moved quickly through the water along the line of markers indicating the location of the underwater net. Man after man dove into the water at each marker as the dory moved along. Each man dove twenty feet beneath the surface to a weighted line underneath the net. Once they reached the line, they cut it, releasing the net so that it could rise to the surface. The dories rowed back to pick up each man when the net was completely free of its weights. Hadari watched as the net floated to the surface, and he blew the conch again, letting the land crew know it was ready.

Captain d'Arnaud and his crew were slightly confused by the actions of the men in the little boats. D'Arnaud saw the rope rise behind his ship as they sailed farther into the cove. He wasn't sure whether to fire at the small boats or turn his guns at the three ships he was approaching.

The crew at the net spools heard the conch shell blow and immediately began cranking the wheels to retract the rope. Slowly, the net began to move toward the schooner. Again, d'Arnaud was confused by this action. What were these people up to?

The net approached the schooner, capturing it and beginning to move it toward the beach. D'Arnaud ordered his men to fire at the beach. He didn't know where exactly, but someone there intended to capture his vessel.

Cannons fired at the beach, shredding low-growing brush and trees. As the schooner came within firing range, the mountain people began shooting at the men on the schooner. The cannon fire from the French vessel had little effect on them because the ship aimed at the ground, expecting their attackers to be on the beach. Men fired their rifles from the treetops so they were not affected by the cannon fire unless their tree happened to be hit by a stray cannonball.

Captain d'Arnaud realized his ship was being towed closer and closer to the shore. It would soon be run aground if he couldn't free his ship. He finally decided to fire his guns at the other ships in the bay.

"All port guns fire!"

A barrage of cannon fire exploded from the schooner. Cannonball after cannonball harmlessly fell into the water far too short of the targeted ships. The rifle fire from the trees began to take its toll on the French crew. Man after man dropped after being hit. Captain d'Arnaud was hit in the shoulder by a slug from the trees. His lieutenant was shot in the left side of his skull and immediately fell dead.

D'Arnaud fell to the deck, grasping his shoulder and trying to stop the bleeding. He leaned on the helm and looked around to see if his crew were still alive. No one on deck stirred. He could hear men below decks who were still manning the cannons. They were shouting, confused, and frightened. None of them dared to come up to the top deck for fear of being shot by one of the tree snipers.

The schooner suddenly lunged to a halt – she had run aground. Raven's men and the mountain people converged on the stranded ship, climbing onboard and searching for anyone on deck who might still be alive.

Raven launched the dories from all three ships with every available man. They rowed to the schooner and climbed aboard. With sword in hand, Raven climbed to the quarterdeck and found the captain bleeding while leaning against the helm.

Breathlessly, he asked, "You are the Red Raven?"

"I am. Were you looking for me?"

"Oui. What will you do with me?"

"I don't know. What did you have planned had you captured me?"

"There is still a price on your head. You would be taken back to France and tried for your crimes."

"What crimes are you talking about?"

"Murder. Piracy. Among others."

"What about the crimes France has committed? Who will pay for those?"

"France has committed no crimes!"

"Certainly they have. Stealing innocent people away from their homes. Allowing them to be sold into slavery. Killing the inno-cent. You don't call those crimes?"

"I call them unfortunate incidents that the world has chosen to participate in."

"Well Captain, I have chosen to fight against such atrocities. These people you see here around you are free, and they will remain free."

D'Arnaud asked, "What do you plan to do with us?"

"I'm going to let King Al Bagani decide your fate. You have come to his land uninvited, so he will decide what to do with you."

The hatch leading to the lower deck was opened, and Raven's men captured all who remained below. They marched them out onto the top deck at gunpoint and waited for Raven's orders. Raven climbed below deck and then to the lowermost deck, where she found Henry Bleaker standing at the door to his cage.

"Raven!"

"Hello, Henry. Are you alright?"

"Aye, Captain! How did I do?"

"Perfect. Let's get you out of here."

Chapter 11

Raven and her men took d'Arnaud and his remaining crew from the ship and onto the beach. They marched the twenty-one captives through the jungle to the mountain's base, where Al Bagani and his people resided. Each of the captives had their wrists tied behind them, which made it uncomfortable for them as they traversed through the jungle; vegetation whipped their faces as they walked through. Flies and stinging insects tortured them as they walked. When they reached the village at the mountain's base, each man was bleeding, swollen from insect bites, and dehydrated.

The prisoners were brought into the clearing where the community fire usually burned. They were forced to kneel in a semicircle on one side of the fire. Al Bagani exited his mud hut, standing on the opposite side of the fire. His bodyguards stood on either side of him, while his son, Abobtu, stood next to the captives. Raven and twenty of her men stood to the side to watch the proceedings.

Abobtu spoke to his father and the people in his native tongue.

"Great Al Bagani, these are the prisoners we captured from the ship that would attack us. They were sent from the French government to raid our village and steal our people just as the others did. What would you have us do to them?"

"My people will offer them to the fire gods!"

Raven understood his rage, but it was misplaced. The French navy captain wasn't responsible for the capture of his people. He didn't have as much claim to these men as Raven had.

"Al Bagani, would you permit me to punish these men? After all, I'm the one they were trying to capture. They had nothing to do with your people being captured."

Al Bagani asked, "What will you do with them?"

Raven replied, "They will be banished! I will take them away to an island far from here where I have left other men before. They will have to try to survive without tool or weapon while on the island. They will be banished and you will not have to be concerned for them again."

Al Bagani consulted with his son, Abobtu, and other trusted advisors in his tribe. Some of the discussion was heated among the men, and Raven could only occasionally catch a word or phrase. Finally, Al Bagani raised his hand to silence the others and spoke to Raven.

"The Red Raven has treated us well. Our people are indebted to you. You may take these men away and see that they bother us no more."

Several of the mountain people still murmured their displeasure.

Raven replied, "Thank you great king Al Bagani! We will see that you are no longer bothered by these men, and if anyone else comes to take your people away as they did before,. we will avenge your people. You now have weapons to fight the slavers. We will bring more powder and ammunition for rifles."

Al Bagani signaled for his men to bring out Raven's gold. Twenty mountain men each carried a small chest and placed it before Raven. Each chest weighed about fifty pounds.

Raven turned to Captain d'Arnaud and ordered, "Have your men pick up these chest and carry them back to the beach."

The captain requested, "May we please have some water before we walk back through the jungle?"

Raven nodded to Hadari, and he had some of his men pass around buckets of water with gourd ladles so the men could drink their fill. Then, twenty of the strongest French were instructed to pick up a chest and carry it on their shoulder.

Raven led the procession through the jungle back to the beach. The captain followed her; the rest alternated between d'Arnaud's crew and Raven's, with Hadari bringing up the rear. Several minutes after they had begun their trek, d'Arnaud asked Raven, "May I ask, what do you intend to do with us?"

"There is an island not too far away, but far enough away that you can't swim back here. You and your men will be marooned there. There are others already there unless they have already perished. I left them there several months ago."

"What sort of an island is it?"

"I don't know exactly. It's a large island. I have no idea if it is inhabited or not. I guess you can let me know the next time you see me."

"And when might that be?"

"Probably never."

Raven led everyone from the seven-mile trail to the beach three hours later. D'Arnaud's men were winded and weary as they each placed their gold-filled chests into one of the dories. The prisoners were scattered among the six dories to be transported back to the ships. Seven men were loaded onto each square-rigged ship while Captain d'Arnaud was sent to *Destiny*. The gold was all placed on *Destiny* until Quartermaster Hamilton could divide it for the crew. All the prisoners were placed on the lowermost deck of each ship, where they were shackled together for the extent of their short journey.

Raven summoned all officers to meet on *Destiny* before they began the journey to Kidney Island. Pharaoh and Attila came over from *Matilda* while Alexander and Daktari rowed from the *Nightingale*. They met Raven and Hadari, John, and Jeffrey in her cabin.

Raven sent Jeremy to find others who would join the ranks as ship's officers. Jeremy returned with Mwindaji, Kiboko, Mkimbiaji, Mchungaji, and Nathan Coates. Once they arrived in the captain's cabin, Raven began making assignments.

"I want to thank all of you for your courageous service to my fleet. As we now have a gunship at our disposal, I need to make changes to our assignments as officers and promotions to men who will serve as new officers. Mr. Ashworth and Hadari will remain as first and second mates on *Destiny*. Pharaoh remains captain of *Matilda*. His new first mate is Mwindaji and his second mate, Kiboko."

The men all congratulated the new officers.

"Alexander will remain captain of the *Nightingale* with Daktari as his first mate. Mkimbiaji is the new second mate."

Again, everyone congratulated the new mate.

"The name of our new gunship will be, the *Lady Falcon*. Her new captain will be Attila. Attila, Nathan Coates will be your first mate and Mchungaji will be your second mate."

Cheers rose among the officers as they congratulated each other. They all drank a toast to success as Raven poured each man a glass of rum.

Raven then said, "Congratulations to all of you! There is one other thing. I want all my ships to fly under the flag of the Raven. I had Mr. Greer make a flag for each ship. As you can see, it is red with a black raven."

Raven handed out the flags to the respective captains and said, "Go ahead and make your way to your new posts. Mr. Ashworth, will you and Attila remain, please?"

Once the others left her cabin, Raven began speaking to Attila.

"Attila, you are now captain of our most important and most dangerous ship. I know you are up to the task I've given you."

"Aye, Raven! You can depend on me!"

"Good! When we are at sea, we will sail in a diamond formation with *Matilda* on my left flank and the *Nightingale* on my right flank. I want you to keep your distance but directly behind *Destiny* about a quarter of a mile behind. You will find sailing a schooner quite different from one of the ships you have been aboard. The *Falcon* will be much faster even with its heavier load of cannons and powder. You will be given a full gun crew and I want you to make sure your men are proficient in firing those cannons with the upmost accuracy."

"Aye, Raven!"

"Good luck, Attila! That will be all."

As Attila left the cabin to transfer to the new ship, John Ashworth was still at Raven's side.

"Papa, I hope you don't think I passed you over to captain one of the ships."

"No, Raven! Not at all! If I'm going to serve on one of your ships, I'd rather it be the one you are aboard."

"Good, because I depend on you and Jeffrey for your council and your companionship. Things just wouldn't be as enjoyable if I didn't have you near me. I missed you so much when we were separated."

John replied, "I feel the same way."

Once all the ships were ready with their newly assigned crews, everyone settled in for the night. At first light, Raven had Hadari give the signal to begin the voyage to Kidney Island. Attila was excited to stand on the quarterdeck of his ship as he gave the command to fall into formation with the other ships. Raven was right about the schooner – it was much faster than the other ships, and he constantly had to order his crew to trim the sails to match the speed of *Raven's Destiny.*

Attila now had forty men on his crew– still not fully manned, but it was all Raven could spare from the other ships until more crew could be found.

Kidney Island was only sixty miles from the Seven Star Cove at Kidney's northeasternmost point. However, Raven was heading for its southernmost tip, which was ninety-five miles from Al Bagani's beach. Raven's fleet arrived at the beach only nine hours after leaving the Seven Star Cove.

Captain d'Arnaud and his twenty-one men were loaded into three dories and delivered onto the beach. As d'Arnaud began to climb out of his boat, he pretended to stumble and fell into Raven at the boat's bow. As he landed on Raven, he grabbed one of her pistols from the brace hanging across her chest. With one swift move, he cocked the pistol and dragged Raven from the dory with his left arm held across her throat.

"No one move!" he shouted as he backed away from the dory.

He spoke to his men in French and instructed them to gather weapons from Raven's men and join him. However, before they could do anything, Raven reached into her leather waistcoat and retrieved the four-inch-bladed knife she had hidden. She swung the dagger into d'Arnaud's right thigh near his crotch and sliced through his femoral artery. D'Arnaud screamed out in pain and reflexively pulled the trigger on the pistol. A shot rang out, causing Raven's men on the ships to take notice. The lead ball from the pistol accidentally struck one of d'Arnaud's men in the head and killed him instantly. D'Arnaud released his grip on Raven and fell into the sand. Raven pulled her other pistol from its brace and pointed it at the other twenty-one prisoners, who were now all attacking her men, trying to take away their weapons.

Raven shouted, "Arrét! Arrét!"

The French prisoners froze as they saw Raven was no longer in d'Arnaud's clutches. Raven's crew threw each man out of the dories and gathered their weapons that had been tossed inside the boats or out onto the sand.

D'Arnaud anguished through gritted teeth as he said, "You have killed me!"

"No, you have killed yourself."

D'Arnaud's blood escaped his leg and soaked his pant leg until the fabric could hold no more. The rest spilled out into the sand and pooled beneath his body. He quickly felt faint from the blood loss and fell backward into the sand before dying soon after.

Raven flicked her wrist as she held the pistol pointed at d'Arnaud's men, indicating they should join their captain on the beach. Each sailor slowly complied, leaving only Raven's crew standing in the boats.

Raven climbed back into her dory and stood holding her pistol, pointing at the men as they all shoved away from the beach. "Au revoir!" she said as the dories rowed away from the beach.

Raven decided to stop at Port Gentil on her way to Port St. Felix. Port Gentil's people might need supplies and want to get rid of some baskets in trade. Raven was sure Señor Rivera would be willing to take them in trade.

It took thirty hours to sail from Kidney Island to Port Gentil, which ordinarily only took twenty-six hours. The seas were rough as the wind blew hard against the waves. The ships rocked through the water in waves as high as ten to twelve feet.

When Raven's fleet finally arrived at Gentil, the beach was abandoned except for the skeletons still hanging in the trees to warn strangers who might come here. André Arsenault's bones were stripped entirely of flesh, and none of his tattered clothing remained. It was an eerie sight even for Raven, who had put him there. She tried not to think about him as she left her ship to find the people of Port Gentil in their little village.

Captain Billings sat on her shoulder as Hadari, Pharaoh, Alexander, and Attila accompanied Raven. Hadari led the way down the path to the little village a mile from the shore. Pharaoh spoke to Raven as they walked along the path.

"Raven, I think I should tell you, we will have a new member of the crew on *Matilda* soon."

Raven was puzzled as she asked, "Oh?"

"Yes, it seems that Rose and I are going to have a baby soon."

Raven was shocked and excited by the news, "How wonderful! Should we go back to the Robin's Nest and set up a place for her there?"

"No, no! Rose wants our baby to be born a sailor. She will remain onboard to have the baby."

Raven replied, "Well, when the time comes, I'll have Mr. Greer join you on *Matilda* to help Rose."

"Thank you."

When they reached the village, Raven spotted Shujaa wa Mfalme immediately: "Salamu!" Raven said.

"Salamu, Shujaa Mkubwa! It is good to see you!"

The women and other village men noticed Raven and her men approaching and gathered around to welcome them.

Raven noticed that many huts had been built since the last time she had visited Port Gentil.

"Mfalme, you have made great progress on building your huts since my last visit."

"Yes, Red Raven. The tools you brought us have been very helpful to us."

Raven asked, "Is there anything else that you need? We are on our way to Port St. Felix and we can pick up anything that might help you."

"Our women are in need of new clothing. Their dresses are worn out and we have no material to make new ones."

"That will be easy. Señor Rivera has lots of fabric. Is there anything else?"

"No thank you! But will you and your men stay and eat with us? We will cook a goat for you?"

"That sounds delicious! We would be honored to feast with you tonight."

The people prepared a feast of roasted goat. They also roasted yams and served fresh guava, bananas, star apples, and breadfruit. The meal was delicious and much appreciated by Raven and her men after eating salted meat and potatoes most days aboard their ships.

When the meal was finished, Mfalme's people filled baskets with fresh fruits and vegetables and helped carry them to the beach for Raven and her crew. They also delivered more decorative baskets for Raven to trade so they could get the fabric they needed.

As Mfalme and the others began to say their goodbyes to Raven and her crew, a young woman ran toward them from the village. She carried a bundle under one of her arms as she breathlessly called to Raven.

"Red Raven! Red Raven!"

Raven turned and saw the young woman calling her name. Raven stepped down from the gangplank onto the dock to meet the girl.

Mfalme asked the girl, "What is it, Mwanamke Simba?"

"Red Raven, I wish to go with you! I want you to teach me to sail on your ship!"

Raven looked her over and noticed she was tall and robust – taller than Raven by two inches. Mwanamke Simba was about the same age as Raven, maybe a year or two older. She had a fierce look in her eyes – confidence.

"Why do you want to come with me? It would be safer for you to stay here with your people."

Mwanamke Simba replied, "These are not my people. They have treated me well, but my people are from a different place. I come from a village where women are trained as warriors. We serve the king as his guardians. We are chosen at a young age to be trained for Walinzi wa Mfalme (The King's Guard). Before I could finish my training, one of my warrior sisters told my captain lies about me. She was jealous of me because I was better than she. She told the captain that I slept with one of the men soldiers which is forbidden. Walinzi wa Mfalme are not to have relations with any man because we belong to our King. I was sent away from our country to be sold into slavery to keep the white man from raiding our village. I want the opportunity to fight against the men who take the women from our villages. Will you please let me go with you?"

Raven was impressed by the young woman who stood before her. She saw much of herself in Mwanamke Simba.

"Why did you not come forward before, when we asked for volunteers?"

"I was sick and did not think you would find me suitable to be onboard your ship. Now I am well, and ready to come with you."

"You will come with me. Simba. . . that means lion doesn't it?"

"Yes, Raven."

"We will be the Red Raven and the Black Lion."

Simba smiled at Raven and giggled. Raven took Simba by the hand and led her onto *Destiny*. The men and women of *Destiny* all welcomed Simba as she walked across the ship's deck.

CHAPTER 12

Raven's fleet sailed toward Port St. Felix once again. Along the way, she began training her new friend, Simba, in the ways of the sea. Raven also trained with Simba using the sword, knife, and firearms. She found Simba already proficient with bladed weapons; however, the long gun and pistol were new to her.

Raven's crew often stopped their usual duties momentarily to watch the two as they sparred with each other. The men were quite amazed at how well both women fought. Jeremy would join in on the training sometimes. Raven was impressed by how well he picked up fighting with his sword. Raven remembered how Captain Billings had trained her in weaponry when she was the same age as Jeremy. She hoped Jeremy would not need to use his new skills anytime soon, but she wanted him to be at least able to defend himself should the need arise.

Daily, Attila's guns could be heard in the distance as his crew practiced loading and firing their cannons. Of course, they fired them without using cannonballs. There wasn't anything they could aim toward anyway. They were only trying to get used to loading, firing, and swabbing out the gun cylinders.

Almost daily, Raven's crew, mostly Africans, would sing as they worked on the ship's deck. The song was nearly the same every time but unlike any song Raven had experienced onboard Captain Billings' *Destiny*. His crews would sing about the seas or some lost love from Ireland. The Africans' songs were more lively – often a chant that was repeated over and over. Someone in the crew would instigate the song by singing a phrase while the rest would respond with a chant.

Leader: "Tutafanya Kazi asubuki!"
(*We will work in the morning*)

Crew: "Fanya Kazi kill situ!"
(*Work every day*)

Leader: " Tutafanya Kazi Mchana kutwa!"
(*We will work in the daytime*)

Crew: "Fanya Kazi kill situ!"
(*Work every day*)

Leader: "Tutafanya Kazi zote hadi mwezi utakapokuja!"
(*We will work until the moon comes*)

Crew: "Fanya Kazi kill situ!"
(*Work every day*)

One day, a young man approached Raven and asked, "Captain Raven, may I play my drum while the men sing their song?"

Raven asked, "Where did you get a drum?"

"I made it while we were waiting for the French ship to arrive."

"Bring it out and let me see it."

The young man named Kujana wa Muziki went below deck, picked up his handmade drum, and brought it up for Raven to see. It was made from a hollowed–out Mahogany tree trunk. He stretched a thin layer of antelope hide across the top and secured it with leather thongs. Muziki then decorated the drum's shell by burning designs around the outside. Raven was excited to see the young man's craftsmanship.

Raven then said, "Let me hear you play, Muziki."

The young man began banging out a rhythm on his drum with a huge smile on his face. Suddenly, all of his African friends began singing once again. The song stirred Raven. She felt happy from the sound of the drum against the voices, but she realized this could be quite disturbing to those unfamiliar with this type of music. Raven felt it might strike fear into the minds of those aboard other ships that they would come against.

Raven watched as Muziki continued to bang out his rhythm. When he looked up to her to receive her criticism or approval, he saw her smile and nod to him. Muziki smiled, too, as he continued to play his song.

Raven walked to Muziki and said, "Put your drum on the quarterdeck so it can be heard by the other ships. We can use it to communicate with the other ships too. Maybe you could build drums for all the ships. The sound of our drums sailing toward other ships might strike fear to those we come across."

Muziki smiled with delight as he replied, "Yes! I will make more drums."

Raven's fleet continued their voyage back to Port St. Felix with troubling winds in their path. Hurricane season was upon them, and they could only hope to outrun the storms heading their way from the west. High winds rocked *Destiny* up and down between tall rolling waves. Raven stood next to John on the quarterdeck as he barked out instructions to the crew.

"Someone, batten down that hatch portal before our lady fills with water and takes us down to Davy Jones! Mustaffa, secure those guns, man! Make sure they don't budge! We can't afford to have someone injured by a loose cannon."

The skies grew darker as the afternoon droned on. The winds whistled and moaned among the ship's sails. The stronger the wind blew, the higher pitch it whistled, chilling the crew to their bones. No one was singing now; their minds were set on the danger at hand. Ropes needed re-tying, hatches needed securing, and sails needed trimming. The men and women of *Destiny* and Raven's other ships worked on it for hours. Their bodies ached from exhaustion. Still, no one dared leave their post; too much was at stake.

They managed to stay ahead of the hurricane, but just barely. If the storms caught up to them, they could be destroyed and most likely perished.

The ships traveled southward while the storms moved eastward, allowing the fleet to outrun the deadly waves. Still, they were tossed about like a flour sack in the sea's rolling waves, and half a day passed before they could take a break from the constant work of keeping their ships afloat. The men and women of the fleet were utterly exhausted.

As the seas began to calm, the crews were allowed to go below decks and rest. Raven fell into her bed and fell asleep quickly, with Captain Billings curled up next to her.

The next morning, Raven had Hadari call the ships together so that she could get a report on each ship's damage. Hadari blew the conch shell, signaling for the ships to converge. Matilda pulled up along the port side of *Destiny*.

Pharaoh reported, "We have a few leaks in the hull we are trying to repair, but nothing too serious,"

Raven asked, "Do you have enough oakum to do the repairs?"

"Aye, Raven."

Nightingale pulled up on *Destiny's* starboard rail, and Alexander reported, "We have some minor tears in the main sail. We will have them repaired soon."

The *Lady Falcon* sailed nearby but was unable to get very close. Attila sent word by having Nathan row over in one of the dories. As Nathan pulled alongside *Destiny*, he reported, "Raven, our rudder is damaged. We are limited in our steering."

Raven asked, "Do you have what you need to repair the rudder?"

"Aye, we just need to replace the steerage rope. It broke during the storm. We'll catch up to you as soon as we are repaired."

"Are you sure you wouldn't like us to wait?"

Nathan replied, "That won't be necessary. We'll catch up to you soon enough."

Raven waved to him and said, "Alright! Keep a sharp eye on the horizon. I wouldn't want you to get caught out here all alone."

"We will!"

Raven instructed *Matilda* and *Nightingale* to sail back into formation as they sailed southward toward the Cape of Good Hope.

Attila remained behind with his crew as they worked to replace the rope that operated the ship's tiller. The old rope was removed and stored below, while a new rope was brought up from the lowermost deck to replace it. The new rope was wound through a series of pulleys and spools, beginning with the steering wheel itself, and then was attached to the rudder from both sides. The rudder would be pulled along an iron rod shaped in an arc called the tiller sweep. It took Attila's crew nearly three hours to complete the repair.

Once satisfied with the repair, Attila ordered his crew to unfurl the sails to catch up with the rest of the fleet.

As soon as the sails were dropped and secured, Attila heard someone from the crow's nest call out, "Ship ahoy! Starboard stern!"

Attila looked over his right shoulder but saw nothing. He then called up to the crow's nest, "How far out?"

"About half a mile!"

Attila asked, "What's their heading?"

"Straight for us, and closing fast!"

"Let me know as soon as you can make out their colors!"

"Aye, Captain!"

Everyone waited anxiously as the approaching ship continued to gain on the *Falcon*. Attila's anxiety grew with each passing minute. It was his first time in command of his own vessel. He had always relied on Raven to give orders whenever danger threatened them. Attila continued to wait impatiently for a call from the crow's nest. Thirty minutes passed when finally the call came: "She's a sloop flying French colors, Captain! She's still heading right for us!"

Attila ordered his men to report to their guns, "All gun crews, man your stations! This is not a drill! Load your cannons and prepare to fire when ordered!"

All available men scrambled to their guns below on the second deck. Powder monkeys began loading magazines with black powder and delivering them to each cannon. The ship's crew was still shorthanded, so each gun crew was responsible for three guns. They were prepared to move from one cannon to the next as the guns were fired. All three of their guns were prepared and loaded to begin the battle. Once a cannon was fired, one of the crew would use a spiral rod to clear the gun of any loose shrapnel from the barrel. The next man swabbed the cylinder clean by shoving a pole with a swab at the end after being soaked in water to clean any debris still in the tubing. The next man placed a gunpowder magazine into the cannon barrel and rammed it with a wood pole to the end of the tube. The next man loaded the barrel with a cannonball. While the gun master set up the gun to aim at his target, another man took the pole with a slow-burning wick on one side and a pointed tip on the other. He pierced the powder magazine inside the cannon with the pointed tip through a hole at the base of the cannon barrel. He then inserted a fuse into the magazine through the same hole. The gun was set. Now, all they needed was a target and the order to fire.

They didn't have to wait long. As soon as the crew had loaded their third cannon, they heard a blast from the approaching ship. A man named Ronald Pearson peered through one of the unused gun holes and saw a cannonball flying toward the *Falcon*. He held his breath as he watched the shot land harmlessly in the water ten feet shy of the *Falcon*.

Then, Pearson heard the order from above, "Ready on the starboard guns!"

Pearson quickly jumped to his position behind one of the cannons. He aimed the cannon at the sloop. A minute later, he heard, "Fire!"

Pearson commanded his man, holding the slow-burning fuse, "Fire!"

He watched to see where the shot might strike the approaching ship. Seconds later, the cannonball fell short of the sloop. Pearson moved to his second gun while his crew began preparing to load the just-fired cannon. He adjusted his aim and then ordered, "Fire!"

The second shot hit its mark but did little damage, striking the sloop's port rail. The rail shattered as it was struck, but then the cannonball rolled along the ship's deck and crashed through the starboard rail before falling into the sea.

Pearson moved to his third gun and aimed once more. As he aimed, he felt the *Falcon* change direction as she swung to her right. Attila was moving into position so his starboard guns would face the sloop's bow—a smaller target for Pearson and the other gunners, but the sloop would find it difficult to fire upon them with the smaller guns that would be on her bow deck.

The French sloop was a fast ship, smaller than Attila's schooner and supporting fewer guns than the *Lady Falcon*.

Pearson waited for the bow of the sloop to line up with his remaining gun. When he had her lined up just right, he ordered, "Fire!"

Again, Pearson watched as his cannonball left the ship and flew toward the French vessel. This time, Pearson's aim was true. The cannonball hit the sloop's bow just below the bow's rail. Wood splintered and shattered into the sea as men could be seen falling into the water from the sloop's bow.

All four of the *Falcon's* gun crews were firing at will toward the ever-approaching sloop. Attila continued to circle the French ship, allowing his starboard guns to fire upon the vessel. Shot after shot struck the sloop, hitting her directly just above and below the waterline. The sloop was damaged so quickly that she barely fired a shot against the barrage of cannonballs coming at her.

Attila watched as the French ship began to sink. He ordered his guns to cease firing. The gun crews watched from the gun deck through the open cannon doors as the sloop descended into the ocean's aqua waters. Attila noticed some French sailors trying to launch smaller escape vessels from their ship. He watched through his spyglass and noticed the French captain approaching one of the small boats. Attila called to the gun crews and ordered, "Take out those boats! If they survive, it will be because they are good swimmers."

Attila knew there would be little chance of the French sailors surviving the ocean this far from shore without a boat. He watched as each of the smaller boats was destroyed while the French sailors tried to escape. Through his spyglass, Attila watched the captain and his lieutenant fly into the air and land in the water as their boats exploded beneath them.

The sloop burned as it began to sink. The *Falcon's* crew cheered, knowing they were successful in their first battle as a pirate gunship. Raven would be proud of them. Attila, too, was proud. He no longer doubted himself as a captain. His decisions against the sloop were vital and had proved successful. Attila looked forward to telling his fellow captains how he and his crew had faired in their first battle.

CHAPTER 13

Raven stood on the quarterdeck, gazing at the stars in the sky. The atmosphere was clear, and the winds were calm as *Destiny* sailed across the sea. Raven could hear gulls squawking as they flew overhead, searching for food scraps on the ship's deck.

Jeffrey walked up to the quarterdeck and stood next to Raven. Captain Billings jumped from Raven's shoulder onto Jeffrey's. Jeffrey rubbed the monkey's head without saying a word. Jeffrey watched as Raven stared into the nothingness. He wondered if she even realized he was standing next to her. Suddenly, Raven grasped Jeffrey's arm with both hands as if to steady herself.

"What is it?" Jeffrey asked.

Raven started to reply, but her knees buckled, and she sank to the deck. Jeffrey grabbed her to keep her from falling. Raven's face rubbed against Jeffrey's, and he realized she was burning with fever. Although Jeffrey was a fit young man, Raven was more than a handful. He called out, "John! Help me!"

Standing at the helm, John quickly rushed over to give his daughter aid.

"What happened?"

Jeffrey replied, "I don't know! She just fainted. She feels like she might have a fever."

John said, "Let's get her to her cabin."

As they picked her up together and carried her below to her quarters, John called out to Jeremy, who was standing nearby: "Jeremy! Go and fetch Mr. Greer! Bring him to Raven's cabin!"

"Aye, Mr. Ashworth!"

Jeremy ran to the other end of the ship where Mr. Greer's quarters lay. He rushed in without knocking.

"Mr. Greer! Mr. Ashworth says come quick! It's Raven, sir!"

"What's wrong, Jeremy?"

"She's fainted! I think she has a fever too!"

Greer gathered his medical kit and followed Jeremy to Raven's quarters. As he entered Raven's cabin, he saw her lying on her bed, with John sitting by her side, looking worried.

"Mr. Greer, what's wrong with her?"

"Well, I don't know just yet, Mr. Ashworth. Let me take a look at her. Jeremy, take the monkey out of here, please. Watch him until Raven feels better will you?"

"Aye, Mr. Greer. She will feel better, won't she?"

"We can only hope, my boy."

Jeremy left the room with Captain Billings on his shoulder. Then Greer said, "I'm going to need to get her undressed and into bed. John, will you help me? Jeffrey, I think it best if you leave us for now. I'll let you know when you can come back."

"Aye, Mr. Greer."

Jeffrey was not happy about having to leave Raven in her condition. He felt he had as much right to sit with her as anyone. However, he understood that seeing the young woman in this compromising situation would be uncomfortable. He dejectedly left the room.

John and Mr. Greer worked together to get Raven ready for bed. They removed her boots and stockings, then her waistcoat and trousers. They left her blouse on for her to sleep in. They lay her down in her bed and pulled up her covers. She was sweating profusely. Greer retrieved a pan of water and a small towel and began wiping her brow, neck, and arms to cool them, hoping to bring down her fever.

John asked, "What do you think is wrong with her?"

Greer replied, "I'm not sure, but I want to check her for any bug, rodent, or viper bites."

Greer began with her head, searching her scalp for signs of ticks or insect bites. It wasn't an easy job since her hair was so long and thick. He searched thoroughly but found no indication of ticks or insect bites. After a thirty-minute search, Greer was satisfied that her head was clear of bites. He had John help lift Raven's body to sit so they could check under her blouse. Greer lifted Raven's blouse to check her back. There between her shoulder blades was a tiny tick. No one would have noticed it unless they were searching for it. Raven probably had noticed an itch back there but tried to ignore it.

Greer rummaged through his medical kit and found a pair of small tweezers to remove the tiny insect. He put on his spectacles to see the tick better. He asked John to light a match and hold it over the area on her back where the tick had begun to burrow itself. They both leaned in for a closer look. Greer captured the tick with his tweezers, then carefully removed it, making sure the head did not remain on Raven's skin. He placed the tick on the table on an empty plate, then had John touch the lit match against the insect.

"Pop!"

The tiny creature exploded and died. Greer then found a small bottle containing pine sap. He took a drop of the sap and covered the reddened area on Raven's back to help suffocate any poison that might still be present.

"Hopefully, we caught it in time. Ticks can be bad news if not treated right away."

John asked, "Do you think we caught it soon enough?"

"I hope so. We can only wait and keep an eye on her. Even if it doesn't kill her right away, it may have lingering effects. She might have spells for weeks when she feels well, then she might fall ill again for seemingly no reason."

John said, "I'll sit with her while she sleeps."

"No John, you've got a ship to run as well as her fleet to watch over. I'll watch her and Jeremy can help when I'm needed elsewhere."

"Alright. But let me know if her condition changes."

"I will. I promise."

The next day, Raven awoke still feeling feverish but was at least conscious. Mr. Greer noticed her opening her eyes and said, "Welcome back."

"How long have I been asleep?"

"Oh, about thirty hours."

"What happened to me?"

"You were bitten by a tick. You have tick fever."

"Oh, no! How bad?"

Greer replied, "I think we caught it early enough."

Raven knew about tick fever from Mr Greer's medical books, which she had read as a youngster serving as a ship's boy on the original *Destiny*.

She asked, "Where was the bite?"

"In the middle of your back. It was a tiny little thing. I almost didn't see it. Just take it easy for a few days. Get plenty of rest and drink lots of water. You'll get through this just fine."

Raven then remembered that *Lady Falcon* was left behind for repairs.

"Have you heard anything of the *Falcon*?"

"Not yet. But it's only been a little more than a day since we left her. It will take a while for her to catch up to us."

"Where's Captain Billings?"

"Jeremy has him."

Raven tried to sit up but faltered and felt sick to her stomach. She groaned as she lay back down.

"Just lie still, Raven. Your papa has things well in hand."

Raven relaxed, then soon fell asleep again.

An hour or so later, a call came from *Matilda*. A man standing in the crow's nest spotted a ship to their aft.

"Ship off the starboard stern!"

Pharaoh waited for clarity. Moments later, another call came down.

"It's a schooner! She's flying a raven! It's the *Lady Falcon*!"

Pharaoh signaled to the other ships that the *Falcon* had been sighted. John Ashworth and Alexander felt relieved to hear Attila was closing in on their location.

John sent word down to Raven's cabin. He thought the news might lift her spirits a bit. Jeremy left the quarterdeck with Captain Billings still perched on his shoulder and moved down to Raven's cabin. He quietly opened the door and peeked in to check on his captain. Raven was still lying on her bed and only slightly asleep.

"Raven?" Jeremy quietly called.

Raven stirred, then sat up.

"What is it, Jeremy?"

"Mr. Ashworth thought you might want to know, the *Lady Falcon* has been spotted. She's quickly closing in on us."

"Come in, Jeremy."

Raven sat up in bed, still wearing her blouse. She rubbed her eyes to clear her head, then said, "Hand me my trousers will you?"

Jeremy looked around to find Raven's trousers hanging over the back of a chair at the table. He snatched them up and handed them to Raven, then waited.

Raven started to pull on her trousers, then looked at Jeremy and said, "Turn around."

Jeremy turned around while Raven stood and pulled on her trousers. She tucked her blouse inside the trousers and then buttoned them up. Raven pulled her stockings and boots on, found her waistcoat, and donned it. She held her hand to Jeremy's shoulder so Captain Billings could take his place on her shoulder. The monkey climbed onto her shoulder and grasped a lock of Raven's hair to hold on as she walked across the floor to the door of her cabin. Jeremy followed her out as she headed to the quarterdeck.

John smiled as he witnessed his daughter climbing to the quarterdeck to join him.

"Have you seen them, Papa?"

"Not yet. *Matilda* spotted them north of us. They should be near enough for us to see within the half-hour."

Raven took a moment to breathe in the salt air as the wind blew across the deck. She suddenly felt refreshed and was glad her fever had passed. She looked to the southern horizon and asked, "Where are we?"

John replied, "We're still about ten days out from the Cape."

Raven ordered, "Trim the sails. Let's wait for the *Falcon*. I want to see how she fairs."

"Aye, Captain."

John called to the crew, "Raise the main sail! Ease her forward at half speed."

Hadari answered from the main deck, "Aye, Mr. Ashworth!"

Raven stood beside her papa near the helm and glanced back occasionally to see if the *Falcon* came into sight. Raven glanced up and saw Simba standing on the main yardarm. Raven waved to her and smiled as Simba waved back. Raven was pleased to see her new friend taking so well to a life at sea. She had no doubts about her ability as a warrior, and now she was proving her capabilities as a sailor.

Matilda called with the conch shell to let Raven know the *Falcon* was closing quickly. Raven looked back with her spyglass and saw her gunship sailing toward them. She smiled as relief flooded her soul. Raven told John, "Have all the ships assemble together."

John replied, "Aye, Raven!"

John gave the command to signal all ships to assemble. Mtoto Jasin blew the conch signal to the other ships and waited for their reply. *Matilda* and *Nightingale* each quickly returned a reply. Each ship came alongside *Destiny* and waited for the *Falcon* to arrive. Half an hour later, *Lady Falcon* came alongside as well. Raven called all captains to assemble on *Destiny*. Pharaoh, Alexander, and Attila joined her on the quarterdeck from their respective ships.

Raven asked Attila, "Is the *Falcon* in full repair?"

"Aye, Raven! And Battle proven!"

"What do you mean?"

Attila said, "Soon after we made our repairs a French sloop followed in our wake. She was fast, so we couldn't outrun her. I ordered our gunners to prepare for battle."

Raven interrupted, "What? You took on a French sloop alone?"

Attila smiled, "Aye, Raven! We were ready for her. I turned the *Falcon* around, and we fired eighteen guns at her until she broke apart. Their officers tried to escape in smaller boats, but we also sank those."

Raven smiled and congratulated Attila, "Well, Captain, I see I chose the right man for the job! Well done! Well done indeed!"

Each of the captains congratulated Attila on his success in bringing down the French vessel, and John and Hadari also congratulated him.

Raven said, "Alright, let's get to Port St. Felix as quickly as possible. We need to make some deals and reward our crew with their shares."

Everyone shook hands and bid each other farewell as they returned to their respective ships.

Fifteen days later, Raven and her fleet pulled into dock at Port St. Felix on the southwest coast of Madagascar. It was midday, and there was a chill in the air. As they pulled closer to the port, they checked the signal flag set up by Señor Rivera to ensure they could enter the port safely. Rivera's servant, Juan, met them at the docks.

"Buenos días, Señorita Raven! How are you?"

"Fine, Juan. I hope all is well here."

"Si, Señorita! All is well. How may I help you today?"

"Is Señor Rivera available today?"

"Oh, si! He is very anxious to see you. He has hoped you would come soon."

Raven turned to Jeffrey and John and said, "Go into the village and see if you can find some more men to work on our new gunship."

"Aye, Raven." Jeffrey replied as he and John walked off the gangplank together.

Hadari remained onboard the ship while the rest of the crew were allowed to explore the village at their leisure. The crews of the other three ships were also allowed to leave their vessels.

Raven followed Juan up the street to Rivera's hacienda. They entered without knocking, and Juan led Raven into Rivera's private office, where they found him studying a chart.

Rivera seemed not to notice the two as they entered, being too engulfed in the map lying on his desk.

"Señor, Señorita Raven has arrived."

Without looking up, Rivera muttered, "Hmm?"

Again, Juan said, "Señor! Raven is here!"

Rivera finally glanced up to see Raven standing before him.

"Oh, Raven! Just the one I've been wanting to see!"

Raven replied, "Are you busy? I can come back later."

"No! No! This concerns you. Come and see."

Raven stood beside Rivera and looked down at a primitive map on his desk. An amateur map maker drew it. Underneath the map were several sea charts stacked up. Rivera had been using them to try to locate the island indicated on his home-made map.

"What is it?" Raven asked.

Rivera replied, "Several weeks ago a Spanish merchant ship arrived. The Capitán brought several items he salvaged from a vessel in the Caribbean. He said the ship was evidently slammed against a reef and although the ship was severely damaged it was only partially sunk. However, apparently the crew was lost."

"Did he give you the name of the ship?"

"Si, the *Crimson Dog*."

Raven's eyes widened as she heard the name.

"Wasn't that Black Jack McGreavey's ship?"

"Si! McGreavey is, or was known for raiding Spanish ships throughout the Caribbean Sea for more than twenty years. No one knows where he has hidden his treasure, until now."

"What do you mean?"

Rivera pointed at the map. "I found this hiding in the spine of that ship's log. It was among other items brought in by Capitán Geraldo. He found it onboard the *Crimson Dog*. Evidently Geraldo had no idea what he had discovered among the wreckage of the ship."

Raven looked more closely at the crudely drawn map. She saw what appeared to be a drawing of a jellyfish lying horizontally in the water, but it had only one tentacle. To the east of that island were two more.

"This looks familiar," Raven commented.

Rivera offered, "I have been searching these charts but haven't identified it yet."

"Let me see."

Raven fingered through the many charts Rivera had stacked on his desk. Most of them covered broad areas of the Caribbean. They needed to be more concentrated on small areas of the sea.

"Do you have any charts that give a closer look at these islands?"

"I'm afraid not. I don't have very many charts."

"Let's go back to *Destiny*. I think I have what we need there."

They rolled up the makeshift map, and the trio began walking back to the docks. Half an hour later, Jeffrey called out to Raven as she and Rivera began climbing the gangplank to *Destiny*.

"Raven!"

She turned to look back at him. Jeffrey trotted over to her and Rivera.

"We're not having a lot of luck finding more crew. I've only signed eight men so far."

Raven replied, "That's fine. I think I know where we can find more. I'll worry about it later. Go ahead and have the men unload the cargo while I work out the details with Señor Rivera."

"Aye, Raven."

Raven, Rivera, and Juan continued onto the ship and entered Raven's cabin. Raven rummaged through her extensive collection of charts before finding a few of the close-up views of the Caribbean.

Rivera took out the makeshift map and unrolled it. Raven looked at the map and noticed some Spanish words at the bottom.

"Can you translate this for me?"

"Si, it says, 'Las Tortugas'. It means turtles."

"Turtles? Hmm."

Raven fingered through a stack of charts again, looking for one in particular. Finally, she found it.

"Christopher Columbus discovered a small chain of islands once he called Las Tortugas. The seas around them were filled with sea turtles. They also had a lot of crocodiles closer to shore. Here it is! The Cayman Islands. Look! See here? This one is shaped like this jellyfish island and there are the smaller islands that McGreavey drew. The treasure has to be on one of these islands."

Rivera's eyes lit up as he said, "Si, Raven! You have found it!"

CHAPTER 14

R aven and Señor Rivera began planning the journey to the Caribbean. Rivera said, "Raven, we must leave right away!"

"We? Are you coming?"

"Si, I want to come with you. It will be a great adventure. This is important for both of us. I can't just wait here for you to come back, I must be with you when you find the treasure."

Raven suggested, "I think we should work out our deal before we take off on such a journey."

"Si, what would you suggest?"

Raven thought for a moment . . . "Well, you are supplying the map, which may or may not lead to treasure. I am providing the ships, the men, the supplies . . . I'll give you twenty percent of whatever we find."

Rivera scoffed, "Huh! Twenty percent? Señorita, I recognize you are supplying much, but twenty percent hardly seems fair. Fifty percent and I will supply your ships for the journey."

Raven wasn't about to give away so much for so little effort, "Twenty–five percent, I'll supply my vessels, and you stay here."

Rivera sensed that Raven would give in very little on this deal, but he didn't want to depend on her honesty to complete this expedition. He trusted Raven to some extent, but treasure such as this might cause anyone to have second thoughts about honesty.

"Alright, twenty–five percent, but I come along. I don't want to miss out on such an adventure."

Raven replied, "I won't be going directly to the Caribbean."

"No? Why not?"

"My crew isn't at full capacity for such an endeavor. I'm going to Lomé to finish out my crew and settle a score. Then we will sail for the Caribbean."

"Who is in Lomé?" Rivera asked.

"It's not so much a who, as a what. There is a slave prison there. Many of my friends from the Gulf of Guinea were imprisoned there. It is a large fortress that holds several hundred slaves. I mean to destroy it so that they will no longer be able to hold people there again."

"Raven, if it is a fortress it will be too dangerous. How will you be able to fight against them?"

"Have you not seen my new gunship?"

"No, I did not notice a new ship."

"Follow me."

Raven led Rivera to the main deck and pointed toward the *Lady Falcon.*

"There she is. I took her just outside the Gulf of Guinea. She's loaded with forty guns and ready for battle. Attila is her captain and he has already tested her in battle. He took down a French sloop about a month ago with only a light crew. I need more men to man all those guns. Lomé is where we will find them."

Rivera asked, "How long will it take for you to find your crew before we can go to the Caribbean?"

"I rate it at, six weeks. Three or four weeks to sail there, attack the fort, and collect the men I need for my ships. It will take another six weeks or so to sail to the Caribbean. Do you still want to go?"

Rivera was silent momentarily as he pondered being away from his business for so long. He also realized that his ordinary comfort of living would be challenged while on a ship. Food would be meager, wine and rum would be limited, and female companionship would be non-existent.

"Si, I will still go with you."

Raven said, "Well then, go and pack your gear. You'll be bunking with the officers. I don't have a private room for you."

Rivera left right away to pack his things. Raven met Juan on the docks to negotiate the sale of her trade goods. Juan was much more accommodating than Rivera in this regard. They quickly settled on a price, and Juan brought Raven a chest of gold pieces to pay for the goods.

Then Raven had all her crew assemble on the docks to receive their shares. To expedite matters, Raven appointed Jeffrey as master quartermaster, a term she came up with on her own. A quartermaster was then assigned to each ship to oversee the distribution of funds to each ship's crew. Jeffrey continued to oversee the payment of *Destiny's* crew while three others were assigned to their respective ships. After each man or woman received their pay, they were allowed to leave after receiving strict orders to report for duty by dawn the following day.

When dawn arrived, Pharaoh was pleased Henry Bleaker was the first man to board the *Matilda*. Bleaker caught Pharaoh's eye as Henry reached the top of the gangplank and noticed a slight upward curl of Pharaoh's mouth. Henry nodded to his captain and continued to his station aboard the ship.

All crew members reported on time, and Raven signaled for all ships to follow in formation as they left Port St. Felix. *Destiny* unfurled her crimson blood sails, and the other ships flew their raven flags as they pulled away from port.

Raven felt her whole strength for the first time in days as she stood on the quarterdeck with Rivera by her side. Rivera asked Raven, "How long will it take us to get the men you need?"

"If all goes well, we should be out within a couple of weeks."

"Why so long?"

"Patience, Oscar! Our treasure will still be there when we arrive on the island."

"But which island? We don't even know which of the Tortugas the map refers to."

Rivera suddenly clutched his gut and winced in pain.

"Ugh!"

"What is it, Oscar?"

Rivera replied, "I am not feeling well."

Suddenly, he vomited over the rail of the ship. Raven took his arm to steady him as she looked around for Jeremy. She found him on the main deck helping one of the crew as they secured the lines of one of the sails.

"Jeremy!"

He looked around. He knew who was calling him, he just wasn't sure where Raven was. Then, he saw Raven standing beside the quarterdeck starboard rail. Raven beckoned him toward her. Jeremy jogged over to the steps leading up to the quarterdeck and reported to Raven.

"Jeremy, take Señor Rivera to his quarters and have Mr. Greer look in on him. He seems to have a little sea sickness."

"Aye, Raven."

Jeremy escorted Oscar to his bunk, found Mr. Greer, and informed him that he had a new patient.

Raven remained on the quarterdeck, enjoying the ocean air. She looked into the skies and across the sea, staring sometimes at the horizon. She watched as groups of sea birds hovered above the ocean surface as they searched for any unaware fish swimming just below the water's surface. Raven couldn't imagine herself doing anything else with her life. She loved the sea, she loved sailing, and she even loved the adventure and sometimes danger it often presented. She would rather be dead than be forced to live on dry land. The sea was her home.

Raven's fleet sailed into the Gulf of Guinea three weeks later. They lingered well off the coast until dusk. Raven didn't want to be so conspicuous as to lower any concerns of those living in Lomé, especially anyone associated with the fortress where the slaves were held.

The ships pulled up about two miles shy of the port and waited. Raven signaled all her captains to meet her onboard *Destiny*. Pharaoh, Alexander, and Attila joined Raven in her cabin with John, Jeffrey, and Señor Rivera.

Raven began, "Here's what I intend to do. Attila and his crew will moor just outside the port within firing range of the fortress. Attila, I calculate the distance to be about a mile from shore, so you should easily reach it with sixteen pound guns. Just make sure you don't over shoot. If you can reach it with the twenty pounders, all the better."

"Aye, Raven."

"Pharaoh, Alexander, we will assemble our men at midnight. Jeffrey, how many men do we have not counting those onboard the *Falcon*?"

Jeffrey replied, "Hmm, I'd say about seventy-five fighting men and women."

"Good. That will be enough. Each of you bring grappling hooks. We will need them to scale the walls of the fort to get in. Here's what I plan for us to do."

Raven laid out the plan to the officers and answered any questions they might have regarding the attack.

Destiny floated into port alone at nearly four o'clock that afternoon. One other ship was resting at the docks. Raven could see that the ship had only just arrived. She hastened to have her crew tie up and secure the ship so she could hurry over to the other ship before its crew set foot on land.

Raven took twenty armed men with her and walked to the ship, the *Roaming Fairchild,* out of Bristol. When they reached the *Fairchild's* gangplank, they met some of the ship's crew as they were leaving the ship.

Raven stopped them as they walked along the gangplank. "Excuse me, before you leave your ship, I will need to speak to your master."

A scruffy but large man looked at Raven curiously and asked, "Why do you want to speak with our captain, Miss? Wouldn't you rather spend the evening with me?"

The man was disgusting and smelled foul.

"No thanks! I'm not in the habit of associating with such putrid smelling varmints as you."

The man's eyes squinted in anger as he reached for his knife. As he did, he heard the sound of twenty swords being unsheathed. He froze.

Raven continued, "Now, please summon your captain to come and speak with me. It is a matter of life or death for him and his crew."

"Aye, Miss."

The man backed away and stumbled back up the gangplank in search of his captain. Just moments later, a man of about fifty years wearing a captain's uniform came to the rail of the *Fairchild* and asked, "What's this about, Miss? Who are you?"

"My name is Captain Ashworth of *Raven's Destiny*. Perhaps you've heard of me? Some call me the Red Raven."

The captain's eyes widened when he heard the name.

"What do you want from me?"

Raven replied, "I want nothing you have, I only want to offer you the opportunity to save the lives of you and your crew."

"And how might we save our lives?"

"By turning your ship around and leaving this port without incident. Something will happen here tonight that you should not want to be a part of."

The captain said, "That's fine, Captain. We will hurry our business and get away from here before night falls."

"What is your business, Captain?"

"Why, slaves of course."

"I thought so. No, you will not be allowed to do business in this port today. There are no slaves to be purchased here."

"I happen to know that there are nearly six hundred slaves available here at any given day."

"I didn't say they weren't here. I said there are no slaves to be purchased here. Now turn your ship around and leave."

The captain looked at Raven, then her men. He then turned to look at her ship.

"You plan to run me off with just these few men here?"

Raven asked, "Captain, do you have your spyglass with you?"

"I do."

"Let me direct you to search the horizon to the south."

The captain took out his spyglass and looked southward. He moved the glass back and forth until he finally saw three ships in the distance, at least half a mile out.

He then commented, "So! I see three ships in the distance. Why should that concern me?"

"Those are my ships. See the one in the center? The schooner is a gunship carrying ten ,twenty-pounders and eighteen, sixteen-pounders. One of those twenty pounders will take down your ship with one shot and Captain, my gunner is an excellent shot. Captain, you might overpower me and my crew here on this dock and you might even purchase a shipload of slaves, but you will never escape this port alive unless you do it now. You've got ten minutes to turn this ship and leave this port. Do you understand?"

The corners of the captain's mouth turned downward as he looked at Raven's cold blue eyes.

"Alright, young miss. Have it your way. We will be leaving now."

As he turned to walk back up to his ship, Raven said, "Captain! Don't bother coming back here. There won't ever be any slaves here anymore once we're finished."

The captain turned and walked away, shaking his head. He hated being bested by a young sprout, especially of the female gender. He called out to his men and instructed them, "Make ready the sails! We're heading west!"

When midnight finally arrived, Raven stood on the quarterdeck, watching *Matilda* and the *Nightingale* pull into port. The *Lady Falcon* followed but remained outside the port within gun range of the fortress. The fortress sat atop a hill overlooking the city of Lomé. Her strong stone walls towered above the jungle wall at thirty feet. Guard towers were built at the four corners of the walls, with walkways leading from one tower to the next around the fort's perimeter. Forty guards patrolled the fort walls on any given night.

Raven assembled her men on the docks for final instructions. Pharaoh, Alexander, and John would remain with the ships, commanding only a crew of five or six men per ship. All others would follow Raven to the fort. Each man would carry only small blades and bows as weapons. Long swords would make too much noise as a man walked along and would be too cumbersome in battle. The bows would allow them to attack from below those who patrolled the walls above. They intended to make a sneak attack so that guns would be useless.

Sixty men and women began sneaking through the city streets. The fortress was about a mile from the bay as the crow flies, but more like two miles on winding roads going uphill. They walked in dim lights of torches hanging from various buildings within the city. They split into four smaller groups of fifteen, taking different routes through town. Hadari led his band directly through the city's center, taking the most direct route. He would be responsible for getting his men to the far side of the fort to attack from the rear. Mwindaji took an easterly route, swinging wide through the city streets where they planned to attack from the east. Kiboko took his band and swung through the left side of the city to attack from the west. Raven led her group straight through, following the first group but lagging thirty minutes behind. She would attack the southern wall of the fortress.

Once through the city streets, the raiders found travel more difficult as they wound through the jungle surrounding the fort. Raven's men were instructed to avoid the road connecting the fort to the city as much as possible, sticking to the jungle's cover.

As they left the lit streets of the city, everyone found traveling in the dark more difficult until their eyes could adjust to the darkness. They traveled quietly through the brush, making almost no discernible noise. When Raven's crew arrived near the south wall, she found two men guarding the stone walkway beneath the towering wall. Each man was armed with a rifle. One guard started his patrol from the southeast corner of the fort, while the other started from the southwest corner. They strolled in front of the wall toward the center of the wall, where they met and sometimes conversed before heading back to their respective corners.

Raven selected two men and instructed them to eliminate the two guards.

"Each of you go to one of the corners. Be mindful of guards patrolling the east and west walls. Once the guards reach the corner and turn to return to the center, attack them from behind."

Each man nodded and proceeded to his assignment. Raven watched as each man crept forward at each end of the wall and hid, waiting for his prey. Simultaneously, they grabbed each guard around the throat from behind and then swiped their knives across their guard's throat from ear to ear. Raven then turned to the archers who had followed her and pointed out the guards on the top of the wall near the towers. Four arrows were released, and four guards fell to the ground thirty feet below.

Raven instructed her grapplers to throw their hooks over the walls for the climb. Six hooks were thrown over the top of the wall and then secured for the climb. Raven's men began the climb up the six ropes. Each man was skilled at such climbs, having worked so long on ships where they were expected to climb rope ladders several times daily. Their strong hands, arms, legs, and toes allowed them to make quick work of the climb up the fortress wall. Raven's climb was more difficult because she wore boots and was no longer used to making such climbs anymore. However, she finally reached the top, where she joined her crew.

Raven searched the other three walls to find her other crew. They, too, were reaching the tops of the walls where they waited for Raven's signal. More guards patrolled the courtyard below, unaware they were being watched from above. Raven took out her spyglass and scanned the courtyard to find the remaining guards. Sixteen guards remained walking along the lower perimeter of the fort. None of them suspected that they were being watched from above. None of them realized that their comrades on the walls and in the towers were already dead.

Raven beckoned the attention of her men, who surrounded the guards from the tops of the walls. The bowmen readied their bows, and each found their target. Then, they awaited Raven's signal. Raven raised her hand above her head and paused, then swung down, signaling her archers to let their arrows fly. Silently, each of the remaining sixteen guards fell lifelessly.

The raiders followed Raven to the prison's ground floor, meeting with their compatriots from the other walls. Raven quietly instructed the men, "Search the guards for the keys to the cells, then free the people. Tell them to stay quiet. Hadari, take some men and open the fort gates."

"Aye, Raven!"

Raven watched from the center of the courtyard while her crew opened door after door, allowing men and women to walk out into the night air, some for the first time in weeks. Quietly, the raiders moved door to door, releasing the captives and telling them to follow silently behind. Three stories of cells became empty in a matter of minutes. Everyone gathered in the courtyard around Raven and awaited her instructions. Hadari and his men opened the large wooden gates at the east end of the fort, and Raven turned to the people and said, "Quietly follow me. You will be slaves no more."

CHAPTER 15

Nearly six hundred people walked out of the Lomé Prison together in the darkness of the early morning. Stars twinkled brightly above their heads as they whispered to one another along the road leading into the city. An hour later, they arrived at the docks and witnessed three large ships in the harbor, with another only a quarter of a mile off the coast. The sight of these ships frightened the people, and they began to murmur. Raven heard some of the comments but didn't understand them all. Hadari walked over to Raven and translated, "Raven, they think we have stolen them away to be our slaves. They are afraid of the ships because they have had people taken away in the ships never to return."

Raven said, "Hadari, gather our people together so I can address them."

Hadari quietly called his men and women together, although finding sixty people among six hundred was difficult. He did find most of them and had them gather around Raven for instructions.

"Scatter and tell the people this: They don't have to get on our ships if they don't want to. They can leave this place and find their homes for themselves. However, if they come with us, we will take them to a place not far from here where they can start anew. We will take them to Port Gentil. Others who are interested can join us and work with us on the ships. I need sixty additional men to work on the gunship. They will get a full share's pay for their work. Go and spread the word."

When Raven's men started spreading out through the crowd, they discovered many people had already begun to sneak into the jungle. Many were already becoming rowdy with fear and antics, starting a commotion. Raven saw lanterns lit in some houses and businesses near the docks. People were beginning to open their doors to see what was the matter. When they saw the large crowd of Africans standing outside their abodes, they quickly shut their doors and locked them.

Raven was concerned with how many were leaving. She didn't want them to go back toward the prison because she hadn't thrown her final stone. She called for Kujana wa Muziki to come to her. When he arrived, she said, "Muziki, call your drummers together and drum out a call to these people so they will return."

Muziki and the other drummers began to beat out a rhythm that he thought most Africans would recognize as a call to re-turn. Gradually, people began to turn and listen to the beat of the drums, and they stopped. Then, many, but not all, began to return to the docks. After many of the people had returned and stood before Raven, she spoke as best she could in an African dialect.

"People! I am the Red Raven! Some of you may have heard of me. I am not here to make slaves of you, but to free you from slavery. I know that many of you want to return to your homes. Some of you can't return to your homes because your leaders have turned you over to the slavers. I am offering you a new life. There is a place nearby that I can take you to start a new life. There are people living there that I freed from slavery in the past and they have built a village. You can join them. I also need able men and women to work for me on my ships. Most of my people were once like you, captured and sold into slavery, but I freed them. Now, they work for me. I can't take all of you as my crew, but I need about sixty more men and women to join me. If you want to be considered for a place on one of my ships, let it be known to one of my crew. I will select new crew members once we have reached Port Gentil."

Nearly four hundred passengers boarded the ships that would take them to their new homes. The rest had already escaped into the jungle to find their way home.

Raven told Muziki, "Signal the *Falcon* to begin firing."

"Aye, Raven!"

Muziki began beating out a rhythm to signal the attack upon the fort. Moments later, a blast could be heard from the bay, and a cannonball could be heard whistling over the ships and toward the prison. The iron ball struck the fort's south wall and opened up a six-foot-diameter hole.

More blasts rang out in succession. Each shot struck its mark against the prison's stone walls. The citizens of Lomé walked out of their houses to see what was happening. They screamed with every cannon blast. Many fled from the safety of their homes into the jungle east of the city, not realizing the attack was not on their homes but on the fort.

Cannon fire continued blast after blast, destroying the seemingly indestructible structure. The southeast corner guard tower collapsed, bringing down sections of the adjacent wall. Cannonballs struck the base of the three-story area of the prison where the prisoners were housed, demolishing it into a pile of rubble.

Attila stood on the quarterdeck of the *Lady Falcon*, barking orders to his gun crew, indicating which areas of the structure remained intact. Ronald Pearson relayed the orders to his gun crews, giving angle adjustment orders to the men and indicating which guns should fire.

In less than half an hour, the prison no longer existed. Only a pile of timbers and stone remained. Dust floated through the air like a cloud of smoke.

Raven instructed her crew to divide the people and load them onto the three ships. The people were in a panic as they boarded the ships. They balked when instructed to go below to the lowermost deck. Again, they doubted their safety among these strangers who claimed to be saving them.

Raven's men yelled to the people, "Go below! We can not leave until the ship is secured! It is too dangerous for you to be above decks!"

Reluctantly, the people finally made their way down into the bellies of the ships. Raven ordered all ships to cast off. Hadari saw something in the city that struck his attention. Soldiers were running toward the docks while fully armed. Hadari called to Raven, "Raven! Raven!"

Raven looked around to see who was calling. She spotted Hadari waving to her. When he saw Raven looking at him, he pointed toward the city where more than one hundred soldiers were bearing down on them.

Raven yelled to her papa, "Mr. Ashworth! Get us underway, now!"

John looked around and saw the soldiers. "Aye, Raven!"

John barked his orders and had Jeremy blow the conch signaling the other ships to depart immediately.

Raven called out to Hadari, "Man the guns!"

"Aye, Raven!"

Hadari put crews on the starboard guns and set them to work while he ran to the bow gun. Hadari yelled, "Fire when ready!"

The starboard guns fired simultaneously into the crowd of soldiers running to the docks. Each cannonball bowled the soldiers down with such force that body parts flew in all directions. Men screamed in anguish who were missing limbs or had holes blown through their bodies but were still alive.

As *Destiny* turned seaward, Hadari fired a blast from the bow gun, taking down another section of the charging soldiers. *Matilda* was next in line to leave the dock, and she fired her guns against the mob of angry and frightened men as well. More body parts flew into the air, and more screams echoed through the streets. As the *Nightingale* began pulling away from the dock, ready to fire her guns, Alexander held fire, seeing that the soldiers were retreating to the city's far end.

As they pulled into the bay, Raven ordered Hadari, "Raise the blood sails!"

Three days later, Raven and her fleet arrived at Port Gentil. It was early morning, and the sun had barely reached the tops of the trees. No one was there to meet them on the shore. Skeletons still hung from the trees along the beach, which was a frightful sight for the new visitors from Lomé.

As Raven began to unload her passengers, she noticed the looks on their faces as they saw the corpses hanging along the shoreline.

"Don't worry!" she said. "These are not meant to frighten you. They are meant to frighten unwelcome visitors."

Everyone gathered along the beach to stretch their legs and explore the once-inhabited village site. The beach was crowded with the nearly four hundred visitors who had just arrived. It became even more crowded when Shujaa wa Mfalme and two other men arrived to go fishing. Mfalme was quite surprised to see everyone on his beach. Then he saw Raven's ship and knew it was safe. He searched for Raven and then saw her as she called his name.

"Mfalme!"

"Raven!" He replied. "It is good to see you. Who are all these people?"

They approached each other, and Raven began to answer, "They, like you, were freed from slavery. We attacked the prison at Lomé three nights ago. Six hundred were freed."

Mfalme replied, "Oh, that is good. But they will just fill the prison up again."

"I don't think so. It's nothing but a pile of rubble now. They are officially out of business."

Mfalme asked, "Where are you taking them?"

"Some of them will work for me just as Mwanamke Simba. But, I was hoping the rest might find a home here with your people. Can you make room for them?"

"If they want to stay, they may. But they must be willing to work. We will not have shirkers in our village."

Raven replied, "Very good! Let's see if we can whittle down the number who will remain with you."

Raven had all the people gather around to see and hear her. When everyone was settled, Raven began to speak.

"Welcome to Port Gentil! This place was once run by a French man who traded slaves. My men captured and killed him and his men when they refused to stop selling slaves. It is now home to people like you who have been freed from slavery. This is Shujaa wa Mfalme! He is one of those I freed not long ago. He and his people have a village not far from here where they are willing to accept any of you who wish to stay and start a new life. If you stay, you are expected to do your part in making it a successful home for everyone. They won't accept shirkers. If you don't work, they will ask you to leave and you will have to fend for yourself. As I told you before, I need sailors to work on my ships. I am willing to take as many as one hundred who are willing and able to live on the seas and work. I won't take just anyone. You must be strong, willing to learn, and able to fight, for that is what we do. We fight for those who cannot fight for themselves as you have recently witnessed. So, if this is a life that appeals to you, remain here on the beach. Mfalme's men will show the rest of you the way to their village. Those who remain will meet with my officers to determine if you qualify to be part of my crew."

Mfalme's companions beckoned those who wanted to live at Port Gentil to follow them down the trail leading to their village. There was much discussion among them as many slowly walked down the trail. Nearly two hundred people remained on the beach.

Raven's officers lined the remaining applicants along the beach in rows. Raven, Pharaoh, Alexander, and Attila walked the rows together to weed out those who were unqualified. Young girls who were younger than sixteen were quickly culled from the group. Raven wasn't discriminating against them; she knew life on a ship would be difficult for such skinny little girls. Several men and women who had remained were ill or injured after staying in the dark, dank cells of the prison. They were also asked to leave.

One hundred and forty men and women remained.

Raven asked her officers, "What do you think?"

Attila said, "They all look like good men, strong and young. The women too!"

Pharaoh replied, "Yes, but some of them may be too strong. Too big!"

Alexander added, "Yes, he's right! We need men and women who can climb the ropes on our ships and will be comfortable at sea!"

Raven then said, "Alright! Here's what we'll do. We'll have a contest. Something tells me many of these people can't swim."

Pharaoh said, "You are right!"

"Well then, we should be able to eliminate them very quickly."

The officers all nodded their approval.

Raven turned to the people still standing in line and announced, "If you can't swim, I can't use you! Those of you who cannot swim may leave now."

Several people looked around slowly, and many began to leave one by one. Raven quickly counted and concluded that one hundred and ten remained.

"Alright! So, all of you can swim, right?"

The remaining candidates muttered amongst themselves.

"Then swim! The first one hundred of you to swim out to my gunship and return will qualify to the next contest. When I fire my pistol you will begin!"

Raven drew her pistol from the brace hanging over her shoulder, cocked it, then fired. **Bang!**

People ran out to the water, splashing against the beach, and dove into the sea, swimming as fast as possible. Others were smarter and waded into the water and began swimming, but they took their time and swam at a steady pace. The *Lady Falcon* was a quarter of a mile offshore, and those who attempted to sprint the whole way would not likely make it. Finally, five men and two women remained on shore. They had lied about being able to swim. They glanced at Raven, then hung their heads as they walked away.

Raven and the officers decided to watch from *Destiny's* quarterdeck. As they watched, they noticed several of the larger men who had swam out with such ferocity were also trying to impede the process of those around them. They would hit someone who got too close or even dunk their head under the water. They ended up expelling more energy than they should have. Some quickly made it to the *Falcon,* while others extended themselves too quickly. Those individuals found themselves floating back to shore, having not finished the race. The first ones to make it to the *Falcon* were soon overtaken by the swimmers who swam steadily. As the steady swimmers passed the sprinters, some of the sprinters tried one last time to eliminate some of the swimmers by trying to hit them or dunk them under the water. In doing so, they used up their last ounce of energy and eventually had to revert to floating back to shore.

Once the competition was over, seven more men and women were eliminated who had never made it to the *Falcon.*

Raven allowed them to rest for half an hour while setting up the next competition. She asked a group of her crew who among them would be willing to climb to the top of the main mast to tie a bell. Many of her men were not so keen to climb for such an occasion, so they looked at each other, trying to decide who Raven would volunteer for the task among them. However, Raven didn't have to make any of them volunteer. She heard someone from the back speak up and immediately knew who it was.

"I will, Raven!"

It was young Jeremy. Raven smiled at her young apprentice and thanked him for his willingness to show up ahead of those with more experience at the task.

"Alright Jeremy! Let's show them how it's done."

Raven handed Jeremy a small bell, which he tied to his belt. Jeremy looked up the mast, took a deep breath, and then began his ascent. He steadily climbed the rope ladder leading to the top of the nearly one-hundred-foot mast. As Jeremy climbed, Raven remembered her first climb up the mast of the original *Destiny* under the tutelage of Captain Billings. She remembered how much effort such a climb takes and how some men she worked with could not make it themselves. It wasn't a task for older men. The contestants watched in awe as Jeremy made quick work of his climb. Within two minutes, he reached the top, tied the bell to the top of the mast, then rang the bell. Jeremy then slid down to the crow's nest to rest momentarily.

Raven yelled to him, "Stay there, Jeremy!"

Jeremy waved his understanding and remained in the nest.

Raven sent the contestants up the rope ladder five at a time. The first five began climbing and quickly slowed their pace. It was more difficult than Jeremy had made it look. The rope was unsteady as they moved up from knot to knot, and the wind played tricks with them as it blew against them. Five minutes passed before the bell rang for the first time. Soon, the bell rang four more times. As each man climbed back down, their legs began to shake uncontrollably. Each one struggled to reach the bottom, but they finally made it.

Groups of five continued the climb throughout the morning until everyone attempted the climb. Seven women could not complete the climb and were thus eliminated, bringing the final count to eighty-five. The others were sent with Mfalme to the village to find their places among the villagers.

Raven called Jeremy and said, "You can come down now! Bring the bell with you! Show everyone how it's done."

Jeremy made the short climb up to the bell, put the bell in his mouth, and removed his belt. He looped his belt over a rope that ran from the top of the mast to the ship's rail. Suddenly, Jeremy dropped from the mast, holding onto his belt. He squeezed his belt against the rope to slow his descent. The people who had struggled mightily to climb back down the rope ladder stared at Jeremy's unbelievable feat. When Jeremy landed on the deck, Raven patted the young man on the back and said, "Well done!"

155

CHAPTER 16

The fleet sailed northwesterly, crossing the equator into the northern hemisphere. As usual, *Raven's Destiny* led the way with the other three ships sailing in her wake. On the twentieth day at sea after leaving Port Gentil, they arrived on the southern tip of Barbados, where they stopped to resupply. Raven found their location on her chart as Cane Vale, a small coastal town rich with trading stations where local crops were bought for export. Sugar cane and tobacco were the main crops grown in the island's southern portion. The land was flat, and the soil was suitable for such crops. The island's northern part was more mountainous and teamed with jungle life, especially opossums, monkeys, and sloths. The green monkeys, named for their greenish-golden fur coloration, were prevalent in the jungles of Barbados.

As they pulled into port, they found another ship had already docked there. It was an English square-rigged vessel, much like Raven's three cargo ships. Raven checked the ship's name painted on its bow. *The Blue Menace* was notorious for its captain and crew: pirates, one and all. Horace Finley, also known as Horrible Horace, was one of the most unfavorable men a seaman would ever want to meet up with at sea. He was ill-tempered, crude, and, most of all, blood-thirsty.

The Blue Menace was no ordinary merchant ship. She was rigged with extra sails, making her faster than most square-rigged ships in the sea. She was also heavily armed. The *Menace* carried twenty sixteen-pound guns on either side of her on the mid-deck and twenty more on the lowermost deck. The *Menace* wasn't used to haul cargo, only treasure. She was manned by sixty of the foulest, meanest, and uncouth individuals who sailed the seven seas.

Raven directed her ships into the docks except for the *Falcon*, who remained nearby in the bay. The crews of Raven's other ships would ferry the *Falcon* any supplies she needed. Attila and his crew watched *Destiny, Matilda,* and the *Nightingale* from the bay.

Raven left *Destiny* in Jeffrey's command while Hadari, Simba, and twelve of her ship's largest, strongest, and most capable fighters escorted her ashore. She met Pharaoh and Alexander on the docks, who each carried their own entourage.

Horace watched Raven as she left her ship and eyed her with lust. He had never seen a more beautiful young woman in all his days. He turned to his first mate and said, "Smyth, go fetch me that wench. I'll have her for my bed tonight."

Smyth looked at his captain and smiled his response. "Aye, Captain! But how? She be completely surrounded by her crew."

"Take forty men with you. Tell em, £20 to the man who brings her to me."

Smyth chuckled as he turned to gather up his crew. Horace watched from his quarterdeck as forty men left the *Menace* to capture their prey. The men snarled and growled as they walked down their gangplank and approached Raven's crew. Smyth called out to the crowd surrounding Raven and said, "Excuse me, Miss! Captain Finley wishes to have a word with you if you please."

Raven stared at the man leading the mob through the shoulders of her men as she replied, "If your captain wishes to speak with me, he is welcome to join me on my ship. I'll be available shortly after I have resupplied my crews."

"I think not, Miss! The captain is very adamant about the matter. He expects me to deliver you to him, forthwith."

Angered, Raven pushed her men aside to present herself to the brash sailor who called for her capture. Smyth's eyes widened when he saw Raven up close and said, "I know you! You're the Red Raven!"

"You think yourself man enough to deliver me to your captain?"

Smyth had to muster his bravery before he replied, "Aye, that I am!"

Raven then said, "Well then, deliver this!"

She drew her knife from its sheath on her belt and quickly plunged it into Smyth's throat, then raked the knife through his jugular and watched him fall to the ground, bleeding and dying at her feet. Finley's men were shocked to see such a lovely young thing kill their first mate right before their eyes.

Raven's men took advantage of Finley's crew's shocked countenance and attacked. Although Raven's men were outnumbered, they were aided by the element of surprise. Blades clanged together, and men cried out in pain and anger as they began to fall to the ground. Simba swung her staff at several enemies, knocking each to the ground, bleeding from their heads. Raven was attacked by another man who quickly tasted his blood when Raven hit him in the mouth with the hilt of her sword, knocking him to the ground. Raven then thrust her sword into his heart and killed him. Finley watched in horror as Raven's small band of protectors quickly overtook his crew. Finley's men were quickly subdued, and those who were not severely injured or killed submitted and surrendered.

Finley wasn't ready to give up even though his men had already done so. He drew a pistol from his belt and aimed it at

Raven's head. However, before he could cock the hammer, the pirate captain felt a sting in his shoulder, knocking him to the ground. Finley had been shot. Raven searched for the source of the bullet and found it on *Destiny*. John Ashworth had saved his daughter. She saw her papa holding a smoking pistol aimed at Horrible Horace.

Finley wasn't giving up just yet. He slowly climbed to his knees and looked around to see who shot him. He found John holding the smoking pistol and aimed his gun at John. Suddenly, a shot was fired from the distance. Finley heard the crack of splintering wood above him. A cannonball struck his foremast, bringing it crashing down to the deck of the *Menace* and on top of Finley. Although still alive, he could not free himself from the fallen debris.

Raven searched to see where the shot had originated and saw smoke billowing from the *Lady Falcon's* gun deck. Raven and her crew raised their arms in victory, recognizing that her gunship had cast the final blow.

They rounded up the last of Finley's crew and lined them up on the docks. Raven then climbed onboard the *Menace* to find her fallen foe. As she stood over him, pinned beneath the ship's mast, she stared in disgust at the once-feared pirate of the Atlantic. Horrible Horace looked up to Raven standing over him and said, "Well, young lass, you've done me in. I'm dying. Go ahead and finish me off."

Raven replied, "Gladly!" Then she pulled out her pistol and shot him between the eyes. Raven stared momentarily at the notorious pirate, who had been no match for her men and their skills. She turned to her crew and said, "Let's see what there is to offer below decks of this bag of barnacles!"

Her crew ran to the *Menace* and plundered the ship, carrying off anything that wasn't nailed down. Raven searched the captain's quarters for anything of value. They divided the spoils between the three ships Raven's crew had docked at the port, then returned to their ships. They found enough food, fresh water, and rum onboard the *Menace*, and there was no longer a need to go ashore to buy supplies. They left the remaining crew of the *Menace* on Barbados to fend for themselves.

Raven instructed Hadari to take a few men and get aboard the *Menace* to steer the ship as Raven's ships would tow it out to the bay. Hadari stood at the helm and steered the vessel as it was pulled away from the docks. Raven's crews pulled the *Blue Menace* into the bay to meet with Attila and her gunship. When they had settled in the center of the four ships, Raven had her men finish plundering the last supplies from the *Menace*, the cannon ammunition and black powder.

They quickly fashioned a transfer plank together, nailing two long boards along the edges, creating a long V. They stretched it from the *Menace* to the *Lady Falcon*, then rolled cannonballs down the board from the *Menace* to the *Falcon*. A similar design was built to transfer the black powder kegs. Once the *Blue Menace* was utterly stripped of anything of value, the other ships pulled away from it out of harm's way, and they watched as the *Falcon* fired six shots into the hull of the abandoned ship to sink her.

Raven and her crew watched as the once terror of the Atlantic slowly dipped beneath the surface of the Caribbean. No one would ever again fall prey to Horrible Horace and his crew.

Raven's fleet began the journey to the Cayman Islands, fully supplied and ready for a long haul to the small island chain. Raven decided to travel to the island farthest east of the other islands to begin their search. This wasn't going to be an easy search. Black Jack McGreavey hadn't bothered to mark his spot on the map with an X. That would have been far too easy. Raven and Rivera sat for hours in her cabin, searching for clues to lead them to the spot on the map where they might find the hidden treasure. Rivera pointed to the east island and asked, "What is this word?"

Raven replied, "Brac! Cayman Brac. It's the name of that island."

"What is this, Brac?"

Raven replied, "I don't know, but..."

She left the table where they had been sitting and walked over to a bookcase at the other end of the cabin. She pulled down a book and began fingering through the pages, searching.

"Here it it! Brac is a Gaelic word. It means bluff. Like a mountain bluff. The island must be mountainous."

Rivera asked, "You have never been there?"

"No, I've never been any farther west than the Bahamas. This is new territory for me."

Rivera offered, "If there is a mountain, the treasure could be almost anywhere. There must be another clue about where we should search."

Raven asked, "Are you sure this was the only paper you found in that book?"

"Si!"

"Were there any other books?"

"No, Raven! It was the only one!"

"Why would Black Jack hide a single page of a map with no indication of where it was or what it might even lead to? We could search for the rest of our lives and not find this treasure."

Rivera replied, "I don't know! We are missing something. We're just not looking at this the right way!"

"Well, I don't know how else to look at it unless you think standing on my head will help."

Over the next three days, the seas were choppy. The skies were nearly black, and torrential rain fell relentlessly. Lightning flashed all along the skies above them as they sailed north toward the Caymans. The winds ripped at *Destiny's* sails, and the other ships were not immune to them. The lightning seemed to come closer and closer to the ships the farther north they traveled.

Raven left the safety of her cabin to walk out on the deck and check on her crew. Rivera remained in his cabin, not wanting to risk getting wet or even being struck by lightning. Raven climbed to the quarterdeck where her papa stood and yelled to him through the whistling winds.

"How bad is it?"

"Bad enough! We've lost the main sail. There's a large rip in it. Mtoto Jasiri went up to secure it until we can repair it."

Raven replied, "What? He's up there now? Get him down! It's much too dangerous in this wind."

No sooner had she said so than lightning struck the main mast at the crow's nest. An orange fireball the size of a large bolder exploded above them. The fire ignited the ropes holding the mast in place. The sails caught fire. An electrical charge radiated throughout the ship, causing everyone's hair to stand up. Two of Raven's men fell from the rope ladders leading up to the main mast where they had been working. Both were dead before they hit the deck. Jasiri slumped over, hanging halfway out of the crow's nest. Raven was sure he must be dead as well. She cringed at the thought of losing the young man. He was only about fifteen years old.

The white main sail began burning. Raven ordered her men to grab buckets to put out the fire. The fire was too high up the mast to reach from the deck, so someone had to climb up and cut it loose.

Raven yelled, "Hadari, get someone up there to cut loose the sail before it burns down the mast!"

"Aye, Raven!"

Before Hadari could give the order, Jeremy was already twelve feet up the rope ladder, heading to the top to cut loose the sail. He must have learned his climbing skills from spending so much time with Raven's pet monkey because he was at the top of the mast in no time. Jeremy took out his knife and began cutting the ropes to free the sail from the mast. Flames burned around him as he cut, but he tried to ignore them. Cutting the one-inch diameter ropes with such a small blade wasn't easy, but Jeremy continued. Slowly, he freed the sail from the mast. Most of the sail was already burning, but he was able to keep it from setting fire to the mast. The sail finally dropped to the deck, where Raven's men doused it with water to extinguish the fire.

Before he climbed back down to the deck, Jeremy ascended to the crow's nest to check on Jasiri. When he reached the crow's nest, he found the young black man had perished. Jeremy found a significant burn mark on Jasiri's forehead, and the boy's right hand looked like a cannonball had blown it off.

Jeremy tied a rope around Jasiri's body and slowly let him down to the deck so that some of the crew could tend to him. Then, Jeremy made the descent back down to the main deck. Raven quickly grabbed the boy and pulled him to her, wrapping her arms around him and holding him. Jeremy felt awkward having his captain hug him like his mother once had, but then he relinquished.

Suddenly, the rain let up, and the skies began to clear. Raven finally let go of Jeremy and examined the ship's damage. Three dead bodies lay on *Destiny's* deck. Her main sail was partially burned, tattered, and torn. Several ropes leading up to the top of the main mast needed to be replaced.

Raven looked at Hadari and said, "Let's check the blood sails. If they are alright, unfurl them and get us moving again as soon as possible. Get someone busy replacing the main sail and the ropes. Have Mr. Greer prepare for a funeral. We have three souls who need burying."

"Aye, Raven," Hadari whispered.

Raven summoned her other three ships to come alongside for a conference. The other ships approached *Destiny*, and they tied themselves together. The officers from each ship met Raven onboard *Destiny* in her cabin.

Raven said, "We lost three men during the storm. Did any of you lose anyone?"

Pharaoh replied, "I lost only one, Jacob Reynolds."

Alexander said, "I lost two, and one more is injured."

Attila said, "I guess we were lucky. No one onboard the *Lady Falcon* was killed. Only minor injuries."

Raven said, "Mr. Greer is preparing our dead brothers for burial at sea. Do any of you need his assistance?"

All shook their heads in reply.

"Then we will bury them at dusk. Attila, prepare six guns to be fired to honor our fallen men."

"Aye, Raven."

When the sun fell below the horizon that night, Raven's ships had separated in preparation for the burials. Hadari blew his conch to signal all was ready on *Destiny*. Alexander returned the call, as did Pharaoh. Almost immediately, six cannon blasts erupted from the *Lady Falcon*. **Boom! Boom! Boom! Boom! Boom! Boom!**

Each ship allowed its fallen to slide into the sea, and they slowly sank into its depths. Muziki and his fellow drummers beat out a rhythm honoring their lost friends.

Chapter 17

Raven's ships sailed through the Jamaican coastline five days after leaving Barbados. Every day, Rivera and Raven searched through charts and ship logs, looking for any clue that might lead them to Black Jack's hidden treasure. Raven stared at the map Rivera had discovered for hours on end. She turned it around and over, looking for some unseen clue she had not yet discovered.

Raven decided to pull into port at Treasure Beach on Jamaica's southwestern tip. She hoped someone there could give her information about the Cayman Islands. Raven assembled her ships and instructed them to remain outside the port while she took *Destiny* into shore. Before she left the ship, she instructed her papa, "If we're not back by sundown, come looking for us."

John replied, "Don't worry, daughter, we'll find you if you go missing."

Raven and Rivera left the ship in search of someone who might be able to shed light on the mystery of Black Jack's map. Most of the inhabitants of Treasure Beach were Taino, a breed of people who had traveled to the island sometime around 700 A.D.

Christopher Columbus discovered the people during his voyage in 1492 and named them Taino, which means good or prudent. The people spoke a dialect of Arawakan, mainly spoken by people who lived along the Amazon River in South America. Taino is a term used to identify an elite social class rather than an ethnic group. The Taino had a matrilineal system of kinship in which lineage was traced through the mother's bloodlines rather than the father's.

Raven and Rivera entered the nearest village and found themselves in the presence of one of the chiefs known as a cacique. The chief's name was Arocoel, which means grandfather. When Raven and Rivera approached the chief while working on his fish nets, the man called over a young man standing by the seashore. The young man came over to Arocoel and waited for instructions.

Raven spoke to the old man and was immediately quieted by his hand, which caused her to pause. The young man then knew why he had been called over: Arocoel needed an interpreter.

"I am Warakaba and this is Arocoel, our chief. He has asked me to translate for him."

Raven replied, "I am Raven, and this is Oscar. We are searching for someone who can tell us about the islands west of here known as the Caymans."

Warakaba translated to Arocoel and then waited for his reply.

"Arocoel says, many people have come and gone over the years while my people have settled here. My grandfather once spoke of a man called Columbus who came to our island. The man was kind and brought many gifts to my ancestors, but they also brought diseases that killed many of my people. Very few men and women survived the sickness. It has taken two hundred years for our people to come back to where we once were. White men keep coming and we are afraid they will bring more sickness and kill us again. We ask that you leave."

Raven said, "Tell Arocoel, we mean no harm to you. We are looking only for information. I will not invade your island with my men, I only want to ask you a few questions before I leave."

Warakaba asked, "What is it you want to know?"

Raven reached into a leather satchel she wore over her shoulder and pulled out a leather-bound book.

"Did anyone who came to your island happen to leave anything like this here?"

She handed Warakaba the ledger, and he thumbed through the pages. He noticed the scribbled marks of black on the pages.

"What is this?"

"It is a sailor's ledger. We use it to write down what happens to us on our journeys so that others can see what we have experienced along the way."

Warakaba briefly referred to Arocoel before saying, "Arocoel had seen things like this before. They are no use to us."

"Does he still have any of them?"

Warakaba replied, "There is a cave not far away where some of these 'books' have been left. I can show them to you. Arocoel says you may take them and go."

"Thank you, Arocoel!"

Warakaba led the way into the jungle down a barely noticeable path. Raven and Rivera followed behind without saying a word. They occasionally passed individuals, primarily women, who were picking fruit from trees in the area. Sometimes, they noticed children who had stopped playing to watch the strangers stalk through their jungle.

After about an hour of trekking through the dense vegetation, Warakaba stopped in front of a small opening on the side of a rocky hill. He pointed to the opening about four feet in diameter and said, "This is it."

Raven asked, "Are you going in?"

"No. It is forbidden. The cave is filled with evil spirits. I can not go any farther."

Raven looked around for something she could make into a torch. There wasn't much to choose from, but she noticed a human leg bone lying at the cave's mouth, halfway in, halfway out. An animal had dragged it from inside, where it had found a meal of human flesh. There was a strip of clothing lying next to the bone on the ground. Raven collected them both and wrapped the cloth around one end of the bone. She took a fire flint from her bag and removed her knife from its sheath. Then she said to Rivera, "Let me have your flask."

"What? Why?"

"I'm going to make a torch."

"With my rum?"

"I'll get you some more!"

Rivera hesitated before handing Raven his flask. Raven poured a generous portion of the liquid onto the rags hanging from the leg bone, then handed it to Rivera.

"Hold this while I start a fire."

Raven gathered tender from brush, leaves, and coconut husks outside the cave and raked her knife across the flint, causing it to spark. After a while, the sparks turned into smoldering embers and smoke. Then, small flames jumped from the tender and ignited a small fire. Raven took the torch back from Rivera and dipped it into the flames. The torch immediately lit and burned steadily.

"Come on."

Rivera followed Raven into the cave while Warakaba waited outside. They had more room inside than Raven had expected. She was able to stand her full length without ducking. She and Rivera walked carefully around the inside of the cave, looking for anything that looked like it might be a ship's log or a journal.

All around them, they found many skeletons lying about. Many of them wore remnants of military uniforms or seaman's clothing. Weapons lay next to the bodies, but they seemed ancient, as if from centuries ago. Swords and knives with old rusty blades lay about. Rats scrambled among the dead, looking for morsels of food that might be available. Cobwebs hung from the cave walls, clinging to Raven and Rivera as they moved about.

Raven spotted a tunnel at the far end of the cave room and moved toward it. Rivera followed closely behind with no light of his own. Raven ducked into the tunnel and used her torch to look around before entering. The next room seemed larger than the first, so Raven entered with Rivera close behind. A steady drip of water could be heard inside the room. More cobwebs covered the walls and ceiling; some were recently constructed by the spiders who occupied them. Raven tried to avoid them as best she could. More skeletons lay about the large room inside the cave. These seemed to have died more recently than those found in the first room. Among the skeletons were mummified bodies which had died more recently. Raven swung her torch, searching the room for any clue of what had happened to these men who breathed their last inside this cave.

Raven knelt beside one of the more recently killed bodies to have a closer look. Raven turned to Rivera and commented, "I don't see any bullet holes or stab marks in any of these bodies."

Rivera asked, "Then, how did they die?"

Raven thought for a moment, then realized how.

"Quickly! We've got to get out of here!"

"Why?"

Without answering, Raven bolted for the entrance of the cave room toward the original entrance. Rivera followed as closely as he could, unable to see where he was going, only following Raven's light.

Raven ducked into the first room with Rivera following but suddenly stopped.

"Listen!"

It was too late. Raven heard someone roll an immense boulder into the cave entrance, blocking their path to freedom.

Rivera asked, "What is this?"

Raven replied, "That's how all these men died. They were lured into the cave, then locked in to die. They all died a slow arduous death."

"How will we get out of here?"

"Oscar, don't panic. We can't get out if we panic. We have to remain calm and work through the problem."

Raven held up her torch and moved around the first room again to see if there were any other passageways besides the one they had already begun exploring. Finally, satisfied that there was only one doorway, she led Rivera back through. Once they were back in the second room, they moved along the walls, searching for any other passage through the cave. Raven heard the water dripping again as she moved farther away from their entrance. She never found another opening in the wall; however, she found the source of the water. It was slowly spilling over the edge of an aperture in the rock wall above her head, one drip at a time.

"Oscar, lift me up so I can see what might be above. This water is coming from somewhere."

Rivera complied, cupping his hands together to make a stirrup for Raven to step into. He grunted as he lifted her upward but suddenly lost his grip, and Raven came crashing down on top of him. As they both tumbled to the cave floor, they landed on one of the bodies. Body parts broke apart as they were disturbed. Flesh-eating insects scrambled across the floor, as did Raven and Rivera. They both scrambled to their feet, quickly brushing the bugs off themselves. They checked each other's backs until they were each satisfied the insects were gone.

Raven looked down at the body they had disturbed and noticed something about it. He had been one of the more recent deaths lying in this tomb. His uniform was somewhat intact, and she could tell he was an officer of some sort. The corpse still had hair from his chin and jaw, the traces of a beard. He had one gold tooth in the front of his mouth and a golden ring in his ear. Raven checked his pockets and found papers folded inside one of the coat pockets. Two documents had been folded together. The first was a letter addressed to Mrs. Angelique McGreavey of Aberdeen, Scotland. Raven read the letter.

My dearest Angel,

It has been such a long time since I have written and I'm afraid this will be my last. I have found myself in a pickle here on this wretched island of Jamaica. My crew and I were lured here, hoping to find another treasure to add to our loot. It seems the people of this island have kept a dirty little secret alive for hundreds of years. They seem a right friendly clan, yet it is only a farce. They promised information about a treasure that could be found in a cave on their island, which they led us to. Once inside, they covered the entrance and sealed us inside. We have found dozens of other poor wretches inside here who have died through the years. Some have apparently been here for hundreds of years.

This is the end, I fear. I will see you and the children nevermore unless we meet in the hereafter. I am sorry I could not be a better husband and provider for you and the children. God bless you in your lives.

Your loving husband;
John McGreavey

P.S. If this letter should find you along with any of my belongings, the key to finding my treasure is on the back of the map which I have drawn.

Raven was astonished to find Black Jack McGreavey lying before her at the bottom of this cave. She now felt desperate to get out because she had a clue to finding the treasure in her hands.

"Oscar, do you realize who this is?"

Since Rivera had not read the letter yet, he was at a loss.

"No, Raven! Who is it?"

"This is the body of Black Jack MeGreavey! This is a letter he wrote to his wife before he died in this cave. It confirms that the treasure is real and that the map is real."

"Does it tell where we can find the treasure?"

"Not exactly. But it does give a clue. He says the key to finding the treasure is on the back of the map that he drew."

Rivera was confused, "But, there is nothing on the back of the map. I have searched it thoroughly!"

"I know! So have I! But we must have missed something. We need to get back to the ship and have another look at that map."

John stood at *Destiny's* rail, searching for any sign of his daughter and her companion. The sun was setting, and he grew more and more worried by the minute. He finally signaled the other ships' captains to join him onboard *Destiny*.

Thirty minutes later, Pharaoh, Attila, and Alexander joined him in Raven's cabin.

As Pharaoh was the last to enter the cabin, he asked, "What is it, John?"

John replied, "Raven gave instructions before she left that we should come ashore and find her if she wasn't back by dusk."

Alexander asked, "How do you think we should handle this situation?"

John replied, "With stealth! We will wait until the village goes to sleep. Then, we'll take most of our men to shore armed to the teeth. We'll search every house and every building until we find her or someone who knows where she is."

Attila asked, "What about if they are unwilling to tell us where she is?"

John replied, "We'll make them tell us. I'll kill every last one of them until someone talks! We'll start with their leader and work our way down if we have to."

Pharaoh said, "Alright, John! We will leave at midnight. Attila, bring sixty of your men to the beach at midnight. Alexander, John, and I will bring twenty men from each of our ships. Make sure everyone is heavily armed and knows what we are about to do. We must be quiet and move quickly. We will search for the leader first. His house will be the largest and probably near the center of the village. Once we have taken him, we can bring all the others out to see that we expect nothing but the truth from them. Someone will speak or they will all die!"

Raven and Rivera once again tried to climb the wall to find the source of the dripping water. Oscar tried again to lift Raven by holding her foot in his hands. He strained against her weight and grunted as he lifted.

"Huh!"

"Just a little more, Oscar!"

"Huh!"

Raven also grunted, "Huh!" as she grabbed for anything she could.

She found a small outcropping of rock on a ledge and grasped it in her right hand.

"Higher, Oscar!"

Rivera changed his grip, lowering his body to one knee where he could come up from below her. He lifted again from underneath, "Huh!"

"That's it!" Raven exclaimed.

She climbed onto the ledge, swung her hand down toward Oscar, and asked, "Can you hand me the torch?"

Rivera took the torch from the floor and raised it toward Raven as far as he could. He stood on his toes and grunted once more, "Huh!"

"It's no use, Raven! You are too high!"

"Try tossing it up onto the ledge in front of me."

Rivera held the torch like a spear with the flame pointing toward Raven. He gently tossed the torch upward toward Raven, then waited.

"Got it!"

Raven left Rivera in the dark as she crawled away from him and farther into the darkness. The space she found herself in was too small to stand in, too short even to kneel in, so she had to crawl on her belly with the torch in front of her. There was a narrow opening through which she was traveling, only about twice as wide as her body. It left little room for Raven to move her legs toward her arms to scoot herself along the damp ledge.

After ten minutes of crawling through the tight passage, Raven found herself at the end. There was no way out. It would have been difficult for Rivera to fit himself through the narrow aperture anyway, but Raven had hoped she could find a way out to find help to rescue Rivera.

There was no way for her to turn around and crawl back to her friend, so Raven scooted her body backward, shoving her body a few inches at a time, then reaching back for the torch so she could drag it with her. After fifteen minutes of strenuous shoving and scooting, Raven found herself again at the edge of the ledge where Rivera waited impatiently.

CHAPTER 18

It was midnight, and the skies were dark and cloudy. No stars shown to help illuminate the night skies, which meant Pharaoh and all the others would be hidden as they infiltrated the village.

Twelve dories carried one hundred and twenty men and women from the ships to the shore of Treasure Beach. All the first mates remained onboard their ships to manage the vessels, except for John, who led one of the raiding parties. Hadari remained in his stead.

Each man was armed with knives and pistols, although knives would be the preferred method of attack for the sake of silence. Each boat was dragged onto the beach and secured when they reached the shore. Pharaoh took charge of the raid and made assignments to each group of twenty. John relented the men of his ship to be led by Mchungaji, the second mate aboard the *Lady Falcon*. Alexander and Attila each led a group from their respective ships, while Kiboko and Mkimbiaji led groups from the *Lady Falcon*.

Pharaoh instructed the groups to split up and encircle the village before any attack. Mchungaji led *Destiny's* group to the far end of the village, making a broad sweep through the jungle to avoid detection. Kiboko's group would flank Mchungaji's group on the left, while Mkimbiaji's group would take the right flank. Pharaoh's group would move straight through the center of the village, searching for the chieftain's house, while Alexander flanked his left and Attila his right.

Fifteen minutes later, Pharaoh heard the first signal blown from a conch shell to indicate one of the groups was settled into position. Then, a second signal was blown. Minutes later, a third blow from a conch was heard. The remaining three signals were blown to let everyone know everyone was in position. No one would be allowed to retreat from the village; it was surrounded.

Kujana wa Muziki began beating a rhythm on his drum. Another joined his beat, and then another until six drums beat the same rhythm. People from the village awakened when they heard the drums. They slowly began exiting their homes to see what was the matter. Chief Arocoel was one of the last to come out of his home. He held a torch in his hand as he left the safety of his abode and searched the area around him to determine what was happening.

Arocoel was immediately met by Pharaoh and his men, who stopped him at gunpoint. The chief was nervous but not frightened by the group surrounding his village. He spoke to Pharaoh in Arawakan.

"What do you mean by invading our island? What have we done to you?"

Pharaoh was confused by the language he heard. It was a tongue he had never heard before. He looked around to see if anyone could help him translate. An older man from Attila's group stepped forward. José Felix appeared of Spanish descent, and Pharaoh had never met him.

"Pardon me, Captain Pharaoh. I believe I can help you talk to this man. He's speaking Arawakan, a language from the Amazon area. I learned it when I was a young lad from my grandmother. She was Arawakan."

Pharaoh asked, "Fine, what did he say?"

"He wants to know why we have come and raided his village."

"Tell him, we are searching for two of our people who came into their village earlier today."

José relayed the message and was met with a confused look from the chief. The chief spoke to José, and José translated.

"He says no one has come into their village for a very long time."

"Tell him, I know for a fact that a woman and a man came into his village today and if he doesn't turn them over to us he and his people will face my wrath."

Again, José translated. After what seemed like a long diatribe of information, José explained, "He says you are mistaken. No one has come into their village today."

Pharaoh drew his pistol and approached the chief, then pointed the gun at the chief's head, touching the man's temple with the gun's barrel. Arocoel suddenly became frightened, and his eyes widened with fear. His hands began to shake. All his people gasped as they witnessed this stranger holding a weapon to the chief's head.

Arocoel protested, saying, "I don't know who you speak of! No one has entered our village today!"

Just as José finished translating the chief's words, a shot rang out in the village. Pharaoh pulled the trigger and ended the chief's life in front of all his people. Women and children cried out in fear while many of the men yelled their protest. Pharaoh took out his second pistol and fired into the air.

"José, tell them this, if they don't tell me what happened to our people right now, I will kill every one of them, starting with the children!"

This statement made even José pause. He wondered, would one of their captains be so cold-blooded as to kill young children?

"José!"

José raised his hands to quiet the crowd before he told them the threat Pharaoh had just made. The people were shocked and angered by the large black man's threat. The Tainos began yelling out to their assailants in anger, and Pharaoh grew impatient with them. He needed to find Raven; it was his only concern.

Pharaoh ordered his men, "Bring the children to me!"

The raiders swept through the crowds of people searching for children. Whenever a child was found, they were brought to Pharaoh and lined up in front of him. Children of all ages were presented to their village, ready to be sacrificed if necessary. Babies were laid on the ground away from their mothers. Young children cried for their parents and reached out to them to be rescued. Each child remained detained by the sailor who had retrieved them from their parents.

While all this was happening, Pharaoh reloaded his pistols and waited. Once all the children had been detained and set before Pharaoh, he took one of his freshly loaded pistols, picked up the nearest baby he could find, and held the gun to the baby's head. The child screamed in anger and confusion, having been removed from the safety of his mother's arms. Pharaoh cocked his pistol and watched the crowd's reaction. More screams of anger echoed throughout the village.

Suddenly, a woman pushed through the crowd and fell at Pharaoh's feet as she cried out, "Mercy! Have Mercy! A cave! There is a cave in the jungle. Your people are in the cave!"

José quickly translated for Pharaoh, who slowly released the hammer on his pistol and handed the baby to his mother.

Pharaoh shouted out, "Where is this cave?"

A man stepped forward and said in English, "I will take you to the cave."

It was Warakaba.

Pharaoh ordered his men, "My group of twenty will follow me! The rest of you remain here and stand guard over the people. Shoot anyone who tries to run!"

Pharaoh gathered his twenty along with Warakaba and walked into the jungle. Several of Pharaoh's men gathered up torches to carry as they trekked through the jungle. Warakaba walked along the path leading to the cave without speaking. Pharaoh followed and watched him closely. Half an hour later, they reached the mouth of the cave. A large boulder was blocking the entrance when they arrived. Warakaba stood at the boulder without speaking.

Pharaoh asked, "This is the entrance?"

Warakaba remained silent as he stood at the boulder.

Pharaoh grabbed the man by his hair and slammed him against the boulder.

"I said, is this the entrance?"

The young man shook with fear but finally replied, "Yes."

Pharaoh threw Warakaba to the ground and ordered one of his men to watch him. He then ordered the rest of his men to remove the boulder from the cave's entrance. Several of the crew gathered to one side of the large rock and began pushing against it to roll it away from the cave opening. They started with eight men pushing against the weight of the enormous rock. Then, two more joined in to help, but still, the rock wouldn't budge. Two more men jumped in to help, then two more. Finally, the rock rolled away from the cave's entrance, exposing cold, damp air.

Pharaoh took a torch from one of his men and entered the cave. Just as he entered, a thought occurred to him. He turned to his men and said, "John and I will go in. The rest of you keep watch unless I call for you."

Pharaoh looked into the sky and noticed the moon's position. He determined it was about three hours until dawn, which meant it was around three o'clock in the morning. John followed Pharaoh through the opening of the mountain wall. They were both surprised to see skeletons scattered about the cave floor. Pharaoh held his torch above his head and scanned the cave walls. Nothing moved except the cobwebs swept by a breeze entering the cave opening.

Pharaoh then spotted another doorway at the far end of the cave.

"This way." he said to John.

John followed without question. Pharaoh reached into the new doorway with his torch to provide light before he entered the unknown room.

Suddenly, his torch was snatched from his grip, causing Pharaoh to stumble into the darkness of the next room. Then, he fell as he received a blow across his back. He grunted as he fell to the damp floor.

John peeked into the room and saw a figure standing over Pharaoh as he lay on the floor.

"Raven!" he exclaimed.

The figure turned to see who had called her name.

"Papa? Is that you?"

Then Raven looked at the body lying on the floor and recognized her old friend.

"Pharaoh! I'm so sorry! I thought they were coming to finish us off."

Raven struggled to help Pharaoh to his feet.

"I'm alright. You just caught me unaware. I'm not hurt."

Raven asked, "How did you find us?"

John replied, "We can talk about that later. Let's get you back to the ship."

Raven and the others stepped out of the cave and found Warak-aba being detained by several of her crew. She glared at Warakaba as she walked past him, leading the way back to the village with Warakaba, Rivera, and twenty of her men following.

John followed closely behind Raven and tried to catch up to speak with her.

"Did you find any answers?"

"We'll talk about it when we get back to the ship. I don't want just anyone to hear what I have to say."

As they reached the village, Raven saw one hundred of her crew guarding the villagers. Children were crying from fear, and the women tried to quiet them and comfort them. Raven paid little attention to the people as she walked into their presence. She stopped momentarily and looked at the body of Arocoel lying on the ground. Raven then looked defiantly into the crowd. It was as if she had taken the time to look each one of them in the eyes while looking right through them. Raven pursed her lips angrily, then walked over to Arocoel's house. She flung her torch inside the hut's open door and watched as it slowly began to burn. Raven then defiantly walked toward the beach.

One by one, Raven's crew took their torches and followed Raven's example. Every house in the village was set afire. The people began to scream and cry out as they watched their homes and all their belongings burn up in the flames.

Raven's crew followed her to the beach and loaded in the boats to row back to their ships. Each crew member returned to their respective ships except for the captains of those ships. They all were dropped off onto *Destiny* to meet with Raven. They followed Raven into her cabin along with John, Rivera, and Jeffrey.

Sunlight peeked through the window of Raven's cabin as they sat around the table together. Jeremy brought in food and drinks so they could eat while discussing the matters at hand. John began the conversation.

"Alright Raven, tell us what happened."

"When we got there, we tried to speak to the village chief. He called over the one they called Warakaba to interpret for us. I guess his interpretations were not exactly concise. He led us to the cave and told us there were ship's logs and journals inside from captains who had come to their island in the past. He failed to tell us those captains never left their island. All those skeletons you saw inside that cave, they were others who had come to their island for one reason or another."

John asked, "How can you be sure they were other sailors?"

"Because we found this on one of them."

Raven pulled out the letter to show everyone. They passed around the letter without paying much attention to its contents. When it arrived in Jeffrey's hands, he read the letter closely. When he finished, Jeffrey asked, "Black Jack?"

Raven smiled and slowly nodded her head.

John grabbed the letter from Jeffrey as John said, "Let me see that!"

John read the letter out loud, pausing between lines as he thought to himself. "What makes Raven think this is from Black Jack?"

Finally, he reached the end of the letter and saw the signature. "Ah! John McGreavy! Of course!"

Alexander asked, "So what does this mean?"

Raven replied, "It means there really is a treasure hidden by Black Jack somewhere, probably in the Cayman Islands."

Alexander then asked, "But how will we know how to find it?"

"Black Jack said the key to finding the treasure was on the back of the map. But, so far I haven't been able to find anything on it."

John offered, "Maybe we have the wrong map."

"It could be, but it's the only map we have and we have been told it once belonged to Black Jack."

Pharaoh then asked, "So what do we do next?"

"We head for the Caymans. We begin to search. We'll divide up into teams and cover every inch of the islands."

Jeffrey asked, "But Raven, do you have any idea what we are looking for? How will we know if we've seen it?"

"I don't know. But, we won't find it by sitting on these ships and thinking about it. My guess is it will be hidden in a cave somewhere on one of these islands. So, we'll start there. I'll take *Destiny* to the first island farthest east; the one they call Cayman Brac. Alexander and Pharaoh, take your ships to Little Cayman and search both sides. Alexander take the north side, Pharaoh take the south. Attila, take the *Lady Falcon* and begin searching the big island. You have the most men, so divide them up into groups of ten and drop them off in different areas along the coast to begin searching. We'll all meet back at the big island in three weeks unless someone finds something sooner. Now, let's get started shall we?"

The captains filed out of Raven's cabin and returned to their ships. John and Jeffrey remained with Raven. John looked at Raven worriedly without saying anything.

"What is it, Papa?"

"May we speak alone for a moment?"

"Yes. Jeffrey, will you excuse us, please?"

Jeffrey slightly bowed before exiting Raven's cabin, closing the door behind him.

"What worries you, Papa?"

"Pharaoh."

"What of Pharaoh?"

"I saw something in him on Treasure Beach that I haven't witnessed in him before."

"What did you see?"

"I saw him kill a man in cold blood because the man wouldn't tell us where you were. Then he was about to kill a baby before the mother came forward and told us where you were. He's beginning to frighten me."

"Don't be afraid, Papa. Pharaoh only did what he thought he had to do to find me. Pharaoh is completely loyal to me. He would do anything to ensure my safety, including killing if necessary."

"But, was it necessary?"

"I don't know. I wasn't there. Do you think you could have gotten those people to reveal where I was without making an example of one of them? Because that's all he did."

"I don't know. But, that baby!"

"Forget the baby, Papa! Did you see how many bodies were left in that cave to die?"

"Well, I saw several, yes."

"You didn't go into the second room where Oscar and I were. There were many more in there, more recent the in the first room, too. We weren't just captives, Papa! There were bodies inside that cave from hundreds of years ago. We were left there to die and Pharaoh did what he had to do to find us. I'm just thankful he was willing to do what was necessary to get us out."

"Yes, of coarse. Please don't be disappointed in me, daughter. I am very grateful Pharaoh was willing to do what was necessary. I guess, it just scared me to think he might kill a baby."

"Don't be ashamed, Papa. You are a good man. Maybe too good to be doing what we are here to do."

CHAPTER 19

The morning air was brisk and moist as *Raven's Destiny* reached the coast of Cayman Brac after being at sea for only six hours after leaving Jamaica. Cayman Brac wasn't the smallest of the three islands that made up the Caymans, but it wasn't the largest. The big island that lay farthest west was shaped like a sea creature with its tail swooping upward on the map. Linearly, the island measured a distance of twenty-nine miles long. The breadth was about six and three-quarter miles wide at the broadest part of the island.

The island in the middle was called Little Cayman and stretched southwest to northeast. It was approximately ten miles long and nearly two miles wide at its widest point. Cayman Brac, the island Raven and her crew would explore, was approximately twelve miles long and one and a half miles wide.

Raven had John direct the helmsman to pull up to the far eastern tip of Cayman Brac. She sent twenty men to explore the island, looking for anything that indicated a hiding place for a large amount of treasure.

The first thing Raven noticed as they reached the island's coast was the number of sea turtles swimming in the shallows. There were so many that it seemed challenging to travel through the water without knocking into several of the reptiles, as they seemed to fly through the waters with their feet flapping like bird's wings. Leatherbacks, Loggerheads, and Green Sea Turtles all swam together through the clear waters along the coast of the little island. Raven kept her eye on one particular turtle for a long time: a giant green turtle whose color pattern looked as if the turtle had swum through a spider's web. Raven watched the turtle seemingly dance along the aquatic stage, giving its most outstanding performance as she swam.

Raven sent two boats to the beach, where the twenty explorers would begin their journey across the island. Before they boarded the small boats, Raven gave them instructions.

"Spread out as you search the island. Don't get too far away from one another. Stay within speaking distance. I don't want anyone out there alone. We don't know who lives on this island, or if they are friendly."

Hadari, leading the group on the island, asked, "What should we look for?"

"Something that doesn't belong. It could be a tree that is out of place, or a cave in a hillside. If you find anything of interest, contact us on the ship. We'll be following along, never too far away. By the way, anyone who finds the hidden place of the treasure will get four shares in the treasure, instead only one."

The men were delighted to hear this and anxious to get started searching. They excitedly climbed into the boats and began rowing toward the beach. Mwanamke Simba was among the crew who would be searching for the treasure. She was glad to be a part of the exploration. She enjoyed sailing with Raven but was delighted to be on dry ground for a change.

Hadari gathered his explorers together on the beach before they set out. They all excitedly listened as he gave them instructions.

"The island is too wide for us to go through it on one pass and be able to see and communicate with each other. We will move along the south side of the island until we reach the end, then we will return to this point by way of the north side of the island. If you stop to investigate anything, let someone know so you don't get separated from the group. If you become injured, let us know so we can get you back to the ship for help. We are all in this together, it is not a race. Keep together no matter what, and no matter what, keep together."

The crew began their walk and quickly discovered that the jungle was dense and full of life. The sound of birds singing and cawing to one another was almost deafening. In his travels, Hadari saw more different kinds of birds with more coloration here than anywhere else. Parrots, parakeets, macaws, and different species of songbirds littered the treetops. Reds, blues, yellows, and greens painted the jungle canopy. Several times, the explorers were thwarted by birds swooping down to run off the two-legged strangers who had entered their territory. The crew found themselves spending more time dodging birds than looking for treasure.

Matilda reached the Little Cayman about an hour after *Destiny* reached Cayman Brac. Pharaoh sent twenty men ashore to explore the southern side of the island. Kiboko led the exploration as it moved westward across the southern side. He gave his group the same instructions Hadari had given his crew: "Stay within speaking distance of each other. Don't get separated. Let someone know if you are stopping to investigate something."

The explorers stretched out across the beach as they began their trek. Kiboko walked in the center of the line that traveled together through the beaches, jungles, and up rocky hills.

Alexander's ship pulled up alongside Pharaoh's as they began their journey. Daktari could be seen leading his group onto the beach, where they would begin their exploration on the island's north side. Daktari and his crew were only fifteen minutes or so behind Kiboko and his crew.

Soon after they began the trek, the groups stood before a large hill covering most of the island's eastern side. The hill wasn't too steep, but traveling uphill would be slow and strenuous.

Large trees of all sorts were scattered about the hillside, both allowing for handholds as they climbed and presenting trouble along the climb by way of the tree's inhabitants. Squirrel Monkeys and Capuchins lived in the treetops. Their screeches and calls were nonstop as long as the invaders climbed upon their hill. The little creatures pelted the men who climbed along the landscape with all sorts of weaponry: half-eaten pieces of fruit, nuts, and, the worst, monkey excrement.

The hill grew taller and taller the farther they climbed. Kiboko stood at one point of the journey at the crest of a bluff overlooking the ocean. The steep ridge stood more than one hundred feet above the ocean surface. Kiboko looked over the edge to see if he could spot any caves within the side of the bluff. A young man named Muski Jahiri came and stood next to him at the edge of the bluff and looked over. As Jahiri looked over the edge, his foot slipped, and he began to fall over the side. Kiboko caught Jahiri by the arm just before he fell over the edge. Both men found their hearts beating more rapidly than they would have liked, knowing each of them could have fallen to their death.

Kiboko said, "Jahiri, go over there, away from the edge to do your looking."

Jahiri nodded to Kiboko and walked away with his head hung low. Kiboko continued searching the escarpment's wall, looking for a passageway to a hidden cave. He watched as the waves crashed against the mountainside, then drew away from it. The sight was nearly intoxicating, watching the water move in and out. The escarpment wall was concave, creating a small cove at the island's south end. The coral reef below created a hazard for any ship or small boat trying to travel through. Kiboko decided it would be treacherous for anyone to try to hide a treasure down there, even if there was a cave below. He stepped away from the bluff and continued his search elsewhere.

After ten hours of searching, the two groups searching on Little Cayman met in a recessed area on top of the mountain where a lake was. A freshwater lake in the middle of a mountain seemed odd to them all but welcoming. Kiboko and Daktari decided their crews deserved a rest for the night. The lake was welcoming as its cool waters relieved them from the island's hot and humid air. Several of the men and women decided to take a swim before settling down for the night.

Blue herons, ibis, and other waterfowl waded or swam in the lake's shallow areas. On the north end of the lake was a waterfall that extended to the top of the mountain, seventy feet high. Most of them chose to swim around the falls, while others swam farther out where the water was quieter.

Daktari and Kiboko stood together at the lake's edge near the falls as they discussed the day's events. They both chose to wash themselves at the lake's edge rather than swimming out in it. Somehow, it didn't seem befitting for either of them to play in the water like children as their crews did. As they finished washing and talked about the day, Daktari looked over the expanse of the small lake and noticed movement about fifty yards out. Something was moving in the water toward a woman swimming in the distance.

Daktari asked, "Who is that woman?"

Kiboko replied, "That is Timbu Msukuri."

Daktari said, "Something is swimming toward her."

Daktari and Kiboko suddenly felt fear for the woman, and they both shouted at her, "Msukuri, watch out! Something is swimming toward you!"

The woman waved to them, not knowing what they were trying to tell her. She was oblivious to the danger that was to befall her.

Daktari began telling everyone, "Get out of the water! Get out, now!"

Those close enough to Daktari heard his words and ran from the lake onto the shore. Others farther away from the bank were beginning to understand that something was wrong but didn't understand why. They slowly began swimming to the bank, and everyone started calling out to those farther away from the bank to return to shore.

Timbu Msukuri didn't receive the message in time. Something under the water grabbed her by the leg, sending an unbearable pain throughout her body. Blood immediately leaked from her leg as she attempted to climb to the water's surface. Suddenly, she felt her body being pulled down into the water. She was in the clutches of a twelve-foot crocodile, and the creature began rolling over and over in the water with the young woman trapped in its jaws. She tried to scream for help, but her screams were mainly silenced under the water. She gasped for breath every chance she could as her face rolled from time to time out of the water. No one could help her. They could only watch in horror as they saw her body rolling over and over in the watery grave of the lake.

Some of the women and younger men began to cry as they realized Msukuri's death was imminent. After several minutes of seeing her roll through the water, they were dismayed as she finally disappeared.

The celebration suddenly turned to mourning of a young woman who was taken too early in life. Daktari didn't even know her, but he was saddened that she no longer existed. The rest of the night was spent in silence except for the occasional sobbing of several of the crew. The treasure was much less important to them all now. They had lost one of their own, and she was taken away too brutally to suit any of them. Eventually, with the exemption of a few guards posted around the camp to keep an eye out for more predators, they all bedded down for the night.

Attila's crew sailed the *Lady Falcon* into the east coast of the Grand Cayman shortly after midnight. They had no reason to begin their search in darkness, so Attila allowed his crew to sleep until daybreak. Attila took the night watch with a few others of his crew to allow Nathan Coates and Mchungaji to sleep. Nathan would lead the exploration on the big island, while Mchungaji would be in charge of the ship while Nathan was on the island.

As morning broke, Nathan began preparing his men for the trek over the island. Eighty men and women would go ashore, while the remaining twenty would stay onboard the ship. Attila had the explorers dropped off on the east coast. Nathan gave everyone instructions once they landed, just as the other officers had concerning staying together so no one would get lost.

The big island was about six and three-quarter miles across, so making one fell swoop across the island with only eighty men would be impossible. It would be challenging even if they had two hundred. Attila planned to move the men across the island back and forth, beginning from the east end. They would move across in a line, about twenty yards between each man, until they reached the opposite beach. Then, they would move down the beach and make another swipe across the island to the opposite beach again. This would continue until the entire island had been covered. Attila figured they could cover the whole island in two weeks if they were lucky, and the ground wouldn't be too difficult to travel through. If they were lucky, the other ships would join them to cover their island and make things go faster.

As they reached the shore and began to exit their boats, Nathan immediately saw that the journey wouldn't be as easy as it seemed looking at a map. Once they got past the beach, the terrain was hilly, overgrown with vegetation, and rocky in spots. Nevertheless, they began their trek in the early morning.

Tall grasses initially obstructed their path, making travel slow and treacherous. Poisonous snakes slithered in their paths, making them anxious as they walked. Some of the areas were marshy, allowing for dangers of another sort. Crocodiles would lay about in the mud to cool themselves. The explorers had to be highly aware of their surroundings to walk away with their lives and faculties intact.

Several times, people found themselves stuck in the mud, needing the assistance of their fellow trekkers to free themselves. The mud also put an extra strain on their muscles, causing them to tire quickly. By the end of the first day, they had only made one pass.

They spent their first night on the southern beach under several palm trees. Those covered in the mud from the marsh washed in the saltwater of the surf. The swells of the tide made it difficult to wash themselves because they were constantly rolled through the waves. Bathing became as tiresome as the trek itself.

The following morning, several of the crew went fishing along the coast to catch their breakfast. They made a quick meal of fish, turtles, fruits, and bread, then returned to work searching for the treasure.

When they lined up to start their next sweep, Nathan had the line switch sides so that the ones who trekked through the mud the previous day were hopefully given a break this day. Not far into the walk, they found a small creek leading through the jungle. At the end of the creek, a small pond about an acre wide. Water-fowl were scattered throughout the pond, walking on stilted legs or swimming with paddled feet. Nathan warned everyone again to watch for crocodiles and venomous snakes.

Not long after Nathan gave his warning, a young man named Msafiri stepped on a snake and was bitten. Msafiri panicked and cried out, "I am going to die! A large serpent has bitten me!"

Nathan ran to him to check, as did two others who were near-by. They found the young man sitting on the ground, holding his leg that was barely bleeding, crying with tears running down his face.

"Help me! I do not want to die!"

Nathan ordered, "Dry it up, boy! You're not going to die. Where did the snake go?"

Msafiri pointed into the brush nearby and said, "Over there, near that small tree."

Nathan and the other men looked around, finally finding a reddish brown four-foot-long viper with black-tipped scales. Nathan chopped off the snake's head, then held up the body and asked, "Does this look like it?"

"Yes, Mr. Coates! That is the snake that has killed me!"

Nathan instructed one of the men to help Msafiri back to the ship to be looked after. Nathan had no idea whether or not the snake was venomous but felt the boy needed looking after in any case. "Here, take this snake with you. Maybe Mwanamki Dawa can identify it. She'll know what to do for him."

Mwindaji wa Swala, who helped the boy back to the ship, had to listen to Msafiri's cries and complaints for the next hour as they returned to the beach. Msafiri was convinced he would be dead before they reached the ship.

Once they reached the beach, Swala signaled for a boat to be sent back to retrieve him and his companion. Another thirty minutes passed before the boat arrived, then thirty more until they reached the ship. All the while, Msafiri was convinced his life was about to end.

Mwanamki Dawa had Msafiri brought into the infirmary so she could examine him. She found that there was some swelling at the bite site as well as redness. She looked, examined the snake, and determined it was venomous. "This is a Racer. I saw one described in one of the books aboard this ship. They call it the Grand Cayman Racer. The bad thing about the Racer is it is venomous. However, the venom isn't harmful to people. You will not die from this bite. You may die of fright if you don't learn how to be brave in these circumstances. You are worse than a little girl. Are you a man or a little mouse?"

Msafiri asked, "So, I am not going to die?"

"Not unless I decide to kill you myself! Stupid boy!"

CHAPTER 20

Raven had her crew leisurely float *Destiny* along the shore of Cayman Brac as her expedition of the little island continued. She grew anxious as she stared at the back of Black Jack's map. She turned the parchment over in her hands. She held it up to the light to examine it more closely. Raven turned the paper over and over, this way, then that way, but nothing revealed itself to her. She grew more and more frustrated.

Oscar sat across from her at the table in her cabin. His head was face down on the table, exhausted from looking at the map. Captain Billings climbed off Raven's shoulder and walked across the table to Oscar, where the monkey started combing through the man's hair, looking for fleas or ticks. Raven let a slight smile approach her lips as she watched her monkey begin grooming her Spanish companion.

Rivera raised his head finally and said, "I don't know, maybe this is all just a waste of time."

Raven replied, "I'm not giving up yet. I know sending those men out to search without an idea of what to look for isn't very productive. But, until we can solve this map it's all we have."

Rivera said, "I have to get out of here. I feel like I'm going monkey crazy."

Raven smiled and replied, "A little fresh air might do us both some good."

They both left the cabin, Captain Billings crouching on Raven's shoulder. When they stepped out onto the deck, the air was brisk. The sun was already lowering into the western sky, fading into the horizon with shades of orange, red, yellow, and blue. It was the end of the second day of their search for the treasure.

Raven stepped up to the quarterdeck, where John searched the island with his spyglass.

She asked, "Any sign of them?"

"Haven't seen them since last night. It shouldn't be long now. Unless they've run into trouble."

Raven remarked, "Let's hope there's none of that. I don't want anyone to get hurt or worse because of some non-descriptive treasure map."

"Don't worry yourself, daughter. There's not a one of us who wouldn't follow you to the ends of the earth; treasure or no treasure."

Suddenly, someone whistled from the crow's nest above. John and Raven looked up and saw the man pointing toward the line of trees at the beach's edge. A group was beginning to appear from the jungle cover and escape its clutches onto the freedom of the sandy beach.

Raven released her breath, which she had not realized she was holding. She slightly smiled when she saw her people walk out onto the beach one by one and begin preparations for the night. Raven tried to count them to ensure everyone was there, but it was like trying to count termites coming out of their nest. Once everyone had gathered on the beach, Hadari blew the signal, indicating all were safe and sound.

Raven told John, "Let's drop the anchor here for the night."

John nodded his head, then gave the order to drop anchor. Rivera excused himself and returned to his bunk to retire for the night.

Hadari and his crew gathered around a quickly built fire to relax after a long day. They were tired, skinned up, scratched, and sore. Many of them had managed to gather fruit while trekking through the jungle. They reached into the sacks they wore over their shoulders and passed around the fruit they had to those who had none. One man showed everyone his mosquito bites from an area in the jungle that hid a small stagnant pond. His body was covered entirely in the raised, itchy bumps from the bites. Mzururaji was so tired that he barely noticed his itching. He lay down while eating an orange and went to sleep before he finished his meal.

The next morning, Mzururaji woke with a fever and chills. His body convulsed from the chills of the fever that had entered it. Someone told Hadari, "Mzururaji is sick! He has a fever!"

Hadari blew his conch, signaling the ship that they needed a boat sent out to them. John searched the beach with his spyglass to see what might be the problem. He saw everyone on the beach gathered around one man lying in the sand. He then spotted Hadari, who was facing him. Hadari began sliding his hands all over his body, first down his face, all the way down his torso and down his legs, then down each arm. John surmised that someone must be sick. He sent out Mr. Greer with two men on one of the dories to find out what was needed.

When Greer arrived, he walked through the sand along the beach until he reached the area where Mzururaji lay. Greer asked everyone to step aside so he could examine the man. When he saw Mzururaji's body covered in the small welts, he asked, "Mosquito bites?"

Hadari replied, "Yes."

Greer concernedly replied, "Hadari, you should have called us last night. Although, it might not have mattered. This man has malaria! He won't likely make it to the end of the day. The poison from the mosquitos is too much. I've never seen anyone bitten so many times. Let's get him in the dory and back to the ship. All I can do is try to make him comfortable."

When he heard the call of Hadari's conch shell and saw Hadari signaling for help, John sent Jeremy to wake Raven. Jeremy quietly knocked on Raven's door and peeked inside to see if she was asleep. He saw her lying in bed with Captain Billings asleep at her head. Jeremy quietly walked to her bedside and placed his hand on her shoulder. Raven took a deep breath and roused from sound sleep. She looked up and saw Jeremy standing over her.

"What is it Jeremy?"

"Mr. Greer has been sent to the island. Someone is either sick or injured. Mr. Ashworth asked me to come for you."

"Alright, tell him I'll be there momentarily."

Jeremy walked out of Raven's quarters and returned to the quarterdeck.

Raven quickly dressed so she could meet Papa up top. As she moved toward the door, she decided she was thirsty, so she reached across the table to pour herself a cup of water. As she reached for the pitcher, she accidentally knocked over a lit candlestick that landed on Black Jack's map. Raven gasped as she witnessed the map ignite and burn around its edge. Raven swatted the flames with her bare hand, quickly extinguishing the flame.

She breathed a sigh of relief, knowing she had nearly lost the only hint of where they might find Black Jack's treasure. She sat at the table to gather herself before leaving her cabin, her face resting in her hands as she leaned on the table with her elbows. Raven wiped her eyes with her fingers, trying to clear her head, when she noticed something on the map. As the map lay facedown on the table, Raven saw a faint image at the map's edge near the place it had burned. The image appeared to be the start of a word. She held the map up to get a better look, but it was too dim inside the cabin. Raven moved to her window and held up the map to let the light illuminate the front of the map as she looked at the back. She saw what appeared to be a cross. Not a cross. It was a "t".

Raven questioned whether or not she was imagining the letter "t" or if it was something else. And how did it suddenly appear? She had checked the back of the map over and over again, never seeing anything.

She fingered the edge of the paper as her mind continued to search for an answer. Suddenly, Jeremy knocked on the door and opened it.

"Are you coming?"

"Wha . . . I'll be right there!"

Raven set the map back on the table as she followed Jeremy out the door. She arrived on deck just as the dory arrived with Mzururaji and Mr. Greer.

Raven asked, "What's the matter with Mzururaji?"

Greer replied, "My guess is swamp fever. Look at all the whelps on his body!"

"Will he be alright?"

Greer looked at her, waiting to make eye contact with her. When she looked at Greer, he shook his head slightly.

Greer said to those carrying Mzururaji's body, "Take him to the infirmary."

Raven followed along. She felt concerned for the young man, but her mind kept seeing the burnt edge of the map. Suddenly, she stopped shy of the infirmary and returned to her Papa.

"Signal to Hadari! Tell him not to proceed until he hears from me."

John blew the conch shell to give Hadari the signal to stay put.

Raven entered the infirmary to check on Mzururaji. She found Mr. Greer applying salve to his bites to ease the itching. Mzururaji's body shivered with fever as Raven approached the table where he lay. Raven knew the young man was at terrible risk of death. She had seen swamp fever before and knew what it could do to the human body. She had seen it ravage sailors when she worked as Mr. Greer's assistant onboard the original *Destiny*. She also knew there was little that could be done for Mzururaji as he lay there suffering, burning with fever and itching uncontrollably.

Mzururaji was just a little older than Raven. He had been a hard worker and an able seaman aboard her vessel. She hated to see him suffer this way. It reminded Raven of seeing her mother suffer so many years ago in their flat in Bristol. Raven was only eleven when her mother fell sick with a fever while Raven's papa was at sea. Raven tried to care for her mother as best she could, but there was only so much a child of eleven could do under the circumstances. Raven constantly bathed her mama with cool compresses. She fed her broth, which she had made from boiling what few vegetables were available to them. They couldn't afford meat, only potatoes, carrots, or turnips. Raven had learned from her mother to use the same vegetables over and over, adding additional water to the broth to make it go further until the vegetables had disintegrated entirely. Sometimes, they could make the broth last for a week with only two small tubers in their pantry.

Rivera entered the infirmary and woke Raven from her trance from the past.

"Is he alright, Señorita?"

Raven took Oscar by the hand and led him out of the room. In a low voice, she said, "I'm afraid there's little we can do for him. He likely won't make it more than a couple of days."

Rivera replied, "I noticed the men on the beach, they have stopped searching?"

Raven nodded and said, "Come with me."

Oscar followed her back to her cabin and waited impatiently for any news she might have to share. He looked down at the table and noticed the burnt edge of the map.

"What happened here?"

Raven replied, "I knocked over a candle and the map caught on fire."

"Oh, it is a good thing you were able to put it out so quickly. We could have lost everything."

Raven said, "I think it might have been a good thing that the map caught fire. Look at this."

She showed him the back of the map near the burnt edge.

"What is it?"

"I think it is some writing that is hidden on the back. I don't know how he did it, but Black Jack hid some information on the back of this map."

Rivera asked, "How can we know for sure?"

"I have an idea."

Raven lit the candlestick and picked up the map. She held the map horizontally to the table and waved it over the flame. At first, she held the map about a foot above the flame. Seeing that it had no effect, she slowly lowered the map closer and closer. Suddenly, letters began to appear, one by one. Then words. Then sentences.

"Look!" exclaimed Rivera.

Magically, clues to finding Black Jack's treasure appeared before them.

The center of the islands would be best
To find the resting of my treasure chest
Not just any hour or any day
But if the time is right, you'll find the cay.
When the moon is high and the sun is low

Would be the best time to find its chateau
The entrance is meager and narrow and small
It's not always visible; some might have to crawl
When the tides are right under a moonlit sky
You'll find your way for the treasure you'll spy.

Chapter 21

Rivera asked, "What does it mean?"

Raven replied, "It's a riddle. Let's take it line by line and see if we can solve it. Look, '*Center of the islands would be best to find the resting of my treasure chest*'. That's easy. The map is of the Cayman Islands, so it must be the Little Cayman since it's in the center. '*Not just any hour or any day, but if the time is right you'll find the cay.*' We're looking for a reef! *When the moon is high and the sun is low, would be the best time to find its chateau.*' Sounds like it might be some particular low tide. '*The entrance is meager, and narrow, and small. It's not always visible, some might have to crawl.*' Alright, so we're looking for maybe a cave? '*When the tides are right under a moonlit sky, you'll find your way for the treasure you'll spy.*' We need to check the tide schedule and figure out how we're going to find this treasure. Oscar! This might be it!"

Rivera laughed and said, "Si, Raven! This is it!"

Raven rolled the map and placed it in a dresser drawer on the inside wall of her cabin. She and Rivera then left her cabin and went up to the quarterdeck. As usual, John was standing near the tiller checking the skies, the seas, and the beach with his spyglass.

"Papa, call back our people. We're at the wrong location."

John replied, "You know where it is now?"

"Not exactly where, but we know it isn't on this island. We need to go to the Little Cayman."

"Aye, Raven!"

John had Jeremy blow the conch signal to the beach where Hadari and his people were waiting. He then sent the dories to pick them up from the beach and return them to the ship. An hour later, Raven had all of *Destiny's* crew back onboard. Hadari was the last to climb aboard, and he went straight to the quarterdeck to meet Raven and John. Jeffrey and Rivera stood on the quarterdeck with them, too.

"Is Mzururaji alright?"

Raven replied, "No, he isn't. But, that's not why I called you back. We have discovered a clue that tells us we're at the wrong island."

"You have? Where do we need to go?"

"We should be at the Little Cayman. We need to sail there to find Pharaoh and Alexander. Then, we'll send word to Attila to meet us there. Mr. Ashworth, set a course for the south side of Little Cayman."

"Aye, Raven."

As soon as the dories were loaded onto the ship, John ordered his crew to unfurl the sails and turn the helm south by southwest. John quickly discovered the winds were not in his favor; they were blowing directly from west to east. So, he had the helmsman turn southward to find a favorable wind to take them to Little Cayman.

Raven and Oscar stood together at the rail, watching Cayman Brac shrink. The sun and the wind were warm against their faces as they looked over the horizon to the fading island. Seven pelicans flew past them westward, gliding only inches above the water's surface. Seagulls circled above the ship, searching for food scraps that might be thrown overboard.

Raven was in her element. She loved the sea. She couldn't imagine ever living anywhere else but onboard a ship. Her mind wandered back to those early days when she was only twelve, serving Captain Billings on his *Destiny*. She was so nervous at first, trying to hide her gender from a ship full of men. Raven remembered how many times someone had nearly discovered her. Then, she remembered the first time. She was punished for stealing a cup of milk and taking it to her papa. She was sentenced to twelve lashes, save one for her crime. Even though it was a crime of ignorance, Raven, or Richard, and she was known by then, took it without complaint. She remembered then the look on Mr. Greer's face when he treated her wounds.

"Oscar, will you excuse me, please?"

"Si, Raven."

Raven left the rail and walked to the infirmary to find Mr. Greer. She found him still tending to Mzururaji and his bites.

"How is he doing?" she asked.

"Oh, not so well. His breathing has become labored. His temperature is much too high. I fear it won't be long, now."

"Mr. Greer, would you mind speaking with me in private for a moment?"

"Aye, Raven."

He followed her into the hallway just outside the infirmary, where they could speak without prying ears.

Raven began, "Do you remember that first voyage we took together?"

Greer smiled, "You mean when you were just a wee lad?"

"The day you tended to my wounds after receiving that lashing, did you know then I was a girl?"

Greer looked into her eyes and very slightly nodded.

"I knew. I also knew you were very special. The way you took your punishment without crying or without protest. Mr. Hardy told me later that he was the one who gave you that cup of milk. You had no idea it was wrong. Hardy feared that you would tell the captain that he gave it to you. But, you never did. That made an impression on Hardy and on Jamie. Neither of them suspected, though. They thought you were the most capable, most reliable young man they had ever met."

Raven then said, "I was surprised when Hardy joined us, but not Mr. Gant."

"Oh, Gant is an old fool. Like I said, he had no idea you were a girl. When he saw you at Port St. Felix and discovered that you were that same Richard Ashworth he once trained, he couldn't accept it. In his mind, women don't belong on a ship. It's bad luck."

Raven asked, "So, you told no one, I mean about me?"

"Never."

Raven looked into the older gentleman's eyes, then kissed him lightly on the cheek.

"Thank you, Mr. Greer."

Greer lowered his eyes and blushed as Raven walked away.

The next morning, after fighting the winds moving against them, *Destiny* arrived on the southern banks of Little Cayman. They found *Matilda* anchored about halfway down the coastline. Raven asked John to pull them up along *Matilda's* rail so she could talk to Pharaoh. The waters were at high tide, so they met *Matilda* about a quarter of a mile off the shore and tied the two ships together.

Pharaoh met Raven on the rail so they could converse.

Raven asked, "Any luck?"

"No, Raven. We haven't seen anything that would indicate a treasure being hidden on this side of the island."

"That's alright. I think we have a better clue now of where to look. Bring all your crew back to the ship and sail around to the other side to find Alexander. Then, both of you come back here and wait for me. I'll go and find Attila and meet you here."

"Do you know what we will be looking for?"

"Some sort of cave that can only be spotted at low tide."

Pharaoh said, "I will ask Mwindaji if he saw such a cave while searching the island."

Raven replied, "I'll see you late tomorrow if all goes well."

Ten hours later, *Destiny* found herself halfway down the southern coast of the big island. The sun had already set, and clouds covered the moon, not allowing Raven or her crew to see well enough to explore the coastline. Reefs and jagged rocks hidden underneath the waterline could be treacherous. So, they anchored in deeper waters and rested for the night.

Raven, John, Oscar, and Jeffrey gathered in Raven's quarters late in the evening to share a cask of rum and discuss the possible events of the next few days.

Rivera asked anyone listening, "Do we know what time the lowest tide will occur?"

John replied, "I measured low tide at around six last night."

Jeffrey interjected, "Yes, but the moon is only at its first quarter phase right now. Don't we need a full-moon?"

Raven replied, "According to the map, it will be the easiest time to find the entrance to the cave. However, with the cloud cover we have been seeing the past several nights, it might not matter what phase the moon is. Without light, we won't be able to see the entrance."

John replied, "Or where to even begin searching."

Raven suggested, "Well, we can't solve this puzzle tonight anyway. Let's all get some rest. We'll find the *Falcon* tomorrow and then worry about where we will begin our search."

Everyone finished their drinks and left Raven's quarters to retire to their own. Raven reclined on her bed with Captain Billings lying at her head on her pillow. She held the map up and studied it. She flipped it over and read the clues once again, then again, and again. Something told her it wouldn't be as simple as finding a cave at the island's edge during low tide. There had to be more to it.

Her eyes began to droop. She tossed the map to the table just a few feet from her bed, closed her eyes, and fell fast asleep.

The next morning, Raven awoke to the sound of the blown conch. She quickly gathered herself and ran up to the quarterdeck. Hadari was manning the ship, standing next to the helmsman. When he saw Raven approaching, he called out to her, "The *Lady Falcon* is approaching from the starboard stern."

Raven looked behind *Destiny's* stern into the distance and saw the *Falcon* approaching them.

"Has she returned your call?"

Hadari replied, "Not yet."

Hadari blew the conch again to signal the approaching ship and then listened. A slight hum traveled across the wind. The *Lady Falcon* returned his signal and sailed directly toward *Destiny*. Raven took out her spyglass and pointed it toward the *Fal-*

con. When the ship finally got close enough, Raven could tell it was still sailing with a light crew. That meant most of their men were still searching for the treasure on shore.

Raven then turned her spyglass toward the shore to see if she could spot anyone on land. The jungle was dense, not allowing her to see much. So, she decided to be patient and wait for Attila and his ship to arrive.

Lady Falcon tied up alongside *Destiny* an hour later, and Attila climbed over to meet Raven.

"Have you found anything?" he asked Raven.

"We have another clue to the map. It tells us that the treasure is somewhere on Little Cayman. Where are your men?"

"We saw them on the other side of the island last night when they completed their trek through the jungle to spend the night on the beach. We can expect them to show up about a quarter of a mile down the beach from here due west. But, it will be later in the day before they arrive."

"When they do arrive, collect them and sail back to Little Cayman and meet us on the south side. I've already talked to Pharaoh. He has gone to meet Alexander and bring him to meet us. From there we will begin our search, but we have plenty of time."

"Why do we have plenty of time?"

"We're waiting for a full moon."

Attila replied, "Aye. We will do as you say. As soon as we can gather the rest of the crew, we will sail to Little Cayman."

While Attila was meeting with Raven onboard *Destiny*, *Lady Falcon's* crew met below decks in the gun room. The first man spoke, "I think they must have found the treasure."

A second man asked, "How do you know?"

"Why else would Raven show up here so soon? They haven't had time to properly search both those islands entirely."

A third man said, "How many men do we have?"

The first replied, "Enough! But the timing will have to be just right. We have to make sure the treasure is onboard first."

CHAPTER 22

The next evening, as the sun was setting in the western skies, the last of four ships arrived to meet *Destiny* off the southern shore of Little Cayman. The *Lady Falcon* had to wait for all her crew to arrive on the southern beach of the Grand Cayman before they could be collected and set sail to meet the others.

Attila informed his crew that Raven had found another clue indicating the treasure would be found on Little Cayman so that they would meet the other ships there on the south beach. Although his crew was tired from long hikes through the jungle, their spirits were uplifted by the news that a new clue had been discovered.

Lady Falcon was anchored near the other three ships parked in the waters off the small island. Then, Attila, Nathan Coates, and Mchungaji rowed over to *Destiny* to meet with the other officers. Ronald Pearson, the head gunner, was left in charge of the crew of the *Falcon* while Attila and his officers were away.

All the officers and Rivera met in Raven's quarters and sat around the table in her room. Jeremy brought in a cask of rum for everyone to partake in. Raven began the meeting by reading the newly found clue on the map's back.

"While your crews were out searching the islands, I accentually discovered a new clue."

She showed them the back of the map and then read the clue.

"The center of the islands would be best, to find the resting of my treasure chest. Not just any hour or any day, but if the time is right, you'll find the cay. When the moon is high, and the sun is low, would be the best time to find its chateau. The entrance is meager and narrow and small. It's not always visible, some might have to crawl. When the tides are right, under a moonlit sky you'll find your way for the treasure you'll spy."

Alexander asked, "Forgive me, Raven, what does it all mean?"

"It's a riddle. They way I understand it, the center of the islands means the Little Cayman. The cay, means the entrance is somewhere around a reef or cay. The entrance is small, so that means we'll be looking for a cave opening. When the tides are right under a moonlit sky, means the entrance of the cave probably isn't visible anytime, so we have to wait until the tide is low and the moon is bright."

Attila asked, "So, do you know where on the island we should look?"

"Not yet. We need to explore the shoreline to see if we can locate a cay or a reef that looks promising."

Kiboko said, "I think I know where to start."

Raven asked, "Really?"

"Yes. When I was on the Little Cayman I found a bluff high above the ocean. Jahiri almost fell over the side of a cliff. It was jagged and steep. He would have died most definitely if I hadn't caught him before he went over the side. That is where I would begin looking."

Raven smiled at Kiboko and replied, "That sounds like an excellent place to begin. We'll start there tomorrow; find the cliff and see what is at the bottom. However, since we are dealing with a situation that is time sensitive, I want us to spread out our dories along the southern shore. We won't have a full moon for another ten days, so let's scout out other locations that might seem promising to us. Look for reefs or cays along the shore. Attila, take the *Lady Falcon* to the north shore and do the same. You have six dories, so you should be able to cover the north alone. Alexander, take the eastern shore and Pharaoh take the west. Chart any likely places and present them when we meet three days from now. Any questions?"

The captains and officers returned to their respective ships, leaving Raven with John, Hadari, Jeffrey, and Oscar still gathered in Raven's cabin. Raven looked at Oscar and asked, "What do you think?"

"I think this is as close as we have been yet. My hopes are high, but I am trying to be realistic. Even if we have narrowed down the search with the additional clues, our window of opportunity is very narrow. My question is, can all of your men be trusted?"

"Probably not. I've always tried to split men up once they have joined our ranks when they have served together on other ships. However, there are always a few malcontents among every group of men serving together. Captain Billings had them on ship too."

"What can you do about it?" asked Rivera.

"Papa, you, Hadari, and Jeffrey will take a letter to the captains; for their eyes only. Have them read it when no one else is around. Have them sign the letter acknowledging that they understand my instructions."

Raven sat down and quickly penned three letters. She sent one with Jeffrey to the *Matilda,* one with Hadari to the *Nightingale,* and one with John to the *Lady Falcon.* Each man left straightaway to deliver their messages while Raven stepped up to the quarterdeck to wait for them to return.

Raven admired the cool breeze wafting across the ship's decks as she waited. The night sky was clear. Clearer than it had been for quite some time. Captain Billings sat on her shoulder and rummaged through Raven's vast red curls. Raven's mind began to wander as she waited. Who could she trust among her crew? She quickly surmised that if anyone would cross her, it would not be the Africans. She trusted all of them. She had given them freedom and a good living on the seas. They had as much money as they could spend whenever they were in port. No, it would be someone relatively new to her crew: someone English, French, Spanish, anyone but the Africans.

Raven had little trouble from those with whom she had served in the past. Most men who knew Raven as Richard long ago found her agreeable, hard-working, and highly intelligent. Henry Gant was one of the few who seemed to dislike her. Gant didn't like anyone. Yes, he admired young Richard as he taught him the ways of a sailor, but they were never friendly. When Gant discovered that Richard was Raven and had the opportunity to join her crew, Gant chose vehemently not to. He would never stoop so low as to serve under a woman. And he let her know it.

Raven turned her attention back to her officers, who were approaching the three other ships under her command. She watched as each man climbed aboard his assigned ship to deliver her message.

Her mind wandered again. How had she gotten here at such a young age? She now had four ships under her command. Most men in her situation would have taken on the rank of Commodore while she chose to remain captain. Was her lack of pride keeping her from naming herself Commodore, or was she unwilling to relinquish her ship's command to anyone else?

Captain Billings chirped, letting Raven know that someone was approaching. It was Jeremy. "Can I get you anything, Raven?"

"No thanks, Jeremy. Would you mind taking the captain below and putting him to bed?"

"Happy to do so."

The boy took the primate, placed him on his shoulder, and left the quarterdeck. Raven was once again left to her thoughts. Her thoughts led her to Jeffrey. She had grown quite fond of him. They had sailed together for two years and had grown closer together. She enjoyed his company and his sense of humor. However, did she love him? She still hadn't decided. She liked the feel of his hand against hers and his body's warmth whenever they stood beside each other at the rail and stared into the horizon. He kissed her once, very gently, but it was one-sided. She had not returned the kiss. She felt guilty but couldn't get bogged down in a romance. At least, not yet.

Something stirred Raven back into the present. A ship suddenly appeared on the southern horizon. When Raven saw it, she heard a call from the crow's nest, "Ship ahoy, off the starboard bow!"

Raven took out her spyglass to examine the scene. Then she called out, "Can you make out her colors?"

"She's flying the Jolly Roger!"

"Drat!" Raven exclaimed. "Who could that be?" She spoke under her breath.

She called again, "Can you determine what kind of vessel she is?"

After a long pause, "She looks to be a sloop! I make out thirty guns! Wait a minute! It's the *Ranger*!"

Raven rolled her eyes and muttered, "Just my luck."

Benjamin Hornigold and his crew aboard the *Ranger* were headed her way.

Raven told Jeremy, who had just returned from putting the monkey to bed, "Sound the alarm. Man the guns. Prepare to be boarded."

Jeremy took out his conch shell and blew the alarm, alerting the other ships that another ship was approaching. The *Matilda* was closest to *Raven's Destiny*, and Pharaoh stood at the rail on the quarterdeck and called out to Raven.

"What are your orders!"

"Ready at the guns, but let them think we are making repairs! Pass the word!"

"Aye, Raven!"

All her ships made ready, manning the guns, but appearing to be repairing their ships. An hour passed before the *Ranger* pulled into the bay where they anchored. Hornigold and ten of his men rowed over to *Raven's Destiny* and asked to board. Raven allowed Hornigold to come up alone.

As he climbed over the rail and approached Raven, he bowed, removed his hat, and remarked, "Ah, Miss Ashworth. We meet again."

"That's Captain!"

"Oh, of course, how rude of me."

Benjamin Hornigold was tall, good-looking, and always charming. But Raven also knew he was ruthless and bloodthirsty. She disliked him immensely but tried to hide her feelings.

Hornigold continued, "I would have thought you to take the monicker of Commodore by now. Are all these ships yours?"

"They are. But I don't feel the need to inflate my ego with such flowery titles."

"I see. I am surprised to see you here. I once heard the French had captured you. I half expected you to have fallen to the gallows."

"They wanted to chop off my head, but I told them I was attached to it."

Hornigold leaned backward and laughed a most pretentious laugh.

"Well, I'm glad to see you're doing well. By the way, I was so sorry to see you leave my company so long ago. What happened?"

"I grew bored with your blockade. I wanted some real adventure."

"Yes, well I see you found it. And, almost lost it with one fell swoop of the axe. What are you doing here, in the Caymans?"

"We're making repairs. I have a few leaks in my hull. Thought we might do a little barnacle scraping when the tide cooperates. What about you? What brings you here?"

"I'm looking for Jack McGreavey."

"Black Jack?"

"Yes, he's an old friend of mine. Have you ever met him?"

Raven replied, "I saw him not long ago. Over on Treasure Beach on the southern tip of Jamaica."

"Oh, pray tell what was he doing in that awful place?"

"He didn't say and I didn't ask."

"Why not?"

"Because it wasn't any of my business. I try to mind my own business. You should try it sometime."

"Yes, well that never really worked for me. I'll have to keep that suggestion in mind, however. Well then, I shall bid you farewell."

Raven stood staring at him without responding.

Finally, Hornigold said, "Yes, of course." then turned around and left Raven's ship.

Raven watched as Hornigold and his boarding crew slowly rowed back to the *Ranger*. He climbed aboard his ship but remained in the area overnight.

CHAPTER 23

Before the sun rose the next morning, Benjamin Hornigold ordered his ship to weigh anchor and head toward Jamaica. Although Hornigold spoke and conducted himself as a gentleman, little was known of his past, and that's the way he preferred it. He never spoke of his upbringing or where he grew up, although it was quite obviously somewhere in England.

He had his ships avoid attacking British merchant ships for the most part, concentrating on Spanish vessels sailing in the area around the Bahamas and occasionally attacking ships bound for Charlestown in the Carolinas.

Benjamin's second in command was a large, burly man with crazy, black eyes. He wore a long black beard, which he sometimes stuffed with lit cannon fuses during an attack to strike fear in those he encountered. Edward Teach was a man not to be trifled with, his demeanor as unstable as his eyes. He spoke with a growl that would frighten a bear. Benjamin, however, seemed to know how to handle the man. He knew Teach was an able sailor who could lead in Hornigold's absence.

Benjamin took a group of twenty sailors to Treasure Beach when they arrived in the bay just off the coast of Jamaica, leaving Teach behind to mind his ship, the *Ranger*. They rowed toward the village Raven had spoken about seeing Black Jack McGreavy. When they arrived on the beach, all seemed to be deserted. No one came out to meet them, and no one seemed to be milling about at all. Typically, in these island communities, they would at least see natives fishing somewhere off the coast in long canoes, or women would come out and happily greet them as they rowed to shore.

Nevertheless, Hornigold and his men marched across the beach and into the jungle, hoping to find someone to speak to about McGreavy. They finally came to a small village that had burned and then been newly built. It seemed uninhabited except for a middle-aged man sitting in front of a hut near the back of the village. Benjamin asked the man, "I say there, Chap, do you speak English?"

The man did not respond except to glance up at Hornigold and then at each of his twenty men who followed.

"Is there anyone here who we can speak to? Anyone who speaks English?"

The man then spoke with a well-worn voice as he called to someone in the distance. Then, the man remained silent once more. A few moments later, a younger man came from the jungle and stood by the first man.

Hornigold asked, "Pardon me, do you speak English?"

"I speak English."

"Well done, my good man. Can you help us? We're looking for an old friend whom we were told might be here on this beach. His name is Black Jack McGreavy."

"There are no white men here."

"Have there been any white men here recently?"

"Yes, white men come, they not stay long. They say they look for man called Black Jack, like you. I take them to where man was and show them. I show you, too."

"Splendid, my good man. We shall follow."

Hornigold and his crew followed the native through the jungle along a well-worn path. They kept watch as they walked, not completely satisfied that they were safe.

They finally arrived at the mouth of a cave in a small clearing. The man pointed to the cave and said, "This where I show white men, last place I see man called Black Jack."

Benjamin said, "Alright, lead the way, I'll follow."

"Warakaba not go in cave. Evil spirit live in cave. Warakaba go back to village."

Hornigold felt uneasy about the situation. Something didn't seem right to him. He turned to two of his men and said, "You two stay here and stand guard while the rest of us go inside. If anything goes wrong, go back and get *Blackbeard.*"

"Aye, Captain."

Benjamin led the other eighteen men inside to search the cave. The doorway allowed a good bit of light to a large room inside. Skeletons dressed in rags lay scattered throughout the room. At the far end of the cave was another doorway. Benjamin stood in front of the doorway to examine it more closely. Suddenly, darkness filled the cave.

Hornigold asked no one in particular, "What happened?"

A voice replied from the darkness, "I don't know, Captain. It appears someone has blocked the entrance to the cave."

"Bless my barnacles! What of the men I left to watch for us?"

"I don't know, Captain. They must have been overtaken by some of the natives?"

The next morning, Raven went up topside and found her papa standing on the quarterdeck using his spyglass.

She asked, "Is the *Ranger* gone?"

"Hornigold left just before dawn."

"Which way?"

"He looked to be heading east, but you never know."

Raven said, "Maybe he'll go to Treasure Beach looking for Black Jack. That should keep him busy for a while."

John smiled at the thought of Benjamin Hornigold getting stuck inside the cave where they had rescued Raven. Raven put her hand on John's shoulder, then rested her head on his other shoulder as they looked out into the sea.

Then Raven asked, "Did you ever imagine us out here together like this?"

"Well, no. But, I never thought you would remain a boy for the rest of your life either."

Raven playfully punched her papa with her free hand, and they chuckled together.

Then John asked, "By the way, what did you write to your captains about?"

"I gave them instructions that all white sailors were to be included in the search for the treasure today along with enough of the Africans to fill the boats."

"May I ask why?"

"The Africans have no reason to cross me. The white men recruited from ships we captured may have reason to steal the treasure for themselves."

"And, what might that reason be?"

"Because they are greedy and think they are smarter than I."

Again, John chuckled at his little girl.

Meanwhile, Attila was making assignments for his boat crews. When Ronald Pearson heard his name called to be on one of the boats, he shuddered angrily.

"Captain, are you sure you want me to go on this search? Who will man the guns in my absence?"

"Mr. Pearson, do you think I am not capable of running a gun crew on this ship?"

"No, it's just that, I feel I would be better suited to stay here and man the guns should they be needed."

"Mr. Pearson, I think you would be better suited to follow orders without question. Do you understand me?"

Ronald looked at his feet and muttered, "Yes, Captain."

"What!?" shouted Attila.

"Aye, Captain!"

"Alright then. Each crew will be searching the shoreline for reefs or cays under the water. If you find one, mark it with a buoy. We have made buoys out of coconuts and painted them yellow. Float a buoy whenever you find a reef so that I can mark it on the chart as I sail past. Understand?"

The men nodded.

"Alright, prepare to move out when the signal is given. We will sail to our appointed place on the island and get started."

Back on *Destiny*, Raven said, "Alright, Papa. Let's begin."

John instructed Jeremy to blow the conch shell to alert the other ships they should begin their search.

Wooooo. Wooooo. Wooooo.

Each ship began its assigned duties. *Lady Falcon* sailed away westward to move to the north side of the island. *Matilda* followed to begin her search on the west end. The *Nightingale* sailed east to search the east side of the island. *Destiny* remained where she was to search the south side.

Each boat carried a five-man crew. Ronald Pearson was surprised to see his companions from his gun crew were assigned to him. He was suspicious because they happened to be the only white sailors aboard the *Lady Falcon*. David Aldridge, James Hunter, John Clarke, and Zachery Thacker were the others assigned to Pearson's boat. Aldridge took the first shift at rowing.

Pulling against the oars, he asked, "What do you think, Ronald? Are they onto us?"

"I don't see how? Has any of you talked to anyone?"

They all responded, "*No!*"

Then Pearson said, "This could be a break for us. If we find the treasure, we can deny seeing it and keep it for ourselves."

Thacker asked, "But how will we get out of here without being seen? Where would we hide it onboard the ship?"

"We won't hide it on the ship. We'll leave it lie where it is and come back for it another day. We'd have to be patient. The Raven will tire eventually and go in search of other treasure. We'll ask to be excused from our duties to join another ship, then find a boat of our own, come back here, and collect the treasure for ourselves."

Hunter said, "What if we don't find it? What if one of the other crews finds it?"

"Then we'll go back to our original plan. We'll find a way to overtake the *Falcon* and use her to steal the treasure away, sink the other ships, and sail off to become rich men."

Raven waited until nearly dark to set her two boats out near the center of the south shoreline. The tide was low, so each would row away from the other, marking the reefs as they traveled. The boats first had to row inland to the island because the ships couldn't get very close for fear they might get stranded on a reef or rock formation when the tide changed. Raven anxiously waited along the rail with Oscar, watching through spyglasses as the boats rowed toward the island. Raven could see the point she was most interested in searching. The bluff Kiboko had described was sitting about 20° east of where *Destiny* was anchored. Raven felt that would be an ideal place for someone to put a hidden cave.

Someone? Who? Raven had never been religious. She didn't know if there was a god. She had never been to church. She did once see a priest. When her mother died, a priest was called in to give her last rights, whatever that meant. There was no funeral. She didn't even know what happened to her mother's body. Some men came in and took her away while Raven wept in her papa's arms. She had seen the dead piled up outside the flat along the streets of Wapping. She had never considered that the bodies had once been people until her mother died. Tears began to run down her face as Raven thought of it. Then she realized her tears and wiped them away along with her thoughts. She had other things to think about now.

Suddenly, Raven realized Jeffrey was standing next to her.

"Are you alright?" he asked.

"Fine. I was just thinking about my past."

"What about your past?"

"My mama. She was sick for such a long time. And, I was so young when she died."

"How old were you?"

"Eleven. Almost twelve."

Jeffrey asked, "And, you were twelve when your papa brought you to sea?"

"Yes."

Jeffrey smiled, "Hmph! I can't imagine you as a boy."

"Well, thank you. I can't imagine you as a girl, either."

"How did you manage?"

"What do you mean?"

"How were you able to conceal the fact that your were a girl to all those men? Did no one suspect?"

"I don't think so. But, one knew."

"Really? Oh, you mean your papa."

"No, not Papa. Mr. Greer."

Puzzled, Jeffrey asked, "Did you tell him? How did he know?"

"Right at the beginning, I got into trouble. I was accused of stealing a cup of milk. I guess I was guilty, but not really. I was given the milk by Mr. Hardy. But rather than place the blame on him, I told the captain that I took it when Mr. Hardy wasn't looking. Anyway, after I received my lashing, I was sent to Mr. Greer to have my wounds treated. He saw my chest and realized I wasn't a boy, but he never said anything and never told a soul."

"My word! Now I know why you two have such a strong bond between you."

"He and I talked about it just the other day. I thanked him for what he did, and didn't do."

Jeffrey smiled again and said, "I think I would have liked to have seen you as a boy."

"Oh, don't be so sure. This little boy could have licked you good."

"I don't doubt that. You still can."

Raven stopped to observe as her first boat reached the shoreline, placed its first buoy in the water, and rowed eastward down the coast. The other boat turned westward but had not yet placed a buoy.

Raven said, "I don't think you've ever told me where you're from."

"There isn't much to tell. I, like you, started out very young aboard a merchant ship."

"The *Matilda?*"

"No, *Matilda* was my second ship. My first was the Lucky Lucy. A ship out of Plymouth."

"Is that where you're from?"

"Yes, I was born there."

"And who were your mother and father?"

" I really don't know. I mean, I know my sir name is Hamilton, but I don't recall ever knowing my parents. I was sent to a boarding school in Plymouth at a very early age. I know someone paid for my schooling, but I never knew who. Anyway, when I turned thirteen, I decided I'd had enough of boarding school. I used to sit in my dorm room, looking out my window at the ships sailing in the docks. I finally got my nerve up to abandon the school and find a ship I could sail with. Lucky Lucy was that ship. I served as ship's boy for two years before I was promoted to third officer. After a year, I found *Matilda* who was looking for another junior officer. I contacted the captain and offered my services."

Raven asked, "Oh, what was that captain's name?"

"Stennet. John Stennet. He was a rude man. Spoiled by his parentage. Not a good sailor at all. We were lost most of the time. If you hadn't come along and rescued me, there's no telling what might have happened."

"Well, I'm happy I could oblige."

Raven looked at her boats again and saw the second boat set out a buoy. She checked the other boat sailing to the east and saw it approaching the high cliffs that Kiboko had pointed out to her. She found she was holding her breath, hoping a reef existed there. Raven picked up her spyglass and watched the eastbound boat rock in the water of the waves. She watched as suddenly, the boat struck an outcropping of jagged rocks along the coast. The water smashed the boat against the rocks, tossing its passengers into the sea. Raven gasped as she saw her men struggling against the waves, continuously smashing them against the rocks and the shrapnel of boat pieces.

"We have to go!" she cried.

She turned to her papa and ordered, "Mr. Ashworth, come about. We need to rescue our men."

John Ashworth looked over his shoulder but couldn't see anything; he was too far away and didn't have a spyglass.

John ordered, "Mr. Finch, come about turning port! Make for that cliff! Don't get us smashed up on those rocks."

"Aye, Mr. Ashworth!"

Raven then turned to Jeremy, who was at the bow, "Jeremy, recall our other boat. We're going to need it to rescue our men."

"Aye, Raven!"

Jeremy blew his conch shell to the western wind as hard as possible. Jeffrey moved next to Jeremy and watched through his spyglass to see if the boat crew acknowledged the signal. The boat was nearly half a mile away and was continuously moving away. Suddenly, Jeffrey saw a man standing in the boat and looking back toward *Destiny*. He waved, letting them know he had heard the recall. Two men in the boat sat side by side, rowing back to *Destiny* as fast as they could.

Jeffrey turned to Raven and said, "They're coming back."

John continued to have the ship turned easterly but waited before letting loose the sails to retrieve the stranded crew. Ten minutes passed before the approaching boat reached *Destiny*. As they came closer, John called out to them, "We need to rescue the other crew. They crashed against the rocks. We'll throw you a line and tow you closer, but don't get too close to those rocks. They'll have to swim out to meet you if they can."

"Aye, Mr. Ashworth!"

CHAPTER 24

Raven's crew set out their first buoy and rowed east to find the next area where a reef lay underwater. Mvulana Mbuzi rowed the boat as the other three began preparing the next buoy. Mti wa Mvua held a yellow coconut while Pua ya Ndege tied a rope to a hook already inserted into the coconut. The last man onboard, Kijana Mkaidi, sat at the boat's bow, watching the waters, searching for the next reef.

Mvulana rowed and steered them toward a high cliff over the ocean. He remembered that Raven had been particularly interested in this cliff, although he didn't know why. The closer Mvulana rowed toward the cliff, the choppier the water seemed to grow. The waves lifted the boat out of the water and slammed it back down repeatedly. The other three men held onto the boat's rim as the waves continually knocked them about.

Pua ya Ndege called out, "I don't think this is a good idea. We should not go any closer to the cliff. Let's put our buoy right here. It will be close enough and we can see that there is most definitely a reef beneath us."

Mvulana replied, "I want to get closer. Raven was very interested in this area. It could be the location she is looking for."

Pua ya Ndege asked, "What exactly is she looking for?"

Kijana looked back and replied, "The entrance to a cave."

Pua ya Ndege asked, "A cave? We can clearly see that there is not a cave in the wall of that escarpment."

Kijana said, "We will not find the entrance in the wall. That would be too obvious. The entrance will be under the water until the lowest tide comes. Then we will be able to see the cave she is looking for."

Suddenly, the waves lifted the boat high above the sea's surface and slammed the boat onto a large rock protruding from the bottom of the ocean. The boat landed with a loud "**_Crack_**" that sent the men flying in all directions. Kijana was slammed against the big rock, where he hit his head and passed out. Waves rolled over his head, trying to rake him into the water like four large fingers clawing at him.

The other three screamed to one another as they tried to swim anywhere that might provide them safety until rescue could arrive. Pua clung to a large piece of the little boat that continued to rise and fall within the grips of the sea's waves. He felt his legs scrape against the rock below the surface. He cried out every time another rock peeled flesh from his legs.

Mvulana and Mti wa Mvua held onto bunches of yellow buoys discarded by the shattered boat. The water tossed them around, and they had no control over where they might end up. Mvulana called out, "Try to swim out into the sea away from the cliffs."

Mti wa Mvua nodded and tried to follow Mvulana into the sea depths away from the jagged rocks. Mvulana looked over his shoulder, searching for the other two men who had ridden in his boat. There wasn't enough light to spot either one of them, so he called out to them.

"Pua! Kijana! Swim out to the sea! Get away from the rocks!"

He called over and over to them but heard no response. Mvulana realized he had made a critical mistake in taking the boat too far inland. He should have done as Raven had instructed and only marked the areas where they spotted the reefs instead of looking for a cave entrance. He felt guilty because he had endangered the lives of the men in his boat. Mvulana looked around to see where *Destiny* was. He was relieved to see that she was turning around to come to his rescue. He only hoped that he and his friends would be alive when the ship arrived.

Mti wa Mvua caught up to Mvulana in the open water, and they floated together, waiting for *Destiny* to rescue them. Soon afterward, Mvulana heard a faint voice call to him.

Mvulana called back, "Pua! Is that you?"

Again, he heard his name called. "Mvulana! Where are you?"

"Pua, I am coming."

Mvulana swam back toward the reef while holding onto some coconut buoys. Pua kept calling for Mvulana, but his call was becoming weaker and weaker.

"Hold on, Mti! I am coming for you."

Mvulana bumped into Pua's body before he saw him. Pua was lying face down in the water. Mvlana quickly rolled him over and checked to see if he was still breathing.

"Pua! Pua!"

Mvulana lightly patted his friend's face, trying to revive him.

"Pua! You must wake up."

Pua suddenly started coughing up water. Mvulana held him out of the water and said, "I have you, my friend. I have you. Look, *Destiny* is coming for us. The Red Raven will be here soon to rescue us."

Pua told his friend, "Mvulana, I don't like the little boats. I want to go on the big ship."

"It's alright my friend. We will be on the big ship soon."

Mvulana chuckled at his friend. He held onto Pua and swam back out to find Mti.

When they found him, Mti asked, "Did you find Kijana?"

Mvulana replied, "No, only Pua."

Pua weakly replied, "I saw him lying on a big rock. But, I don't know if he was alive. I couldn't get to him. The water was too strong."

Mvulan replied, "Don't worry, Pua. We will find him when Raven gets here."

As they waited for *Destiny* to arrive, the three shivered as their body temperature dropped. Each man was exhausted from trying to stay afloat. The coconuts helped, but there weren't enough to entirely suspend them out of the water.

Finally, *Destiny* arrived. The three men watched as the dory rowed toward them. They heard the familiar voice of their friend, Mwepesi, call out to them.

"Ahoy, my friends! Are you alive?"

Pua replied, "Only barely."

"Well, come! Let's get you into this boat and take you back to *Destiny*."

As they began pulling the three stranded men into the dory, Mwepesi remarked, "These are the three biggest fish I have caught all day."

Then Mwepesi noticed someone was missing. "Who else was on your boat, Mvulana?"

"Kijana. He is stranded on a large rock deep within the reef. I don't know if he is alive or not."

Mwepesi said, "Alright, we will get you back to *Destiny* and then Raven can decide what to do about Kijana."

They all rowed back to the ship, where the dory was pulled up by Raven's crew using pulleys. Once the men were back onboard, Raven asked Mvulana what happened.

Mvulana replied, "I am sorry, Raven. It is all my fault. I went too far into the reef looking for a tunnel instead of just leaving a buoy."

"Where is Kijana?"

"He was stranded on a large rock inside the reef. We couldn't get to him. I don't know if he is alive or not. It was too dark to see. I should never have gone in there."

"You're right. There is no treasure worth the life of even one man."

Raven then turned to her entire crew and announced, "There is no treasure worth the life of one man. If we can't do this by being safe, then we won't do it at all. Do you understand?"

A small mutter came from her men.

"Do you understand!"

This time, the men responded with more commitment.
"*Aye, Raven!*"

Raven turned to John and said, "We'll stay here until we can see well enough to decide what to do about Kijana."

"Aye, Raven."

Raven spent the rest of the night in her cabin thinking about the mistakes made already in searching for this treasure. How many men would she lose in this endeavor? She thought, "*It is one thing to lose men in battle trying to free men from slavery. It is another to waste lives searching for a treasure that might never have existed. Even if it does exist, it isn't worth the lives of my men to find it.*"

Raven lay on her bed without undressing and closed her eyes, trying to escape everything in the moment. She only wanted to sleep. She didn't want to think about it anymore.

Morning came quickly. There was a rap on her door. Then, another finally woke Raven.

"Enter!"

Jeremy stuck his head into her room and waited for Raven's response before entering.

"What is it, Jeremy?"

"Mr. Ashworth has sent for you, Raven. It's daylight and they've spotted Kijana."

"Is he alive?"

"Don't know, Raven. He's not moving. He's laid up on a big rock in the reef."

"Tell Mr. Ashworth I'll be right up."

"Aye, Raven."

Moments later, Raven joined John and Jeffrey on the quarter-deck.

She asked, "Where is he?"

John handed Raven his spyglass and pointed toward where Kijana's body lay. Raven looked through the glass to find Kijana. There he lay, nearly face down. He did not move. She couldn't see him breathing.

"Let's go get him. Get the dory ready. Jeffrey you come with me along with two men. Bring some blankets."

Jeffrey snapped to, and followed Raven's orders. "Prepare the dory!

He then pointed to two men, "You two, you'll be rowing the boat."

"*Aye, Mr. Hamilton.*"

Then, a voice from the crowd of men said, "Wait! I want to go."

It was Mvulana. Jeffrey began to say, "Alright go..."

"No!" said Raven. "You will not go."

The crowd of men on deck hushed as Raven spoke.

"Mvulana, you have done enough. You will remain here and receive your punishment."

Then Raven looked at Jeremy and said in a low voice, "Get me the whip."

Without speaking, Jeremy ran across the deck to a peg on the wall where the whip rested. He took the whip down and carried it back to Raven. Many of the men gasped when they saw Raven holding the whip. She had never punished anyone on her ships before. They thought she must be mighty angry to use the whip on one of her men.

Raven raised the whip above her head for all to see her. She looked at Mvulana and asked, "Is this what you deserve for your mistake?

Mvulana looked down with tears in his eyes and replied, "Yes, Raven."

"Did you disobey my orders yesterday by taking that boat into the reef?"

"Yes, Raven."

"Mvulana, why do you think you deserve the whip?"

"Raven, if Kijana is dead, I deserve worse. I should die for my mistake. I don't deserve to live."

Then Raven asked the crowd, "How many of you men have felt the whip?"

Many of the men raised their hands and murmured. Some were Africans, and some were White. John looked at his daughter wide-eyed. He had never seen her this upset before, and he was afraid of what she might do next.

"I too have felt the sharp sting of the whip's bite. I was twelve years old when my captain ordered that I receive twelve save one. Mvulana, you will not receive the whip as your punishment. Your punishment, and I say this knowing well, will be much worse. You will live out the rest of your days knowing very well that if Kijana dies, it was at your hand."

Mvulana began weeping aloud as he listened to Raven's words.

"And, whether he lives or dies, your next pay will be cut by three-quarters. Whether it be this treasure, or whether it be the taking of another ship, you will receive only one-quarter share."

Through tears, Mvulana replied, "I don't want any share in it."

Raven said, "You will take it. It will serve as a reminder of your mistake."

Raven turned to John and nodded as she returned the whip to Jeremy. John then ordered, "Man the boat! Lower away!"

Raven, Jeffrey, and the two men Jeffrey had selected climbed into the dory and prepared to row away. Each of Jeffrey's men grabbed an oar and began rowing toward the reef. Although the tide was no longer at its lowest level, the seas had calmed from the day before. They could row into the reef without much incident, although occasionally, they did bump into a rock below the water's surface. They finally reached the rock where Kijana's body lay. The rock was almost completely submerged from the change in the tide. Raven stepped out of the boat and onto the rock. She knelt to check to see if Kijana was still breathing. If he was, it was so faint she couldn't discern it. She lowered her head and put her ear to his chest to listen for a heartbeat.

"He has a heartbeat, but it's faint. Let's get him in the boat."

Jeffrey's men reached over the side of the boat, grabbed Kijana, and pulled him into the boat. Raven followed, then began wrapping the injured man with several blankets she had brought. They rowed back to the ship as quickly as they could.

Upon arrival, Raven called up to John, "Get a hammock! We'll use it as a sling to bring him up."

John did as Raven requested, and very soon, a hammock was lowered over the side of the ship and down to the boat. They placed Kijana in the hammock, then Raven straddled him and steadied the sling as it was raised to the ship. When it reached the rail, Raven ordered, "All the way up, and over."

The sling cleared the rail and was then lowered to the deck. Raven stood and said, "Get him to Mr. Greer."

Four men carried Kijana to Mr. Greer's infirmary so the doctor could examine him. Raven went back to the rail where Jeffrey was now climbing back up. She spoke to the two men still in the dory and said, "You men stay in the boat. I want you to continue the search. I'll send two more to help."

"*Aye, Raven!*"

Raven told Jeffrey, "Get two more men in the boat. Send down some more buoys and have them continue the search for coves heading east. We'll take *Destiny* around to the other side of the island and meet up with *Lady Falcon* and get one of the boats to finish the search on this side. And tell them to stay out of those reefs!"

"Aye, Raven!"

CHAPTER 25

Raven directed John to sail to the other side of the island to find the *Lady Falcon*. They unfurled their sails and sailed east to the end of the island. As they rounded the bend in the shoreline, they saw the *Nightingale* anchored in the bay on the island's east coast.

When *Destiny* got close enough, Raven pulled beside the *Nightingale* to speak with Alexander.

"How is your search going?"

"We have nearly finished this end. There was only one reef to be found and it was on the southeastern shore."

"When you're finished here, send your boats back around to the south and help with the search there. We had some trouble last night and lost one of our dories."

Alexander asked, "Is everyone alright?"

"Kijana is badly injured. I don't know if he will survive or not. Mr. Greer is looking after him now. Make sure your men know not to go into the reef. They are only to mark them with the buoys. We'll explore them later when the tide is at its lowest."

"Aye, Raven."

Raven gave the order to proceed north along the shore; they turned west, looking for the *Lady Falcon*. Thirty minutes later, Raven spotted the *Falcon* resting halfway down the coastline. *Destiny* pulled up along the *Falcon's* port side so Raven could talk to Attila.

Raven asked Attila, "How is the search going?"

"Better, now that we have daylight. We should be finished later this evening."

"When you finish, I need you to move your boats to the south shores. Alexander will be moving that way. His crew is almost finished on the east side."

Attila asked, "Have you had any luck on the south?"

"Only bad luck. We lost one of our boats because they got too close to the shore. They crashed and we have an injured man."

"Anyone I know?"

"His name is Kijana Mkaidi."

"I do not know him. I hope he will be alright."

"Thanks! I'll see you when I get back to that side. I'm going to find Pharaoh, now."

Attila waved to Raven as she sailed away, heading west.

Raven noticed very few buoys floating in the water as they sailed along the north shore. She counted only four as she made it to the end of the island and turned southward. Just as she rounded the bend in the shoreline, she spotted the *Matilda* anchored. *Matilda* was already loading her two dories onto the ship. Raven had John pull alongside the other ship so she could talk to Pharaoh.

Raven asked, "Have you had any luck?"

"We found two reefs, and marked them. This end of the island seems to be mostly sandbars. How about you?"

"We're still marking reefs. We ran into trouble last night. One of our boats got too close to the rocks and wrecked. One of our men is in bad shape. Everyone is moving to the southside again."

"We are on our way."

Raven continued back to catch up with her boat crew on the island's south side. When she arrived, she found the *Nightingale* and the *Lady Falcon* moored together, waiting for her to arrive. *Matilda* was only ten minutes behind her as she arrived.

The ships all rested in the waters before the prominent escarpment where the boat wreck had occurred. Raven's single boat rowed back to *Destiny* and was loaded back onto the ship. All the captains moved over to join Raven on *Destiny* to plan their mission's next steps. As they sat around the table in Raven's cabin, Attila asked, "How is your man?"

Raven replied, "The last I heard from Mr. Greer, he was not doing well. His head was injured and he spent the night on a rock where he nearly froze to death."

Pharaoh asked, "What is our next step in this search for the treasure?"

Raven said, "It's a bit of a waiting game, now. The tide needs to be low enough and the moonlight just right for us to see the entrance to the cave, if it's there."

Rivera frustratedly interjected, "It has to be there! We just have to find it. We have come so far and learned so much from the map. It has to be here somewhere."

Just then, a knock came to the door.

Raven said, "Enter."

Jeremy stuck his head in and waited for Raven to recognize him.

"Come in, Jeremy. What is it?"

Jeremy entered the cabin and sheepishly replied, "It's Mr. Greer, Raven. He sent me to tell you that Kijana has died."

Everyone's countenance dropped when they heard the news. Raven said, "Tell Mr. Greer to prepare the body for a funeral. As soon as he is ready, we will bury Kijana."

"Aye, Raven."

Raven went back to her meeting. "We need to set up watches at each of the buoy locations. How many buoys did each of you set out?"

Attila replied, "We set out four on the north side."

Alexander said, "We only had two."

Pharaoh replied, "Only one on the westside. It was mostly sand over there."

John said, "We marked six locations on the southside."

Raven said, "I want us to set up lookouts at each location over the next few nights. I don't know exactly what to look for, but there should be some kind of indication during the moonlit sky to tell us where to look. Keep an eye on those reefs. We should have a full moon in four nights, but let's not wait til then. Keep someone on those reefs every night until we find something, or until we decide there is nothing."

Rivera started to object, but Raven interrupted him. "I know, I know. We will find it. Don't worry, I'm not giving up yet. But, I don't intend to stay here for the next year searching for a myth. Now, I have a man to bury. All of you may stay if you like or you may return to your ships and prepare for the night watch."

Everyone decided to stay for the funeral, even though some didn't know Kijana Mkaidi. Raven walked up to the quarterdeck and waited for Kijana's body to be brought out. Mr. Greer had wrapped the man's body in a tarp and tied it up with ropes and weights so it would sink to the bottom of the ocean. Four men carried the body out and placed it on a plank resting on the port rail. As everyone gathered around to pay their respects, Raven began to speak.

"We commit our brother to the depths of the sea to rest for eternity. Kijana was a good man, full of spirit, and a hard worker. I take responsibility for his death. I should not have sent you out in the night with such rough waters. I apologize to all of you for my mistake. I deeply regret that such a good man is lost because of my mistake. May God have mercy on his soul."

Mvulana Mbuzi watched with tears in his eyes as his friend slid down the plank and landed in the water. Slowly, the body sank to the ocean floor, never to be seen again. As everyone dispersed, Mvulana remained at the rail, looking into the water, thinking about what he had done to his friend.

Mvulana and Kijana came from the same village. Mvulana remembered their lives together as boys. He was a year older than Kijana and had always looked after him like a little brother. Mvulana remembered the day when the slavers came and took them away. They were down by the stream that ran through their village, watering and tending their village's goat herd. At least twenty men surrounded their small village and collected all the young people between thirteen and thirty.

There weren't many of them. The village was made up of only sixty or seventy people, most of them old women. The twenty or so of them taken that day were led to a large boat on the river about ten miles from Mvulana's home. They were shackled together on the boat and forced to sit out on the open deck without shelter from the hot African sun that beat down on them. They traveled by river for four days before they reached their destination, the slave fort at Lomé, where they remained until Raven and her men rescued them.

Now, Mvulana was left without his childhood friend, who had been the only one remaining in his village clan. It was his fault Kijana was now dead, and he couldn't forgive himself for it.

Mvulana slowly turned away from the ship's rail. Like a zombie, he walked away, not seeing anyone or anything around him. He was in a trance that led him to the cannon station at the ship's starboard side. Mvulana took a rope hanging nearby, tied it to his leg, then the other end around one of the cannonballs. He lifted the cannonball from the stack next to the big gun. Mvulana then sat on the rail, swung his feet over the side, and allowed himself to drop into the water.

The splash alerted Hadari, who was standing watch on the quarterdeck. Hadari ran to the starboard rail, where he had heard the splash, and looked over the side. He saw ripples in the water, showing that something significant had dropped into the sea, but he had no idea what it might be.

Hadari then walked to the main deck near where the splash had occurred to get a closer look. Puzzled, he looked around, searching for anything out of place. Then he noticed it. The pyramid of cannonballs stacked next to the cannon was missing the one on top of the stack. It usually held twenty-six balls but now only had twenty-five.

Hadari swiveled his head, looking for anyone who might have tossed one into the sea. No one was around. He looked in the water again, but nothing surfaced to the top or floated below. He then remembered. . . Mvulana had been standing at the opposite rail for a long time after Kijana was buried. *Where was he now?*

Hadari was unsure what to do. He looked around again to see if anyone else on deck might have heard the splash. No one was around; they were all in their bunks. He felt he had no choice but to wake Raven and report what he had heard.

He rapped on the cabin door loud enough to wake Raven if she had been sleeping. She was not.

"Enter!"

Hadari opened the door and walked inside.

"What is it, Hadari?"

"Raven, while I was standing watch on the quarterdeck, I heard a loud splash on the starboard side of the ship. I went to investigate but saw no one there. When I looked around, I noticed a cannonball was missing from the stack. Someone must have dropped one into the sea, but I can't imagine why?"

Raven furrowed her brow as she contemplated Hadari's report. Then, she realized what it might have been.

"Hadari, where is Mvulana?"

"I don't know. He was standing on at the port rail for a long time after we buried Kijanan."

Then he realized what must have happened and said, "Oh, no!"

He and Raven ran onto the deck to search.
Raven said, "Go below and see if he is in his bunk."

Hadari ran below with a lamp and woke everyone, calling, "Mvulana! Mvulana! Are you down here?"

He woke everyone with his calls. Pua, whose bunk was close to Mvulana's, said, "He is not in his bunk. I have not seen him."

Hadari ordered, "Everyone, look for him, now!"

The crew scrambled from their bunks and searched every inch of the ship. Everyone called Mvulana's name over and over as they searched. It was so loud that no one could have heard him had he answered. Raven checked with John and Mr. Greer, and neither had seen Mvulana since the funeral. Eventually, everyone was back on the main deck without knowing what had happened to their fellow crewman.

Raven beckoned everyone to silence. "Hadari has informed me that one of the cannonballs is missing from the starboard gun stack. Since that is where he heard the splash, I can only deduce that Mvulana carried one of the cannonballs into the sea with him. We must assume he has taken his own life.

I know the last two days have been difficult for us all. Let this be the last loss we experience in this matter. We are all weary and frustrated, but take heart. . . if you allow it to be, there will always be another day. Now, everyone, return to your bunks."

CHAPTER 26

*D*estiny's mood was solemn for the next couple of days. Everyone continued their usual duties, but rather than the usual banter between sea mates, they were quiet. Nature must have sensed the somber mood because the skies clouded to a hazy gray. Rain was visible from the ship but was well to the south of them and moving east. A pelican landed on the forecastle and squawked most of the morning. John eventually grew tired of it, walked over to the forecastle, and shooed the bird away.

Raven was concerned that the weather might not cooperate with their plans for the night. She had ordered her boat crews to keep vigilance at each marked reef in hopes of finding the location of the treasure Black Jack indicated on his map. Cloudy conditions might cover the moon, not allowing the location of the treasure to be discovered. The moon was scheduled to be in full phase in two nights. However, Raven hoped that with clear skies, there might be enough light from the moon at only near full phase. She would have to be patient and wait to see.

Jeffrey, Oscar, and Raven spent most of the day sitting in Raven's cabin, discussing various scenarios of where the treasure might be hidden.

Oscar offered, "It seems to me that the treasure is in an underwater cave. Why else would we be looking for a reef?"

Jeffrey rebutted, "Then how will we find the treasure if it is underwater? None of us can breathe underwater."

Oscar thought for a moment, then replied, "Pearl divers! We can hire pearl divers to get the treasure for us."

As the discussion continued, Raven left her cabin and went up to the quarterdeck, where John stood. She stood beside her papa, took his arm, and held him close.

"What do you think, Papa?"

"About what?"

"About all this."

"If you mean life at sea, I like it."

"I mean, about this treasure. Is it worth it?"

"Do you mean, worth the lives we've already lost? Worth the lives we are likely to lose yet? I don't know. Is any treasure worth all that?"

"That's what I think, too."

They stood together silently for a time. Then, Raven offered, "I think of Mama a lot."

John smiled, "And what do you think about her?"

"I think she would not recognize me. I think she might not like what she sees in me. I'm not the little girl she played dolls with while she lay in bed sick. I'm not the little girl who shook with fear anytime there was a knock on our door. I'm not the little girl who hid in the bed under the covers whenever a storm came at night. I'm not the little girl who cut out paper flowers for Mama when she wasn't feeling well. I'm not the little girl she once knew."

"Oh, but you are; and so much more. You're still that kind little girl who cared for and loved your Mama. But, you're also brave, and smart, so capable. Raven, how many men follow you? I follow you. I depend on you. You are the most capable captain I have ever sailed with on these seas. I want never to sail with anyone else."

Raven said, "Sometimes I wonder what I would be doing if I weren't at sea. Would I be a lady dressed in fine clothes? Or would I live in a small flat like Mama, struggling to stay alive?"

"Your Mama was sick. It was a shame she had to die at such an early age. But, you have the world open to you. You can go anywhere you want and be anything you want. You are the Red Raven! So, fly high, my dear!"

Raven hugged Papa's arm tighter as she looked up at the escarpment. The cliff towered over their ship. It must have been at least two hundred feet high. The limestone side of the mountain wall was streaked with white stripes where the rain had made the limestone bleed. She saw several places that jutted out from the wall where birds had made their nests. Then, Raven saw a seagull fly toward the wall about halfway up and then disappear into the wall. The bird had evidently built her nest in a small pocket in the mountain's wall. Raven thought how nice it would be to fly anywhere she wanted.

Suddenly, Jeffrey appeared by her side. "Are you alright?" he asked.

"Yes. I just needed to get some fresh air."

"I know what you mean. Oscar was using up all the air in there."

Raven smiled. "He is just excited. I hope he won't be too disappointed if we don't find the treasure."

Jeffrey replied, "Ah, I think not finding the treasure is out of the question as far as he is concerned."

After a moment of silence, Jeffrey said, "Well, I will leave you two for now."

"Wait. Will you walk with me?"

"Yes, of course."

"Papa, will you excuse me?"

"Of course."

Raven and Jeffrey walked down the steps to the main deck along the starboard rail. The wind blew Raven's hair, whipping it into her face. She pulled her hair away from her face, then took Jeffrey's arm and stood close to him as they looked out over the water at the western horizon. The sun was about two hours away from disappearing into the western seascape, changing from its bright white light into pail hues of orange. It looked to Raven like a giant peach hovering in the sky.

Raven sent a boat to watch the first reef to her east. The other ships were covering all the other reefs around the island. She watched as the dory rowed away. In her mind, she wished them safety.

As the night sky closed in on them, Raven began to feel anxious. She looked at the sky often to see what kind of visibility they might have. Clouds moved in and out quickly as time passed. Twenty people stood at the rail watching the escarpment, searching the water below it, and watching the nearly full moon as it moved across the sky.

When the moon finally moved directly over the escarpment, Raven found she was holding her breath. Unfortunately, a large cloud covered the moon when it was directly over the reef. The cloud lingered and increased in size as time passed. When the cloud finally cleared, the moon was far to the west of their location.

Raven said to everyone, "Alright! We'll try again tomorrow night. Everyone get some sleep."

Oscar was dismayed as he slowly returned to his bunk to retire for the night. Unfortunately, the next night was no better. Again, clouds covered the moon most of the night, preventing light from shining upon the reef.

Rivera was frustrated beyond end. His demeanor changed drastically from a well-mannered, delightful businessman to an aggravated and impatient child. He was incorrigible. Raven tried encouraging him, saying, "Oscar, did you *really* think it would be so easy? We still have time. The moonlight will certainly be available one of the following three nights. Besides, tomorrow is the night of the full moon.

Rivera tried to calm himself. "Of course you are right, Raven. I apologize for my behavior. I'm sure you are correct. Tomorrow night will be best."

The following night was much different. The skies were clear, the stars twinkled like fireflies, and the moon in its full phase could not have been any brighter. Everyone onboard *Destiny* impatiently waited at various locations on the rail as they waited for the moon to move into its proper position so it could do whatever it was supposed to do. Raven and the others would alternate watching the moon and watching the cliffside. Raven had to occasionally drop her chin to her chest to stretch out the muscles in the back of her neck, which were tired from constantly looking up.

The moon's reflection moved through the ocean's surface, slowly creeping toward the ship and its occupants. The water seemed abnormally calm that night. The tide was at its lowest since Raven and her crew had come to the island. The reef seemed to come to life before their eyes; coral outcroppings were everywhere. Starfish, crabs, and octopus could be seen crawling along the tops of the coral, disappearing beneath into little caverns below the surface.

As the moon moved directly above them, Raven watched as what seemed to be a small pool appeared in the middle of the reef, about twelve feet from the original shoreline, which was now above the water's surface. The pool was black among the orange, green, and yellow corral that grew around it. However, as the moon continued to travel directly above *Destiny*, the blackness of the pool changed. The moon's reflection rested in the pool, which gave it a bright white illumination.

Everyone onboard the ship was amazed at the spectacle they witnessed as the cave they had hoped to find revealed itself to them. Raven could hear the oohs and ahhs of her crew as they stood around her, watching the reflection come to life. Raven looked up to see where the moon was in the sky during this phenomenal event. Looking up, she noticed something else: high above them on the escarpment wall where she had previously witnessed birds landing in a nest. Raven saw several birds circling an opening in the wall. Somehow, the moon's reflection had created a light that traveled from the pool up the inside of what could only be a cave, and it disrupted the birds as they roosted for the night.

Raven pointed and exclaimed, "Look!"

Everyone followed her gesture to a point on the wall where light was escaping from the cliffside.

Raven then said, "That is how we will enter the tunnel. We need to get up to the top and lower ourselves down."

Everyone began to cheer and celebrate as they realized the treasure could be a reality. Oscar, John, and Jeffrey all took turns hugging their captain as they celebrated their discovery of a point of entry into the cave they had hoped to find.

Someone fired a shot into the air in celebration, causing the four men occupying Raven's dory and watching the next reef to take notice. The men watched as everyone on the ship celebrated together. Pua, who was at the oars, said, "Come on! They have found the treasure. We must go back and help them celebrate."

One of his companions replied, "Yes, they are not doing it right."

They all laughed with excitement as they swiftly rowed back to the ship.

CHAPTER 27

On the island's north side, Attila stood on the quarterdeck of the schooner, *Lady Falcon*, and searched the shoreline. Nathan Coates reported to him as the sun rose above the eastern horizon.

"Any sign of them yet, Mr. Coates?"

"No sir, Captain."

"How about the other boats?"

"All other boats have reported in and are ready to sail."

"Who was on the last boat yet to arrive?"

"Mr. Pearson and his crew, Sir."

Attila paused before replying. "I think this is just what Raven had feared. All of Pearson's crew were white were they not?"

"Aye, Captain. And there's another man missing. Peter O'Neal, along with several long guns and pistols. I fear we have a mutiny, Sir."

"It appears so, Mr. Coates. Make ready to sail. We'll head to the southside and report to Raven."

"Aye, Captain."

Raven and her crew rose early the next morning even though they had made a long night of celebration. Everyone was anxious to start rescuing the treasure from the depths of the escarpment's cave.

She had her crew load one hundred-foot lengths of rope onto the dory, as well as grappling hooks, pulleys, and torches. Raven chose Hadari, Jeffrey, Mti wa Mvua, Pua ya Ndege, Mwindaji Chui, Mfugaji wa Mbuzi, Mwanamke Simba, and Jeremy to make the first trip to the island to begin the ascent up the escarpment. Raven brought Jeremy because of his diminutive stature, which might come in handy inside a cave, and she brought Simba because of her extraordinary fighting talent.

Jeremy was excited for the opportunity to go ashore. He was rarely allowed to leave the ship because of his age. But over the past two years, Raven had spent much time teaching the now fifteen-year-old to fight with bare hands or weapons.

Pua and Chui rowed the dory to a spot on the island just east of the escarpment. Once they reached the shore, Raven instructed Mfugaji and Mti to row back to the ship and bring the next group to shore. They would need many more men and women to retrieve the treasure from such a precarious location.

The first group carried the gear into the jungle with Hadari in the lead, cutting a trail with his machete. Traveling through the uncut jungle and uphill would be a challenging task. Most of the trek was made one step at a time, with long pauses in between while Hadari slashed at the vegetation blocking their path to the top of the escarpment. After an hour of cutting a path, Hadari had to relent his spot to Pua, who took over for a while. Monkeys and parrots watched from above as the group slowly entered the jungle. Jeremy continuously looked up into the trees, trying to spot one of the little primates. He hoped he could capture one so Captain Billings could have a companion. As they walked underneath a large Mahogany tree, Jeremy spotted a strange-looking creature hanging upside down from a limb. The animal had long grappling hook-like claws that it used to travel along the limb slowly.

"Look Raven!" he said as he pointed to the creature. "What is it?"

Raven replied, "I think it is a sloth. I have never seen one, but I have read about them. They are slow moving creatures; that's why they are called sloth."

"Are they a kind of monkey?"

"No, they are related to anteaters, I think."

Jeremy watched the creature, waiting for his next step. "Odds, bodkins!"

Raven smiled at Jeremy's amazement.

Six hours after their journey began, the group reached the top of the escarpment, which they were delighted to see was quite open. The landscape was scattered with large boulders of limestone that seemed to be crawling out of the top of the mountain. Small patches of grass and other vegetation cropped up here and there, but most of the area was bare.

Just as they made it into the clearing, the next group arrived at the top of the mountain with Mfugaji leading the way. Raven turned back to meet the second group and spoke to Mfugaji.

"Did you have any trouble?"

"No, Raven. The trail was quite easy for us."

Have any of the other ships arrived yet?"

"Not yet. But, we tied the dory up tight to the shore. They should be able to see where we landed when they near the beach. And your trail was easy to follow."

Raven smiled and said, "Alright, let's get to work."

Raven led the way as they approached the edge of the cliff. She carefully looked down over the edge but couldn't see anything except the sea beneath them. She decided to lay on her belly and told Jeffrey, "Hold onto me while I have a look."

Jeffrey grabbed a handful of the back of Raven's britches as she slowly crawled forward to look over the edge. Raven looked down over the cliff's edge and searched for the cave opening. She swiveled her head back and forth, searching for the cave. The side of the escarpment was so steep that she couldn't see an opening anywhere. Then, she noticed birds flying and circling an area below and to her right. The birds seemed to be flying out a very short distance from the side of the cliff, then disappearing into the escarpment.

"Pull me up."

Jeffery pulled her away from the cliff's edge and helped Raven to her feet.

"We need to move farther down about twenty yards. I think the cave is about fifty or sixty feet below."

Everyone followed Raven as she led them twenty yards to the west. Raven lay on a grassy spot at the edge, and Jeffrey grasped her britches again to steady her as she looked over the edge. As Raven crept forward, the ground beneath her suddenly gave way, and the top half of her body fell over the side. Raven yelled, "Ahh!"

Jeffrey pulled back on her waistband, trying to keep her from falling over the edge. Simba and Jeremy grabbed Raven's feet to help keep her from falling.

Jeffrey yelled, "Hang on, Raven! We've got you!"

The three pulled Raven to safety, and she sat on the ground, trying to catch her breath.

Jeffrey asked, "Are you alright?"

Raven nodded her head without looking up at Jeffrey. Then she said, "The good news is, the opening is directly below us, about seventy feet."

Jeffrey helped Raven to her feet as she looked around at her crew, watching her wide-eyed. When Raven saw the concern on everyone's faces, she said, "I'm alright now. Let's get started."

The first thing they did was build a tripod out of logs they cut from nearby trees. They attached a pulley to the tripod's top and ran a rope through it. Raven grabbed the rope's end and tied it around her waist, but Pua stopped her.

"Wait, Raven. Let me go first. We need you here to lead us. If it is safe, then you can follow."

Raven relented and allowed Pua to go down to the cave opening first. Pua tied the rope around him and allowed the loop to slip underneath his arms. Raven handed him a lit torch to carry with him as he went. He then began his descent down the side of the mountain. Slowly, six men allowed the rope to slip through the pulley so that Pua could work his way down to the cave's opening. Several minutes later, Pua reached the entrance.

He called out, "I'm here!"

Pua reached out with the torch to peer inside the opening but saw nothing but darkness. He carefully pulled himself into the cave for a closer look. Once inside, he loosened the rope and pulled it over his head, letting it drop outside the cave so it could be pulled back up to the top for the next person to be let down.

Raven wrapped herself into the rope loop and took a torch as she descended to the cave. Halfway down the side of the escarpment, she heard a scream from the cave. "Ahh!"

Suddenly, thousands of bats flew out of the cave and swarmed around the opening.

The scream continued, "Ahh!"

Bats continued to swarm below Raven as she descended. A black cloud of bats hovered below Raven just outside the cave. Bat squeaks filled the air as the winged mammals swarmed around the cave opening. Amid the squeaks, Raven could still hear Pua's screams.

After several minutes, the bats eventually flew away from the cave, looking for another place to continue their daytime sleep. Raven finally reached the cave opening and held her torch just inside as she peered into the darkness.

"Pua?!" she called out.

No one answered.

This time, she called out more loudly, "Pua!"

A quivering little voice like a mouse came back, "I am here."

Raven saw the flicker of light emitting from Pua's torch.

"Stay there, I'll come to you."

Raven crawled into the cave on all fours, searching for the frightened young man who had ventured in alone. As she crawled, something sticky clung to her hands. She lifted one of her hands to sniff the substance, then said, "Ugh! Bat guano!"

Raven continued to crawl, searching for Pua. Finally, the shaft opened into a larger room, where she found Pua huddled beside a wall.

"Pua, are you alright?"

"I think so. But, next time I will let you go first."

Raven chuckled to herself as she moved closer to Pua. She sat next to him and sat with her back to the cave's wall. She held out her torch and found they were now in a room that expanded twenty feet in all directions, and the ceiling was at least twenty feet high. From the ceiling, crystal stalactites hung, flickering in the torchlight. Raven surmised that the stalactites caused the light phenomenon when the moonlight struck the cave the previous night.

Raven stood up to inspect the room more carefully. When she reached the center of the room, she saw a wide opening in the floor that expanded twelve feet in diameter. She held her torch over the opening but couldn't see the bottom.

Just then, Jeffrey entered the room.

"Jeffrey, send word back, we're going to need more rope."

"Aye, Raven."

Jeffrey turned back and called to someone behind him, "Tell Hadari to send down more rope!"

A call came back, "Aye, Mr. Hamilton!"

Jeffrey stood up and noticed Pua still sitting against the cave wall. Jeffrey walked over to where he saw Raven's torch burning and asked her, "What happened to him?"

"He's upset. It seems he had an encounter with about a million bats."

"That will do it." Jeffrey replied.

Simba was the next to enter the cave, and then Jeremy fell close behind her. Shortly afterward, Chui dragged one hundred feet of rope behind him.

John stood at the helm, watching *Matilda* pull into the nearby bay. When John looked to the east, he also saw the *Nightingale* coming. Both ships pulled nearby and anchored closely to *Destiny*. Pharaoh and Alexander left their respective ships and joined John on the deck of *Raven's Destiny*.

Pharaoh asked John, "Did you have any luck?"

John replied, "We did," then pointed to the escarpment.

"They're up there now entering a cave that the moon pointed out to us."

Pharaoh and Alexander took out their spyglasses and pointed them at the side of the mountain, searching for any sign of Raven or her men. Pharaoh spotted it first, a man being let down the side of the mountain by rope. The man entered a black hole in the side of the mountain, then disappeared.

"I see it."

"Where?" asked Alexander.

"It is about one hundred feet from the bottom. Look for a rope hanging down from the top. A man just entered a hole in the side of the mountain."

Alexander looked again and *still* saw no one, but he finally spotted the rope being drawn back up to the top. He then watched as another man climbed over the cliff's edge and was lowered to a hole in the escarpment's side.

"I see it!"

Alexander looked at Pharaoh and said, "I am going up there."

"Yes, I want to go too."

They rowed back to their ships and gathered men to take to the island. *Matilda* took twenty men to the island, while the *Nightingale* sent twenty-two. They were loaded with equipment and supplies as they rowed down the coastline, searching for a landing place to go ashore.

Eventually, they found Raven's dory tied up on the beach, and all four boats made their way to that location to begin the trek up the mountain.

Edward Teach was concerned that the captain hadn't come back. It had been three days since Hornigold had taken a group ashore to search for Black Jack McGreavy. Teach knew it might take a while to search the area the young girl had called Treasure Beach, but his gut told him his captain was in danger.

"Wilmington, stay here and guard the ship. I'm going to search for Captain Hornigold. I fear something may have happened to him."

"Aye, Mr. Teach!"

Teach took an additional twenty men ashore to search for their missing captain and his crew of twenty. They left at dusk and carried torches to light their way. Teach followed the clearly marked path from the beach to a small village where several huts had been built. As they entered the village, the pirates were rudely greeted by thirty men holding primitive spears. One of the men approached the invaders and spoke in English.

"Why are you here? You are not welcome."

Teach replied, "We're looking for our men. They came here three days ago and haven't returned."

Warakabe replied, "We have seen no one for many days. No one has been here. Now leave or you will be killed."

Teach's eyes seemed to suddenly glow as he stared into the eyes of the one who spoke.

"You are lying, and you will tell me now where my men are or we will tear this village apart looking for them."

Warakabe said something in his native tongue, and his men immediately pointed their spears at the invaders. Teach looked like his eyes were going to explode from his head. He quickly reached for the pistol he held in his belt, cocked the hammer, and shot a man standing next to Warakabe.

The whole village gasped in terror as they watched one of their own fall to the ground, dead. Teach grabbed Warakabe by the throat and lifted him off the ground, then brought him closer to his face so that they were eye to eye. Teach replaced his pistol into his belt and drew another to point at Warakabe's head.

"Now, tell me where my men are or I'll kill every last one of you."

Warakabe lied again, saying, "We have seen no white men."

Teach pointed his second pistol at the older man sitting in front of the hut, who had been quiet but staring wide-eyed. He fired the pistol and watched the man fall over dead. The villagers cried out mournfully as they saw their new chief fall over dead.

Blackbeard shouted, "I can do this all night if you want!"

Warakabe tearfully replied, "No! No! Your men are in a cave not far from here. I will take you there."

"Tell your men to lay down their weapons."

Warakabe spoke to his people, and watched as every man laid down his spear and stepped back.

Teach ordered his men, "Tie them all up so they can't move. The women, too."

His men obeyed the order, and soon, everyone in the village except Warakabe was bound and immobile.

Teach then ordered, "Let's go! Two of you stay behind and make sure they don't move."

Warakabe led the way at gunpoint as they wound through the jungle, making their way to the cave where Hornigold and his men were imprisoned.

When they reached the boulder covering the cave entrance, Teach asked the man, "They've been in there three days?"

"Yes."

Teach motioned for his men to remove the boulder to get inside. Once the entrance was cleared, Teach forced Warakabe to lead the way into the cave. As they entered, called out, "Benjamin Hornigold! Hornigold, are you alive?"

No one answered. As torch after torch entered the cave, saw several men leaning against the cave walls alongside several skeletons of long-dead men. Teach spotted the captain in a corner of the cave and motioned for one of his men to see if Benjamin was still alive.

The man checked the captain and replied, "He's alive, Mr. Teach, but just."

"Let's give them some water and get them out of here."

After receiving water and a small amount of food, Hornigold and his men were able to get to their feet with some help.

"Thank you, Mr. Teach. I'm very happy to see you."

"Aye, Captain. I'm happy to see you ain't dead."

They all returned to the village and found everyone as they had left them. Teach shoved Warakaba over to the side to be with his villagers, then asked Benjamin, "May I have the honor, Sir?"

"By all means, Mr. Teach."

Teach looked at his men and ordered, "Fire the village! Kill the men!"

Enthusiastically, Teach's men set about torching all the newly built huts in the village. The men and women screamed in terror as they watched their homes go up in flames, again. Once all the huts were burning, the pirates moved toward the village men and began shooting and stabbing all of them. The women cried the more as they saw their men being put to death. Some of them began to wonder if they would be next to be killed. Then, they began to fear for their children. Although they were still stunned by the broad killing spree they had just witnessed, they were somewhat relieved to see the white men turn and walk away.

CHAPTER 28

Once Teach and Hornigold were back on the *Ranger,* Benjamin returned to his cabin to recover from his ordeal. As Blackbeard followed him inside, Benjamin said, "Edward, take us back to the Bahamas. We need more ships."

Pharaoh and Alexander led the groups through the jungle path Raven's group had cleared. The trek only took an hour for them to reach the top of the escarpment. In the distance, they spotted Hadari and others standing at the cliff's edge. Pharaoh called out to Hadari and waved. Hadari looked back and recognized Pharaoh, and waved back.

When the new groups reached Hadari, Pharaoh asked, "What have you discovered?"

Hadari replied, "The moonlight revealed a cave to us. It is about seventy feet below. Raven and some others are down there now, searching the cave. I have no idea what they have found."

Alexander asked, "What can we do to help?"

"Nothing yet. We are waiting for Raven's instructions. All I know is she sent word a few minutes ago to send down more rope, so they must be going down even farther into the mountain."

Pharaoh asked, "How many are down there?"

"Eight, so far."

Pharaoh said, "I want to go down there. Lower me down."

Hadari pulled up the rope and handed the loop to Pharaoh, who slipped it over his shoulders and around his chest. He then walked backward to begin his descent. Ten men held onto the rope to let Pharaoh down to the cave opening. Pharaoh was a large man, six feet three inches and at least two hundred and fifty pounds. All ten men strained against Pharaoh's weight as they lowered him to the cave opening. When he finally reached the cave's doorway, Pharaoh reached in to pull himself inside. He quickly found the opening to be too small for his large frame. No matter how he twisted or turned, his broad shoulders wouldn't fit into the small opening.

He finally called up, "It is no use! I can not fit into the cave. Pull me back up."

Hadari and the others quickly discovered ten men weren't enough to raise Pharaoh back up. Two more men were added to the rope line, pulling against the great warrior's weight as they pulled him back up.

Pharaoh stood up, removed the rope, and asked, "Who did Raven take with her?"

Hadari replied, "Jeffrey, Jeremy, Simba, Pua, Chui, . . ."

"I get it. They are all puny human beings."

Alexander asked, "Will I fit?"

"No, Alexander. Not even Hadari will fit. We will have to stay here and wait."

Alexander then suggested, "Well, maybe we should set up camp. We might be here for a long time."

Pharaoh replied, "That is a good idea."

Then, Pharaoh instructed his men to set up temporary shelters while they all waited to hear from Raven.

Chui handed Raven the rope, and she began making a loop at one end so that she could be lowered into the twelve-foot-wide hole in the cave's floor. Raven decided to check the depth, so she dropped her torch into the hole. They watched as the torch fell several feet. It continued to fall until the torch's light was the size of a chicken's egg.

Raven commented, "I hope a hundred feet of rope will be enough."

She looped the rope around her body, underneath her arms, and waited while Jeffrey, Simba, Chui, and Pua took the rope in their hands to lower her down. Jeremy watched Raven as she dropped herself over the edge and descended into the dark hole.

When she reached twenty feet below the surface of the cave floor, Raven found herself in nearly complete darkness. She looked up at her companions and saw Jeremy holding a dimly lit torch, looking over the edge. When she looked down, the torch's light had become the size of a grapefruit, although the light was still dim. Twenty more feet, and the grapefruit had become a coconut. The floor beneath her began to glow and brighten. Raven could finally see the rocky bottom of the cave floor. After eighteen more feet, Raven found herself standing on solid ground.

"Alright, I'm at the bottom!" she called up.

Jeffrey called down, "What do you see?"

Raven loosened the rope and let it drop to the floor, then picked up her torch and began to explore the bottom. She walked first to the nearest wall behind her. The wall was nearly smooth after centuries of water erosion down the fifty-eight-foot tube she had just descended. The walls sparkled against the light of her torch, giving Raven hope that there might be more to them than just Limestone.

"Gold? Diamonds?" she wondered.

The closer she got to the wall, the more she realized it was *simply* Limestone. She moved around the perimeter, searching for a place where the treasure might be hidden if there was indeed a treasure to be found. She turned around to look at the opposite walls and noticed two openings at the cave's far end. She stepped closer to the doorways and noticed they were both large enough for her to fit through reasonably easily.

She decided to check out the first cave on the right and entered with the torch leading the way. In the distance, she heard Jeffrey calling, "Raven, are you alright?"

"I'm fine! There are two tunnels here. Give me a moment to see if they lead anywhere."

Raven slowly continued into the first tunnel, swiping cobwebs away from her face as she walked through the darkness. Something crunched beneath her foot. She held the torch down to examine her boot and saw she had stepped on a small crab.

"Ugh!" she said, then continued to move along.

The tunnel sharply turned to the right, then again to the left. The height of the tunnel changed, becoming shorter. Raven had to duck as she continued to walk through. Another turn to the left, and then, the tunnel ended.

Raven sighed as she realized she had reached the end. She carefully turned and walked back the way she had come. She could hear Jeffrey calling her again as she returned to the tunnel's entrance. She chose not to respond until she safely reached the cavern where she had started.

"I'm alight, Jeffrey! The first tunnel was a dead end. I'm going to try the next one."

Jeffrey and the others impatiently waited as Raven moved to the second tunnel to continue her exploration. This tunnel was much wider at first, at least six feet wide. However, the height was only about five feet, meaning Raven had to crouch to walk through it.

As she entered the tunnel, she noticed her torch flicker. She momentarily paused as she realized fresh air was wafting into her face. With hope-filled anticipation, Raven walked farther into the tunnel. She made another sharp turn to the left, and the tunnel narrowed slightly, but not so much that the average man couldn't pass through it. Raven welcomed the fresh air entering her lungs through the tunnel, and she hastened her step, searching for the end.

The end came suddenly, but not as she had expected. Raven discovered another hole in the floor of the tunnel. A four-foot diameter hole that dropped straight down once again. She thought about dropping her torch down the hole again but thought better of it. If it were very deep, she would lose her light and find her way back to the cavern in total darkness. Instead, Raven chose to travel back through the tunnel to the cavern and get help.

When Raven finally reached the cavern she called up to Jeffrey, "Jeffrey? I found another tunnel that drops below this cavern floor. I'm going to need more rope and more torches."

Jeffrey answered, "That's fine. Pharaoh and Alexander's men have arrived to help. We will come down to join you until more rope can be brought into the cave."

Raven asked, "Any word from Attila?"

"Not yet. No one has seen them of late."

"Come on down, and bring some food if you have it."

"Right away," Jeffrey replied.

Attila sailed the *Falcon* eastward, searching for his missing dory. It had been more than twenty-four hours since he sent it to watch one of the buoy locations. It had not escaped his attention that a crew of only white men manned the missing dory. Five men were sent out on the boat together, led by the gunner, Ronald Pearson. Also missing were David Aldridge, James Hunter, Zachery Thacker, and John Clarke. Attila also discovered that one other white man, Peter O'Neal, was *also* missing from the *Falcon*. That meant all six white crew members of the *Lady Falcon* were now missing, along with one of the dories.

Attila sailed to the spot along the coast where his missing crew had been sent. The yellow buoy still floated in the water, but the dory was nowhere to be found. Attila decided to sail farther along the coast and look for his crew. The water had grown choppy along the coastline, so Attila feared the little boat might have been dashed against the rocks and lost. He had his lookouts watch for debris from a possibly fractured boat.

The *Lady Falcon* reached the end of the north shore, so Attila had his helmsman continue to follow the coastline heading south. He noticed black clouds rolling in as they eventually turned westward. The waters grew choppier as they crashed against the rocks along the shoreline.

Attila took out his spyglass and searched the western horizon. He spotted three ships moored ahead but couldn't tell if they were Raven's ships. They continued sailing forward, waiting for a closer look. They continued as they sailed along, looking for their missing dory.

A mile farther down the coast, Attila spotted the remains of a small boat. It was the correct shape and size of the missing dory. The remains of the little boat were scattered among the large rocks that protruded out of the coastline. Attila used his spyglass, hoping to find the missing men from his crew. Then he saw what he thought might be a body stretched out on a large rock about twenty feet from the beach.

Attila said to Nathan Coates, standing nearby, "Take a look. Does that look like one of our men?"

Coates looked through his spyglass at the body lying on the rocks. The body was somewhat mangled, its arms and legs turned in directions they shouldn't have. But the clothing was recognizable. The shirt was striped horizontally with red and white stripes. Only one man wore it on the *Lady Falcon*.

"That looks like James Hunter. He's the only one I know on this ship that wears a red and white shirt."

Attila asked, "One of the white men?"

"Aye. He was on the gun crew with Ronald Pearson."

Attila thought momentarily before saying, "He'll have to stay put until the water calms. We can't risk another boat trying to fetch the body of a possible mutineer."

Attila stared at the body momentarily before giving his order, "Continue sailing west."

"Aye, Attila!"

Raven stood outside the tunnel entrance, waiting for Jeffrey and the others to arrive. Moments later, Jeffrey, Simba, Pua, and Jeremy joined her on the cavern floor.

Jeffrey told Raven, "I left Chui above to direct the others as they arrive."

Raven nodded her agreement and then showed Jeffrey the tunnel she intended for them to explore.

"The one on the right is a dead end, but this one leads to another tunnel shaft."

Jeffrey asked, "Any idea how far down it goes?"

"Not yet. I was waiting for an extra torch before I tested it. I didn't want to get stuck in there without light."

Jeffrey told the others, "Stay here while we check it out. Wait for the rope."

Simba nodded and said, "Aye, Mr. Hamilton."

Jeffrey followed Raven into the tunnel as she wound back and forth until finally reaching the opening of another small cavern where the next tunnel shaft lay.

"Alright." Raven said. "Here it is."

She held her torch over the four-foot opening, letting it drop into the darkness below. They both watched as the torch seemed to travel in slow motion several feet below. Then, the torch stopped, and the light suddenly disappeared.

"Drat!" exclaimed Raven.

Jeffrey replied, "What do you think? Did the light extinguish or did it go so deep that we can't see it anymore?"

"I think it must have hit the water. I'm sure it fell at least fifty feet below before it hit bottom."

"Well, if that's the case, it could have hit a.puddle of water left from the high tide, or it could be the cavern below is filled with the sea."

Raven replied, "In either case, we need to get down there and see what lies beneath."

Jeffrey said, "I'll go back and see what's holding things up on that rope."

Jeffrey returned to the tunnel carrying his light, leaving Raven alone in the dark.

CHAPTER 29

Raven sat alone in the dark, her back to the cave wall. In the distance, she could hear water dripping from a ceiling somewhere. Suddenly, something crawled across her hand. She nervously shook it away and instinctively brushed her hands all over her body, trying to free anything crawling over her. Raven usually wasn't skittish, but the thought of the unknown gave her the creeps.

Raven tried to occupy her mind elsewhere while she waited. What would she do with unlimited riches? Would she still sail the seas? Maybe she would travel to parts of the world she had never heard of, somewhere in the Far East. She could sail the Pacific Ocean. She had once heard of Islands in the Pacific where money wasn't necessary. People only worried about basic needs: food, shelter, and clothing. Some didn't even worry about the clothing part. Raven wasn't too sure about the clothing part.

Jeffrey finally arrived with Simba, Pua, and Jeremy. Others from Pharaoh's and Alexander's crews were starting to file in behind throughout the tunnels and caverns. Pua dropped the rope on the cave's floor and began tying a loop so that someone could be lowered into the next cavern. Raven reached for the loop as Jeffrey stopped her, "Wouldn't you like me to check this one out?"

"I would not. No one is going into the unknown except me. I won't risk the lives of anyone else."

Jeffrey knew it was useless to argue with her, so he relented. Raven looped the rope around her and under her arms and began descending into the four-foot-wide hole. She held a new torch in her left hand as she traveled downward. The tunnel changed shape and size the farther she traveled, sometimes narrowing and sometimes widening. At its narrowest point, it was still at least three feet wide.

The air changed inside the tunnel as she moved downward. It became cooler and more moist. The dripping sound she had heard from above increased in volume as she moved closer and closer to its source. The tunnel walls were wet with condensation. When Raven finally landed at the bottom, she stood in three inches of water. She looked around the floor and found her torch, which she had dropped from above, searching for the cavern floor. The cavern itself was tiny compared to the others she had already explored. The room opened up into a room about twelve feet in diameter. The cavern's ceiling was about eight feet high at its highest point. More stalactites reached down from the ceiling, but they weren't very long like the ones she had seen in the cavern above. Raven searched for another tunnel or room within the cavern. Two more tunnels opened up away from the center of the cavern.

Raven called Jeffrey, "Jeffrey, can you come down?"

"Coming!" he answered.

Jeffrey waited until Simba and Pua joined him in the cavern so they could lower him down to join Raven. Jeffrey heard Raven's caution as he descended into the tunnel, "Be careful! The floor is filled with water."

"How deep?"

"Only about two or three inches."

When Jeffrey reached the bottom, he discovered that the water was deeper than Raven had said. He stood in six inches of water.

"I thought you said it was only a couple of inches?"

Raven came closer to where she saw Jeffrey's torch burning. "What are you . . ."

The water was twice as deep as when Raven arrived only moments ago.

"The tide is rising!" she exclaimed.

"We've got to get out of here before we're trapped."

Jeffrey called up to those waiting above and said, "Simba! We're coming back up!

Jeffrey looped the rope over Raven and prepared her for the ascent.

"Alright! Pull her up!" he called.

Immediately, Raven began rising up the tunnel. The ascent seemed slower to Raven than it had been coming down.

"Hurry up!"

After what seemed like an hour to Raven but had only been five minutes, Raven reached the tunnel opening and found Simba and Pua at the top. They pulled her out of the tunnel as she said, "Quickly! The tide is coming in. We've got to get Jeffrey out of there."

When the rope reached Jeffrey, the water had risen to his knees and filled his boots. He wrapped the loop around his body underneath his arms and tugged, letting them know he was ready for the ascent. With Raven's help, Simba and Pua pulled Jeffrey up to safety.

Raven asked, "How long have we been down here?"

Jeffrey replied, "I'm not sure, but if the tide is coming in it must be getting on toward dusk."

Raven said, "Let's get back to the top and we'll sort things out tomorrow,"

As they returned to the top of the escarpment, they left the ropes rolled up at the entrance of each tunnel shaft. Climbing up each rope took a little longer because they picked up additional people along the way who had begun their descent to meet Raven. Two hours passed by the time everyone reached the top of the escarpment.

When Raven exited the final tunnel and was pulled up, she looked out to the ocean and saw that the *Lady Falcon* had arrived. When she reached the cliff's edge, she saw Pharaoh and Alexander waiting for her.

"How long has Attila been here?"

Pharaoh replied, "Only about an hour."

"Is he on his way up?"

"I think not. Take a look."

Pharaoh handed Raven his spyglass so she could get a closer look. As she began looking, Pharaoh remarked, "He is missing one of his boats."

Raven took a closer look and realized Pharaoh was right. "Any idea why?"

"No, Raven."

Raven said, "Send one of your men down to him. Tell Attila I want him to report to me."

"Aye, Raven."

"Oh, and have your men bring up more torches and pitch. We're going to need as many as we can manage."

"Aye, Raven."

Hadari led the crews as they made camp for the night. They cut small trees to use as tent poles, and sail canvas was stretched between them. It would also allow them shade in the day as they stood working at the top of the escarpment out in the open.

Pharaoh, Mwindaji, Alexander, Jeffrey, Hadari, and Daktari sat with Raven around the campfire while waiting for their fish to be roasted over the open flame.

Hadari asked, "How was it down there?"

Raven replied, "Hadari, be glad you are a large man. It is dark, wet, sometimes cold, and there are tiny creatures crawling around.

"Hadari said, "Ah, Raven, that doesn't scare me."

"Really? I've seen you dance a jig trying to avoid a dragonfly swarming your head."

Everyone laughed aloud.

Pharaoh added, "And don't forget the snakes."

More laughter erupted. As things settled and the laughter ended, Hadari asked, "No, really. What is it like down there."

Raven replied, "Well that first drop is about sixty or seventy feet. The tunnel where the bats were living is small."

Pharaoh interrupted, "I can attest to that."

Everyone smiled.

"Then you have to crawl about twenty yards on your belly through bat guano."

Hadari remarked, "Oh! Is that what I smell?"

"Then it opens into a cavern about twenty feet wide with a twelve foot wide hole in the center. You go down the hole for about sixty feet where you find another cavern. There are two tunnels, one going to the right, and one to the left. The one on the right is a dead end. Follow the tunnel on the left for about fifteen yards until you find another small room with an another hole about four feet wide. Then down another fifty feet. This shaft is shaped like an hourglass, but it's no problem to get through. At the bottom is another cavern about twelve feet wide with two more tunnels.

That's as far as we got before the cavern started filling with water. We'll continue our search tomorrow early."

Alexander then said, "Well, let's eat our fish and get some sleep. The morning will come quickly."

Just as they started to bed down for the night, Attila and ten of his men arrived. Raven rose from her blanket and met Attila away from the others.

"Is everything alright?

Attila answered, "We have a boat missing and six of our men. We think we found the boat smashed on the rocks just east of here and one of the men lying on a rock is probably dead. The water was too choppy for us to rescue him."

Raven asked, "What of the others?"

"No sign of them. They could all be dead, or they might be somewhere on the island."

"How are the rest of your crew?"

"Nathan and Mchungaji have everything under control. No one will board the ship without being noticed."

"Good. Stay here for the night, then leave eight of your men in the morning when you go back. We'll need them to help here. When you get back tomorrow, send me another twenty men to help here. Hopefully, they will be needed to carry the treasure down to the beach so it can be loaded onto the ship."

Attila smiled at the thought and said, "My men look forward to it."

Five men huddled under a tall Mahogany tree in the twilight on the island's south side. David Aldridge suffered a wound at the back of his head, where he had scuffed against a rock as their boat was tossed against the shore. Ronald Pearson had received only minor injuries to his back, legs, and arms; scrapes against his skin left his body raw and burning while exposed to the salt water. Zachery Thacker had twisted his right ankle trying to climb out of the ocean when he slipped on a slick rock and landed in the hole within another rock. John Clarke somehow survived the turmoil after swallowing at least a gallon of salt water, which he, in turn, vomited once he reached dry land. Peter O'Neal only had the breath knocked out of him after being catapulted through the air when the small boat rammed into the rock that created James Hunter's demise.

James was only twenty when he joined Raven's crew a year and a half ago. He had been one of Matilda's original sailors when Raven captured her. Jeffrey Hamilton knew James well because Jeffrey had served as the ship's second mate when she was captured. James ended up on the *Lady Falcon* after the schooner was captured when Raven swapped crew members around to give the new ship some experienced sailors.

The men huddled together to warm themselves, not wanting to draw attention to themselves by building a fire. Aldridge asked, "Well Ronald, what do we do now? We have no boat."

Pearson replied, "That won't be a problem. The crews from the other ships have to get to the island. We'll take one of their boats when the time is right."

Zachery asked, "When will the time be right?"

"When I say it's right."

Peter asked, "What do we do until then?"

"We'll hold up here until we get dry and mended. They still haven't found the treasure, so there's no rush. Then we'll make our way to where they're landing their boats and wait for a chance to steal one. There's no need in us revealing ourselves until we let them do all the heavy lifting. Once the treasure is onboard the ships, we'll pick the easiest target and overtake them."

Clarke asked, "What about weapons? How are we going to overtake one of the ships without weapons?"

"We've got knives ain't we? And whatever else we can find along the way. Clubs, hammers, swords, guns; whatever we can get our hands on when we hit the ship."

David remarked, "I hope it's the *Falcon*. She's faster and smaller than the other ships, and she's got more guns."

"Aye," said Ronald. "But I think Raven will want to put all the treasure onboard *Destiny* before it's meted out. She'll have Mr. Hamilton divide it all up before any of the other ships sees a farthing."

CHAPTER 30

R aven woke early to bright sunlight beaming into her canvas shelter. Tropical birds, sea birds, and monkeys announced to the world that a new day had begun. She wiped the sleep from her eyes as she sat up on her bedroll and looked around to see who else might be awake. To her surprise, most of the camp was already bustling, preparing for the day.

Jeremy entered Raven's tent, holding a cup of tea.

"Good morning," he said as he handed Raven the cup.

"Good morning, Jeremy. Is everyone up?"

Jeremy smiled as he replied, "Everyone but you."

"Yes, well, I needed some extra sleep after a day of crawling and climbing throughout the mountain."

Jeremy chuckled as he replied, "I don't doubt that. I wanted to wake you earlier, but Mr. Hamilton told me to let you sleep."

Raven sipped from her tea, then asked, "What, no crumpets?"

"Would my lady settle for some fresh mango?"

"Ooh, yes, please."

As Raven nibbled on the mango and sipped her tea, she asked, "Is everyone here and ready to get started?"

"Attila's men haven't arrived yet, but everyone else is ready whenever you are."

Raven shoved the last bite of mango into her mouth and replied while chewing, "Well if they are waiting on me, they are stumbling backward."

She handed Jeremy the empty tea cup and strolled to the tripod where everyone else had gathered. "Good morning," she said to all.

Everyone replied a collective, "*Good morning, Raven.*"

"Let's get started, shall we?"

Raven took the rope and looped it under her arms in preparation for the descent of the cliff. She walked to the cliff's edge, then turned with her back to the sea and began climbing downward over the side with her crew holding the rope taut, her right hand on the rope while the torch was in her left. Raven walked backward down the mountainside with her body parallel to the ground below. Her crew released the rope a handful at a time, allowing her descent. Raven felt a sensation of floating on air as the wind blew through her hair. She glanced over her shoulder to see nothing but the rope holding her up. Step by step, she descended, and seventy feet later, she reached the cave.

Raven peered into the tunnel opening as she waved her torch around inside, looking for the bats that had occupied the crevasse the day before. She listened inside for any movement or communication from the leathery little creatures who climbed the walls and defecated on the cave floor. Satisfied that, for now, it was safe, Raven pulled herself inside the tunnel. She removed the rope and let it drop so it could be pulled back up and used to bring down the next traveler.

Raven crawled through the tunnel, sometimes on her belly, sometimes on her knees. The bat guano was still there, and the smell was, once again, overwhelming. Then suddenly, she heard the screeching of the winged creatures as they exploded into a swarm of frenzy, flying straight to her and through the tunnel. Raven ducked and covered her head, waiting for the swarm to subside.

Everyone else watched from above as the bevy of bats flew out of the mountainside and twisted around overhead before disappearing into the jungle. Pua shuddered as he watched the bats, then said, "I'm glad she went first this time."

One by one, Raven's people followed her into the darkness of the mountain, Jeffrey first, then Simba, Jeremy, Pua, and on and on. By the time Attila's men had arrived, twenty people had already entered the caves to continue their search for the treasure.

Twenty more men entered the cave, following the others into darkness and the unknown. The new men were nervous as they descended the escarpment exterior and entered the cave opening. Each man held a torch, which eased their fears but didn't completely extinguish their questions about the dark unknown. No one had warned them of the sticky, smelly, tar-like substance they would be crawling through as they made their way twenty feet back into the mountain.

Raven waited for Jeffrey at the edge of the first cavern. The rope they had used the previous day was waiting for them at the edge of the twelve-foot hole in the cavern floor. Raven secured the rope around herself and waited for Jeffrey. Jeffrey lowered Raven fifty-eight feet into the blackness of the hole, then waited for Simba and Jeremy to join him so they could lower him in to join Raven.

Raven waited for Jeffrey at the left doorway, and they traveled together, weaving their way to the next small cavern. The next rope lay on the floor at the four-foot opening, which would send them another fifty feet down.

Again, Jeffrey waited for Simba and Jeremy to join him so they could lower him down through the hourglass-shaped shaft. Once he arrived and joined Raven, they stood before the two remaining tunnel openings that Raven had yet to explore: Jeffrey on the left and Raven on the right.

Jeffrey walked through the opening cautiously with his torch in front of him. He kept his free hand against the rough wall, feeling his way as he stepped forward, half-step by half-step. The tunnel abruptly turned left after twenty feet. Jeffrey continued another forty feet slowly. The tunnel narrowed until it was barely wide enough for Jeffrey to squeeze through, then opened back up. Then, suddenly, the floor ended. Another hole opened up below him, but only about eighteen inches wide. Seeing there would be no way through, Jeffrey muttered, "*I've been kimbawed!*" His heart dropped as he turned to walk back and find Raven.

When Jeffrey reached the entrance to his tunnel, he found Simba, Jeremy, and Pua waiting for him.

Jeremy asked, "Did you find anything, Mr. Hamilton?"

"Not even a cat's whisker," he replied.
Then Jeffrey asked, "Has Raven made it back?"

"No, Mr. Hamilton," Jeremy replied.
"Well then, let's have a look, shall we? Pua, stay here until someone comes to relieve you. Then follow along."

"Aye, Mr. Hamilton."

Jeffrey, Simba, and Jeremy entered the second cave to find Raven. The tunnel was six feet wide in most areas, allowing easy travel. Each held their torch above their heads as they traveled through. The cave's floor was by no means level; it tilted first to the left, then to the right, winding back and forth, turning this way, then that, then this again. Then, the trail opened to a gaping room below and to their right. The walkway traveled downward with only a space of three feet wide for them to navigate across. The ledge began to spiral downward to the right, sweeping a wide turn for one hundred yards, ending at the bottom into a room that spanned more than one hundred feet across. Jeffrey looked to his right as he walked down the spiral trail and saw Raven's torch burning in the distance below. The light was dim and didn't give enough illumination for him to see beyond Raven's presence.

When the three finally reached Raven at the bottom of the cavern, they found her staring at something they had not yet seen. The cavern floor stretched for about twenty yards in every direction but was surrounded by a pool of water except for the strip of rock that Jeffrey and the others had just walked across to join their captain.

They all stood next to Raven and looked across the pool that wound around the tiny island on which they stood. Across the circular pool was a shelf of flat rock circling the cavern. Lining the walls of the cavern were sea chest after sea chest, overflowing with gold and silver trinkets, broaches filled with emeralds, rubies, diamonds and sapphires, gold and silver coins, and larger items that had been crafted from gold or silver.

Raven and her crew stood in awe of the great riches that had been hidden so many feet deep in the belly of the mountain. As Raven slowly turned, looking at every inch of the cavern, she finally noticed an opening at one end where the water entered the cave. As she walked closer to examine the doorway, she realized this was the opening she had seen from her ship on the night of the full moon. The cave opening in the water was large enough to get a small boat through, but dealing with the tides would be difficult. The large boulders outside the cave lining the reef would make traveling to collect the treasure treacherous. The alternative was to carry everything back up the mountain from the inside: time-consuming and treacherous.

Raven started counting the sea chests that rested on the stone shelf. The chests were of various sizes, ranging from small ones, about twelve inches by eight inches, to larger ones, two feet by three feet by two feet tall. The gold filling the larger chest would be much too heavy for them to carry up to the top, so Raven decided burlap sacks might be the best way to carry out the treasure.

Raven asked Jeffrey, "How much treasure do you estimate?"

"Raven, I wouldn't know where to begin a guess. I've never seen so much gold in one place in my entire life. I doubt the king himself has seen this much gold."

More of Raven's crew found their way into the belly of the mountain, where the treasure rested. Soon, there was so much torchlight in the room that Raven and the others could see the expanse of the treasure all at once and grew more in awe of it.

"Jeffrey, send word up to my captains. We need every burlap sack onboard the ships. Send them all down here along with grappling hooks at each ascension point. We'll set up a relay to carry the sacks up to the top of the mountain, then down to the beach where the dories are anchored, then out to *Destiny*. We'll carry the sea chests out last once they have been emptied. Let's get to it."

"Aye, Raven."

Word quickly went up the chain by word of mouth until it reached Hadari, Pharaoh, and Alexander, who had been waiting impatiently at the top. The three men danced in celebration like three young schoolgirls as they heard the news that the treasure had been found.

Pharaoh sent word back to *Destiny* and the other ships that the treasure had been found, so the ships should send the gear they would need to bring it out of the mountain's depths. News traveled slowly along the chain and even slower to the ships that waited in the ocean.

Oscar Rivera stood next to John Ashworth on *Destiny's* quarterdeck as word of the treasure was relayed to them. They, too, jumped and celebrated together. Soon, all the ships received the news and began sending the supplies and gear needed to retrieve the treasure from the mountain.

Two hours later, Raven received the first burlap sack, and her people began filling it with gold and silver. The sacks usually carried about fifty pounds of grain but now held between seventy-five to one hundred pounds of treasure.

Once a sack was filled, they tied it up with small woven rope, and it was carried to the first ascension point, where it was hooked with a grappler and raised from the depths of the cave. Forty men and women lined up like a bucket brigade at a house fire to move the treasure up through the mountain tunnels and caverns. It took forty-five minutes for a treasure sack to reach the top of the mountain. The last section, the final twenty yards before exiting the cave, took the longest time because the sack had to be dragged behind the carrier while crawling on his belly. Once pulled up the outside of the mountain escarpment, the sacks were stacked near the tents to await transport to *Destiny*. Four men were placed at the stack to guard the treasure should someone try to steal any of it, whether it be someone from Raven's crew with sticky fingers or pirates from another outfit who might also be looking for Black Jack's treasure.

That first night of removing the treasure, Raven went up top to sleep. While she was eating her evening meal, she beckoned Pharaoh and Alexander to join her. When they sat beside her, eating their supper, Raven spoke to them quietly so no one else could hear.

"I need some coconuts."

Confused by her request, Alexander asked, "Did you say coconuts?"

Raven looked into his eyes and nodded.

"How many?"

"Lots and lots of them. Stack them over there."

CHAPTER 31

The moon and stars were hidden by dark clouds as Ronald Pearson and his cohorts sneaked to the part of the beach where the dories were anchored. They were ragged and still wounded days after having crashed their boat on that very shore two weeks before.

They survived on the fruit they foraged from the jungle trees and small sea creatures, such as crabs and sea turtles, that had wandered onto the shore. After having rested and recovered, they were ready to implement Pearson's plan.

Pearson jumped into one of the boats Raven's men left at the shore, grabbing the oars as he sat in the middle of the tiny vessel. Then Aldridge and Thacker joined him while Clarke and O'Neal pushed the boat into the water before jumping into the boat as well.

They quietly rowed farther east along the shore, choosing a spot where they could hide the boat until it was time to move onto *Destiny*, which had been loaded with the treasure. Pearson guessed that most of *Destiny*'s crew would be ashore helping to collect the treasure from the island. If they could row over to her at night without being detected before the crew returned, Pearson and the others could overtake the remaining crew and steal the ship away.

David Aldridge had been sent two nights earlier to spy on Raven's crew at their camp on top of the escarpment. From his hiding place, Aldridge could see that the treasure had been found and was being stacked in the middle of the clearing, close to the area where sleeping quarters had been set up.

He watched as four men stood constantly watching over the treasure as it was brought up from the side of the mountain. David tried to count the sacks as they were stacked, but he had yet to learn how many had already been set in the stack.

Pearson sent Aldridge back each night to monitor the camp and report when he thought they might be ready to transport the treasure to *Destiny*.

Spirits were high as everyone worked together, moving the treasure up to the top of the mountain. The Africans broke out in song as they moved the sacks of treasure upward through the darkness of the mountain's caverns and tunnels.

"Kunguru Mwekundu anasafiri juu ya maji
(The Red Raven sails on the water)
Yeye ni shujaa hodari
(She is a mighty warrior)
Ametutajirisha kwa hazina
(She has made us rich with treasure)
Tunakuheshimu Kunguru Mwekundu
(We honor you, the Red Raven)
Kunguru mwekundu ametutajirisha
(The Red Raven has made us rich)
Kunguru ametutajirisha.

(The Raven has made us rich.)"

Raven was pleased to hear her people sing again. It seemed such a long time since they had sung while doing their work. Their song echoed throughout the mountain caves. She and Jeffrey stood by and watched the men and women as they sacked up the treasure and lifted it out of the cave's depths. Jeffrey kept a log of everything being placed in the sacks so that they could be tallied and distributed in the proper shares. Once the treasure was loaded onto *Destiny*, Jeffrey and the quartermasters from the other ships would divide it up, twenty-five percent being set aside for Señor Rivera. The rest would be divided into their proper shares to all the crew and distributed.

One hundred fifty-two sacks were eventually carried up from the mountain's depths. They worked ten hours a day for eleven days before all the treasure had been extracted from the belly of the mountain. The sea chests were brought up after the sacks were stacked above ground. Thirty-five chests could be used to store either part of the treasure or other items Raven might need. Raven decided to give each of her officers one of the larger chests so they might have a secure place to store their shares. It took an additional day to bring up all the chests.

Twelve days after discovering Black Jack's treasure, Raven and her crew began carrying it down to the ten dories still available to her. Six boats had been anchored on the island, so they were loaded first. Only five were present when Raven and the others arrived.

"Jeffrey, were there not six boats here? Where is the other boat?"

"I don't know, Raven. Maybe it was taken back to resupply at some point."

Raven's thoughts rolled through her head as she suspected something else was happening here.

"Alright then, keep a sharp eye out. Remember, we've got some missing sailors out there somewhere."

"Aye, Raven."

Ten sacks of treasure were placed on each boat, and two men, rowing over to *Destiny*, would transfer the treasure to the larger ship. Jeffrey rode along with the first dory to ensure the treasure amount never changed as it was loaded onto *Destiny*.

Raven instructed, "Jeffrey, have all the other dories sent back to help out here."

Jeffrey waved back to her and replied, "Aye, Raven."

Jeffrey was glad to see that the sea was calm that day. The water looked more like a sheet of glass than the ocean as they effortlessly glided through the sea. As they reached *Destiny*, John met them at the starboard side to welcome them back. Ten men besides John were aboard *Destiny* as Jeffrey approached them. All eyes were upon the dories as they rowed to the ship.

Meanwhile, on the port side, another boat approached from the west. No one spotted the dory as it came alongside *Destiny*. Everyone on the other three ships was also watching Jeffrey and his boats rather than watching for the enemy craft that might approach.

Ronald Pearson led his tiny band of bandits over the port-side rail. They hid behind the forecastle while the sacks were being loaded onboard. Each man brandished a knife, but they also found belaying pins they could use as clubs if needed.

As Jeffrey boarded *Destiny*, he shook hands with John, who congratulated Jeffrey and the others for a job well done.

Jeffrey then said, "Raven has requested all available dories to go to the island to transport the treasure."

"I'll signal them right away."

Mr. Greer joined them on the quarterdeck and asked Jeffrey, "Is all well? Has anyone been injured?"

"Nay, Doctor. All is well. Surprisingly so, since we have held ourselves in deep peril these several days."

"Glad to hear it, Jeffrey. I look forward to seeing what all of you have discovered and brought forth."

The first fifty sacks were brought onboard and stacked on the main deck while Jeffrey tallied all that had been delivered. As soon as all had been loaded onto the ship, the ten men making the delivery shoved away from the ship and rowed back to the island.

Jeffrey and John stood by the pile of sacks on the main deck, admiring the large amount already placed on the ship.

John asked, "How much more is there?"

"There are 152 sacks of treasure, so if all goes well, the rest should be loaded by twilight.

"My, my! That much! We should all be able to retire after this."

Jeffrey smiled and asked, "Where would you go if you could retire? Back to England?"

"Oh, no. I'd find me some island here in the Caribbean and live on the beach. Grow old without a care in the world. How 'bout you?"

Jeffrey shrugged, then said, "I don't know. I'm a little young to retire yet. There's still a lot of the world I haven't seen yet. Besides, I doubt our captain is ready to retire no matter how much gold she has."

"Yes, I'd say you're right. Gold is only part of her mission. There are more important things she wants to accomplish in life. I've never known anyone so passionate about a cause in my life, except maybe her mother."

"Really? Raven's mother was passionate? About what?"

"Mostly about poor, motherless children. She would skip a meal very often so that street orphans could have a morsel to split among themselves. We had very little when she was alive, but what we had, she was willing to give away. I think that's why she died at such an early age. She never ate enough to keep her health."

"Does Raven know that?"

"I doubt it. She never let on to Raven about it. As far as Raven knows, her mother died of typhus. And, she did, but she could have overcome her illness quite possibly if she would have taken better care of herself."

Suddenly, five men came out of hiding behind the forecastle brandishing knives.

"Hold it right there, gentlemen."

Ronald Pearson stood close by, with Aldridge, O'Neal, Clarke, and Thacker on each side of him. Jeffrey and John raised their hands but didn't seem overly concerned with the would-be thieves.

John said, "Well, Pearson. We wondered when you might show your mutinous face. Where have you all been hiding these past weeks?"

"Oh, we've been nearby, don't you worry. Just waiting for the right time to collect our pay."

Jeffrey asked, "What pay?"

Pearson pointed at the burlap sacks and replied, "This pay. The treasure."

"Oh, this treasure? Oh, alright. Go ahead. Open it up, let's see what you've won shall we."

Pearson looked confused as he looked down at the pile of burlap on the deck. He said, "Go ahead, Zachery. Open one up. Let's see what we've got here."

Thacker took his knife and cut the small rope of one of the sacks to open it. He then dumped the sack over to empty its contents. Out onto the deck rolled twenty or more green coconuts.

The thieves stared, confused and angry.

Pearson demanded, "Check the others!"

All four of Pearson's compatriots cut open all fifty sacks, hoping that at least one contained gold.

"Say, what is this?" Pearson asked.

"This is your treasure, Mr. Pearson. Compliments of the Red Raven." Jeffrey replied.

Pearson and the others decided to attack Jeffrey and John because of the farce they had been led to. However, the ship rocked to its port, causing the coconuts to roll across the deck and underfoot of the would-be attackers. They tripped and fell just in time to be greeted by twenty men climbing aboard *Destiny* from all sides, including Raven, Pharaoh, Attila, and Alexander. Raven quickly approached Pearson and held him to the deck at the point of her sword.

"Mr. Pearson, I see you finally decided to come back to us. I'm so happy to see you. We've missed you, terribly."

Ronald lay on the deck, snarling and sneering as Raven spoke. "What have you been doing these past weeks?"

"Honestly, Captain Raven, we've been trying to get back to the *Lady Falcon* but our boat ran aground. We were just trying to get back to our duties."

The other men nodded in agreement to Pearson.

Raven challenged, "So, not only are you a thief, but a liar as well."

"No, Captain. It's the truth I tell you. Right, lads?"

"*Right.*" they all agreed.

"Hmm, cowards, too."

Raven announced, "I hate cowards worse than I hate thieves and liars."

Jeffrey asked, "What should we do with them?"

"Shackle them and stow them in the lower deck for now. I'll deal with them later. We have treasure to load, now."

CHAPTER 32

Once the prisoners were secured below decks, Raven set about having the treasure transferred to *Destiny* to be appropriately divided and stored away for the voyage back to Port St. Felix. As the treasure was brought onboard *Destiny*, Jeffrey, his quartermasters, and Señor Rivera counted and divided it into fourths. Rivera's fourth was taken to the lowest deck and stored separately from all other stores. It was locked away, and only Raven and Rivera had a key to the lock.

The remaining treasure was divided in half: half to be divided amongst the crew and officers and half to be held aside to replenish supplies for the ships when needed. Each ship would be given a portion of the treasure to use as cash on hand should it be separated from the rest of the fleet. Jeffrey then meted out the proper shares to each ship according to how many men or women were aboard each ship, as well as the officers.

The *Lady Falcon* carried the most crew to operate the guns aboard her, and since they were now short six sailors, Raven needed to make changes again to her crew. She transferred Henry Bleaker from *Matilda* to the *Lady Falcon* to serve as gunnery mate. Bleaker had served Raven well as a spy but was also proficient at artillery commands. It was a promotion for Bleaker to a mate's position so he would receive a mate's share based on the Articles of Code.

Jeffrey divided 12,160 pounds of treasure into shares, giving Rivera's portion through gold and silver items, such as urns, platters, and flatware. He reserved coinage for the men, making it easier for them to stow with their personal gear and more accessible for them to spend once they reached a destination that allowed them free time.

He dispersed the treasure among the quartermasters of each ship, and the dories transferred it over. All the men and women excitedly gathered on the main decks of the ships and waited for their names to be called out to receive their share.

According to the Articles of Code Raven's crew adopted initially, the treasure was portioned out as follows.

The captain is to have two whole shares; the first and second mates are to have one share and one half; the doctor, junior officers, gunner, and boatswain, one share and one quarter; and all other crew, one share.

Although still retaining the title of captain instead of commodore, Raven agreed to accept three shares instead of two. All the officers voted on this, and it passed unanimously. Therefore, Raven received £11,564.16. Pharaoh, Alexander, and Attila each received £7,709.44. As junior officers, John Ashworth, Hadari, Mwindaji, Kiboko, Dakari, Mkimbiaji, Nathan Coates, and Mchungaji each received £5,782.08. Jeffrey Hamilton, Mr. Greer, and Henry Bleaker each received £4,818.40. Every other man on each ship received £3,854.72 pay for their efforts in the search for the treasure. The average pay for a sailor on a merchant ship was only £30 per voyage, and sometimes that voyage might take more than a year to complete.

After receiving their shares, everyone celebrated on each of the ships. Several casks of rum and ale were brought out to allow everyone to imbibe for the special occasion. Raven and her captains allowed everyone to drink until they passed out. The officers partook in the rum and ale but remained sober to watch over the ships.

Five men sat shackled together in the lowermost deck of *Destiny* while the celebration took place. Pearson seethed in anger as he heard the muffled sounds of celebration above. Each of his men took their turn at chastising him for getting them into their predicament.

Thacker said, "That could be us up there."

Aldridge added, "It should be us up there."

John Clarke asked, "Got any ideas how we're going to get out of this mess?"

O'Neal asked, "Yeah, what are they going to do with us, do you think?"

Ronald Pearson said nothing. He stared into the darkness as his temper boiled.

The party finally ended three hours past midnight. Men and women were passed out in their bunks, lying on the quarterdeck and the main deck, and one even managed to climb up to the crow's nest, where he passed out with his feet hanging out of the top of the nest.

Once daylight came, the officers encouraged the inebriated sailors to make their way down into their bunks so the sun wouldn't bake them to death. Raven and the officers took turns keeping watch and sleeping while the crew recovered from the party.

At midday, Raven escorted Jeremy to the lowermost deck to feed the prisoners. Jeremy passed out a portion of bread and a cup of water to each of them. As Raven approached them, Zachery Thacker asked, "Please, Captain, what do you intend to do with us?"

"I haven't decided, yet."

Aldridge said, "Please don't kill us, Captain. We had no intention of harm. We just wanted the treasure. We didn't hurt no one."

"What about, Hunter. You got him killed, didn't you?"

"That weren't our fault. The sea took him," cried O'Neal. "Besides it was all Pearson's idea. We just went along with him. We weren't gonna kill no one."

"O'Neal, when you sleep with pigs, you're bound to get muddy. How much treasure do you think you would have been expecting per man if you had been successful?"

Clarke replied, "I was hoping to get enough to buy my own farm somewhere. Maybe £200?"

"What about you, O'Neal. How much were you hoping for?"

"Oh, I thought I might get as much as £500. I could retire with that."

Raven asked Jeremy, "Jeremy, how much was your share in the treasure?"

Jeremy smiled and replied, "Almost £3,900, Raven."

"Blimey!" Aldridge replied. What's a boy like you gonna do with all that money?"

Jeremy shrugged and replied, "I dunno, maybe buy a monkey?"

Raven smiled at Jeremy's innocence before saying, "Let's go, Jeremy. I'm sure these lads have a lot to think about."

Jeremy and Raven climbed onto the main deck, enjoying the bright sunlight and the calm wind kissing their faces.

Jeremy asked, "What do you intend to do with them, Raven?"

"I dunno. What do you think I should do with them?"

Jeremy thought momentarily and then asked, "Well, they didn't kill anyone, did they? Maybe not getting a share in the treasure is punishment enough."

"You're forgetting, Mr. Hunter was killed due to their actions. Tell me, do you think you could ever trust these men again? I can't."

"Well, will they be killed?"

"I don't know. I think I'll leave it up to the captains to determine what punishment these men deserve."

The next morning, all the ships were called together to decide the fate of Ronald Pearson and his men. The ships were all tied together so everyone onboard could hear the proceedings. Pharaoh, Attila, and Alexander moved on to *Raven's Destiny* for the trial.

Raven had the accused brought up from below decks and placed on the quarterdeck so everyone from all four ships could view them. Some men climbed the riggings of their ships to get a better look, while others gathered at the rails to get as close as possible.

Raven began speaking to the crowd, "These five men are accused of mutiny, theft, and murder. Witnesses will be brought forth to testify of their deeds. We begin with Captain Attila."

Attila stepped forward to the rail on the quarterdeck to give testimony.

"Captain Attila, when did you suspect something was wrong with this group of men?"

"When you told me."

"And, what did I tell you?"

"You said I should put all the white men in the same boat when we were searching for the treasure."

"Did I tell you why you should put them in a boat together?"

"Aye, you suspected they were up to something and you wanted them together so it would be easier to keep an eye on them."

"Was there a time when you realized my suspicions might be warranted?"

"Yes, about two weeks ago when we were watching the buoy locations to try to find the correct location of the treasure. The boat that the white men were using never came back. All the other boats came back at the appointed time. We did not see the white men's boat until we came to meet with you. We saw the boat crashed against a big rock. James Hunter's body lay on the rocks. We could only assume he was dead. We could not retrieve his body because the sea was too rough."

"Thank you, Captain. Do any of the other captains have a question for Captain Attila for the record?"

Both Pharaoh and Alexander shook their heads. Neither would ask the question if they had it. They both had too much respect for Raven to question her judgment or her ability to find the truth.

The two younger men, Zachery Thacker and Peter O'Neal quivered in their boots as they stood at the rail. O'Neal began crying openly. Pearson sneered at the boy and said, "Stop it, you nit! You think they're going to pity us?"

Raven asked so everyone could hear, "Do any of you men have anything to say for yourselves?"

Thacker replied, "It was all Pearson, Captain! None of us wanted to do it. He said he'd slit the throat of the first man who crossed him. That's what happened to James. James wanted out. Said he'd have no part in going against you."

"Shut up!" exclaimed Pearson.

"But Pearson cut his throat when James tried to leave the boat. Then Pearson threw him out of the boat onto the rocks. Once we got to shore, Pearson destroyed the boat and drifted the pieces into the sea to make it look like an accident."

"Shut up! Shut up! Shut up!"

Raven looked to the others and asked, "Is this true?"

One by one, the men replied, "*Aye, Captain.*"

"Pearson?"

"No, it's not true! These nits are trying to lay it all on me. It was all Hunter's idea!"

Raven replied, "I doubt that very seriously."

Raven looked at her captains and asked, "Have you any more questions?"

Each shook his head without saying anything.

"Very well. Ronald Pearson, I find you guilty of sedition, attempted thievery, theft of one of my boats, and murder."

She looked at Hadari and said, "Take him away and hang him from the yardarm."

Hadari and John took Pearson by the arm and dragged him down to the main deck. Raven's crew murmured and sneered at Pearson as he was led through the crowd to the main mast. Hadari took a rope and made a noose, then swung the noose over the yardarm and grabbed it as it fell back down to him after looping itself over. Hadari loosened the noose, slipped it over Pearson's head and around his neck, and then tightened it. Hadari then looked to Raven for instructions.

Raven nodded. Hadari and John began pulling on the rope, lifting Pearson into the air as he struggled against it. He widened his eyes as he realized he couldn't breathe. He couldn't cough, and he couldn't talk. He kicked his feet, trying to free himself or at least find relief. His face turned red, and he drooled as he gritted his teeth. His body convulsed and rocked. Everyone watched:

some seemed to enjoy the spectacle, while others gasped in horror. Zachery Thacker cried as he watched the man die. He cried out of fear and regret. He cried at the horror that he would be next. He lost control of himself and his bladder. He urinated on himself as he continued to watch. Peter O'Neal also cried as he watched. He had never seen anyone hanged before, and the thought that he would be next frightened him so that he lost control of not only his bladder but also his bowels, making an awful mess of his trousers.

When Pearson's body finally stopped struggling, Raven nodded to Mr. Greer to check to see if the man had died. Greer felt in the wrist of the body as it hung from the yardarm. After a few seconds, Greer turned and nodded to Raven, indicating Pearson was dead.

"Take him down, remove his shackles, and throw him into the sea. Let him sleep with Davey Jones. He doesn't deserve a proper burial."

Raven then turned to the other four men standing at the rail on the quarterdeck. The two younger men were still crying. Aldridge and Clarke wore solemn looks on their faces as if knowing what their fate would be now. Raven walked down the line of men, looking each one in the eyes as she did. She turned to the crowd and announced, "I'm still not sure how much these four men are guilty of. I feel positive that the younger two had very little, if anything to do in this matter. I think David Aldridge and you, John Clarke, had more to do with it than you are admitting to."

She then announced so everyone could hear, "Each of these men will be given the benefit of the doubt. They will be separated to serve on separate ships and each will be demoted to cabin boy. They will be given the dirtiest, menial jobs available on the ship. They are not to be mistreated, and they are not to be spoken to unless it is to instruct them to do a job. If they are spoken to derisively, the guilty person will trade places with him. Once we reach Port St. Felix, they will be allowed to leave and seek other employment should they wish. Until then, no one will harm them. Is that clear?"

A low rumble traveled through the crowd.

"I said, IS THAT CLEAR?"

"*Aye, Raven!*"

CHAPTER 33

Raven made the assignments, sending Peter O'Neal back to the *Lady Falcon*, John Clarke to serve on *Matilda*, and David Aldridge to the *Nightingale*. Zachery Thacker would remain on *Raven's Destiny*, and Jeremy would be promoted to Junior Officer. He would assist the first and second mates with duties on the ship's deck and take turns at the watch.

Jeremy was very excited to learn of his promotion. He was only fifteen but had learned much from his captain since coming aboard *Destiny* nearly two years ago with his father, Isaac, a helmsman on the ship. Isaac, too, was very excited for his young son. Raven had worked extensively with Jeremy, teaching him navigation, seamanship, and fighting skills. Jeremy was proficient with firearms and swords, although his hand–to–hand combat skills needed improvement. He and Simba continued to work together so that he could improve his fighting skills.

Zachery Thacker was three years senior to Jeremy and was taking a demotion from seaman to ship's boy. Yet, he took the demotion gratefully as he considered the alternative. He could have been hanging from the yardarm with Pearson. Zachery was shunned by most of the crew while working on *Destiny*. Most completely ignored him as he moved about the ship, performing his duties without complaint. Many would turn their back to him whenever he approached, but no one dared say a word of belittlement about or to the young man for fear Raven would hear about it.

Raven also took one of the boats from *Lady Falcon* so that each ship could have at least two.

Once everyone was dispatched to their proper ships, Raven ordered them to set sail. An azure sky dotted with cottony white clouds covered them as they began the journey back to Port St. Felix. No one was more excited to depart the Cayman Islands than Oscar Rivera. He stood on the quarterdeck beside Raven as she directed Hadari to set sail. Kujana wa Muziki and his drummers beat a rhythm on their drums as the four ships swiftly moved through the ocean waves.

Destiny bounced headlong across the sea as she gained momentum aided by the winds. Seagulls circled above the ships, searching for a scrap of food that might have been dropped on the decks. They screeched in a constant barrage, creating a song that could be heard above the sound of the ships as they crashed through the waves.

Raven asked Rivera, "Are you ready to get back home?"

"Oh, Si. It feels like I have been away so long now, but it will be worth it. I only hope that Juan has not sold my business in my absence."

Raven replied, "Juan would never do that, would he?"

"Oh no, Raven. I make a joke. Juan would never go against me, although, I am sure he is very worried about how long I have been gone."

"Well, you must reward him generously once we get back. I'm sure he has earned it."

"Si, he is a hard worker and very loyal. He will soon be very rich."

Raven smiled as they stood together, looking at the beautiful horizon they sailed toward.

By the end of the first day, Raven's fleet had traveled nearly 250 nautical miles and was entering the waters around Jamaica. Raven swung her ships, giving the island a wide berth, hoping to avoid Hornigold and his ship should they still be in the area. Raven had her ships turn southeasterly as they approached the island, keeping to the open sea. Hornigold would be unhappy if Raven had sent him there to find Black Jack McGreavy when McGreavy was already dead. If Hornigold happened into the cave that Raven and Rivera had been trapped in, his anger would undoubtedly increase with intensity.

The next three days, they continued southward into a chain of islands that ran northeasterly to southwesterly from Antigua to Trinidad. Waves were building as they neared the South American coast, and storm clouds began to form.

Raven navigated a path south of Grenada and north of Trinidad, hoping to avoid the pirate Hornigold and his fleet, knowing he mainly directed his attention to the north in the Caribbean. Other ships were spotted along the coast of Trinidad and Grenada, but so far, Raven had managed to miss Hornigold. Raven sailed with her white sails displayed, hoping to avoid any attention from the French navy, which would more than likely be in the area of Grenada.

With *Destiny* in the lead, *Matilda* on her port flank, and the *Nightingale* on her starboard flank, they sailed through with little attention, or so it seemed. The *Lady Falcon* followed the others about a half-mile behind, knowing that if trouble should arise, Attila could come to aid very quickly with the speed of his schooner.

Two miles after Raven passed Grenada, six ships gathered in her wake, which seemed to have been coming from the north. Still a quarter-mile behind *Destiny*, the unknown fleet fell in behind *Destiny*, *Matilda*, and the *Nightingale*.

Raven heard one of her men call from the crow's nest, "Ships off the port stern! They seem to be in pursuit!"

Raven asked him, "Can you tell who they are? Are they navy or private vessels?"

The lookout checked his spyglass momentarily before responding, "They're not navy! Looks like they're flying Jolly Roger!"

"Drat!" Raven said under her breath.

She then turned to Hadari and said, "I need as much speed as we can manage. I fear it might be Hornigold coming after us."

"Aye, Raven."

Hadari ordered the crew, "All hands, make ready the guns! Full speed ahead!"

Then Hadari blew the conch shell, letting the other two ships know they were being pursued.

Pharaoh and Alexander prepared their ships for battle and full flight to outrun their pursuers.

Raven ordered Muziki, "Give the signal to change formation. I want us to split up and be ready to attack if need be."

"Aye, Raven."

Muziki beat out a rhythm familiar to his counterparts aboard the other two ships. They, in turn, beat out a return signal and let their captains know what Raven wanted them to do. Alexander split right, while Pharaoh split left, widening the gap between the three ships. All ships increased their speed, ignoring the chop of the waves, making the ships ride like rocking horses through the seas.

Attila heard a call from above as his lookout announced, "We're falling behind, Attila! The other ships have left us behind!"

Attila ordered the speed to increase by adding more sails to the mix. The schooner quickly picked up speed and began to gain on the sea. The *Lady Falcon* rocked through the waves, rising and falling as the seas became more perilous.

After fifteen minutes of increased speed, another call came from above, "Attila, there are six ships in pursuit of Raven and the other ships!"

"Can you tell who they are?"

The lookout used his spyglass momentarily before replying, "Pirates! I'm not sure who, but they're flying the Roger!"

Attila ordered, "All men make ready your guns! Mr. Coates, I need full speed, please."

"Aye, Attila! Full speed."

The crew dropped all sails aboard the *Falcon* to allow them to catch as much wind as possible. They quickly increased their speed, no longer traveling at ten knots but now sailing at fifteen knots and quickly gaining on Raven's pursuers.

When *Destiny* came into view of Attila's lookout, he announced, "*Destiny* is sailing straight ahead now within a quarter mile. The other ships have split off right and left."

Attila realized what Raven had in mind. They had discussed various strategies throughout their tours together on *Destiny* before Attila was appointed captain of the *Falcon*. Attila ordered, "Mr. Coates, come about 10° starboard. We'll attack from the right as we come alongside the enemy ships."

"Aye, Attila!"

Then Attila ordered, "Mr. Bleaker, man your port guns as well as your bow and starboard guns. We'll be attacking with the enemy on our port."

"Aye, Attila!"

Henry Bleaker called his gunners together to give instructions. He still didn't have enough men to man all the guns on the ship and still didn't know his crew—he barely knew their names. "You there, take your gun crew and man the bow gun. Be ready if any ship that isn't flying our colors should pass in front of you. Sir, take another group to the bow and do the same."

"Aye, Mr. Bleaker!"

"The rest of you, man the port guns. Each crew prepare six guns in succession. That gives us eighteen shots against the enemy at a time. Once your guns have fired, prepare them for the next round."

"Aye, Mr. Bleaker!"

Hornigold's fleet, which did not have the weight of gold and silver in its cargo holds, quickly overtook Destiny. Raven prepared all her guns but paid particular attention to her stern gun at the rear of her vessel.

"Jeremy, take a gun crew to the stern and when the closest ships is in range, see if we can take out their sails."

"Aye, Raven!"

"Mr. Ashworth, keep our heading and hold her steady if you please."

"Aye, Raven!"

John nodded to Isaac, who was at the helm, and Isaac returned his nod. Raven looked to her right and saw the *Nightingale* slowly moving away from her side. She turned about and saw *Matilda* doing the same but to the left on her port. Then Raven watched as two of Hornigold's ships turned off to pursue each ship, cutting away from her.

"Good job, Benjamin." she said quietly. "You're doing just what I'd hoped you would."

Two ships pursued each of Raven's lead ships, and the *Lady Falcon* came up behind unnoticed. Hornigold's *Ranger* was the ship at the rear, allowing his other ships to remain in harm's way should they be fired upon. The last ship was nearest *Destiny*, directly in front of the *Ranger*.

Jeremy loaded the small six-pounder gun on the stern and aimed directly at the bow of the pursuing ship. He watched as the ship rocked up and down in the water and counted in his mind to calculate the timing of his shot. When he was sure he had it just right, he waited until the following ship dipped into the sea and began to come back up out of the water.

"Fire!"

"*Boom!*"

Jeremy watched as the cannonball flew through the air and struck the hull of the pursuing ship, blowing a six-inch hole at its keel. Jeremy smiled and turned to see if Raven saw his shot. She had. Raven nodded her approval at the young man and said, "Keep it up."

Jeremy's shot wasn't enough to cause immediate damage, but the hole would steadily allow the sea to enter the ship's hull and eventually sink her. Men aboard the enemy ship scrambled, seeing the damage to their bow. They tried covering the hole with little success. The ship then fired against *Destiny*. The shot missed severely, dropping short of its target because the ball had not been appropriately packed before firing the gun. The mistake also created a crack in the cannon tube, making it useless for the rest of the battle.

Hearing that his hull was damaged and his bow gun was inoperable, the captain called to fall away from pursuit, leaving the *Ranger* to battle *Destiny* alone. Hornigold, seeing his lead ship veer off to the left, had no choice but to pull up in pursuit of *Destiny*. Benjamin watched as the crew of the damaged ship began abandoning the ship, launching their lifeboats to escape and yelling, "Blimey, you sour dog! Where did you learn to sail a ship?"

Raven turned to Muziki and said, "It's time, Muziki!"

Muziki beat out a new rhythm to the other ships, and Hornigold watched as Raven's three ships turned, changing their positions. *Destiny* and the *Nightingale* sharply turned to port while *Matilda* turned to starboard. They wove past each other while presenting the 24-pound guns toward the enemy. Simultaneously, eight heavy guns fired at the enemy.

Boom! Boom! *Destiny* fired her guns at the *Ranger*, striking her foremast and damaging her rigging. The foresail fell to the deck, causing the *Ranger* to lunge backward like someone had suddenly applied a brake.

Attila watched as he passed the line where *Ranger* floated in the water too far away for the *Falcon* to fire a shot to sink her. Attila continued his wide pursuit, coming up on the two ships that had been in pursuit of the *Nightingale*. As Alexander moved to the port side, surprising the two ships following her, Attila came up just in time to fire upon the two ships. Eighteen port guns blasted in succession as the *Falcon* passed the first ship. The damage was so bad that the ship began to sink immediately. However, before the crew could abandon the ship, an explosion rocked the ship when one of Mr. Bleaker's shots struck the magazine house of the ship, obliterating the ship. Not a soul survived the explosion.

As *Destiny* and the *Nightingale* passed *Matilda*, they fired upon the two ships pursuing *Matilda*. **Boom! Boom! Boom! Boom!**

The first ship in line was struck on its port side as it turned in pursuit of *Matilda*. Before the ship could fire a shot, a cannonball disabled her rudder, and she had no choice but to raise her sails and surrender. But Raven wasn't interested in prisoners, only escape.

The second ship received strikes, one at the forecastle blowing it into pieces, and the other struck the mainsail's rigging, causing the ship to slow to a near halt.

Raven instructed Isaac to sail back to the *Ranger*.

John asked, "What? Why would you sail back into harms way? We've won the battle."

Raven smiled maniacally and replied, "Papa, it's not about the battle. It's about the war. I want to get a closer look at Benjamin's face."

Raven slowed her ship as she came along the *Ranger*. She saw Hornigold standing on the quarterdeck, exasperated.

"Are you alright, Benjamin?"

"My Lady Raven, come back to gloat did we?"

"Absolutely. Did you find what you were looking for in Jamaica?"

Benjamin bowed and shook his head, "For such a beautiful young woman, you certainly are devious."

Raven smiled again and replied, "Yes, aren't I? Benjamin?"

"Yes, Raven?"

"Don't ever come looking for me again. I won't be so generous next time."

Raven turned to Isaac to let him know he could turn the ship around and head for Port St. Felix.

Hornigold stood beside his second in command, Edward Teach, and softly said, "Fare thee well, fair maiden."

CHAPTER 34

Raven changed course, sailing east by southeast toward the Gulf of Guinea. Hurricane season was upon them, so they would need to be vigilant in watching the skies to the west and the south so they might change direction if need be. She didn't have a definite destination other than eventually delivering Oscar back to his home at Port St. Felix. She didn't have a definite timetable to abide by, so she was free to change course whenever the need arrived.

They had traveled nearly two thousand miles when a storm was noticed toward the east. Raven set a new course south to avoid the storm. They sailed along the coast of South America, passing the equator when Raven decided they needed to resupply before continuing east.

Raven checked her charts and chose Natal as their destination. Natal was a coastal town on the coast of Brazil, initially settled by indigenous people of the Amazon River area. However, on Christmas Day of 1599, the Portuguese came and made it theirs, thus giving it the name Natal, which means Nativity or Christmas.

Raven set a course for Natal and arrived there the next day. Nathan Coates was fluent in Portuguese, making arranging a trade for supplies much easier. Natal was a place, unlike most areas in the Caribbean and South America. The soil was too sandy to grow sugar cane, but they raised cattle. The residents jerked the beef, called carne de sol or sun meat, and sold it as an export.

The ships pulled into port and docked together along the pier. All the crew were excited, knowing they had money to spend in port. Raven advised her crew to spend only some of their money here, especially not on spirits alone. She knew it would be impossible for them to spend all their money since they had so much to spend, but they might lose it by gambling or theft. They would be allowed to go ashore during eight-hour shifts. Someone had to remain onboard to look after the ships.

"Don't take all of your money with you. Keep most of it locked up here on the ship. Be aware of those who might take it from you. Have fun, but be back here sober by the beginning of your shift."

Raven, Jeffrey, and Nathan Coates left to seek someone to help them supply the ships. As they met together on the pier, Oscar Rivera called to Raven.

"Raven, would you mind if I come along?"

"Certainly, Oscar. You're welcome to come."

Rivera quickly stepped down the gangplank and joined the trio as they set out to find the supplies they needed to finish their voyage. The little city was finer than Raven had expected. The streets were paved with cobblestone, allowing wagons and coaches to travel more easily than if the sand had not been covered. The buildings were brightly painted with warm summery yellow, orange, and light blue hues. Merchants lined the streets selling wares of fruits and vegetables, fish and shellfish, jewelry and trinkets.

Raven approached a young woman with a cart beside the street, selling melons, sugar apples, cashews, and papayas. The woman had roasted the cashews and portioned them into small burlap sacks. Raven bought a bag of the nuts and tried them.

"Mmm! These are delicious, Oscar. Have you ever eaten cashews?"

"No, Raven."

"Here, try them."

Raven passed the bag around for her companions to try. The warm, nutty flavor was delightful.

"I want more of these to take to the ship. Nathan, ask her where we can buy more of these. Much more."

Nathan asked the young woman where they could find an ample supply of the nuts to take to their ship. She pointed out a large building several blocks away that supplied merchant ships.

Nathan told Raven, "There is a supplier several blocks away called Potiguara Merchant Warehouse. They supply most of the merchant ships that come into port."

"Nathan, how do I say, thank you?"

"Obrigada."

Raven handed the woman a gold coin and said, "Obrigada."

The young lady replied, "De nada, Senhorita."

They continued down the cobblestone street past shops of all sorts. The people of the town waved to them and called out in an attempt to sell them something. Raven smiled politely at them but continued to walk. A few minutes later, they stood in front of a large gray stone building with wooden double doors that stood eight feet tall. The doors were attached to the door frame with black wrought iron hinges. One of the doors was ajar.

Raven and the others stepped inside and found the inside much cooler than on the streets. They saw another set of doors at the back of the building, which was opened, allowing a breeze to flow through the warehouse, cooling its contents—large divided areas lined up in the warehouse, creating aisles for customers to walk down. There were large wooden crates filled with various fruits and vegetables. One of them contained cashews. Burlap sacks filled with cashews that had already been roasted to remove the caustic liquid of the nut's shell filled the bins.

Farther back in the warehouse were stacks of wooden barrels. Writing burned into the sides of the barrels read, "Carne bovina Salgado," which translates as "salted beef."

"Looks like we've come to the right place," Raven said.

Suddenly, a short, dark-skinned man approached them and spoke in Portuguese.

"Good day, gentlemen, and young lady. I am Thomas Legarea. May I help you in some way?"

Nathan spoke, "Yes, we have four ships docked at the pier. We are traveling to Africa and need to resupply. We were told you could help us with that."

"Oh, yes sir. I can help. What is it you need?"

Nathan turned to Raven and asked, "He wants to know what we need."

"Tell him, forty barrels of beef, eight of those large crates of melons, four crates of the sugar apples, and one hundred sacks of cashews."

Nathan raised his brows at her request.

"What? I just discovered I like cashews, is there anything wrong with that?"

"No, Raven. Nothing at all."

Nathan relayed the message, and the gentleman delighted in the larger order.

"Come with me. We will begin filling your order right away and decide how much you will pay."

Thomas led them into another room much smaller that served as his office. He wrote the order on a piece of parchment using a quill and ink, then handed the order to one of his associates, who would begin filling the order.

Thomas announced, "This is quite an order. I may just close for the day after it is filled. Just kidding, we never close. How will you be paying? English pounds?"

Nathan replied, "Pounds. We can pay in gold and silver."

Thomas replied, "The total comes to five thousand réis which is equal to roughly, £700."

Nathan translated to Raven, "£700 for all of it."

"Wow, that's more than I had expected. Ask him if he will deliver it to the docks for that price?"

Nathan asked, received an answer, then replied, "He says, yes."

Raven turned to Jeffrey and said, "Pay the man."

Jeffrey replied, "I didn't bring that much. I'll have to go back to the ship."

"Alright, do so. Oscar and I will browse around town a bit while you go. Nathan can stay here and wait for you. Oscar and I will meet you back at the ship."

Jeffrey nodded, then left to retrieve the money to secure their purchase.

As Raven and Oscar left the warehouse, they turned left and proceeded farther down the street. A few moments later, Raven heard music from somewhere nearby. She followed the sound until they turned the corner and found a courtyard in front of a larger stone building. The building seemed to be some sort of public office building. The courtyard in front was lined with large Mahogany trees outlining a stone-paved path leading up to the front doors. A band was playing music the likes that Raven had never heard before. A combination of brass bugles, drums, and stringed instruments played a lively tune to which many of the town's residents were dancing.

Raven and Oscar stood in the crowd to watch and listen as the people celebrated and danced. Many of the people clapped along with the music as others danced together. Raven, moved by the music, began clapping along with everyone else. Suddenly, a young man approached her and said something she didn't understand. Oscar was able to pick out a few of the words, and he said, "The young man wants to dance with you."

The young man held out his hands to Raven, to which she balked at first. However, the music was so tempting that she relented, took his hands, and danced with him among the crowd. Oscar smiled to see Raven enjoying herself. He said to himself, "*A young señorita should dance like this rather than always fighting someone.*"

When the music finally stopped, Raven bowed to the young man, then turned back to find Oscar. She saw him in the crowd, clapping his approval. Raven breathlessly joined him once again. "I have never danced before," she said.

Oscar replied, "You should dance often. It suits you."

They left the courtyard to return to the ship and join the others.

Rivera and Raven arrived back at *Destiny* just before dusk. The last of the supplies was being loaded onto each of the ships. They climbed the gangplank and walked to the quarterdeck where John was standing. John noticed a broad smile across his daughter's face. He smiled in response. It had been long since he had seen her smile like that.

Raven asked John, "Oh, Papa! Has everyone come back to the ships yet?"

"Not yet." Then John remarked, "You seem very jolly. Have you been partaking in liquid spirits?"

"No, Papa. Not at all, Papa. I and Oscar have been enjoying the spirits of music and dance. I have never had so much fun before. The people here are wonderful."

John then asked, "Tell me something else. Why do we need one hundred sacks of nuts?"

Raven giggled as she said, "I have just discovered that I like cashews."

John smiled and shook his head.

CHAPTER 35

Sixteen days after leaving Natal, Raven and her fleet were approaching the Cape of Good Hope. Temperatures dropped as they moved farther from the equator into the southern hemisphere. Light snow began to fall onto the decks of the ships but melted immediately because the deck boards were saturated in salt water. As Raven stood on the quarterdeck next to John and Jeffrey, they could see each other's breath in the cold, crisp air. Jeffrey and John's ears were red, as were the tips of their noses. Raven's nose was red also, but her long, curly locks covered her ears, protecting them from the cold.

Three days later, they found themselves at the southern tip of the Cape. The weather hadn't changed; temperatures in the teens still froze them, but something curious appeared on the eastern horizon. A call from *Destiny's* crow's nest said, "Ships ahoy! Port-bow!"

Raven called back, "How many?"

A moment later, "Six. . . no, seven!"

Raven called her captains to join her on *Destiny* to discuss the matter before the approaching ships got too close. Pharaoh, Alexander, and Attila rowed over in their small boats along with two of their men to row the boats. They climbed aboard and met Raven in her cabin.

She began by saying, "I take it you've seen the approaching ships from the east?"

Pharaoh replied, "Aye, Raven. Do you know who they are?"

"Not yet. We need to be ready though. I've instructed Mr. Ashworth to take a wide path to try to avoid them. If they change their course and come at us, we'll know they mean trouble."

Alexander asked, "What do you want us to do?"

"Let's widen the space between us, as we did against Hornigold. Attila, stay back and be prepared to attack should they fire upon us. We'll weave the ships back and forth again. It seemed to work well last time. If we can, however, let's outrun them. I'll signal with the conch . . ."

Suddenly, Hadari interrupted, and he quickly opened the door without knocking.

"Raven, the ships are close enough to see who they are!"

"What colors are they flying?"

"French! They're frigates!"

"*Drat!*" said Raven to herself.

Alexander asked, "Can we outrun them?"

"Not likely."

"Well, can we out maneuver them?"

"Maybe. We only have three choices: sail straight into them, wait here and fight, or swing southward and see if they follow."

Pharaoh said, "You know I hate to run away from a fight, but I say run."

Attila asked, "What's it going to be, Raven?"

Raven paused before replying, "Hadari, have Mr. Finch change course, 45° starboard. We'll see if they try to intercept."

"Aye, Raven. 45° starboard."

Raven then said, "Let's see how they react. Gentlemen, I'm afraid you'll have to stay onboard for now. There isn't enough time to get you back to your ships. Hopefully, your officers can handle things without you."

Seven French frigates sailing from the French island province of Mayotte were sailing southward near the Cape of Good Hope when a seaman spotted a group of ships sailing toward them. "Ships ahoy, mon Capitaine!"

"How many?"

"Four ships, mon Capitaine!"

"Can you see their colors?"

"Not very clearly, mon Capitaine. They are red with some kind of emblem in black. They appear to be merchant ships, though they are armed. One of them is a schooner and is set for battle. I count, eighteen guns on their port."

The captain ordered his helmsman, "Stay the course until we can make their colors."

"Oui, mon Capitaine."

As the French ships reached the southern tip of Africa, the captain had his helmsman change course to follow the shipping lane through the Cape of Good Hope.

"Helmsman, come about 60° starboard."

"Oui, mon Capitaine, 60° starboard."

Captain Jean Louis Mont Blanc had served in the King's Navy for twenty-three years, the last ten as captain. He wasn't tall, about 5' 9", and his build was slight. He was always clean-shaven, adequately dressed, and never seemed caught off guard. In the past ten years, he had seen numerous battles onboard his ship, the Tempête, translated as the Tempest.

Mont Blanc was a fierce fighter at sea, well–educated in the art of combat, and had never lost a battle. He, like his name, was immovable like a White Mountain. He stared straight ahead, wondering what this small fleet of merchant ships could be up to. Although it wasn't uncommon for merchant vessels to travel in groups, they rarely were armed. Mont Blanc suspected they were English privateers, although the colors weren't correct. Who would be flying red colors?"

As they neared the small fleet of merchant ships, another call came from the frigate's lookout. "I've got it, mon Capitaine! They all fly a red flag with a black bird as an emblem."

"*A black bird?*" He thought to himself.
Then he realized, "Might it be a raven?"
"Oui, mon Capitaine! It could be a raven."
Mont Blanc smiled as he realized his luck.
"All hands prepare for battle! We've just located the Red Raven! Signal the other ships to prepare for battle!"

The men scrambled to their guns. Mont Blanc took out his spyglass and pointed it toward the cluster of ships approaching him. Looking through the glass, he noticed the approaching ships were changing course and trying to run away.

"Lieutenant, change course to intercept those ships. Don't let them get away."

"Oui, mon Capitaine!"

The lead frigate turned hard left, trying to cut the ships off before they could get around the French ships. The frigates turned quickly, almost keel–hailing themselves over into the sea. The turn was too abrupt, causing many French sailors to lose their footing on deck. Several of them slid downward, slamming into the starboard rail and each other.

Once the ship was righted, the men scrambled to man their stations. The frigates were now on course to cut off the opposing ships to keep them from escaping. But suddenly, Raven's ships turned and performed a maneuver that confused the French. *Destiny* continued forward while *Matilda* and the *Nightingale* crisscrossed in front of her. They split from the formation, trying to lead some of the frigates away from *Destiny*. The *Lady Falcon* was bringing up the rear in an attempt to attack the lead enemy ship. *Falcon* turned, allowing her starboard guns to face the enemy. Nathan opened fire on one of the frigates that had released from its formation and was now attacking *Destiny*. Eighteen guns fired in succession upon the frigate as it fired upon *Destiny*. Six of the eighteen cannonballs struck the frigate. One shot knocked out their foresail. Three shots entered its starboard hull. Another shot missed the ship but collided with six sailors, killing them instantly. The final hit was just below the water's surface at the ship's bow, causing the ship to take in water and slowly sink. The hole in the front of the ship caused a decrease in its speed, making the ship sink faster and faster. The crew had to abandon ship, many climbing into lifeboats, while others could only try to swim away from the wreckage.

The French were now down to six ships. *Destiny* continued to sail directly, trying to escape the blockade and into safety. Raven fired her two port guns as quickly as they could as a deterrent against the enemy ships, but only minor damage was done. *Matilda* ran a block across *Destiny's* port bow, trying to draw fire from the frigates. Raven saw this and asked Pharaoh, "What does Mwindaji think he's doing?"

"He is trying to save you."

"Well, I don't want him to save me. I want him to save himself."

Matilda fired her two starboard guns at the frigate closest to her, striking the ship's main mast. The main sail fell to the deck, covering most of the crew and not allowing them to fire against *Destiny*. *Matilda* fired again, hitting the frigate's hull near the water's surface, causing the ship to fill with water. Another French crew found themselves abandoning ship. However, the frigate behind them fired on *Matilda* and struck her in her forward hull, causing enough damage that she began to sink. *Matilda's* crew rushed to lower their boats into the water to escape the sinking ship.

Raven gasped as she saw her men trying to escape the sinking ship. Her thoughts returned to when she watched one of her other ships sink with two of her original men aboard. Tears came to her eyes, and she tried to brush them away and concentrate on the battle at hand.

Seemingly, out of nowhere, the *Nightingale* swept in to block *Matilda's* crew from being fired upon while they attempted to escape their sinking ship. Daktari fired his port guns at the closest frigate, hitting its port hull and damaging the forecastle. She then reloaded and aimed at the next available frigate, hitting it twice in its port hull, but the damage was too high to cause leakage.

The *Lady Falcon* began a sweep past the French fleet, constantly firing as she passed through. She damaged four of the frigates but not enough to sink them. Then, a barrage of cannonballs hit the *Falcon* in her hull on the second deck, damaging many of the cannons. One shot hit the powder room, igniting the black powder, which exploded and sent the *Falcon* flying into the air piece by piece. No one survived the blast. What was left of the *Lady Falcon* quickly sank to the bottom of the sea.

Raven stared in horror as her gunship exploded before her eyes, killing over half her men. Anger swelled within her as she saw her men place themselves between her and the enemy.

"We've got to get out of here! Tell *Nightingale* to pull out!"

Pharaoh replied, "No, Raven! It will do no good. They are sacrificing themselves to save you. It is what we have all agreed to do. You can not stop them."

"But I didn't ask them to do that!"

"No. But everyone on these four ships has only one purpose here. You saved us all from a life of slavery and suffering, and because you did, we will give our lives to save you, no matter what."

Raven openly cried aloud as she watched the *Nightingale* being struck over and over until she and her crew sank into the depths of the ocean. Then she saw *Matilda's* men in the small boats as they tried to row to safety. But the two tiny boats were struck by cannon fire and quickly sank, killing all who were aboard. *Destiny* sailed away eastward while Raven stood at the stern rail crying. She looked at the sea behind her, seeing pieces of flesh, wood, and canvas sails floating on the surface. Alexander, Attila, and Pharaoh walked up and stood by her side as she wept.

She watched as the remaining frigates limped away in the opposite direction, choosing to fight another day instead of pursuing her further.

Captain Jean Louis Mont Blanc walked to the stern of his frigate and watched *Destiny* sail away.

"Bon voyage, Red Raven. Until we meet again."

CHAPTER 36

Raven finally walked to her cabin, closed the door behind her, and sat on her bed. Captain Billings came and climbed onto her shoulder, sensing she needed comfort. Tears still streamed down Raven's face as she stared into nothing. Then she lay down, curled into a ball, and cried some more.

"Why? Why would they do that? I didn't ask them to save me. I don't deserve to live. I've gotten too many killed with my schemes and dreams. They might have all been better off if I had never saved them from slavery."

John quietly entered her room. "I know what you're thinking."

Startled, Raven sat up and wiped away her tears.

"What am I thinking?"

"You're thinking that those who lost their lives today would have been better off never knowing you. You're thinking, if you hadn't freed them from slavery, they'd all still be alive."

"How could you know that?"

"Because, that's what I would be thinking if I were you. But, it isn't true, Raven. You gave every one of those men and women freedom and hope. You gave them lives of excitement and won-der. They saw places and things they would never have seen if they had ended up at the end of a chain in some cotton field in Carolina. You taught them to fight, and laugh, and love freely. And, even though their lives were short compared to most, they lived fully. Don't take away the sacrifice they made for you by blaming yourself for their deaths. You didn't take their lives away from them, you gave them life. And you didn't take life away from them, they freely gave it so that you could be saved, just as you over and over again saved them."

"Oh, Papa, I feel you are right, but I still blame myself."

"Don't blame yourself. Blame the French. Blame those who have attacked you and your crews. Blame those like Hornigold, and Arsenault, and d'Arnauld. But, don't blame yourself. Everyone is counting on you, and everyone expects you to lead them. Wherever you lead, even if it's into the depths of hell, we will follow you."

A knock on the door interrupted them.

Raven sniffed away her tears before saying, "Enter."

Zachery Thacker entered her cabin carrying a tray with a bottle of rum and a glass. "Pardon me, Captain. Mr. Greer asked me to bring you this."

Raven smiled at the young man as she replied, "Thank Mr. Greer for me, please. And, thank you, Zachery."

"You're welcome, Captain."

Fifteen hundred miles later, the weather warmed, and so did Raven's disposition. She stood on the quarterdeck with her remaining officers, John, Hadari, Pharaoh, Alexander, Attila, Jeffrey, and Jeremy. They stood silently together as *Destiny* floated into the bay at Port St. Felix. Oscar Rivera walked up to join the others as the pier appeared. Raven took out her spyglass to check the flag pole. The white flag waved in the breeze, and the signal to stay away was displayed. However, no sooner than Raven saw the signal, the flag started moving down the pole. Juan changed the signal to give them a clear signal.

Raven told the others, "Looks like all is well. We're free to pull into the port."

Oscar smiled as he saw his home port ahead. "It is so good to be back. I look forward to finally getting off this ship. Uh, no offense."

"None taken," Raven replied. "What will you do now that you are rich?"

"Ah, well my dear, the first thing I will do in honor of you and your crew is, I will do away with all slave trading. Nevermore will I buy, sell, or trade slaves. You have converted me."

Raven smiled and replied, "Glad to hear it. Do you think you can survive here without trading slaves to the merchant vessels?"

"I think so. I will find something else the merchants want. Maybe I will go into the cashew business."

Raven replied, "Save some for me."

Destiny slowly pulled up to the pier, and two of Raven's men jumped to the dock and tied off the ship. The gangplank was dropped into place so the crew could leave the ship when ready. Raven asked Hadari, "Would you please have some of the men help Señor Rivera with his cargo?"

"Aye, Raven."

Rivera turned to her and said, "Thank you, my dear. You have been a most excellent host and I could not have asked for a better partner in this endeavor."

"Oscar, the next time you come across a treasure map. . . let me know."

Rivera smiled, then turned away and walked back to his cabin to gather his things.

John asked her, "What now?"

"Now, we will take a break. Let the crew go into town and spend their money. We'll stay here for a few days if we can. Hopefully no one will come along and try to kill us. Then, we'll go back to the Robin's Nest and decide what to do."

After the ship was secured and all the sails were raised and tied up, John released the crew so they could go ashore. Raven asked her three captains, "Did all of you lose your shares during the battle when the ships sank?"

Alexander replied, "Ah, sadly, yes."

Both Pharaoh and Attila nodded their heads in agreement.

Raven replied, "Well then, we will have to compensate each of you. I can not have my captains going ashore with empty pockets."

Each of them smiled and thanked Raven.

As the crew began leaving the ship to enjoy themselves, Raven spotted Jeremy about to cross the gangplank. "Jeremy! Can you wait a moment?"

Jeremy waved and stepped back onto the ship. Raven left the quarterdeck and walked over to meet Jeremy. "Would you give me a moment before you go ashore? Let me go back to my cabin, then I'll join you momentarily."

"Aye, Raven."

Raven walked to her cabin, opened the door, and retrieved her leather satchel, which she sometimes wore over her shoulder. She took a small bag of coins from one of her hiding places, dropped the bag into the satchel, and then walked out to join her young friend.

"I'm ready," she said as they walked down the gangplank together.

Jeremy asked, "Where are we going?"

"I want to take you to one of the first places I ever visited after becoming a junior officer aboard the original *Destiny*."

"Are we going to a pub?"

"No! You are still too young for that. Stay away from those places, do you hear me?"

"Aye, Raven. Then where are we going?"

"You shall see."

They walked through the streets together, light-footed and gay. Raven was finally feeling like her old self. They laughed together as Raven pointed out various shops along the way. Once in a while, a young girl about Jeremy's age would meet them on the street and smile at Jeremy as they met. Raven would tease Jeremy, poke him in the ribs with her elbow, and say, "She likes you, Jeremy. I can tell."

Jeremy would blush, and Raven would laugh harder.

Finally, they reached their destination. At Seafarer's Tailor Shop, young Richard Ashworth bought his first officer's uniform, compliments of Captain Billings.

Jeremy asked, "What are we doing here?"

"Well, I can't have my newest junior officer looking like a ship's boy, now can I? We're here to get you fitted with a new uniform. This is where Captain Billings bought me my first uniform when I made fourth mate."

Jeremy smiled as his eyes widened. He never expected to be wearing a fine officer's uniform before. Even Raven's captains didn't wear a uniform. They typically dressed in leather britches and linen shirts like Raven. Jeremy walked around the shop looking at all the fine clothing: dress coats, waistcoats, boots, hats, and white pants typically worn by naval or merchant ship officers.

He marveled at how fine they all looked and felt to his touch.

Samuel Tate approached the two as they wandered through the shop and asked, "May I be of service to you, Miss?"

"Mr. Tate, so nice to see you again. It has been such a long time."

"I'm sorry, Miss, have we met?"

"Well, yes. But of course, you would not remember me. I was once a young officer on Horatio Billings' ship, the *Destiny*. My name was Richard Ashworth at the time. I was posing as a boy, then and my father and I came in to get a new uniform when I made fourth mate."

"How long ago?"

"Let's see, I guess that would have been five years ago."

Tate replied, "Well, I can see you are no longer a boy. Grown up a bit, haven't you?"

"Aye, Mr. Tate. That I have. This is Jeremy Finch, my newest junior officer, and I want him to dress the part."

"I see. Would you want him to have the standard officer's uniform then?'

Raven smiled as she looked at Jeremy, then replied, "I think not."

Raven noticed Jeremy's countenance fall a bit.

"The typical officer's uniform is too formal, too . . . pretty. Jeremy is a buccaneer. He will need a uniform more befitting a man of the sea."

Jeremy's countenance rose again, and he smiled.
Tate replied, "Well then, leather britches, maybe a leather waist coat. A jacket, boots and a hat to match?"

Raven smiled and replied, "Sounds about right."

"Well then, let's get you measured young man and then get you fitted. I've got just the right thing for you."

"Thank you, Sir." Jeremy replied.

Mr. Tate had Jeremy stand on a stool while he took out a tape to measure him from head to toe. He wrote down each measurement, then began gathering clothing he thought would be the correct size for the young man.

"Here you are, my boy. Take these behind that screen and try them on."

Jeremy gathered the clothes into his arms and went to the screen to change into his new clothes. Raven waited patiently for her young friend to try on the suit that would soon mark him as her junior officer. She thought about the time she had stood behind the very same screen to try on her new uniform; how uncomfortable she was as she tried to hide from the tailor, who had no idea she was a girl instead of the boy he saw before him.

Jeremy walked out from behind the screen wearing the full uniform: brown leather britches, a waistcoat and overcoat, a black felt hat, and black boots that reached nearly to his knees. Underneath the leather was a white linen shirt.

Raven suggested, "Are the boots alright? Would you rather have brown?"

Jeremy replied enthusiastically, "I like the black ones."

"Alright. How about the size? Do they fit alright? Do you have room to grow a little? You know, you haven't stopped growing yet. You don't want to outgrow them before you reach port somewhere to buy new ones. Then you'd have to go around everywhere barefoot."

Jeremy replied, "Their fine. I have plenty room to grow."

"Well they're not too big, then?"

"No, Raven. They're just right."

"Alright then. How's everything else? Turn around."

Jeremy slowly spun around so Raven could have a look.

"Hmm, fits nicely. My don't you look dashing. Those young ladies we just saw on the street won't be able to resist you, now."

Jeremy blushed again and replied, "Ah, come on, Raven."

She smiled, walked over to him, and hugged him. He hadn't received a hug from anyone since his mother passed away.

Jeremy asked Mr. Tate, "How much do I owe you, Sir?"

Raven said, "Oh no you don't. This is my gift to you."

"But, Raven, I have plenty money. I can buy it myself."

"Of course you can, but you wouldn't want to take a pleasure away from me would you?"

Jeremy paused, smiled, and said, "Thank you, Raven."

"You are most welcome. Mr. Tate, better throw in a belt as well. He'll need something to hang his knife sheath onto."

"Yes, of course."

Raven paid Tate, and she and Jeremy left the shop and returned to the ship.

Oscar Rivera met Raven three days later at the pier as she prepared to leave Port St. Felix. Pharaoh stood nearby and counted the crew as they returned to the ship after three days of revelry.

Oscar asked Raven, "Where will you go, now?"

"We're going back to our little hide out in the Gulf of Guinea, a place we call the Robin's Nest."

"What then?"

"The usual. We'll find some more slaves to free, more gold to collect, maybe a new ship to expand my fleet again."

"Raven, you have no need for all of that, now. With all the treasure you found, you could settle down, start a family..."

John interrupted, "Make me a grandpapa."

John then left, not wanting to receive Raven's wrath.

Rivera continued. "You can do anything you want now. Why keep putting yourself in such dangerous situations? Why not take it easy? Live the life of luxury. You can afford it."

Raven smiled and replied, "Because it's my destiny."

About the Author

 Michael L. Clark was born in Tacoma, Washington, but grew up mainly in the south. Over the years, he has worked as a farmhand, elephant handler, zookeeper, restaurant manager and owner, musician, cake artist, and rural mail carrier, all while honing his craft as a storyteller.

Clark's debut series was inspired by his many trips down the Natchez Trace. The stops along the Trail mentioned the people who once lived on the trail but gave limited information about their lives. Clark began to wonder about their stories and imagine traveling back in time to live among them and learn more. That desire sparked the idea for his first novel, The Shimmering, which has since evolved into a series of time-traveling Historical Novels.

His fourth novel, Ambush at Horse Creek, is the first of many books he calls The Young Americans series. Each story depicts a young person growing up in a historical situation. Ambush is about a teenage boy who rides for the Pony Express.

His latest series, The Red Raven, is based on pirates who operated during the early 18th Century.

More Books from Michael L. Clark

The Shimmering

The Diary of Gus Childers: The Shimmering Book 2

The Prophet: The Shimmering Book 3

Ambush at Horse Creek

The Red Raven